THE LA

Christie Dickason was born in America but also lived as a child in Thailand, Mexico and Switzerland. Harvard-educated and a former theatre director and choreographer (with the Royal Shakespeare Company and at Ronnie Scott's among others), she has now lived longer in London than anywhere else. She has two very large sons and two small cats. Besides writing books and musical libretti, she gardens and climbs the occasional mountain.

CHRISTIE DICKASON

The Lady Tree

HarperCollins*Publishers*

HarperCollins*Publishers*
77–85 Fulham Palace Road,
Hammersmith, London w6 8jb

The HarperCollins website address is:
www.fireandwater.com

This paperback edition 1999
1 3 5 7 9 8 6 4 2

First published in Great Britain by
HarperCollins*Publishers* 1993

This novel is entirely a work of fiction. The names,
characters and incidents portrayed in it are the work of the
author's imagination. Any resemblance to actual persons,
living or dead, events or localities is entirely coincidental.

ISBN 0 00 651357 3

Set in Sabon by
Rowland Phototypesetting Ltd,
Bury St Edmunds, Suffolk

Printed and bound in Great Britain by
Caledonian International Book Manufacturing Ltd, Glasgow

FOR MARJORIE, MY MOTHER,
WHO MADE THE FIRST GARDEN IN MY LIFE

Acknowledgements

My heartfelt thanks to the National Trust staff and volunteers at The Vyne, Hampshire, who generously helped me to recreate the world of Hawkridge House.

Also to Juliette Brown, Theresa Cederholm, Sheila Cooper, Frank Horack, David Massa, Anna Powell, Leo Solt of Indiana University, Dr Stephen Wyatt, and the staffs of the Royal Horticultural Society Gardens at Wisley, the Royal Botanic Gardens at Kew, the Chelsea Physic Garden, the Cambridge University Botanic Garden, and the Weald and Downland Open Air Museum, for encouragement and education in the religion, politics, law, finance, natural sciences and 'garderobe problem' of the seventeenth century.

To Nick Sayers, my editor, and to my agent, Andrew Hewson.

Author's Note

Between 1634 and 1637 a part of the Dutch economy surged out of control. Mad speculation pushed the market above rational limits. Special stock exchanges were needed to deal solely in the single commodity involved. Investment syndicates were set up in inns and taverns. Ditchdiggers and washerwomen gambled as wildly as merchants and aristocrats. The crash in 1637 was as spectacular as the Wall Street Crash of 1929, and, in the aftermath, as many men were said to have committed suicide.

The commodity which ruined so many lives was not silk, nor gold nor spices, nor even opium, but the tulip bulb.

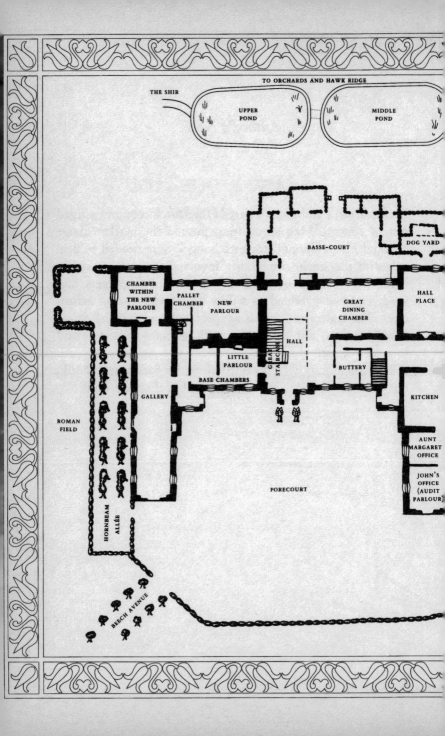

TO ORCHARDS AND HAWK RIDGE

THE SHIR

UPPER POND

MIDDLE POND

BASSE-COURT

DOG YARD

CHAMBER WITHIN THE NEW PARLOUR

PALLET CHAMBER

NEW PARLOUR

GREAT DINING CHAMBER

HALL PLACE

HALL

LITTLE PARLOUR

GALLERY

BASE CHAMBERS

GREAT STAIRCASE

BUTTERY

KITCHEN

ROMAN FIELD

AUNT MARGARET OFFICE

JOHN'S OFFICE (AUDIT PARLOUR)

FORECOURT

HORNBEAM ALLÉE

BEECH AVENUE

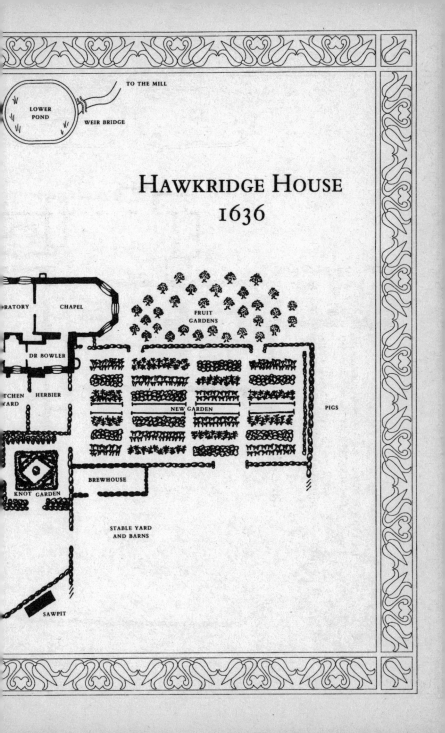

TO THE MILL

LOWER
POND

WEIR BRIDGE

HAWKRIDGE HOUSE
1636

RATORY   CHAPEL

FRUIT
GARDENS

DR BOWLER

TCHEN
YARD   HERBIER

NEW GARDEN   PIGS

BREWHOUSE

KNOT GARDEN

STABLE YARD
AND BARNS

SAWPIT

Part One

Prologue

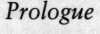

Majestic Wealth is the holiest of our gods.

Juvenal.

AMSTERDAM, FEBRUARY 1636

The room glinted with brass and gold but smelled of damp wool, nutmeg, cloves, sewage and burning fat. In the dim yellow light of thirty tallow candles held aloft by gilt fantasies of mermaids and dolphins, three men waited in uneasy silence. The Englishman, who looked pastel, insubstantial and overfrilled beside the two black-clad Dutchmen, peered down from an open window into the cavern of shadow beneath the massive bow of a moored ship. Although he stood in a house on dry land, the dark rim of the window seemed to shift. The floor tilted. The fat tree-trunks of the ship's masts, tops far up out of sight in the night sky, swayed almost imperceptibly, not quite close enough to touch. He swallowed against the ghost of nausea that tickled his stomach unpleasantly.

Ships rubbed and shouldered each other for dock space as far as he could see to either side. The small red eye of a watchman's lantern etched a slow path through the black, gently heaving thickets of spars and rigging.

I should have refused to come, he thought. *Made them send someone weighty enough to decide such things.*

But he knew that he had been sent precisely because he

was unremarkable. The men who made the decisions paid men like himself to take the risk of looking like an ass. He shifted aching shoulders inside his doublet and cursed the damp.

Anyway, he couldn't afford to refuse a commission.

The house stood on a dock on the Amstel River. The moored ships creaked and scraped. A far-away sailor shouted to another. On the dock just below the window the shadow of a dog nosing among the stacked bales, barrels, and coiled ropes suddenly erupted into a frenzy of barking. The three men inside the room lifted their heads.

In another room of the house, a bad-tempered viol was groaning and complaining again and again through the same four phrases of a French dance tune. The barking stopped.

'Not yet.' Vrel, one of the two Dutchmen and the owner of the house, settled his bulk back into his carved and gilded chair. He sat squarely at the end of a long heavy table as if he expected a dish of roast meat to be set in front of him, but diamond and ruby rings flashed uneasily in the candlelight as his short, strong fingers opened and closed over the lions' masks of the arm ends.

Simeon Timmons, the Englishman, now eyed his host. An agent had to be civil to everyone, but Timmons was struggling with Cornelius Vrel.

A mannerless frog in black silk and fine wool stolen from the English, or near enough stolen, thought Timmons viciously. Hunkered down here smugly among his gold plates and drinking cups, his Toledo blades, Venetian candleholders, and Turkish rugs that covered every flat surface like a plague of multi-coloured moss. Stinking of the spices that had made him rich.

His stomach contracted with a pain like hunger. How he lusted to be such a frog!

Timmons lived to serve other men's wealth. As a third son with two healthy older brothers between him and the family money and lands, he had to live on his wits. He fed and supped on envy and hope to sustain himself in the hard but necessary work of being civil at all costs. Even to former enemies who now smiled and allowed you to admire booty pirated from English ships. No matter that Dutch and English merchantmen were at this moment blowing each other out of the East Indian seas for the sake of cinnamon and cloves. No matter an uncle massacred by the Dutch at Amboyna thirteen years before. Civil and smiling, Timmons made a career trotting to and fro like a market pony, laden with information, propositions, money, documents, promises or silver spoons.

The third man in the room asked a question in Dutch.

Timmons turned to study him with carefully neutral eyes. Named Blanket or Banquet or some such Dutch torturing of vowels, in his late fifties, a little older than Vrel, a head taller but half the weight. As they waited, he had been strolling aimlessly around the room.

Busy coveting the Chinese porcelain and gilt plates, thought Timmons. He heard the anxiety now in the man's voice and wished he could understand the question.

Vrel replied in a voice as chilly as the night air. Blanket (or Banquet) sank his skinny neck and long head back into his shell of black merino and Brussels lace. He turned away to study a set of golden spice scales.

Whatever it is, thought Timmons, Vrel is firmly in control. He shivered. His fine, light-brown hair lay damply clumped against his narrow head. His long thin face slid unchecked down sagging light-brown moustaches and a small pointed beard. A newly-fashionable flat collar drooped limply over narrow shoulders which were betrayed by the new, unpadded style of English doublet. His lace tie, lace cuffs and lace boot tops had all lost their starch in the damp sea air. A more confident man would not have left his wool cloak at his lodgings in the name of fashion.

An ecstasy of barking erupted on the dock.

Vrel was already on his feet. 'He's here. Follow my lead, Blankaart!' he ordered. 'Listen to me very carefully. Don't let your enthusiasms run away with my money . . . !'

A commotion mounted the stairs outside the room. On the dock, the dog still barked.

The newcomer blew into the room like a storm at sea, brushing aside the servant who had brought him up, bellowing words of greeting, his wide hat and cloak flapping, the soft barbs of a scarlet feather in his hat quivering like a virgin's knees. Timmons took a step back towards the safety of the wall.

'Mynheer Vrel . . . Cornelius!' The man clasped Vrel's large hand with one even larger. He slapped at Vrel's upper arm, rustled his lace cuffs, shook his beard and flashed white, white teeth. 'If you ever want to deal in secret again, roast that dog!'

Vrel pulled himself out of the maelstrom. 'Have you left a man on watch?'

'Who do you think is being eaten down there now?' The newcomer focused on Timmons the suddenly still eye of the genial storm. '. . . And is this your speculatory Englishman?'

Timmons stiffened at the tone and cursed the ugly, unintelligible foreign words.

'A mere envoy from the English merchants, chasing after the Dutch lead as always,' said Vrel. 'He won't say how much they can afford to invest.' He switched to English. 'Mr Simeon Timmons, this is Mynheer Justus Coymans.'

Coymans raised his wide-brimmed hat to the Englishman and switched to English also. 'Mynheer Timmons. You're a man of genius to come to Holland at this time to do business!'

'To see if there is any business here worth doing,' said Timmons, more stiffly than he intended. He stayed well out of Coymans's reach.

'No fear,' said Coymans. 'There's no business like it in the world. Forget the Caribes and the Indies! I shall make you as rich as your English king would like to be.'

Timmons's long face sketched a polite smile below its waterline of moustache. 'As I'm not privy to his Majesty's ambitions,' he said, 'that tells me nothing.'

'Rich enough to build a fleet of new ships to wipe the Spanish off the seas,' said Coymans cheerfully. 'And the Dutch.' His teeth showed in the candlelight; his eyes were hidden by the shadow of his hat.

'Amen to the Spanish.' Timmons hesitated. But there was now altogether too much self-satisfaction in the room. He could not resist the lightest of slaps. 'But I believe that our two countries are supposed to be at peace.'

'Ignore politics! They exist only to serve trade.' Coymans snatched off his short cloak and tossed it to the servant. 'Let me show you something more powerful than cannons, more intoxicating than a religious war.'

He seated himself uninvited in Vrel's chair at the head of the long table. From his pouch he took a linen-wrapped parcel which he placed with a flourish on the rug-covered table in front of him. He raised both hands like a wizard poised to enchant and looked up at Vrel.

'Cornelius. *Voilá*! *Ecco*! *Mira*! The new Indies here on your own table!'

Timmons winced at the theatrical excess and peered sceptically through the dim yellow light at the dirty little parcel. He felt the budding of ass's ears begin to prickle at his scalp.

'The *Admiral den Boom*,' said Coymans, and waited for cheers and applause.

Vrel didn't move closer to the table. 'How much?'

Coymans flashed his teeth at Timmons. 'I hope your English clients are more fun to deal with. Cornelius here has no taste for the flourishes that make work into fun. "How much?" he asks. Just like that! Clunk! When I hadn't even finished telling him the whole wonderful story.'

'So tell it,' said Vrel. Coymans was right – he had little patience with whimsy. He went straight for the adding, the subtracting and, most vital of all, the multiplying.

'My *Admiral* here is a miracle,' said Coymans, still including Timmons in the blast of his focus. He dropped his voice to a dramatic stage-whisper. 'He fathers his own offspring without a mother! Would that we all could . . . think of the strife it would save mankind!'

He's going to wink now, thought Timmons with alarmed distaste.

Coymans winked. 'And I have brought Mynheer Vrel the *pater* and two sons.' He leaned forward and hooked his audience more firmly with sharp chilly eyes. 'One son more than God the Father Himself!'

Then Timmons saw the irony behind the chill and felt an uneasy respect. Here was a performer of far greater range and subtlety than himself.

'Like a good pimp, I have brought more than asked for but not more than is desired.'

'You have brought me three *Admirals*?' The pitch of Vrel's low steady voice climbed at least two tones.

Coymans let a beat of silence cut through the candlelight. 'The only three in the world.'

'Impossible.'

'I made sure of it.' Then Coymans added a few swift sentences in Dutch.

Whatever he said shifted the set of the muscles in Vrel's face. The merchant walked to the open window and pretended to look out. He was close enough for Timmons to hear how fast and shallow his breathing had become.

'One thousand florins,' said Vrel.

Timmons understood that much.

'Ptsh,' said Coymans sadly. He drew his knife and cut the leather thongs around the parcel. He laid the knife on the table, then delicately, precisely, unfolded the linen cloth. In its centre lay an irregular egg of dried grass tied with reeds. Coymans cut these bindings. With large-knuckled, reddened fingers he probed the grass, parted it tenderly and pressed it aside. Then he leaned back in his chair.

In spite of himself, Timmons moved closer.

Three onion-like bulbs lay in the grass nest. Each was cased in a papery skin the colour of chestnuts and bearded at its base with a fringe of dried white roots.

Timmons was shocked by how ordinary they looked. Coymans had somehow persuaded him that there really was something wondrous in that packet. Timmons had begun to persuade himself that he wouldn't have to tell the obvious truth when he returned to London – that the Dutch had gone mad and there was no salvation there for the desperate Englishmen. Now the prickling on his scalp grew more insistent.

One thousand florins for those . . . onions!

Coymans lifted one bulb out of the nest into the candlelight, his red fingers as gentle as if it were a phoenix's egg. '*Ecco!* Look there!' He placed a blunt red finger lightly on two tiny, tooth-shaped bulblets just above the union with the roots. 'Two more infant *Admirals*, which will grow to blooming size in three short years. Then there will be five true *Admirals*, all of the same unadulterated substance. Not a rich man's original and four cheap copies for *hoi polloi*. What other commodity can perform this magic?'

When Vrel did not answer, Coymans interrogated Timmons. 'Can gold multiply its true self? Or a porcelain jar? Or a painting?'

Timmons shook his head in helpless assent.

Vrel collected an arrangement of dolphins and mermaids from a sideboard and carried the extra light to the table. 'Blankaart!'

Blankaart leaned forward over the table and extended his wrinkled neck out its lace collar. 'May I?' He picked the largest bulb from the nest and sniffed it. Then he held it close to the candles, turning it in his fingers. '*Tulipa*,' he announced at last.

Coymans blew like a surfacing whale. His moustaches heaved upward on the force of his irritated breath. 'Of course it's a tulip! I don't trade in turnips! Vrel, can't your tame botanist do better than that?'

'Probably not the common Turkish type,' continued Blankaart resolutely, with one eye now on Vrel. 'It's darker and a little longer from base to nose. But an *Admiral den Boom*? Hard to say without seeing it in bloom.'

'It's more expensive to buy in bloom,' said Coymans to Vrel. 'Buy now, in the dry. The advantage will be yours when you sell again.'

'Blankaart?' demanded Vrel. 'What's your advice?'

'If you buy now, you must trust your dealer.' Though Blankaart's voice was flat, his botanist's hands cradled and caressed the smooth chestnut-coloured shape.

A bad actor, thought Timmons. No help to Vrel. In all my ignorance, I could serve better than that.

Coymans's teeth showed briefly in the shadows of his moustaches. 'A cheat can sell only once. I intend to last in business till I'm old as Methuselah.'

'I'll agree a price now but wait till the thing blooms before I pay you,' said Vrel.

'Then I'll sell tomorrow in auction in the *collegium*, as I am bound to do by law,' replied Coymans. 'I'm only risking a private sale because *you* asked it.'

Vrel made a small nervous swing back toward the window. 'Add four barrels of nutmegs, and seven bales of wrought silk.'

Coymans laughed. 'For three? And two offsets? Think what you would have to pay for three bulbs of *Semper Augustus*! Ten times that. And the flames of the Roman emperor are a tiny candle next to the meteor of our own Dutch sailor!' He turned to Blankaart. 'Is that true or not, high priest of things botanical?'

Blankaart swallowed audibly and looked at Vrel. 'The true *Admiral* is a very rare bloom . . . if you can be sure of him. That is the problem. Being sure.'

Vrel sent a dragon's jet of rage toward his perfidious ally.

'The *Semper Augustus* has become a whore with too many masters,' said Coymans. 'And too many little bastards. You alone in Holland would rule our *Admiral*.'

'I'm not a washerwoman or streetsweeper,' warned Vrel, 'who'll give my life savings to some tavern rogue in exchange for an onion.'

'And I'm not a Batavian spice farmer who will accept any price you offer just because your company has a big ship with four hundred guns on it.'

There was a pause.

'Tch,' said Coymans. His moustaches danced like playing dolphins. His teeth appeared and disappeared. 'Oh, Vrel . . . !'

'You've heard my last offer. One thousand florins, the nutmegs, and the silk.'

For a second, Coymans did not move at all. Not a hair, nor ruffle, nor swag, nor fold. Not a moustache. Not a finger. Then he held out his hand. 'May I have that bulb back?' he asked Blankaart politely.

Blankaart returned it with treacherous reluctance.

'How can I raise your value?' Coymans enquired of the bulb. 'Tch.' One moustache arched briefly. He dropped the bulb onto the floor and stamped on it with his boot.

Blankaart gave a strangled yelp of protest.

Coymans stamped again, and ground his sole against the polished wooden floor. He held his boot aloft and peered past it at the white mess on the floor. Then, with his knife, he scraped the rest from the sole of his boot.

'Only two left in the world now,' he said cheerfully. 'And the two infants. We must rethink things a little.'

In the silence, Timmons noticed that the bad-tempered viol had stopped. A nearly-guttered candle on the table sang a high, tiny note. Blankaart coughed.

After a long moment, Coymans pushed the grass nest along the table to Timmons. 'While our friend thinks, would you like to hold a fortune in your hand? Feel for yourself the weight and texture of true wealth?'

Timmons hesitated.

'Go on. I trust you.'

Timmons crossed to the table and picked up a bulb. He turned it curiously in his thin hand. He was only an agent, not one of your gentleman enthusiasts, had never handled such a thing before. Smooth and shiny, like satin against his thumb. Hard under its crisp papery skin, with grey scarring around its neck like a hanged man.

It could just as well be an onion, he thought. How can anyone tell?

He had never before in his life thought about tulips, and certainly not in the same way as spices, or coal, or Baltic grain and oak. He weighed it in his palm.

'Vrel?' asked Coymans.

Vrel still stared at the juicy pulp on his floor. He was breathing heavily now.

'Vrel?' Coymans plucked the last bulb from the grass nest – the one with the two offshoots – and dropped it on the floor. He raised his boot.

'No!' cried Blankaart. 'Please!' He dropped to his knees and snatched at the tulip bulb. 'Ough!' He grunted as Coymans's boot pinned his hand against the floorboards.

'Wait!' Vrel wrapped himself with his thick arms and rocked in an agony of indecision. 'This house . . . and its contents.'

'Not enough.'

Vrel pulled a spark of red fire from a finger of his left hand and dropped it on the table in front of Coymans. Then a chip of ice. 'Let me think!' begged Vrel. 'I was prepared only for one . . . Only expected to pay . . . Just give me a moment to think!' He added a band of gold and a cold tapestry of pearls to the other rings in front of Coymans.

Coymans leaned over and picked the bulb up from the floor. He put it back into the nest, crossed his arms and waited, with his eyes on Vrel's face.

In the following silence, an extraordinary thing happened to Simeon Timmons. The chestnut-coloured tulip bulb in his palm began to change from the ordinary piece of vegetable matter which a few seconds before he could think of only on a slice of bread. First it grew heavier and heavier in his hand, until it was as heavy as the high stacks of bales on the wharf. Heavy as a ship's load of barrelled nutmegs and pepper. Heavy as the wood and stone and brick from which men build palaces. As heavy as gold.

The shiny chestnut skin grew translucent. In the heart of the bulb, Timmons saw the growing glow of the ruby ring, the diamond, and the pearls. And deep among all these fires flickered the small glints of greed in the eyes of Cornelius Vrel. In his hand, Timmons held possibility. For the men in London. And for himself, perhaps, at last.

Only a few years earlier, all the riches of the East Indies had been mere possibility. Travellers' tales. Speculative dreams. Then brave men, with wit, patience and imagination had turned possibility into the reality of ships, spices and empires.

They sent me from London to assess possibilities, thought Timmons. Am I brave enough to tell the Company to forget Baltic grain, Chinese porcelain *kraacke-ware*, nutmegs and gold? For the possibility I am holding in my hand? For onions?

One

May 22, 1636. Sun at last. A sad cold night. Hot bed
cucumbers in bud under handglasses. First swallow. Too
much to do before Eden opens her gates. The Serpent
stirs.

> *Journal* of John Nightingale, known as John Graffham.

At fourteen he had been dangerous. At twenty-six, he feared,
he had become merely reliable.

John crunched across the gravel forecourt of Hawkridge
House in long angry strides, scattering geese and speckled
goslings. A yellow cur from the stable yard trotted purposefully after him with its nose stuck to his heavy work boots
to read his morning of horse, herb, pigeon and pig.

John stopped abruptly and glared over the high brick forecourt wall. In two days, even reliability would be stripped
from him.

'Heads down, lads,' muttered a man with a rake.

Fourteen men and women, cottagers and workers on Hawkridge estate, watched him sideways as they weeded, raked
and polished.

'Poor man,' said a young weeding woman under her breath.
She hoiked a plantain rosette out of the gravel of the forecourt
with a stubby knife and tossed it into a wooden trug.

'Poor us,' said her companion who squatted beside her in

a crumple of woollen skirt. She uprooted a hawkbit. 'He's family. He'll be all right.'

The two women waddled their bunched skirts forward like a pair of geese to attack a young colony of Shepherd's Purse.

'He'll see us all right too,' said the first woman.

'. . . if he's here to do it.'

They twitched their goosetail skirts forward again, eyes still on the dark, curly-haired, bearded storm which had blown itself to a brief stop in the centre of the forecourt. What would the Londoners make, they wondered, of a gentleman with such brown hands and arms, who wore coarse linen shirts rolled to the elbow and a leather jerkin? Each then looked down into her private fears. Change was almost never good.

John's black brows, as delicate as a woman's, dived fiercely together over a long, fine but slightly skewed nose. Light grey eyes gave him a wolfish look. A labourer who was oiling the iron forecourt gates turned uphill towards the road to see what had caused that grey-eyed rage, but he pursed his lips, puzzled. Beyond the forecourt wall, the avenue of beeches that curved down from the road to the house rustled peacefully with sea-green early leaf. High up, near the road, a cottager swung his scythe through the long grass, wild campions and meadow cranesbills. A spotted flycatcher dropped from a beech into the grass. Sheep munched.

The yellow cur waited a moment, then sat and pressed its muzzle against the man's thigh. John's brown hand stroked absently. The dog brushed the gravel with its tail. It sighed with delight. The man did not usually stand still for so long.

Above John's head a breeze rippled and lifted the corners of scarlet and yellow curtains flung out to air over the sills of the upper windows of the pink brick house.

John closed his eyes. He hated to think about himself. A man should be master of his mind. Instead, his had mastered him, and he had no time for such weakness.

28

He flew through the ring of fire, fell like Icarus away from the dreadful heat of the sun.

He squeezed his thoughts smaller and smaller until they shrank to the feel of the cold, friendly nose in his palm.

The fire leaped, closed its claws on his scalp and lit the arc of his fall.

Indignant and terrified, he shaped his palm to the dog's flat furry skull.

'What's wrong with me, eh boy?' he asked the dog, under his breath. 'Why has this come back to me now?'

The curly yellow tail scraped twice across the gravel. John looked down, suddenly jealous. I want to live just like you, in a rich web of scents, he thought. To chase rabbits, dig badgers, beg kitchen scraps, lift a hind leg where I like and mount an occasional bitch, with no grief for the past or fear for the future.

He looked back towards the house and caught the two weeding women eyeing him. Everywhere on the estate, that same look in everyone's eyes – a mix of curiosity, pity and glee – had maddened him ever since the news of his uncle's death had arrived.

'Good morning, sir!'

John wrily noted their confusion as they dropped their eyes, but missed the note of affectionate respect.

His uncle, Sir George Beester, had died three months ago, five years after buying a baronetcy from King Charles and eighteen months after the death from dysentery of his only child, James. The news of Sir George's death reached Hawkridge House three weeks after his burial, along with the news that his heir was now the only son of his only brother, John's younger cousin Harry. John was unfortunately in the female line.

Harry had inherited everything, as was the practice in order to keep estates intact: the Somerset wool-producing estate, the London house, the business interests, the title of baronet and Hawkridge estate. In two days, Harry's carriage would roll through the gates and dump into all their lives not only Harry, but his London friends, London servants, London in-laws, and rich new London wife. In two days the real master would arrive to claim his own.

He would take back from John the control over every penny spent. He would decide what work was or was not to be done, and who would do it. He would choose who could live in which cottage and who would use which field. He could turn any person he pleased off the estate, to go and make a living somewhere else if they could.

No one asked me to meddle for the last eleven years, John told himself. It suited me. Now I must accept the truth that Harry can turn me out of my own bed if he likes. He stared at the iron gates through which the alien carriages would roll.

Tuddenham, the estate manager, waved from the top of the long drive that curved down from the brow of the hill between the avenue of beeches. He loped down the hill, bald as a stone and lopsided from an accident with a cart. John crossed his arms and waited, happy to be distracted from both Cousin Harry and the remembered fire.

'The holes by the gatehouse is filled now, sir,' said Tuddenham.

'Keep two men working on the road itself till we can hear their carriages creak,' said John. 'Muddy or not, Hampshire roads are better than what I hear of London streets.'

Tuddenham looked with approval at the scraping, pulling, raking and polishing in the forecourt. 'You've got them all on the hop this morning, sir. The fox is nearly at the hen-house door, eh?' His voice was a touch too hearty.

John bared white teeth, whose full number and colour were a mark of privileged diet, as were his full head of dark acorn-coloured hair and neat, healthy, curling russet beard. 'And aren't we all shuffling on our perches!'

Tuddenham slid him a sharp, oblique glance. 'You'll stay, won't you, sir?'

'I don't know.'

The scarlet and yellow curtains snapped overhead in the silence that followed. Both men looked up. A housemaid leaned dangerously out of an open window to polish the diamond panes of glass. As she rubbed, the top of a blanc-mange breast quivered in time with her skirts. When she felt the men's eyes on her, she rubbed harder. The two men glanced at each other and smiled, rescued from awkwardness by the shared perfunctory lust.

'I must go finish the accounts,' said John. He gave the dog's nose a final rub and went reluctantly into the cool shadows of the big house.

The estate audit room at the front of the east wing served as his office. John ignored the accounts on his table. He ran his hand along a whale's rib that hung on one wood-panelled wall and waited for his spirits to lift. But he stayed rooted in his office tucked behind the housekeeper's room, within smell of the kitchens, instead of swooping along the bone, through time and space on the steed of his imagination, onto the bloody sea-tossed deck of the ship that had captured the beast. An early flesh-fly buzzed in tight circles near the ceiling.

He turned next for comfort to the coffers that held his books, but his teachers and friends, Pliny, Columella, Cato, Varro and Virgil, lay unbeckoning in their caskets, as mute as the dead men that they really were.

John grew frightened. He did not recognize this state of being.

He opened the drawers of his collection, on which he spent every minute he could spare from estate work. He gazed with rising panic at lizard bones, rare seeds (among them a plum-stone carved with the Passion of Christ), green and scarlet beaks, three strange fishes turned to stone, eighty-six labelled eggs, a dried elephant's pizzle, shell creatures, and minerals that looked like toadstools. A few weeks ago, these had shimmered with import, like sun on the horizon of the sea. Now they lay slack in their drawers, as dull as the eye of a dead trout. Not even his oddities stirred him.

With his forefinger, he stroked his strand of fleece from a borometz. He had pursued the creature for uncounted joyful hours through the multi-layered ambiguities of the classical authorities – a plant-animal, a sheep that grew on a tulip stem and died when it had grazed a full circle. The crinkled wool looked very like the tufts snagged by bushes from his own sheep. He knew now that he had never believed.

He closed the drawer and stepped to the window, desolate. Once, with the passion and joy of secret vice, he had arranged, listed and described, in meticulous categories, drawer by drawer. For eleven years his hungry mind had chewed on these fragments of the forbidden world and been almost satisfied. He had never imagined that this passion might abandon him so abruptly.

He pressed his forefinger hard against a spike of a swollen blow-fish on the windowsill. His blood ran as slowly as chilled grease.

Lord, don't let this strange, fearful torpor be envy of Harry, he begged. Send me a more dignified demon to wrestle. The fly circled his head.

He pushed open the window and sniffed the medicinal tang of rosemary and thyme, sweetened by the citrus tinge of freshly clipped box. From his bedchamber above the office, he could clearly see the entire labyrinthine perfection of the Knot Garden which had been his first mark on the estate, made eleven years ago.

Harry will find more than I did when I skulked here to hide as a fourteen-year-old outlaw. Immaculate brick walls instead of rotting wattles, woodpiles stacked neatly as carpets, a herd of sheep with the new short-staple fleece, and new gardens in which (however temporarily) Nature's rush to disorder has been checked. Even the cabbages in the Field Garden grow as neatly as French knots in a lady's embroidery.

His chest felt tight. He circled the room and alighted at his table again. He fingered the lists that had shaped the last weeks. The black lines through each task were crossing off the rest of his life. Little remained to be done.

Even his Aunt Margaret's chaotic domestic kingdom was reasonably in order. Feather mattresses were laid over the straw in the guest beds, and the grooms in the horse barn had extra rugs. Each time John passed the kitchen, some new panic there was breeding still more meat pies, braided cakes and vats of brawn. Sixty smoked hams hung from spikes beside twenty-eight flitches of bacon. Fifty hens were at this moment losing their heads and four pigs dangled nose-down dripping into pails in the butchery shed.

He picked up the accounts. Under them lay a letter from his cousin. John put the accounts down again, on top of the letter. He stirred his ink and began to cross out items on his aunt's latest provision list with fierce blobbed lines.

Ten pounds of nutmegs. Done! Two hundredweight of sugar. Too expensive – use honey instead! Cinnamon . . . He threw down the pen and ran his hands through his hair.

Fear.

He swallowed. His demon was not Envy. It was Fear.

He pulled Harry's letter from under the accounts. The fire dream had returned, for the first time in many years, the night that the letter arrived. Blotched and smeared, scrawled from edge to edge in a schoolboy hand, the letter looked harmless enough, like Harry.

. . . I beg you, dear coz, to prepar me a triumf worthy of a new Cesar (yore littel cozin and former play mate) who hardly knows himself yet in his new elavashun but likes it WELL ENOUGH.

I will bring my new wyf (more anon) and, alas, a stern senator of Rome (her unkel and gardian, with his wyf) Who would like to pluck off my laural wreeth. But better, I will also bring a deer new frend who carrys wate with our French Qween and has a very speshul purpose to you, coz, in making his visit . . .

John re-read the last sentence twice. A cold weight settled in the bottom of his stomach. He ran his eyes blindly over the rest.

. . . need decent lodging for 8 grooms, 2 women, 6 coach horses, 4 cart ox . . . new shirts payed by me to all the estate . . . Guest mattresses please be dry and free of mice . . . silver piss pots if possible for guests . . .

He smoothed the letter on the table. Surely he had been forgotten in Whitehall by now. He was exaggerating his own importance. But Fear tightened its armlock.

His hand stroked the corner of his chin where a scar interrupted the neat beard.

'. . . a deer new frend who carrys wate with our French Qween and has a very speshul purpose to you . . .'

Harry means nothing by that. He's a self-absorbed cheerful fool, not a traitor. I seek a false importance, John told himself. To make up for the fact that when Harry arrives, I will become who I really am – no one at all.

He kicked away his stool and left the office. Fear slid at his heels after him.

The wood-panelled corridor smelled of cheeses and spilled cider. John passed the open door of the housekeeper's sitting-room and office that guarded the entrance to the locked storeroom. The centre of his aunt's untidy web was empty. His Aunt Margaret, unmarried and a tough, dry-fibred weed of a woman surrounded by a halo of fluff, was elsewhere leading

34

her house staff in a concerto of rising panic. John heard her voice faintly through the open windows.

'Agatha! Agatha, where in Heaven's ... here, take this corner!'

Beyond the housekeeper's room lay the kitchen. As John entered, a twelve-year-old housegroom who was counting candles nodded with moving lips, still counting. John turned right, through the long, narrow scullery and smock-room, and stepped out into a narrow, brick-paved alley. From beyond a brick wall at the left end of the alley, the dog yard in the *basse-court* echoed with yaps. Straight ahead, across the alley and through an arch lay his gardens, where man could constantly repeat the perfection of beginnings.

The herbier came first, built in the elbow where the chapel met the house, handy for the kitchen pots and for the still-room in the *basse-court* at the back of the house. A south-facing wall trapped the sun, to develop the herbal essences and ripen the grapes on the knotted Muscadine vine pinned to the wall.

The woody herbs in the long strip beds had been clipped that morning. John inhaled the brutal scent of bruised rue and the resin of the rosemary which he permitted, as a fond indulgence, to sprawl across the paved walk like a woman's skirts. He tried to admire the naked, weedless dirt between the demure ranks of infant borages and clary.

I have been forgotten in London.

This likely truth did not cheer him as much as it should. He bent and pulled up a minute speedwell, then passed through a second arch into the Knot Garden.

He had reclaimed this square of earth from bramble and breeding rabbits and it still, though not today, gave him stabs of pleasure which he tried to see as satisfaction with honest labour, not wicked pride. Box entwined with germander outlined a four-cornered device of interlocking squares. Within these living walls, sharp-cornered as newly-planed wood, sat thymes, lavender cotton, wood strawberries and auriculas, which would cover the earth in full summer and delight all his senses.

The device itself was framed by a square of brick herring-bone walks. Outside these walks lay a further square of four long beds in which grew John's fragile darlings, his objects of study and his roses.

Not a leaf out of place. Not an unruly twig to nip. John plunged onward into the New Garden.

Where the Knot Garden was for contemplation, the New Garden filled bellies. It was nearly a hundred paces end to end and walled with brick to the height of eleven feet, with a low double brick fruiting wall as its long axis. That morning two gardeners were ridging the cucumbers in a hot bed made of horse-dung, built by John according to the Roman model. Eight weeding women sidled on their haunches along rows of feathery carrots and blunt young cabbages. Four more, under the eye of Cope the chief gardener, tended newly sprouted beans and lettuces. Birds perched in lines on the wall tops, waiting to swoop on the beetles and grubs so kindly being turned up for them.

My *hortus conclusus*, thought John, as Cope hailed him. Where I emulate the closed Garden that God built around all that he valued, to shut out the wilderness. In two more days, my Eden must open her gates.

'... finches,' Cope was saying.

'Hire more boys to drive them off,' John heard a distant self reply. 'We'll need all our fruit with this plague of guests.'

The two men walked a moment in silence. Cope stooped and pulled an early radish. He rubbed it clean against his leather apron, then gave it to John to taste.

John bent his senses to the peppery crunch and the prickle of hairy cloth-like leaves, but was distracted by the anxiety in Cope's eyes.

'An excellent radish, Cope. And the gardens are as ready

as imperfect Nature can ever be. My cousin will be pleased.'

'And you, sir?' Cope was Cope junior, about John's age and new to his responsibilities, trained by his father who had died that winter. John filled him with terror relieved by moments of shared satisfaction.

'Adam's own Paradise was never finer,' said John. He tossed the radish leaves into a trug and fled before he was tempted to add that his opinion no longer mattered.

The three fishponds lay in a line behind the house, parallel to its length. They were fed from the western end by the slow, brown Shir which flowed lazily through them, gathered energy at the weir, slid a little faster toward the mill pond and then pounded along the race. John had diverted a channel from above the ponds through the cellar of the house to provide storage for wine and food that was cool on the hottest summer day. And though John's tidying grip had loosened around the ponds, Nature still served man obediently with carp, pike, freshwater eels, rushes and willow withes.

The spring ducklings were already half-grown and the colour of dead rushes. A drake flapped on tiptoe along the surface of the middle pond, then lurched suddenly into the air. The accompanying clamour in the reeds died to an absent-minded murmur. John reached the bottom pond, crossed the narrow plank of the weir bridge and marched up the slope of Hawk Ridge into the precise grid of the orchard he had made.

Bees plunged in and out of the mud and wicker skeps John had set among the trees. The medlars were already blown. The Swan's Egg pears had set. The buds of the later pears and apples were still tight and pink as toe-tips on the angled grey spurs. John emerged from the trunks of Great Russetings and Billiborues onto the grassy crest and looked back down at the house. In the grass at his feet, a runaway hen peered anxiously over the rim of an abandoned bucket where she had laid secret eggs.

*   *   *

Hawkridge House sat low in the valley, astride the buried stream, a modest H-shaped hall of pink brick, with a fine stone porch in the centre of the cross bar and a small crenellated chapel crouched on the north-east corner. She had been built with her head down just after King Henry died, when too many noble rumps were aiming at the same time for the English throne.

I do not aspire, the house seemed to say. I am one of the blessed meek.

The house and her estate had remained unraped while ambition and politics had burned greater manors and lopped overweening heads elsewhere.

John looked down at the single storey of the *basse-court*. Stillroom, dairy, dog yard, laundry, schoolroom, storage sheds, around a paved yard. Behind this fruitful jumble, the north front of the house rose like a smooth tawny forehead. Sun glinted on her leads and warmed the rosy brick of her dormers and crenellations.

Mine for eleven years, in truth if not in law. The womb of my invention, chief object of my will, the only true measure of my life on this earth. For the last eleven years I have hidden in her safe embrace.

John loved her as if she were a woman. Now he was preparing her for another man.

He stamped down on his jealous rage, but felt a new wash of fear. A void opened. There was nothing left for him to do. He could not see himself three days from now.

A bee rattled in the grass near his feet.

Even Nature rules against me, he thought. Take bees, a model of loyalty to the common good. When their kings become too numerous, they reluctantly destroy them.

He walked on, across the crest of Hawk Ridge, down through the hazel copses that gave game birds cover and up the steeper slope of the beech hanger.

Among the beeches stood the Lady Tree. Like her sisters,

she was grey-trunked and copper-clawed now in the late spring. Pale sea-green leaflets were just twisting clear of their translucent claws. Like her sisters, she had been coppiced a hundred or so years before, her leading shoot cut out for firewood or a fence pole by an assart-holder or poaching peasant. Their side branches had grown into similar goblets around empty centres. Unlike her sisters, she was more than a tree.

I should cut her down, thought John as he always did. She's too disturbing to be part of God's design. But who on this estate would do it?

One of her branches had grown, not up but out, at the height of John's hip, into a naked woman.

She was a little larger than life-size, stretched full length half on her side, shameless as if she waited for her lover. Her head and arms were hidden inside the trunk from which her two armpits arched. The armpits led to two breasts, tightly nippled with broken branch stumps. A ribcage, then a rounded belly and perfect navel. A bulging mound of Venus, then two voluptuous thighs began to curve gently upward. Above the thighs, stretched two slim calves. These elongated themselves, divided like a mermaid's tail, divided again, then again into arching, springy branches as regular as lace.

She feigned sleep, one eye open to see what the man was up to. Yet another visitor. So many this spring. Never so many before.

She shook her amber claws, as pointed as frost, from which the pale green leaves already escaped.

Do I bless or curse? she asked, as she asked all visitors. Take your chance. I'm as sure as life, no more, no less. I make no false promises, but my roots reach far beneath your feet. Plant your deepest desires between the knobby curves, under my moss, and see what grows. Take a chance.

*   *   *

39

The earth between her roots was pocked with fresh mounds. John counted seventeen. A garden of fears and desires. He knelt and dug. He found a slip of parchment tied with hair, a prayer in misspelled Latin – Deliver Us from Evil.

He sat back on his heels and let out a shaky breath. Amen.

In other years he had found phials of menstrual blood and other vital fluids, names, pieces of silver, knife blades. His eyes traced her armpits, her breasts, her belly, her sex, and followed her legs upward. A fresh rowan wreath hung around one of her knees like a loose garter. High on the main trunk above her invisible head, someone had skewered a thrush.

I wonder if Dr Bowler knows who his real rival is on the estate, thought John.

So, she said to the man. You have finally realized that I am stronger than that garden of yours down there, that so-called little paradise behind her brick walls. Her space is full of silent battles. She is eaten up by her enemies. So small, so insignificant, so thorough, they eat holes in her walls and undermine her paths. She is dying from within. Take a chance with me!

Defiantly, he placed his left hand on the meeting of her thighs, to prove what or to whom, he was not sure. When Harry comes and I'm kicking my heels (if indeed I'm still welcome) I'll draw her for my collection. An oddity.

Her bark was as firm as bone, and delicately rough like a woman's fur. The pointed shadow under his fingers shook desire loose from its lashings at the back of his mind. He remembered the white, quivering flesh of the maid on the high windowsill.

It has been so long! he thought suddenly. Months without a woman, ever since my weeding woman Cat married her cooper and moved from the house to the village.

He leaned his forehead against the grey trunk. Lord help me! he thought. Not this as well.

Lust had found the crack in his wall that both fear and envy had missed. The flood broke through. His knees weakened. His throat felt swollen. His skin grew cold and damp. Fear and appetite tumbled together. Reason and good intent spun away downstream like dead leaves. He squeezed himself down onto his boot heels among the roots of the tree and pressed his back against her trunk.

I must be ill!

He thrust his hands into the leaf mould. His head fell back against the grey bark.

Lord, are you listening? I do not envy my cousin! I will not! I have had more than most men. I am grateful.

Nevertheless there was that other ghostly man with a different name, whom John had last known when he was fourteen.

I don't know what he might have been today.

Dark emptiness scoured his gut. He felt as hollow as a bee tree, as fragile as a dried snakeskin. A breeze slid into his open collar, stroked his brown neck and teased the ends of his hair. The tree shook her mermaid tail gently above his head.

Spare me from envy. *Absit invidia*. Let there be no ill will. Ill will is unreasonable, and I have made myself into a reasonable man.

The tree lifted her branches on the back of the breeze and let them fall again.

John shivered.

I thought I was brave. But I am afraid, Lady. I fear. I fear and I want. Oh, how I want my own lands again. My own name. A reason for my life!

Once, rustled the Lady Tree. Once you had it all. Once. Once.

Then to her taunt, she added temptation.

Ask. Ask.

*　　*　　*

41

He flew through the ring of fire like a trained dog at St Bartholomew's Fair. The flames jumped, clamped their claws into his scalp and rode him in a bright arc to the ground.

☙

John had been a child of ivory beauty. Even in babyhood his fingers were long and slim, his legs straight and finely-shaped. His skin was smooth at a time when a third of the people were pitted with pox. He read at four and showed early promise in Latin, Greek and Hebrew. By five he had proved to be well co-ordinated, good at riding, swordplay and all the other male games which keep thoughtful, intelligent boys from being laughed at by their peers. His grey eyes, at seven, already caused stabs of female anticipation. In short, he was a prince in a kingdom that knew his worth.

His paternal grandfather, Howard Nightingale, had been young and ambitious when King Henry annexed Catholic lands after the English split with the Church of Rome. Though the son of a London brewer, the grandfather had been well-educated and found a patron to provide three years at Oxford, from where he had emerged with a fair knowledge of law. In exchange for loyal services to several influential Tudor lords, Nightingale was given a confiscated Catholic estate, Tarleton Court near Hatfield. Shortly after, he bought a second once-Catholic estate, Farfields, for a token price and set his family on the ladder to power. John's parents were still only the middling sort of gentlefolk, but by the time he was born late in their marriage they had prospered enough to buy two more estates.

They were overwhelmed that their only surviving child should be one such as John. They prayed that he live to manhood, masked their doting with severity (which did not fool their small son in the least), acquired still more land to

42

swell his fortune, and bought him a gentleman's education to shape him for a life of influence at the court in Whitehall. He would have been a blind saint if, from an early age, he had not been infected by their sense of his destiny. By miracle, he was not a monster.

Both his own nature and his parents' good sense guided him toward civil manners and a burning concern for others, who included not only his parents and his nurse, but the house families in the Nightingale estates, his many cousins, the young stable grooms who played with him, his horses, his dogs, a hen with a twisted leg, a papery globe of tiny spiders glued to the tester of his bed, butterflies doomed to short lives, and one particular piglet whose death made him refuse bacon between the ages of four and six.

In 1617, when he turned seven, the time came to place him out. His father wooed a London lord on the fringes of the Court to take his son into the noble household for polishing into final splendour. The lord agreed. Master and Mistress Nightingale accompanied John to London from Tarleton Court, their chief estate, north of Hatfield. John's father had business in the city with a tanner who bought hides from him, as well as with an impoverished knight with a small estate to sell. John's mother seized the chance to visit her wool merchant brother, who was still plain Mr George Beester, in his London house rather than on his distant Somerset manor.

They set out at dawn. While a horseman could reach London in one long day, their coach needed at least two on the muddy track which served as a road. John hung out of the window until he bit his tongue going over a bad bump. Then he begged a ride on top with the driver and footman.

A unexpectedly swollen ford cost them three and a half hours by bumpy lane upstream to a place where the coach could cross. John was briefly entertained by his father's angry and puzzled speculation why some idiot had dammed the river just downstream. But as the party lacked men to tear the dam down, the detour had to be made. They were still at least two hours away from their inn and deep in the shade of a forest of oaks and beech when the sun set. The footman lit the carriage lamps. Bored and hungry, John fell asleep with his head on his nurse's lap.

He half-woke to urgent adult voices. The coach rocked violently. The inside lantern swung like a ship's lamp in a storm. But the coach had stopped rolling.

'Are we there?' asked John. His mother grabbed his arm as if she meant to tear off his sleeve. John sat up, wide awake.

A man screamed in the darkness outside the coach. The scream died abruptly. John's father threw himself against the inside of the coach door.

'Richard! Who is it? What do they want?' asked his mother.

His father didn't seem to hear her. Dimly, in the swinging arcs of lantern light, John saw the continent of his father's back bunch and quiver under his coat. The coach rocked harder. The darkness outside moved and flickered with orange light. John heard crackling and smelled oily smoke.

'Oh, sweet God!' cried his nurse.

His mother whimpered once, like a struck dog.

His father cried out and fell across John's legs. A comet blazed through the coach window. Hungry stars spilled onto the crowded, heaped-up yards of gown, cloak, lace and petticoat. The stars bit. Flames ran around the edges of sleeves and spread across skirts. His mother screamed; her hair had caught fire. The coach filled with the smell of burning silk and wool, and seethed like a bag of drowning cats.

Still screaming, John's mother hauled him from under his father's dead weight and thrust him into the air, through the burning hoop of the window like a performing dog at St Bartholomew's Fair. The flames in his hair sketched the arc of his fall against the night.

*　　*　　*

John stood so abruptly that he hit his shoulder against the ribcage of the Lady Tree.

I am ill, he thought. Soul sick.

He wished that Dr Bowler, the estate parson, were as confident in advising the soul as he was in making music.

I can't welcome Harry in this state.

He shook himself like Cassie, his wolfhound. The world tilted. He put one hand on the tree to steady himself.

Dizzy and hollow. Diseased in his soul. No way to head into a new, unknown life.

He lifted his hand from the belly of the tree. He should not have come here. She always unsettled him.

He slid back down the slope of the beech hanger on last year's dead leaves, towards the mill pond. Often before this he had found his reason again in that dark water, when he had thought it was lost.

The mill still slept its winter sleep, locked up around the last season's chaff and dust. The big wheel dripped, heavy and unmoved by the trickle of the closed-off race. The mill pond above the race, where Bedgebury Brook joined the lethargic Shir, brimmed with melted snows and spring rains not yet needed to grind corn. The surplus tugged at the tips of arching grass blades as it poured downstream through the open sluice.

John stepped out onto a stony shelf above the pond. Another self looked back up from the dark water. A cloud of early gnats hung and sideslipped just above the surface. To his right the Shir ducked in and out of the trees, back upstream toward the three fish ponds, in slow green bends. Silver teeth of young nettle leaves and dark matte-green lance-heads of burdock grew at his feet. Across the pond, black-trunked willows eased into leaf. The branches of a fallen willow drew v's on the current. The stream, the pond, the plants, the trees, and his reflection wavered as if John looked through the uneven glass of a window pane.

A fish leaped. John's reflection heaved and rippled. He stripped naked, drew a deep breath and dived.

The icy water, still cold from the winter, peeled him as cleanly as a willow rod. It stripped away thought, leaving a pure white core of muscle and bone. He surfaced, gasped, shook his head like a dog, alive with the shock. Cold eddies caressed his toes in the brown-green depths. Icy liquid fingers squeezed his balls tight into his groin and tugged gently at the dark hairs on his arms and shins.

He coiled and slid under again. He turned among the fragments of floating leaf and weed, opened his eyes to look up through the faint cold green light to the silver underside of the water, his eyelashes heavy with bubbles. He knifed deeper. Let himself drift upwards through the layers of warm and cold water until he burst through the silver into the air.

The air flowed freely into the crevices around his heart. He took a deep breath and felt his weight lighten. He pulled himself back below the surface and swam until the water threw him up again.

One foot touched ground. He stood and scooped the water in cupped hands over his head. When the last drop curved behind his left ear and fell from his lobe, he scooped again. Then again. His skin quivered under each delicate, chilly blow. He shook his head, opened his eyes and saw the woman standing on the far bank.

Cat. His former weeding woman, now married to the cooper. Who had deserted his garden and bed for a lean-to attached to the cooperage in the village. The gnat swarm sideslipped between them. Her shape quivered.

'Good day, Cat.'

'John.' She moved from the bushes that hid the mouth of the path onto the ledge beside his heap of clothes. 'I had forgotten how long and lean you look. Sleek as an otter with your curls plastered back. I thought I'd always remember, but it goes so fast.'

'And there's another to remember now instead.'

She smiled. Neither of them moved. John stood naked in the green-brown water up to his chest. The woman, in a dirty brown wool work skirt, unlaced bodice and linen shirt, looked down as she rerolled one sleeve to her elbow. Finally she nodded equably. 'That's so.'

'Is all well?' He hadn't seen her since the wedding. He didn't know whether he had avoided her, or she him.

'More than well.' She made no move to leave.

John began to feel foolish. He was too fragile, just now, for games. He looked at his clothes. Cat followed the direction of his glance.

'No need to feel modest with me,' she said, but her eyes grew suddenly uncertain.

A shiver of possibility rippled over John's skin. He swam two slow strokes back across the pond towards Cat and his clothes. Then he stopped and looked at her again.

'Oh, John,' she said. 'I followed you here. A married woman. Isn't that wicked?'

'Only if you leave me now.'

Cat stepped back off the ledge. 'This way,' she said, 'along here.' She picked her way around the pond edge, over kingcups and mud to a thicket of yellow-green willows. She parted their curtain with her hands and vanished like a player from a stage.

John waded from the pond, shedding water like a ship in a storm and slipped after her into the green haze. A sudden lustful hope nearly blinded him. Cat stood by the leaning trunk of a mature tree, thick-trunked herself but still graceful. He had seen her dark blond hair, now caught back in a cap from her square-cornered face, drifting as loose as the willow fronds on the water. His gut lurched and his member stiffened.

'You say things are more than well with your cooper,' he said thickly.

'And I mean them to stay that way.' She looked him in the eye. 'We're a good solid match. But I've thought of you . . . and how sudden I married. I'm sorry I didn't tell you sooner.'

'Did you follow me just to apologize?' Lust teetered towards humiliated rage. She had flushed him into the open only to leave him there.

'No. I thought you'd not object to one last time.'

He couldn't speak. His mouth dried. His pulse drummed in his ears. In his strange ill state, he had misjudged her. He had forgotten her inability to toy with what she saw as the truth. At times her solid directness had weighed him down when he had wanted apostrophes, trills and flourishes in their passion. Now she held him in place.

She offered her mouth for him to kiss, then leaned back in his arms. He sank his face into the warm curve of her neck. She smelled strong but sweet, like his herbs.

'I wanted to see,' she said dreamily, 'how it is, just once, when we don't fear making a little bastard. I mean one last time, don't mistake me.'

'No,' he promised, with his muzzle in the cup above her collarbone.

They had seldom mistaken each other, which was why he had liked as well as desired her even when he hankered for something more.

Cat broke back out of his embrace and lifted the hem of her skirt. 'Here, let me dry you a little.'

'Come back!' He slid his wet arms under the petticoats, feeling for her warm skin. 'Oh, sweet Heaven, you're so warm, and I'm so cold!'

'Not for long.' She rubbed his bare chest and then his thighs. 'You are a fool to swim so early.'

He grinned suddenly. The wolf eyes gleamed. 'But look what it brought me!' He felt suddenly easy with her again, as he had for two and a half steady years before she married the village cooper, when he had watched her crouched near him in the gardens intent on slaughtering infant weeds and only half-aware of his eyes. He slid his hand into her bush. 'No fool, Cat. Not at all.'

She hissed between her teeth, blinked, then smiled into his eyes. She pulled her low-cut bodice from her shoulders and eased her brown nipples up into the reach of his mouth and fingers. He pressed her back and down. She twisted away.

'Not on the ground. I can't carry all those witnesses on my back and sleeves and hair. Here. Come over here.'

She leaned forward with her hands on a willow trunk, her skirts and petticoats bunched across her back. He thrust himself home between her magnificent haunches.

A familiar place he thought he had lost. Warm, friendly, familiar.

'Oh, God!' she said, muffling her voice. 'Oh yes.' She pressed her forehead against the tree's bark. 'Oh yes!'

Never to leave, never to leave. Warm, deep, dark, and infinitely friendly. He was all right again. Solid. There.

Need pushed him too fast. Sooner than he wanted, than he meant, he muffled a shout, sighed from his toe-tips and laid his head between her shoulder-blades. Their ribs heaved in unison. Pond water dripped from the ends of his hair onto her bare brown skin.

'I would have liked a longer farewell feast,' he finally said. 'A Roman banquet of courses.' He leaned his hands on the tree, with an arm on either side of her.

She turned to face him, her back now against the tree. 'Don't be a fool. You've never been one before.' With her thumb, she wiped water from his black brows. 'A good hearty tup, my love. More than enough, and right for now.'

She was a good-natured woman, even though she would not have said no if John had offered more, back when she had not had an offer from the cooper, a kind man of her own estate in life, with a skill which would always be needed by civilized man.

49

She stretched her handsome face up and kissed him. "'Twill do me nicely. We're neither of us love-sick idiots.'

At that moment John was not so sure. His spasm had eased his fear, but not the yearning in his bones. The woman in his arms was generous. Her generosity moved him towards words he knew he might regret.

She held out the front of her dress and tucked her teats back into their nest. Then she ran her hands along his arms. 'You're bumpy as a plucked hen. I'd hate to be the death of you from ague. You'd best go get dry and clothed.' One finger stroked his cold, limp member. 'And find some other way of keeping that warm.'

'None better than you,' he said.

'Words to warm me to my grave.' She ducked under his arm and began to shake down her layers of linen and wool.

He plucked a grey-green willow-leaf dagger from the front of her thick, wavy hair.

'We'll still smile when we meet?' she asked.

'Why not?' He drew the leaf down the ridge of her nose, then handed it to her like a rose. He watched her think. Then she decided not to say more. John was relieved. He was not angry at her marriage; he understood her necessity. He himself was not a fit husband for anyone. He was grateful to her for two and a half years of ease and delight. And yet, something coiled deep in his gut was best left undisturbed.

Cat ducked her head suddenly in the ghost of a curtsey. Gathering her ease around her like a cloak in cold weather, she turned away through the willows, back along the muddy bank. John parted the willows to look after her. He would miss watching those haunches shift their weight from foot to foot as she advanced, crouching, along a row of carrots or borage. When she disappeared he felt hollow again. Another line drawn through his life.

He began to tug his clothes back on over damp, sticky skin. At least the madness was gone. Between them the cold water and Cat had flushed it out even if they had not truly eased him. As he hauled at his boots, John decided that although he was still not his former self he should be able to throw his new demon in a worthy fall or two.

On the way back upstream towards the fish ponds, he paused to listen to the voices of the water – treble gurgles, alto murmurs and a low pounding bass pulse in the shadows of the bend.

'Gone, gone,' said the water. 'On. On.'

The pale wolf eyes stared at a patch of froth which struggled for ever above the same stone to race upstream.

I have found my reason only to lose it again, he thought. He could not shake off a troubling fancy that he had just been paid an ambiguous bribe by the Lady Tree.

Two

May 23, 1636. Water horsetail in bloom. 2nd swallow.
Apple buds relaxed, about to blow, very late. A second
dry day. I hide in small things.

> *Journal* of John Nightingale, known as John Graffham.

'I don't know how Harry can ask it of us!' Aunt Margaret
wailed. She yanked her skirt hem from the closed door of the
housekeeper's office, where it had caught. Stiffened hip joints
gave her small figure the rolling walk of a sailor.

John looked out of his aunt's window into the immaculate
forecourt. The geese had got in again and left grey-green
droppings. If only he could freeze all living things until Harry
Beester and his Londoners had arrived tomorrow.

'All those extra grooms and maids and Lord knows who
else! We should have slaughtered another dozen pigs last
autumn!'

Her fingers moved even more intently than they usually
did, constantly checking the location and solidity of things –
her belt, her slightly weak chin, her skirt, her keys.

'Your brother was still alive last autumn,' said John with
careful mildness. 'No one could have known. Least of all
Harry.'

In his head he tested the words 'Sir Harry'.

Mistress Margaret shifted the mess of papers on her table.
She shook her fluffy silver head grimly and frowned past the

end of her generous nose at unavoidable disaster. Her fingers found her handkerchief in her left sleeve and assessed its lace trim. 'We can't bake enough pies for so many in that little oven. Agatha Stookey's taken hysterical on me. Sukie Tanner's about to drop her whelp and is no use to me in the kitchen, and there aren't enough silver ewers for the guest chambers and . . .' Her nose twitched, her small lower lip tucked itself even more tightly behind the upper one, and she burst into tears.

Before John could invent words of comfort, she steered abruptly into the true heart of her panic. 'What will I do if our new lady turns me out?' she wept. 'George left me nothing to live on . . . a few pound a year for clothing . . . ! Do you think he made it clear to Harry that I've nowhere else to go?'

John could not comfort her without lying. He did not know how the new Lady Beester from London would arrange things for her predecessor. He felt a quick spasm of guilt at his earlier self-concern.

He knew how little of her own his aunt had. Since reaching his majority he had paid out on behalf of his uncle the various annuities incumbent on the estate, including his own modest one. After Sir George died, John had carried on paying without waiting for legalities to be sorted out. His aunt, never married, was a tough, wiry little creature, but inclined to come adrift at the edges. She wouldn't survive anywhere but here, where she had lived and more than earned her keep, unofficially, for the last thirty years.

'I can't imagine that warm-hearted Harry would let her do such a thing,' said John. Harry could, however, do as he liked.

'Harry's such a *fool*!' Aunt Margaret wailed and buried her face in her handkerchief. 'Always has been. Anyone can turn him.' Over the top of the handkerchief a suddenly malevolent grey Beester eye found John's. 'She might make him turn *you* out too! And where could you go? Carrying the mark of Cain as you do? *I* know what happened, even if the rest don't. You've nowhere safe to go, except abroad with all those foreigners! Worse off than I am, poor lamb. We must stick together, John. We must help each other!'

John closed his fists tightly around cold fingertips. 'Have faith in Harry. He may be a fool, but he's a good-natured one.'

'Titles and ambition have changed people before now,' muttered Mistress Margaret.

'We must pray for the best, then. Do our duty and trust in the just reward. And who knows? Harry may have changed for the better. He seems to have made a sensible marriage.'

'You're too good, John. No matter what they say you've done. You should have had Hawkridge House ... Harry hasn't visited in years ...'

'There's no question of "should",' said John between his teeth. 'After Cousin James, Harry is your brother's heir.'

'Harry will despise the place,' said Aunt Margaret. 'He'll visit once and run straight back to his precious London ...'

'Then we'll all go on just as before, contented as larks.' John fled into the audit office, away from her quavering voice and spiked briar thoughts.

He turned all his attention to the delicate task of re-carving the point of a quill pen from his table. He split the point unevenly, cursed, and began again.

'John ...!' The voice of Dr Bowler wavered in through the open window. The old parson stood on the gravel of the forecourt. 'Can I have a word? Do you have a minute ... I won't need long. It's just that I'm having a little trouble ...' Bowler's high white bald forehead gleamed in the sun. His slightly-close-together eyes were even more anxious than before a sermon. 'I know you're busy ...'

'Come round,' said John. 'I'm doing nothing important.' He threw knife and quill violently down on the table.

It's like before a storm, he thought. All the livestock have the jitters. Including me.

Bowler was usually an ally. He had been John's tutor and was now his chief drinking companion in the evenings. But since the news of Harry's coming, Bowler had become morose and silent. He had stopped playing his viol and could no longer be tracked through the house or the gardens by his constant cheerful bumble-bee humming of hymns and glees.

The parson was better at music than religion. He had an authority with his flock when he mustered them into choirs which deserted him entirely when he was asked for moral certitude. John's request for a full musical consort for Harry's arrival should have excited Bowler into a melodious frenzy.

Instead he hid away in his small apartment of rooms behind the chapel, where he leafed wanly through sheaves of musical scores. He chose tunes, then rejected them. Picked others, rehearsed them twice with his musical conscripts and gave up in despair.

'John!' exclaimed Bowler in a tone of discovery as he edged through the office door. 'I'm so glad I found you. You know that we've been practising ever since you told me . . . Do you think Harry . . . Sir Harry, that is . . . expects us to be note perfect?'

'Perfection's not possible in this world. Just catch the spirit.'

'He'll have changed,' said Bowler, 'since I taught him. Not that I taught him for long, nor very much, I'm afraid.' He sighed. 'He was never . . . not like you . . .' His voice trailed away. His worried eyes crouched close together like small animals seeking comfort.

He opened a coffer of books and peered in. Many of the volumes were his gifts to John.

'A requiem, John. That's what I will be conducting. A requiem.'

'What nonsense!' bellowed John, suddenly beside himself. He wanted to kick his table. Bowler never moved in straight lines. That was why he could never string together a coherent sermon nor teach Greek grammar. 'What utter nonsense! Who's dead?'

'Coherence,' said Bowler.

'What?'

'It's a requiem for coherence.' The old man held firm with dignity against his former pupil's outburst. 'You know I have trouble with my grip at the best of times. I'm afraid, John. I'm getting too old . . .'

John pulled himself back to order. Bowler had taken the wind out of him. What he felt for his old tutor was as close to love as anything he felt for anyone, including his fondness for his aunt.

'Do you think Harry . . . Sir Harry . . . will appoint another parson? Although that wasn't what I meant by coherence . . . I wouldn't presume to hymn my own demise. Although I don't know what I would do without the tithes.'

'I'll do my best to see that he doesn't appoint another,' said John. 'But I can't read even my own future.'

'It's like waiting for death,' said Bowler. 'Supposed to be all right if you've done the right things, but you never really know. The Greater Power either tosses you up one way or chucks you down the other. I dare say one manages either way, but I must say I find the waiting most unsteadying.'

'If there is justice, Doctor Bowler, you will be one of the chosen.'

Bowler demurred, modest but also amused. 'You haven't had much to compare me with. But you're kind, John.' He seemed to feel better than he had when he arrived. 'I suppose I should go visit Sukie Tanner, though she's quite unrepentant about this child of hers . . . child-to-be, that is. At least my dutiful stone won't be the first one cast at the poor girl.'

After Bowler had left, John paced tight circles, aped by the fly still there from the day before.

He still felt as fragile as a shed snake skin. He could not contain everyone else's fears.

'. . . the mark of Cain,' his aunt had reminded him.

If they had hanged me after all, I think I would have felt like this the night before.

Dr Bowler had left the book coffer open. John lifted out a volume of Virgil's pastoral poems and opened it at random.

Fortunate senex, ergo tua rura manebunt.
Et tibi satis . . .

Fortunate old man, so your land will still be yours. And it's enough for you . . .

His eyes leaped away and onward.

Fortunate senex, hinc inter flumina nota . . .

Happy old man! You will stay here, between the rivers you know so well . . .

He slammed the heavy leather covers shut. Traitors everywhere, disguised as former friends! Columella, Cato, Varro, Pliny . . . He did not trust himself to test any of the others either, in his present mood. He replaced the *Eclogues* and spun around to the end window that looked out onto the forecourt. The geese had gone, but their route was clearly marked. John's left hand touched the left corner of his jaw where the skin puckered over the bone.

Let the storm break! Thunder, lightning, hail – whatever wrath the Heavens may thunder down tomorrow. Lord, just end this waiting!

🙶

May 24, 1636. A cold sour night but sun again today. Soil in the Far still too wet to sow beans. Do I end with unsown beans?

Journal of John Nightingale, known as John Graffham.

There was still no movement on the road. John shifted his body unhappily inside its carapace of stiffened and padded pale-blue silk. (Harry had sent the doublet and new, narrower trunks from London, to be sure that John looked like the cousin of a rising baronet.) Two immaculate white cuffs of Brussels lace fell over the tops of his green kidskin boots. Two more half-hid his brown hands, which were half-raw with scrubbing. He looked more elegant than he felt. Even in baggy work clothes, his physical outline was naturally precise. With the curly acorn-coloured hair trimmed and the right corner of his neat beard shaved to match the bare scars of the left corner, he looked very much at home in clothes that he wore only under duress.

From the small stone entrance porch, John surveyed the players in Harry's requested triumphal masque. He saw ominous portents of comedy.

Below him in the forecourt, Dr Bowler sat on a stool in his best black coat, viol against his ear, picking with irritation at one of the strings. A glass of cider leaned dangerously in the gravel at his feet. A distant sheep was bleating a half-tone higher than the string. Three estate workers, washed, brushed and polished, lounged against the pair of stone eagles that flanked the porch, with their wooden pipes under their arms – descant, alto and bass. The cooper's drum lay abandoned on the gravel; he had no doubt gone in search of his bride Cat.

John stared at the drum. She'd have had me, he thought with a renewed jolt of loss. I should have taken her and not worried what a bad bargain it made for her.

Mistress Margaret darted out of the doorway onto the

stone porch. She was trussed, painted and frizzed for a court ball, but a line of sweat glistened on her wrinkled upper lip, her stiff, pleated muslin ruff was askew and she had lost one of her garnet earrings. 'Anything?'

'Not yet,' said John.

'The mutton will dry out if they don't come soon!' She darted away again in a rustling of rose silk and muslin. 'Agatha! Agatha!' John heard her cries fade away through the main chamber.

A welcoming feast (perhaps now a little overdone) waited in the Great Chamber. Sir Henry Bedgebury, the local magistrate, and Sir Richard Balhatchet, who had been Knight of the Shire before Parliament was dissolved, both attended, suitably dressed, in the Long Gallery with yet another bottle of the estate's best ale.

John glanced back at the cooper's drum. You did the right thing, man. Don't add to the weight already on your conscience.

He went down the three steps from the stone porch, across the gravel forecourt to the off-centre gate. He ached to yank open the scratchy collar of Harry's lace-trimmed shirt and to haul at the excess cloth bunched in his crotch, but too many eyes were on him.

'He should be the one,' said the descant player to the alto, as John walked away. 'Not that London cousin.'

Dr Bowler squeezed his eyes more tightly shut and focused his entire being on tuning his string.

All the estate residents were ranged under the beeches along both sides of the drive – the tenant cottagers and their families, the housed labourers (mainly unmarried) and the poorhouse elders. The men stood or sat uneasily in their best Sabbath clothes, which included the new shirts Harry had ordered. At the sight of John they jumped to attention, hands and caps raised high in over-eager greeting.

'Morning, sir! Good morning! A nice dry day for it, sir!'

Their eyes weighed his unusual elegance, probed his face, and slid away.

They half-want a cockfight, thought John with clarity. My mettle and spurs are being sized up.

The women and girls eyed him over knitting or mending.

'Oh, you do look fine, sir!' called one of the older, bolder ones. Not like a stable groom today. But handsome either way.

'That Cat was a fool,' a young, unmarried woman muttered. 'He's not set on a gentlewoman. *I'd* have played him better. Had him fast enough.'

'And where would you be after today, then?' asked a friend.

'I wouldn't care!'

Among the fragrant green swags of ivy and lavender hung on the gate were tucked white and green bunches of sweet woodruff as delicate as silk French knots, against the plague which already festered in London again this summer.

John smiled to himself, a little grimly. A small gesture made by the helpless in the face of the uncontrollable.

He strolled back toward the porch. He felt numb.

Harry, thought John, come now! I can't take any more waiting! We're all as ready as we will ever be. Our bodies have exhausted themselves to make up for the shortcomings of our hearts and souls.

'Still nothing?' called Aunt Margaret breathlessly from the porch door. As she squinted past John, she tapped her handkerchief with great delicacy against her upper lip. 'Disaster, John! We can't find the new barrels of ale, the ones from Sir Richard . . . ! They're not in the cellar! Help me, John!'

'I'll look in the *basse-court*,' said John with resignation.

The missing ale was not in the *basse-court*, the buttery, the stable yard, or the stream-cooled cellar. Unable to force himself to look further, John placated his aunt with fourteen bottles of Flemish wine which he had meant to save for a later occasion. He lifted a spider's web from the pleats of his lace cuff and dusted the left side of his padded silk breeches.

Then he went into the stable yard. He stood quietly for a moment in the warm, dust-filled air of the horse-and-hay barn. Constellations of bright motes swarmed in a shaft of sunlight that cut low through the open door across the cobbled floor. His own cob and Aunt Margaret's mare, along with all twenty draught animals, had been turned into Mill Meadow. The stalls were clean, their floors covered with fresh straw. The iron manger cribs held hay, and buckets of corn stood ready for the London animals. When John came into the barn, two sparrows flew out of the nearest bucket onto a beam above his head to wait until he had left again.

The coach house next to the horse-and-hay barn stood wide open and empty. The estate's heavy old wooden coach had been hauled to the side of the cow barn, complete with two nesting hens, to give cover for the coaches of Harry and one of his guests. Two stable boys pumped water into the horse trough with the intense purpose of fire fighters at a blaze.

John left the stable yard through the gardens and went around the chapel into the *basse-court*. In the dog yard he leaned into the pen of a pregnant deerhound bitch. She lifted her head and licked his fingers.

'Oh, Cassie! Cassie, you silly, sloppy beast! I'm not your master now. We must all learn new manners.' He held her head in both hands. They gazed into each other's eyes. 'Can't you see into our future as your namesake could?'

She thumped her massive tail against the side of the pen and tried to jump up to place her paws on his chest. He pushed her gently down and turned away.

He left the *basse-court*, heading for the orchard. The damp grass darkened his new kidskin boots like spilled ink. At the crest of Hawk Ridge, the hen still cowered in her bucket. John lifted her gently to count the chicks.

Six. Carefully, he removed the bad egg which had not hatched and laid it in the grass away from the nest. The apples were in full blow at last. He laid a hand on one of the wicker bee skeps set among the trees. It vibrated with life.

He looked down through the blossom at the *basse-court* frozen in unlikely tidiness, the walled gardens suspended in temporary order. Life-in-waiting, a state only briefly possible to sustain. The fish ponds glinted like polished pewter plates. A flotilla of ducks drifted out of the reeds, full of faint inconsequential gossip. From the water meadows to the right came the constant, ragged bleating of sheep.

I can't bear it! John thought suddenly. His throat felt as if he had swallowed a hot coal. I can't accept! Harry and his new wife won't love you as I do.

He heard shouts, faint and far away, from the gatehouse beyond the top of the beech avenue. The bell on the brewhouse tower began to clang as it did for meals, festivals and prayers. The back of a dark, lumbering tortoise hauled itself over the crest of a far hill and sank again into the trees. John gathered himself like an actor pushed onto the stage or a criminal shoved at the steps of the scaffold. It had to be done. He yanked at the fabric bunched in his crotch, shook out his cuffs and stalked down the hill toward the house, stiff with a curious mixture of terror, excitement and rage.

Can I call him 'Sir Harry' without laughing? he wondered in the midst of his panic. A scrappy young cousin who arrived in my life as a poor second to a litter of staghounds when I was four! John picked his way between the grey-green turds which an escaped goose had left on the stone path of the hornbeam *allée* at the end of the west wing.

And what will his rich London woman be like? Do I still remember how to talk to a lady?

When clean, the carriage would have been burnished and studded with brass and copper, but after two and a half days on the road from London it was thickly frosted with mud.

The horses were splattered to the chest, the mounted grooms to their knees. But the estate residents, freed from waiting, played their part undeterred. The mud-caked tortoise heaved and swayed down the drive through cheers and showers of posies. Boys fell from the trees like shaken nuts and capered alongside. The five musicians in the forecourt clutched their instruments in damp hands.

The carriage rolled through the forecourt gate onto the relative flatness of the pounded gravel. Four yellow posies revolved, stuck to the mud, two on its front right wheel, two on the back. The carriage stopped.

Dr Bowler raised his bow with an authority he never showed in the pulpit. The cooper rattled a drumroll. The parson swayed like a tree in a blast of wind, then launched into a galliard, followed in lurching panic by the descant, alto and bass.

Sir Harry's flushed face appeared at the coach window. A housegroom leaped forward to open the door at the same time as Harry's own footman. The assembled house staff cheered on cue. A tossed posy hit the groom. More cheers from the top of the drive signalled the approach of a second coach.

As Sir Harry bent forward through the coach door and stepped to the ground, Dr Bowler switched to a march. Sir Harry raised his arms in greeting to the assembled crowd, provoking a second cheer from the housemaids and grooms. Sir Harry, the new master of Hawkridge House, had arrived at last and he was magnificent.

Caesar to the hilt, thought John. He had grown tall, long-legged and wide-shouldered. No longer the scrappy young cousin. The jolt of surprise was a little unpleasant.

'Oh, isn't he fine!' cried a maid.

Harry's blond hair curled to his ivory ear lobes, his horizontal moustache gleamed with pomade. His cleft chin was clean-shaven. A lace collar as large as a shawl set off his pink, square-cornered handsome face with soft dark-pink mouth and long-lashed blue eyes. His nose was a little short to have been Caesar's, but it was straight, with nostrils which seemed permanently flared in eager questioning of a rose, a lady's nape or a new soup.

Wide butterfly leathers flapped on his boots. An embroidered silk garden grew on his pea-green doublet, which also boasted slashed sleeves with satin linings, triple cuffs and enough lace to have bloodied the fingers of all the grandmothers of Bruges. He was like nothing they had ever seen before at Hawkridge House, and he was theirs. His staff cheered one last time with even more fervour than before. John quivered with a spasm of betrayal.

Then he stepped forward.

'My dearest cousin!' cried Harry with determination.

'Welcome . . .' John swallowed. 'Welcome, Sir Harry.' He bowed.

There! I said it, he thought. A little stiffly, but it's out.

'Thank you, John,' said Harry. 'It's good to be home.' His eyes flicked away from John's.

John wondered if he had seen fear in Harry's eyes.

Then Harry took a deep breath and with a rush of his usual boisterous enthusiasm flung his arms around John, and squeezed him hard.

'Can you believe it, cousin?' He breathed a hot, happy gust into John's ear. '*Sir* Bloody Harry? Me?'

Washed by suddenly remembered warmth, John pounded his cousin on the shoulders, relieved that the words now came easily. 'Who better, coz? Who better? And you look every inch a conqueror!'

'And you, John. And you. Quite splendid! Almost a courtier. Though the waist could be a little higher . . . Not at all like the rustic pose of your letters.'

If Harry also felt a twinge of unpleasant surprise, thought John, he hid it graciously.

They parted. Sir Harry moved on to Aunt Margaret's curtsey.

'You've grown, Harry,' she said, dry-mouthed and too flustered for protocol.

'Older, wiser and much richer, Mistress Margaret.' Harry grinned wickedly.

A crowd of estate workers jostled at the forecourt gate, pushing each other aside for a better view of the new master.

The cooper rattled a finale; the music died. John presented the vicar, who had once been tutor to them both.

'Doctor Bowler!' cried Harry. 'Enchanted to see you again. All the more so now that I've escaped your rod at last. A charming country tune, that was!' He clasped the hand that still held the bow.

As John opened his mouth to introduce the maids and grooms of the house family, something moved in the door of Harry's coach.

A thin child leaned out, pale with chalk powder, a smear of red across her small mouth. Her wiry red-gold hair curled around her face and was caught up in a knot at the back of her head in the latest London fashion. Below the stylish frizz and a pair of pearl and diamond ear-drops, her neck glowed bright purple, right up to the edge of the rouge and powder mask. She hauled at her green silk skirts, levered them through the door and jumped to the ground, spurning the hand of the groom.

John saw a flash of two thin ankles in knitted silk stockings. The ties and swags of her dress jounced and settled around two mouse-sized slippers of embroidered dark green kidskin. She twitched her stiffened stomacher back into place. In the startled silence that followed her sudden descent, she stood by the coach glaring at the ground, stiff-armed, with fists pressed against the front of her green silk skirt.

What is Harry doing with that sulky child?

Instantly, John answered himself. He was startled and appalled. Distracted by meeting Harry, he had forgotten the new wife.

The crowd at the gate edged into the forecourt.

Harry looked as startled as John felt. He extended a hasty hand. 'Mistress, come meet my cousin, John . . . Graffham . . . who has tended things here so well for me, as I can already see.'

Obediently, she scraped her skirts across the gravel to stand beside Harry with eyes lowered under eyelids as smooth as washed pebbles. The red smear remained set in an unfriendly pinch.

'This is Mistress Zeal . . . Lady Beester . . . my wife.' Though Harry met John's eyes squarely, his lashes beat a tattoo against the tops of his pink cheeks.

'Welcome, my lady,' said John. He bowed, then took the small, uncertainly extended, barely unclenched hand. It felt no more substantial than a dove's foot and was ice cold. 'Hawkridge House has been in a lather these last weeks, trying to make itself worthy to be your new home.'

The sulky eyelids lifted briefly. John saw grey-green eyes filled with panic. Then the lids dropped again. John released the cold hand and stared down at the top of her red-blond hair. Coppery tendrils at her temples clashed with the violent purple colouring her neck and small flat ears. Her white-painted face was still marked by the fierce dash of compressed, red lips. The nails of the hand were chewed short.

She's no more than twelve, thought John. And young for that. Too young to change nests yet. He knew all about nest-changing. He felt a rush of pity toward a young animal harnessed too soon.

'Madam!' said Harry sharply. 'Come meet your new household. Mistress Margaret Beester, my aunt . . .'

The panic flashed at John again. The girl let out a shaky sigh, picked up her skirt, and moved forward up onto the porch into the icy blast of Mistress Margaret's basilisk gaze and crocodile smile.

'How was your journey, my lady?' asked Margaret. Her eyes took inventory as fiercely as a bailiff. Her upper lip glistened unwiped, and her remaining earring trembled with her emotion.

The new Lady Beester inhaled, looked at the twenty or so faces, including Harry's, that attended her reply and closed her mouth again.

John was distracted by the arrival into the forecourt of a second carriage as muddy as the first.

'I hope, my lady, that you will approve of my efforts,' he heard Aunt Margaret say as she took the new mistress in charge. 'This is Agatha Stookey, the chief housemaid ... Roger Corry, housegroom ...'

John turned his back on the stammering curtseys and blushing bows.

The second coach stopped behind Harry's, drawing twelve estate workers and eight goggling boys in its wake.

'Sir Harry! Is this your stern Roman senator?' called John.

'Oh, Lord!' cried Harry in dismay. He reappeared on the porch. 'Where's Doctor Bowler! Why isn't there music? Where is everyone?'

The parson leaped back to his stool and snatched up his viol. The pipers dived for their pipes. The cooper, however, stayed where he was, bent over a wheel on the offside of Harry's coach.

'Where's Aunt Margaret?' begged Harry. 'And the house staff ... They were just here!'

The parson began the galliard for the second time, minus the drum.

'You can't possibly expect my niece to make that journey more than once a year,' complained Samuel Hazelton, a lean sixty-year-old in Puritan black with a complexion like tree bark. He shook and brushed himself with a great rustling of silks and travelling wool. 'We left Edward mired down just outside Windsor. He took a horse and went to dine with a friend in Eton while his men dig his coach out . . . How can so much mud get inside?' He beat with his hand at the end of a black silk jacket sleeve. 'Mistress . . .' He turned back to reel in beside him the square-cornered woman, also wearing black silk, who had just descended from the coach. She waved aside a posy offered by one of the weeding women.

'Samuel Hazelton, my wife's uncle and former guardian,' explained Harry, *sotto voce*. 'And his wife, Mistress Hazelton.'

'All the way from Rome,' murmured John. He dropped back as Harry moved forward in welcome.

Even as he bowed stiffly to Sir Harry, Hazelton's eyes moved swiftly, taking stock of house and men. He already knew Harry's worth as a husband to his niece. He had still to determine the soundness of his own social and political investment in letting the young cockerel marry her.

Mistress Hazelton's eyes were glazed. She had been sick from the motion of the coach.

'Mistress Hazelton, Master Hazelton, my cousin Mister John Graffham.' Harry pushed John forward with the air of offering a plate of sweetmeats.

'Mr Graffham! I have looked forward most eagerly to meeting you,' said Hazelton. The stock-taking eyes examined John.

A sharp-eyed pirate's face coupled to a forced mildness of manner, thought Hazelton with interest and surprise. A pirate pretending to be a monk. A broken nose and woman's brows . . . it's the face of a licentious Corinthian, not a simple country Corin. Not over-eager to please like his cousin. He's assessing *me*. Looks good for what needs doing.

*   *   *

John stiffened under Hazelton's open appraisal. *There's more here than mere manners. What has Harry told these strangers?*

Don't panic, man, he then told himself. *The man called you Graffham, not Nightingale.*

'Your reputation as a botanical enthusiast spreads farther than you may realize,' said Hazelton.

John achieved a social smile. John Graffham, enthusiast of Botany and student of Agriculture, had nothing to hide.

'A good friend, Sir George Tupper, is an enthusiast like yourself,' said Hazelton. 'He tells me that you have written excellent advice on replicating certain bushes, or some such thing . . . I don't know a fig myself about the domain of Flora . . .'

'I am flattered to be so much talked about,' said John. He was, in fact, shocked. 'But I'm merely a countryman who observes what lies around him.'

'More than that, coz!' exclaimed Harry, pinkly eager and delighted that his introduction was going so well.

'A man in tune with the preoccupations of his time,' said Hazelton. 'A fortunate thing to be. We must speak further.'

Mistress Hazelton looked past John into the house.

Two large muddy carts pulled by equally muddy oxen heaved into the forecourt. Behind the carts trudged Harry's hunter, ridden by yet another groom. Two dogs and five boys bounded alongside.

'If you will excuse me,' said John, 'I'll see them into the stable yard.'

'Until later, then,' said Hazelton.

Thoughtfully, John watched Harry lead his new family into his new domain, heralded by the fourth repeat of the vicar's march.

There's probably nothing to fear from Hazelton, he decided. *If the dear friend who carries weight at court is no more danger than that Puritan guardian of the little wife, I* can leave the past alone after all. Do what needs doing now, and learn what Harry plans for my future.

Harry had brought seven waiting men and two pages. Hazelton five men and one page. Lady Beester and Mrs Hazelton had two women each. The carters made four more. Even without the servants who accompanied the 'dear friend's' coach which was yet to arrive from its mud puddle outside Windsor, they were already four over the expected number.

'We'll have to use the Lower Gallery as a dormitory for the men servants,' John told Aunt Margaret under his breath. 'Lay them out like flitches of bacon.'

'I'll wring his knightly neck!' she said. 'I'm happy to say that Agatha has agreed to let Mrs Hazelton's waiting woman share her bed.'

'Oy! Another coach!' shouted one of the cottager boys from his perch in the beech avenue. 'A coach! A coach!' The cry passed down the drive.

The bell began to clang again.

John was on his way back to the house after seeing to the supply carts and settling the eight visiting coach horses. 'Go fetch Sir Harry,' he ordered a groom. 'And Mistress Margaret.'

'Where is everyone?' asked Harry a moment later. 'Damn! Have all the cottagers left? Where's Bowler? I don't pay him just to sit there and drink my ale and debate whether or not we have the right to impose the Book of Common Prayer on the stiff-necked Scots.' He searched the forecourt with anxious eyes. 'Don't we even have the bloody pipes?'

Aunt Margaret's pale damp face arrived in the door, framed in limp white curls. 'If you want your guests to dine, you must really let me get on with things,' she announced in despair. '. . . Sir Harry,' she added in quick afterthought.

'Does it matter so much if you welcome your dear friend without your armies behind you?' asked John.

Harry pulled his lips back in a nervous grimace. He straightened the front of his flower-garden doublet and bent to flick at the ruffled garters that decorated his shapely knees. 'This is one with influence, John. The one I must woo. The one in the Queen's eye. The one I really wanted all this *for*!' His voice was plaintive as a disappointed child's.

John counted another five serving men as the last invading coach rolled into the forecourt. Four more coach horses and two mounts.

'I must alert the stable boys,' he said, 'or we'll have a shambles in the yard.'

Harry clutched John's sleeve. 'Don't leave me now, cousin!'

The footman leaped down and opened the door. The circular top of a feathered hat appeared, followed by the shoulders of a red coat. The man straightened and stepped to the ground.

'I hope, Sir Harry, that your cellar and kitchen can make up for that appalling journey.' Edward Malise removed his hat and ran his fingers through his heavy straight black hair. The falcon-nosed face was sulky and tired. 'I'm bruised from nape to heel and dusty as a church.'

Harry's hand pushed on John's elbow. John did not move. As he stared at the newcomer, the hair lifted on the back of his neck and on his arms under the sleeves of his new shirt.

'It will be a pleasure to try to console you, Edward,' said Harry uncertainly. He glanced at his cousin in covert bewilderment. What on earth was wrong with him?

John's lips tightened across his teeth. His breath shortened, and his muscles coiled themselves like springs on his bones. His fingers became knives.

'My dear Edward, this is the cousin we discussed.' Harry's distant voice was nearly drowned by the pounding in John's ears. 'John Graffham ... Master Edward Malise.'

John braced himself for Malise's gasp of recognition. His hands felt themselves already closing around Malise's throat.

But the dark eyes passed over him. 'Delighted,' Malise said wearily. 'Our botanist. Sir Harry has sung your praises, sir. We shall talk more later when I have recovered.'

Confused and unbelieving, John licked dry lips. He bowed curtly, sucked in a deep breath. Made the thick dry lump of his tongue shape words. Malise seemed not to know him, but he would never forget Edward Malise.

Seven-year-old John flew through the ring of fiery tongues, out of the coach window, like Icarus falling away from the dreadful heat of the sun. He trailed flames like a comet, wrapped in his own screams and the smell of burning wool and hair.

His face smashed into the dirt and stones. He felt hands drag him away from the coach and beat out the flames on his hair and clothes. He clawed back toward the burning coach and his parents trapped inside. His mother was a shadow dressed in flames, a burning goddess with fiery hair. She screamed and screamed. Hands pulled at his coat, dragged him away into the darkness.

He saw men's legs on the far side of the coach, and logs braced against the door, to hold it closed. The four coach horses shrieked and reared in their harness. The offside bay twisted and bucked, its foreleg tangled in the logs of the roadblock. A man darted and dodged through the black smoke, trying to cut the horses free. Others, stippled by flames then blurred by smoke, jammed the far-side coach door closed with logs.

'*Mother*!' His scream was lost in the furore of terrified horses, shouting, and flames.

The hands hauled at John's jacket.

'Please, Master John!' begged the voice in his ear. 'Before they take notice of us . . . !'

The silk-padded upholstery, heavy dried-wood frame and pitch-covered roof of the coach burned fast. The screams stopped. In this new silence, the flames cracked loudly. Sparks drifted up into an orange-lit canopy of blackening leaves. The men around the coach dropped back. Now on his feet, John followed the Nightingale groom through the brush towards the road beyond the coach.

'There's justice done,' grated a smoky voice from the group beside the coach. 'A just death to thieves and plunderers, and the courts and King be damned!'

The Nightingales' coachman lay dead on the ground, his cut throat spreading a black pool across the orange-lit ground.

'Ralph! It's Cookson . . .' John started to say.

The groom clapped an urgent hand over the boy's mouth. 'He's past help, Master John. Let's get you away while they're still busy!'

The coach lurched sideways and settled unevenly like a dying stag still trying to stand. Three of the horses, loose at last, darted and whinnied, dragging the men who clung to their leathers. The bay had fallen out of sight and was still.

In the confusion of logs and bodies, a face suddenly stood out brightly in a shudder of firelight. The head was turned to the side. The brow, cheekbone and chin of Edward Malise glowed hot orange. His single visible eye was alight with a terrible glee. Then he turned suddenly, the eye caught by movement in the brush. He seemed to look straight at John.

'Run, Master John!' whispered Ralph. He shoved the boy deeper into a thicket and drew his dagger.

'We missed a brace of them,' said the smoky voice. 'Over there!'

Three of the men beside the coach drew their swords and turned to black silhouettes against the flames as they moved towards the groom.

'Run! To London. To your uncle. For the love of God, run!'

It was told for months, until a new excitement made fresher telling, how a singed, dazed and smoky boy wearing ashy tatters of silken clothes had staggered into a cottage on an estate six miles from the ambush, announced that he was Master John Nightingale of Tarleton Court and demanded to be taken to his uncle George Beester in London to tell him that the Devil had killed his father and mother. He had then sat down in a large, carved chair-of-grace and fallen soundly asleep as suddenly as if struck by a magic spell.

'My dear Edward,' said Harry, 'let me begin to make it up to you at once. Food and drink are waiting for you inside.' He shot John a disappointed, reproving glance. No help there. His cousin John needed a good shaking up and brushing off before he could be trusted in elevated company. Harry felt the chill of imminent disaster. His joy when Malise had agreed to visit Hawkridge House had drowned his common sense.

I should have come down here first, to make certain the place does me credit! Please God, at least let supper be worthy!

John stood like a man who had just been clubbed. Upright but unbalanced, a sawn tree just before it falls.

'Shall I take the coach round?'

John looked up blankly at a strange face above yellow livery.

Harry had betrayed him to Malise.

'Sir?'

'What do you want?'

'The coach . . . where, sir?'

John frowned in confusion. The coach had burned so fast. Pitch-covered roof and dried wood frame. He had begged the screams to stop. And then the meaning of the silence had shrivelled him into a tight, cold ball of ice.

'Sir?'

John looked up again. A London voice and curious eyes.

Malise's coach was here in the forecourt. The Serpent had arrived at Hawkridge House. But the Serpent had been in Eden from the start. Must get a grip on myself, thought John. Deal first with Malise's coach. Then deal with Harry . . . And then Malise.

'Through that gateway,' said John. 'Someone in the stable yard will help you . . . Down, boy!' he called to the yellow cur that danced among the fetlocks. The heavy wooden coach swayed and jolted through the gate to the stable yard, the cur trotting behind.

Oh, Harry! thought John. Harry! Harry! Harry! This is worse than all the rest. He held onto one of the stone eagles with both hands and waited for the sensation of falling to pass.

'There you are!' said Harry reproachfully, emerging onto the porch. 'Why didn't you come in? Sir Richard and I more than had our hands full. Our aunt veers from gawping to squawking . . . Old Doctor Bowler's no better than he ever was, is he? Still goes red as a cock's comb when you so much as look at him . . . used to make me want to climb under the pew, the way he darted at his sermons like a panic-stricken mouse. What the Hazeltons and Malise make of him, I hate to think!'

Harry mistook his cousin's unnatural stillness beside the eagle for contemplation. 'It hasn't changed since I last visited,' he said. He surveyed the forecourt from the top of the steps. 'More's the pity. Not like the two of us, eh? Lord, how long ago was it? Remember riding these eagles? Not changed one bit. Still, being so far from London . . .' He put one arm around John's shoulders, but quickly dropped it again. He might as well have embraced the eagle. 'You must show me my new property before dinner. I want to learn the worst. There's just time for a quick look. My guests mustn't see that I'm as ignorant as they are.'

John turned a cold assessing eye on this stranger from London whom he must call 'Sir', who rode a coach instead of a modest cob, sweated in silks instead of wool and glowed moistly with nervous ownership.

'A good-natured fool,' John had assured Aunt Margaret. But loyal. Or so Harry had seemed, many years before.

'Titles and ambition have changed people before now,' she had replied.

'John?' asked Harry uncertainly. He was puzzled and a little alarmed by John's gaze. He looked suddenly shy.

I see no guilt in those blue eyes, thought John, just the ghost of the younger cousin I so often pulled away from the consequences of his own silliness. Or has he learned guile along with the names of good tailors and hatmakers?

'I'll show you, if you like. Do you want to start with business or pleasure?'

Harry lifted an eyebrow. 'Pleasure first, of course, coz. I never have it any other way.'

A touch over-hearty, John noted grimly. 'Get back to work,' he shouted at three grooms who were grinning through the stable-yard gate.

John led the way down the steps onto the rolled gravel of the forecourt. 'I had the chapel newly roofed last year; the bills are in the accounts I have waiting for you . . .' He looked up at the square gap teeth of the chapel's crenellations at the east end of the house.

'Oh, coz,' said Harry. 'Is this what you call pleasure?'

It is for me, thought John. But he said, 'Only a taste of Purgatory on the way to Paradise. I'm afraid I just have a business habit of mind.'

'That's splendid, John,' said Harry. 'It's a habit I must study now that I'm a man of means. But later!'

Before Malise, John would have smiled. Now he stared bleakly at his younger cousin.

They turned right through a small gate out of the forecourt

into an *allée* of pleached hornbeams that faced each other along the west wing like a long set of country dancers. Harry assumed the abstracted enthusiasm of a man at an exhibition, hands clasped behind his back, chin leading. His blue eyes filled with memories and calculations. He nodded graciously at two awe-struck sheepmen beyond the wall.

I'm certain that Malise didn't recognize me, thought John as they walked. Is it possible?

'My fields?' Harry stepped carefully over some green-black goose turds and stopped to survey the green slope beyond the outer row of hornbeams and a low stone wall. 'They haven't been sold off?'

He had time to prepare himself for our meeting, decided John. He pretended strangeness in front of Harry.

'My fields?' repeated Harry, a little more loudly.

Sheep grazing in Roman Field below the beech avenue raised their heads at the sound of his voice. The afternoon sun glowed pink through their pricked ears.

John finally heard. 'Yes. The nearest, here across the wall is the Roman . . . Roman coins were dug up there years ago. Beyond that lies King's, and then our water meadows, there behind the beech ridge and along the Shir. Two years ago, as you will see in the estate accounts, I bought more good grazing from the Winching estate when the widow died. Hawkridge now runs from Winching Hanger across the road, that way . . .' He pointed back up the hill past the top of the drive. 'All the way past Pig Acre to that second wood there, on that hill above Bedgebury Brook. The limit that way is the field you can just see below the east end of Hawk Ridge, called the Far.'

He counted the sheep that munched down toward the water meadows. The ewe pregnant with late twins was not eating but lay awkwardly on the ground. As he watched, she rose then lay down again. He must send someone to see to her.

But it's not my job now to think like that. One way or

another, this life was now over. But he would not go back to prison. He would never surrender to the rope or block.

They reached the far end of the hornbeam *allée* and passed through a gap in a shoulder-high yew hedge into a flat empty green kept tightly shorn by grazing geese, a quiet green room enclosed by high, dark-green aromatic walls.

'The bowling lawn.'

'Bowling,' said Harry dully. 'Not much in favour now in London. I must do something with this.'

A blue and white cat slipped onto the green from under the hedge, froze when it saw the two men, flattened its ears and streaked under the hedge towards the fields.

Water glinted through a gap in the yew hedge. Harry crossed the bowling lawn in long-legged strides.

'This is better!' he cried.

From the north-west corner of the house they now looked along the north front and over the *basse-court*. A little farther on, the river Shir slid like oil over a small weir into the highest of the three fish ponds, dug before any man or woman on the estate could remember.

'Now here . . .' Harry said, 'I see possibility! We make these ponds into one long lake, the full width of the house. Try to imagine, coz, if you can . . . statues. And water jets. A bronze of Nereus, just there below the weir.' He looked around for his cousin, faltered slightly at John's set face but surged onward. 'Conjoin the ponds and there's room for all his fifty sea-nymph daughters around the edge!'

John lifted his eyes beyond the ponds to the smooth swell of hillcrest that rose from the orchard blossom like the naked shoulder of a woman from her smock. He had swallowed a brand from the kitchen fire.

This time, I must kill Edward Malise, he thought fiercely.

'What's all that?' asked Harry, pointing at the jumble of brick buildings and walls that jostled against the back of the house.

'That?' John stared as if unravelling the well-known corners and jogs for the first time. '. . . The *basse-court* yard . . .'

Two hens scratched in the arch of the gate which opened onto the ponds from the yard between the dairy house and a storage shed.

Not so fast, John then decided. It may be possible that he didn't recognize me. I may have time to think what's best to do. But how, dear God, do I deal with my cousin?

'Come with me!' Harry ordered. He strode along the bank of the pond, to get a more central view of the *basse-court* and the north face. 'Oh, John! This is quite wonderful! I can see exactly . . .' He pulled John round by the arm to face his vision. 'We'll knock all those old buildings down. Make a new ornamental lawn between the house and the ponds . . . Can't you see it? Grass from there to there!' He threw his arms wide like a bishop gathering his flock in a spiritual embrace. 'Not Hatfield perhaps . . .' Harry laughed with the pure pleasure of his vision. 'But the best in Hampshire!'

In the eleven years since Malise and I last met, thought John, I have changed from boy to man and sprouted a beard. From fourteen to twenty-five. He was already twenty-seven then. Perhaps he really doesn't know me!

'Then . . . !' Harry pulled again at John's sleeve and pointed at the house. 'Leave aside all those little sheds and things. Try to imagine a portico centred between the wings in place of that old-fashioned porch.'

There was no reply.

'John? What do you think of my idea of a Greek portico in place of that old porch?'

John focused on his cousin again. 'No portico, Harry,' he said quietly.

'The first on a private house,' insisted Harry. 'A portico in the new classical style, like the Queen's banqueting house just built in Greenwich. I shall build the first in Hampshire. The

King himself might come to admire it. Oh, coz, we shall have such fun putting this place right!'

'No,' said John in a voice like a scythe.

Harry faltered and dropped in mid-flight. 'What's wrong?' He licked his pink lips and swallowed. The long-lashed blue eyes blinked, and looked away. 'No, I know.' Then, 'Please don't look at me like that! It makes me feel five years old.' Harry frowned across the ponds as John had done earlier. He squared his shoulders. 'Very well. I owe you honesty, though I had hoped it would not need to be said.'

John did not breathe.

'I want you to stay here,' Harry said thickly. 'Did you think that I can't see how much you do . . . have done? I need you to stay.' He cleared his throat and hauled an uncertain smile onto his face. 'Cousin, with my ideas, your organizing and my wife's money, we shall have more fun than you can imagine!' He waited for John's gratitude and relief.

'Harry, who does your dear friend Edward Malise think I am?'

'What?' Harry looked startled, then defensive, then a little sulky, the way he had used to look when Dr Bowler asked him to conjugate a Latin verb. 'What do you mean? The same as everyone else, I suppose . . . You're my cousin who has been running my estate.'

'And my name?'

'Your name?' Harry now looked angry, as if John were unfair to ask him something he didn't know but might have remembered if John hadn't worried him by asking about it.

John waited.

'Whoosh.' Harry shook his head. 'I don't understand. It's John Graffham. Or have I got that wrong too?'

John walked to the edge of the pond. A grey and white feather bounced gently on the ripples behind a swimming duck. If Malise did not know him, then why was he here?

'John?' Harry felt that both his explanation and invitation

had been handsome enough to merit a better response. I won't wheedle or apologize any more, he told himself. My cousin will just have to accept the new order and his place in it.

Eleven years ago, Harry was only nine, thought John. And no doubt as self-absorbed as he is now.

Harry cleared his throat and said firmly, 'Nothing will change that really matters.' He nodded toward the *basse-court*. 'I'm sure you can find somewhere else on the estate for all that!'

'I can always chop down the orchard to make room,' said John.

'You're not serious.'

Hot rage suddenly swelled in John's chest and throat, and banged in his temples. 'That "old-fashioned" porch suits the house!' He thrust his fists together behind his back. 'It's the nose it was born with,' he shouted. 'Why cut it off and try to make a duck's bill grow instead?'

Harry stepped back in alarm. He's mad, he thought, with sudden clarity. After all these years of sequestration down here. To get so hot over something like this. Mad, of course! This place would drive *me* mad!

'Why change what needs no changing?' John clamped his teeth down on his anger.

Stop this! he ordered himself. It helps nothing.

'You ride in like one of the Four Horsemen,' he bellowed, 'swinging your blade, mowing down everything in your path . . . !'

'John!' Harry's alarm grew. He glanced toward the house. Perhaps he should call for help.

'And the worst of it is, I believe that you may not even know what you've done!'

They stood, both breathing hard, staring at each other, equally afraid of the next moment.

'I'm sorry,' said John.

Harry breathed out. This was the old John again. 'It's

already forgotten.' He felt the rich joy of magnanimity. He nodded. 'I'm sorry too, if I've upset you in any way. I remember you were kind to me when I was small. I would hate to repay you badly.'

Only with Malise, thought John, suddenly exhausted. This scene has nearly turned comical.

Gossipy quacks from the reeds near their feet wandered inconsequentially through their silence.

Harry took a deep breath. 'I'm not as much of a fool as I suspect you may think me. Please don't be offended, but being hidden away down here has kept you unworldly. I've learned things in the last few years that you can't know. Will you hear me?'

Let him talk, John told himself. If he's guilty, he'll betray himself; he can't help it. 'Teach me. Make me worldly.' And he turned away towards the weir bridge below the bottom pond.

Harry followed. 'How long have you lived here?'

'Eleven years steadily, and childhood sojourns before that.'

'It's very pleasant, I'm sure,' said Harry. 'But a man can rust here.'

'Yes,' agreed John. 'I'm sure he can.'

'In London . . . in the real world . . .' Harry was still wary of his cousin's strange temper. John had always been quick to flare and quick to forgive, he seemed to remember, but it was a great many years since they had last played together. And even then Harry remembered John mainly as reliable for piggy-back rides and rescues, not closely observed beyond his uses.

When John did not growl or start to shout again, Harry continued.

'I now live in the larger world, coz, where power and influence stretch wider than the limits of a single estate, a single parish, or even a whole county. You have no idea how much appearances matter out there! The way things look is how men believe them to be. And what men believe becomes the truth. I mean to be rich and influential before I die.'

He fell into stride beside John.

'I must begin by being seen at all,' said Harry.

'Is that why you married that little girl, so her money would make you visible?'

Two precise, round, pink spots bloomed on Harry's fair cheeks and one in the centre of his forehead. 'Isn't a rich wife every man's ambition? Don't fault me for it. You should congratulate me.' He walked two steps. 'Your own future depends on her wealth!'

John raised a neutral enquiring eye.

'You know as well as I,' said Harry, 'that our uncle left a title that needed renewing, some run-down houses, great bundles of land and almost nothing to live on! And I can see already that this place won't produce enough to feed a fasting saint.'

'We manage, but then we have no worldly ambition to be seen. Quite the contrary. How old is she?'

'Fourteen.'

'She looks younger.'

'Not too young to wed, just young to bed. I'll entertain myself elsewhere while I wait.' Harry's blue eyes slithered toward John. 'It's only contract marriage, coz. Take off that episcopal face. I merely tied her fortune up safe on contract before some other aspiring esquire did. Hazelton has to make the best of it, and me!'

His good humour reasserted itself at this triumphant thought. 'Do me justice, coz. Her uncle had his own favourites. How do you think I snatched her from under their noses?'

John shook his head.

'She wasn't afraid of me! I wooed as if she were little cousin Fal . . . told tales, sang her songs, and generally made an ass of myself. I swore love and passion too, and all the things she expected to hear, but it was kindness that won the day.

I even promised her I won't insist on my bed rights until she's ready. I could see that she was afraid of the others . . . enter Big Brother Harry! All games, jokes and an occasional careful tickle.'

'You relieve my mind,' said John. 'Tarquin is not come to Hawkridge House. I hope you mean to go on kindly.'

Harry missed the irony and swelled to the allusion. 'I owe her the kindness. Her wealth is my philosopher's stone. With it, and my new lands, the base metal of Harry Beester, plain gentleman, will be transmogrified into Sir Harry Beester, man of note!' He listened happily like a bad actor to the echoes of his own voice.

One corner of John's mouth lifted in spite of himself. Harry had not changed. Only his size, clothes and moustaches.

They crossed the weir bridge at the bottom of the lowest pond and continued back along the far shore, at the foot of the orchard slope.

'You're still thinking what a fool I am,' said Harry. 'You have that distant adult look. But I really have learned something worth knowing.' He stopped and reached out to grasp John's arm and full attention. 'Men's eyes used to pass through me, John. I was an inconvenient mist between themselves and more important things. You can't imagine how it feels when you don't really exist.'

John looked away.

'But after Cousin James dried up with dysentery and left me as Uncle George's sole heir . . .' Harry shook his head and smiled at the thought. 'Men began to *see* me. I'm there now, filling up a real space. Their gaze warms me as if the sun had come out. I like it, John. I like it so very, very much! And I will not let myself decay back! I couldn't bear it!'

He held out his arms to the house across the pond. 'This estate is my new dignity. With your help, my wife's money, and the changes I imagine, it will become my glory!'

Even as a small boy, John had not needed his mother's

admonition to look after Harry – Harry had so obviously needed looking after. John had never been able to stay angry long with such cheerful self-satisfaction. Even now, he almost envied it. Surely not a traitor, merely a fool. This conclusion made him very happy.

'Oh, Harry,' he said. 'My dear cousin.'

'*Pax*, then?'

John shook his head helplessly. If Harry had betrayed, he didn't know it.

'So we're agreed.' Harry considered a cementing embrace but decided instead to lead briskly onward beside the pond. 'After we dine, I'll show you the Dutch pattern books for houses and gardens that I brought from London. The Classical orders are explained – Doric, Ionic, and Corinthian. Fireplaces and lintels, pilasters and friezes. All there for us to harvest for our own use ... Those geese do get everywhere, don't they?'

John absolved his cousin and steadied himself for supper with Edward Malise. In any case, you can't kill a man over a dining table, he told himself wryly. Not with ladies present.

'For God's sake, John, don't desert me as you did this afternoon,' whispered Harry when they met in the New Parlour an hour later. 'I need your help! Do what you can with Mistress Hazelton, and don't let Sir Richard drink any more!'

Sir Harry ushered his guests into the large dining chamber at the back of the house which had once been the Great Hall. A tiny knife jabbed his stomach. He would have killed to be in the corner seat of some safely distant tavern with a quart of ale in his hand. In the last hour while being brushed off for dinner, he had become less and less sure whether to claim Hawkridge and its residents as his own or to reserve the right of distance from any possible disasters.

First there had been John's strange behaviour by the ponds. Then the realities of mended and faded curtains and hangings.

He had spied a dog's marrowbone in the entrance hall and chased a cat from his bed. The pisspot in his own bedchamber, though spotless, was only plain white porcelain. The chapel was smaller than he remembered. (And the female acrobats and monkeys carved on the stalls lost charm when seen through the eyes of Puritan house-guests.)

Sir Henry Bedgebury could wait no longer and had left on urgent business. His aunt was nearly weeping because it was closer to supper time than dinner and claiming that the mutton was overdone. And there was some other palaver about missing ale.

Harry needed to become angry, to belch out his nervousness in justified irritation.

'John!' hissed his aunt. She beckoned from the door of the buttery.

John stepped into the small chamber.

Aunt Margaret closed the door and locked it. Her bunch of keys clattered in her shaking hands. 'That's the brother isn't it . . . that man who came last?' Her whole being quivered with panic.

'Yes.' John laid the admission down like a heavy load.

'What will you do now?'

'Dine.'

Aunt Margaret twisted knotted fingers together against her lace apron. Her eyes opened wide like a terrified rabbit. 'How can you joke? He'll have you arrested again. You have to get away! How could Harry bring him here? I told you he couldn't be trusted any more . . . !'

'Aunt!' John laid his hand on her arm the way he would soothe a frightened dog or horse. 'Malise may not recognize me.'

'Then why is he here?'

'That's what I must learn.'

'How can I serve him dinner? And sit there as if nothing's

wrong? And what if he does recognize you? How can you possibly . . . ?' Her right hand tried to pull the fingers off her left.

'Darling aunt, listen to me!' He took both of her hands in his. 'Are you listening?'

Mistress Margaret nodded distractedly.

'You saved my life once before, when the soldiers came looking for me, eleven years ago. I need you to do it again. I need you to be just as calm and wily now as you were then. Pretend I really am John Graffham, an inconsequential by-blow nephew who washed up on your doorstep. Worry only about the sauces and the joint. Show Harry that he hasn't inherited a lower circle of Hell. I need you to forget that you are a good, virtuous woman. You must lie your head off . . . deceive so well that you believe it yourself.'

Mistress Margaret gave a quivery sigh. 'These things get more difficult . . . Of course, I'll try. But John . . .'

'Our guests are waiting for your incomparable meat pies. To battle, my Boadicea of the pots! Distract the enemy with titbits. Feed him into harmless, full-bellied sleep.' He took the keys, unlocked the door, and pushed his aunt towards the dining chamber.

'Be seated,' cried Harry to his guests.

Mistress Hazelton frowned at a carved wooden pilaster set into the wall, from which a bare-breasted nymph offered passers-by an overflowing basket of fruit.

Harry noted her frown. The little knife stabbed again just above his navel.

The dining chamber at the back of the house, however, offered no excuse to purge Harry's emotional wind. The diamond window panes glistened in the late afternoon sun. On every window ledge, John had set blue and white Turkish ceramic pots of late white tulips. Their faint, sweet, green scent twined itself into the smoke of apple logs and rosemary branches that burned in the great plastered brick fireplace to cover the smell of must and mice. One of Harry's own London hounds snuffled and twitched before the fire as if it had always slept there. Harry quivered like dried grass and watched his guests for the direction of their breeze.

At least, he thought, Hazelton seems so far to approve of Cousin John, in spite of my cousin's odd humour. Can't tell what Malise thinks. Please God, let it work. Let them see that I can offer something in my own right. That they must reckon with my advice in the future.

Edward Malise looked out of one window. Samuel Hazelton gazed appraisingly out of another across the yard and outbuildings of the *basse-court* towards the swell of the orchard ridge beyond. The trees were carved in high relief by the slanting rays of the sun.

'It's a poor view now,' said Harry. He winced at the row of churns airing outside the dairy room and at a hen balanced on one leg in the middle of the courtyard to scratch itself. 'But I'll soon put that right. You must imagine the sweep of a lawn where that jumble of a courtyard is now, and a lake beyond! Please do come sit down.'

'It's not a bad view,' said Hazelton pleasantly. 'A scene of good husbandry and industry. In your circumstances, Sir Harry, not to be dismissed.'

All three Londoners gave John a quick look.

John's stomach tightened with renewed alarm. What was that about? he wondered. I feel the hunt is on but don't know from which thicket the hounds will appear.

Harry flushed.

'But there's nothing wrong either in wanting to put things right,' said Hazelton, making peace again.

Harry took John's former chair in the centre of the table. He ached for a gilt Venetian candlestick and Italian glasses, but he could not fault his aunt's muster of the resources she had.

The long, heavy oak table, pulled out from the wall into

the middle of the room, smelled sweetly of beeswax. The wood of the carved oak stools gleamed, and their faded red and green needlepoint cushions were brushed clean of dog and cat hair. (Harry pined for chairs but supposed that he was grateful to be spared the humiliation of benches.) The linen tablecloth was sunbleached to an irreproachable white. The pewter plates and cups shone like water on a bright day. Mistress Margaret had even found, somewhere, a silver spoon to set at each place.

Soon, thought Harry, when cousin John has carried out his task for us ... Then I will buy silver plates, Venetian glasses with spiral stems and lugs, and the French forks they are now using in Whitehall.

Harry called for his knife case and that of his wife, which was a very expensive wedding gift from himself. He hoped that Malise, sitting across from her, would notice the fine Spanish workmanship of both leather and steel.

'Welcome,' said Harry. He raised his glass. 'To the renewed life of Hawkridge House.'

The food, though plain, was plentiful and appetizing: glazed meat pies, the troubling joint of mutton (not ruined by the delay at all), a ham, a platter of spit-roasted doves and woodcock, a deep brown, pungent fricassee of rabbit. There was an excellent chicken cullis served as soup, flavoured with ginger and rose water, and some not-bad wine that his cousin had managed to find.

('Do we deny Sir Richard?' Harry had whispered frantically to John in the parlour. 'Or else risk offending the Puritanical conscience of the Hazeltons? Though I think I may once have seen Master H. take a glass of claret.')

Harry's guests set to with appetite. The three housegrooms and two kitchen maids served without splashing gravy or stepping on toes. So, although his aunt's spoon rattled against her plate with every bite, Harry had to turn his discomfort elsewhere for relief.

His wife drew his nervous eye. She sat hunched and silent beside his cousin John, across the table from Edward Malise. Since arriving, she had spoken seven words. Harry had counted every one.

He opened his mouth to force her to speak. Then he closed it again. Best not to call attention to her. For the first time since getting her in his sights at the boarding school in Hackney, he wondered whether the advantage of her money would make up for the hobble of her gaucherie.

Zeal Beester was more content than she looked. After her parents died of the plague when she was eight, though her money kept her fed and housed, she had grown used to being dismissed as a social creature. It often seemed easier, if not more pleasant, to accept dismissal than to struggle for notice. Relegated to silence, she at least had time to think.

She studied the company from under the washed pebble eyelids. What were the rules here? Who had to be flattered and who really held the power? Who might become a friend?

She noted that Harry's ease had slipped. On one hand, she was disappointed in her husband's shaky grasp on his new role. On the other, that same look of anxious bewilderment on his handsome face had made her decide to marry him. It was as if, without meaning to, he had trusted her with a secret.

'More wine, my lady?'

The young groom stared at her with wide brown eyes.

That's me, Zeal thought in astonishment. She nodded. As she sipped, she eyed Mistress Margaret Beester, her husband's unmarried aunt who seemed to serve as housekeeper. And who bared her teeth at Zeal when she meant to smile.

She hates me, thought Zeal. Wishes I'd never come.

She was used to that, too. In cousins forced to share their beds with her when she suddenly arrived, in girls already at school with alliances firmly made. Zeal looked at Mistress Hazelton. In aunts whose own children had all died and who couldn't forgive the ones that lived when no one wanted them.

Zeal pushed a piece of mutton around her plate with her knife.

Harry's cousin John, who sat on her right, just might be a friend, unless he turned out to be Harry's rival and enemy. He clearly had been in charge before Harry. He had tried to make her feel welcome. She was sorry she had been too tongue-tied to let him know that she was grateful for his kindness.

She glanced at his preoccupied profile. Handsome, but not as beautiful as Harry. Harry was gold, his cousin steel. Or perhaps copper, because of the colour of his hair. A strange, mysterious man. He seemed upset about something. Wound up tight, as silent as she was. She wondered what would happen when he came unwound.

He glanced at her suddenly. Zeal blushed and looked away. He had a look that you had to let in. It didn't just rest on the surface like a look from Mistress Hazelton or that Malise man across the table.

As for the shy old parson – he acted even more frightened than she felt.

I think I can manage this crew, thought Zeal. Particularly when the Hazeltons and Edward Malise go away again.

Samuel Hazelton cleared his throat. 'Excellently fresh pie. In London they're so often tainted by overlong keeping.'

'*Et un très bon vin*,' said Malise civilly. He swirled his glass and drank again.

'*Oui*,' agreed Mistress Hazelton. She glared at Zeal as if the girl had missed a cue.

'Thank you,' said Harry, deeply grateful for any crumbs of reassurance.

Then Harry heard only the sound of chewing. Where, oh where is the easy London wit? he raged in despair. How Malise must be suffering after all his suppers at court! Harry now glared at wife, cousin and aunt.

My wife is hiding in her mutton. My aunt may be able to provide a decent meal but should stay in the kitchen where she doesn't have to talk to proper gentlefolk. And as for John! Useless! All he can do is stare into his wine, mute as a stone!

'. . . The Common Book of Prayer,' ventured Dr Bowler timidly from the far end of the table. 'What is your opinion, Master Hazelton? I mean, in Scotland . . . ? To send English soldiers? I mean, do we English have the right . . . ?' He retreated, blushing into the depths of his wine cup while Hazelton sought a diplomatic reply.

'Too serious and too military a subject for the ladies,' said Harry reprovingly.

'And too expensive! The Crown'll cry for another tax!' Sir Richard Balhatchet, Harry's neighbour, grown graciously drunk as fast as possible, began a discourse on the iniquities of the King's endless new taxes as if there were still a Parliament and he were still a member of it.

As Balhatchet spoke, Samuel Hazelton assessed the serving men's clothes, the wine, the Delft charger on the mantelpiece, the Turkish rugs on the wooden floor, the two life-size portraits of a man and woman, one at either end of the room, with daisy-eye faces in the centres of white ruffs as large and stiff as cartwheels. 'You must mend that road,' he said suddenly.

'As soon as possible!' agreed Harry. 'I had no idea it was so bad!'

Sir Richard was diverted onto his second favourite subject – the lack of good ferries and fords. 'It's all right for you Londoners who can travel by river.'

'I'm not so sure,' said Malise. 'An acquaintance of mine rolled off a barge only last week, into the Thames above

Windsor, coach, coachmen, grooms, pillows, curtains and all.'

'I am grateful,' said Mistress Hazelton, 'that to get to our own country house we have to travel no farther than Hackney.'

There was another silence.

John looked across the table at Malise trapped between Mistress Margaret's pale, watery terror and Mistress Hazelton's black, blunt displeasure. Malise had the smooth, short, rounded forehead and curved beak of a falcon.

The man's eyes met his. John held the eyes with a thrill of expectation, but Malise looked away with a small puzzled frown. Then he resumed his faintly bored civilities to the women on either side.

John's throat had closed against his food. He finally managed to wash down a bite of rabbit fricassee with wine. He did not believe that even Edward Malise, for all his lies, could hide recognition.

'I beg your pardon, Sir Richard?' John had not heard the question. He missed its repetition as he concentrated on placing his wine cup steadily back on the table.

'I said, I never knew you were such a scholar and enthusiast, Mr Graffham!' bellowed Sir Richard. 'Letters in Latin to all those Flemish and Netherlandish chaps, Hazelton here tells me. A dark horse after all these years!' He addressed the table at large. 'A hard-working fellow – more than's right or good for him. Always up to his elbows in muck when I see him, or on his belly with his eyeball up a cowslip! Who'd have thought all that Latin and Greek! How did you come to be such a botanical scholar, sir?' His red-rimmed eyes were slightly accusing.

'Under the benevolent rod of our own Doctor Bowler,' said John.

'A natural instinct for scholarship. *Ab incunabilis* . . . from the cradle,' mumbled Dr Bowler, both pleased and appalled by suddenly becoming the centre of attention again. 'A privilege and a pleasure . . . I offered only the discipline. The appetite for learning is his own . . .' He dropped a piece of bread into his lap and fumbled after it.

'Are you any one sort of enthusiast, Mr Graffham?' asked Malise suddenly. 'Of roses? Vines?'

Hazelton leaned forward into the conversation.

'I study all that grows on this estate,' said John.

Malise studied him now.

'Are you an enthusiast, sir?' John asked levelly. Still no flicker of recognition. But the man was digging deep into his mind, under the casual talk.

'Not in the least.'

'Nor I,' said Hazelton. 'A mere merchant . . . crops of cargo and specie for me. But talk of petals and broken colour and blooming seasons has grown most amazingly fashionable among my London friends.'

'Like Sir George and his roses,' said Harry eagerly.

'Ah, yes, Sir George – a fellow shareholder in the South Java Trading Company,' explained Hazelton, 'who called your reputation to our attention. He claims to ignore anything that grows lower than his knees. Stiff joints, he says. Mr Graffham, can you look lower than your knees?'

'Nothing in God's creation is beneath interest,' said John lightly. 'Even below my knees.'

'Amen,' said Hazelton. He glanced at Malise.

'I would like to retire and recover from that appalling journey,' announced Mistress Hazelton suddenly. She pushed away a plate with a half-eaten quince cake.

Hazelton finished his silent conference with Malise. 'And I,' he declared, 'would like to take a little air. Sir Harry? A gentlemen's stroll? Malise?'

His giving of orders was subtly done. Dr Bowler blushed at the omission of his name.

'Splendid!' cried Harry. 'John, you lead the way to the gardens, and I'll explain our plans for the lawn and portico!'

John was sure that Hazelton had a different purpose.

'Forgive me,' said Sir Richard, levering his bulk up over his feet, 'if I take to my horse while the sun's up.' He leaned over the table, braced on his knuckles and puffing in triumph.

'Why not stay the night, Sir Richard, I beg you,' said Harry. Aunt Margaret gave John a quick, horrified look.

'Be a pleasure, young Harry,' said Sir Richard. 'A true pleasure. But needs must. Duty. Y'know. In the morning. No, best if off I go!' He pushed himself upright and balanced uncertainly.

They rustled and scraped and bowed and murmured as they rose and the women took their leave. At the last moment, one of the serving men spat on the floor behind Mistress Hazelton's chair. For one moment, Mistress Margaret forgot Edward Malise and planned a murder of her own.

'I'll join you in the gardens,' said Harry. 'When I have seen Sir Richard safely off. I leave you till then in my cousin's care.'

'I don't know why,' muttered Mrs Hazelton to her husband, 'I really don't know why we paid to school her! She sat there like a turnip . . . didn't take the chance when Master Malise spoke in French. I told you it was a waste of time to send her to Paris with Lady Chase. No one would ever guess what she has cost to educate!'

'With her own money,' said Hazelton.

'Which could have had other uses.'

'It has, mistress. It has,' said Hazelton. 'And lack of charity makes your face unbecomingly red.'

John led them out of the main door, across the forecourt and into the Knot Garden. Along one wall the white tulips glowed in the dusk. Against the opposite wall the red tulips punched soft dark holes in the evening light. Hazelton sniffed the air, which was faintly perfumed with honey. There was also a not-unpleasant undernote of dung newly ridged along the lines of germander and box.

'How it refreshes the soul to contemplate the works of God,' said Hazelton. He strolled beside John; Malise walked behind. 'The city is now almost entirely the work of man.'

'You might detect the hand of man even here,' said John amiably.

'Yes,' said Hazelton, sniffing the air again. 'But only as Adam was the first gardener in God's Paradise.'

They circled the central device in silence. John wished he had Malise in view.

'Perhaps you can answer a question I have often asked,' said John. 'Does vegetation in Paradise, whether on earth or elsewhere, show the same natural rage for disorder that I find here in Hampshire?'

Hazelton glanced at John to check his tone. 'All disorder is unnatural. Divine order is the natural state. Here in Hampshire you wrestle with the corruption of Man's Fall.'

'Do you mean to say that slugs and caterpillars might respond to increased piety and prayer?'

This glance from Hazelton was longer and held a glint of amusement. 'I suspect that they're susceptible to good works.' He raised his voice. 'Edward, are not Mr Graffham's tulips very fine?"

Come to your point, man! thought John. 'I ordered them from Leyden. It's now possible to write to dealers in the Netherlands for their bulbs and fruit trees.'

'Have you been to the Low Countries?'

John shook his head. 'But I mean to go before I die. I hear that they have fields of flowers as we have meadow grass.'

Hazelton actually smiled. 'I may be able to help.'

They passed under a gated arch into the New Garden, where the central walk was lined by chest-high fruiting walls.

The pale green fish skeletons of espaliered peaches and apricots were not yet in full leaf. At the far end of the fruiting walls, the two night-watch mastiffs, Bellman and Ranter, raised large heads and rumbled in their throats.

John whistled. The mastiffs wagged ox-sized tails. Then John finally allowed himself to turn to look at Malise.

Malise stood braced in the arch that led from the Knot Garden as if he had just stumbled and caught himself. John's nape bristled.

'Now, Mr Graffham,' said Hazelton. 'I'm not a man to tie conversation into diplomatic knots, nor, I suspect, are you. Please sit down.'

Hazelton settled his black folds and pleats on a wooden bench. John sat beside him, trying to listen.

Malise stared into a gooseberry bush.

At last! thought John.

'Master Malise and I have descended on your cousin like the Egyptian plagues before he has even had time to sleep in his new bed because we need to speak with you urgently. You must go to the Netherlands for us.'

John kept his eyes on Malise. He barely heard Hazelton's extraordinary command.

'Your two tracts on fruit-growing,' went on Hazelton, 'have given you a modest but solid reputation in the circle of botanical enthusiasts which seems to be growing daily. That stiff-kneed friend I mentioned at supper, Sir George Tupper, has recommended your reputed good sense, education and energy.'

John wasted no words on modest demurral. Any minute, Malise would lift his head.

'And your cousin, of course, chimed an eager echo,' said Hazelton. 'Will you help us?'

'Us?'

'The South Java Trading Company – members include myself, Master Malise, Sir George, as it happens, and several others whom I doubt you know. And Sir Harry, of course . . .'

'I'm sorry,' said John. 'I can't help you.' He stood up.

'Have the courtesy to let me finish, sir!'

'There's no point.'

Hazelton inhaled sharply. His thin dry face turned dark red above his white collar. He was seldom dismissed so abruptly.

Edward Malise raised his head. He listened, but did not turn around.

'Please forgive any offence my refusal gives,' said John. 'But I am not your man.'

Hazelton steadied himself. 'I misjudged you, sir. A man of sense would at least hear me out. I haven't given you any reason yet for refusal.'

'None that you know.' John was still watching Edward Malise.

Malise turned his head and met John's eyes.

Silence pressed down upon the evening air.

The waiting had ended. Now would come Malise's denunciation, his call for armed men, his summons to Sir Henry Bedgebury, the local magistrate. But Malise's teeth stayed clamped tight against his tongue.

Hazelton shifted on his bench. He had suddenly ceased to exist, and he did not like it any more than he liked to be refused. He had had three surprises today, which was unsettling for a man who understood how both God and the world ticked. This cousin had been a pleasant surprise. An educated villain suited their purpose perfectly.

But then came the villain's impertinent refusal. And now, it seemed, there was bad feeling between Edward Malise and a man he had pretended not to know. The non-existent Hazelton looked from one pair of eyes to the other. Worse than mere bad feeling. Graffham and Malise would clearly be happy to slit each other's throats. Hazelton had stubbed his toe on two mysteries. In business, mysteries were usually expensive.

At last, Hazelton broke the silence. 'We have no time for niceties,' he said. 'Mr Graffham, tell me what stops you so absolute before you even know what we want.'

'I am truly sorry . . .'

'Hear me out or say why not! I would have expected more manners from you!'

'I hope that you are gentleman enough not to insist on pressing an impossible case.'

'Leave it, Samuel!' said Malise sharply.

Hazelton stood up. His face turned puce. Twenty years of money-making, silk nightgowns, a large town-house in London, and a deciding voice in the Court of Committees of a royally chartered trading company had not yet hardened him to an insolent command from a man who fancied himself a social better.

'There you are!' cried Harry from the archway into the Knot Garden, before Hazelton could think how to reply. 'Sir Richard's safely off, and I've ordered pipes laid out in the parlour. Just before I left London, I managed to buy some of the new Virginia tobacco . . .'

'Please excuse me,' said John. He bowed and slipped out through a small gate in the side wall.

Harry watched him go in astonishment. 'What's wrong with my cousin?'

Hazelton's rage spilled onto Harry. 'You mistook him, Sir Harry. Wasted my time and Master Malise's with this junket down here.'

'What has he done?' cried Harry. 'How do you mean, "wasted"?'

'He won't even to listen to our proposal!'

'He *must*!' Harry looked ready to burst into tears. 'It's so perfect!'

'Nothing is, in this world,' said Hazelton with fury. 'But I had hoped for something better than this! I'm going back to the house. With luck, I can stop the unpacking in time to save restuffing it all. I'll set off back to London first thing in the morning. Malise can do as he likes.'

'But we're to dine with Sir Richard tomorrow! And there's the hunting . . . Your time won't be wasted. I've planned so much . . . !'

Hazelton turned brusquely to Malise. 'If that idiot Graffham won't do it, we're almost out of time to find someone else!'

'Let me try,' begged Harry. 'I'm sure I can talk him round!'

'You were sure of him before,' said Hazelton.

'I think,' said Malise carefully, 'that perhaps I should speak with him.'

'John?' Harry laid his ear against his cousin's door. 'John? Are you there?' He opened the door onto a dark, empty room. 'He's not here,' he said over his shoulder to Edward Malise.

'Clearly not. Where does he keep his sword?'

'I don't know.' It seemed an odd question. After a second, Harry shuffled cautiously into the shadows of John's room. 'It's here. On a peg, with his belt.'

'Then he hasn't left the estate,' said Malise. 'I'll try him again in the morning.' He leaned through the door and peered around the darkened room.

'Shall I send a man to look for him in the barns?' asked Harry. 'Maybe he's not back yet from whatever he does at night.'

'I'll find him in the morning. He can't hide for ever.'

'You must forgive his bad manners,' said Harry in anguished apology. 'Cut off from decent society for so many years. But he has a good heart and a good brain. You'll respect him once you get to know him, Edward, I promise you.' Harry began to feel angry now. He shouldn't need to apologize for something which was really nothing to do with him. Some things really were going to have to change and his cousin had better get used to the idea! Starting with the right way to treat guests!

Three

John stripped off his blue silk suit, climbed naked into the enclosing shadows of his fourposter bed and drew the curtains against the world. He lay stiffly against his pillows, listening to his man Arthur settle the bedchamber for the night. Suddenly, he leaned over and threw the bed curtain open again.

'Arthur. My leather jerkin and the woollen breeches.'

He climbed anyhow into his clothes, thrust on his heavy boots. When Arthur had gone back to his pallet on the antechamber floor, John let himself through a small wooden door into the narrow passage within the wall. The passage, barely wide enough for his shoulders, led down a thread of staircase into the *basse-court* at the corner of the Hall Place below the dining chamber. John did not want to meet anyone at all.

From the *basse-court*, he saw a flickering light move through the dining chamber toward Dr Bowler's tiny apartments behind the chapel. His aunt's windows on the first floor glowed.

The hens are still restless, John thought. In spite of their amiable-seeming fox.

He unbolted the gate at the back of the dog yard and flung himself out into the night.

Through the taste of blood in his mouth from his broken nose, John smelled the burning wood and tar of the coach.

An orange-lit circle blackened and spread on the leaves over-head. He choked on the vile smell of charred meat.

He found himself panting on the crest of Hawk Ridge. As he looked down at the house, Aunt Margaret's window went dark. Dr Bowler's bedroom window was hidden by the chapel. The house was so changed that he hardly knew what he was looking at. Behind the dark windows of the east tower lay the face he had seen lit by the flames of the burning coach.

When he finally woke, a day and a half after the startled farmer had delivered him to his uncle, his mind had been washed clean as a pebble in a stream.

'The Devil stole your memory,' his Uncle George later told him. 'There was a smell of sulphur on you when that farmer brought you to me.'

John had remembered only a headache that lasted for weeks, and the sharp, jagged edges of broken teeth.

'How many men were there?' his uncle had begged. 'How were they dressed? Were they vagabonds? Highwaymen? Soldiers?'

The boy seemed not to have heard the questions. He had stared out through the diamond window pane at the wavering lines of the world beyond, his mind filled with the blurred shadow of a bird on the sill outside.

'Colours, John? Livery? Badges?' Solid in his chair, holding tight to the arms, George Beester (still plain mister) had reminded his nephew of a painting he had seen of King Henry. He watched his uncle's soft, fish-like ellipse of a mouth open and close above a square jaw.

'John? Did you hear a name called out? Titles? Anything Frenchified? Were any of them gentlemen? I must have evidence!'

The seven-year-old John squirmed on his stool and shook his head. The answers his uncle wanted so badly jostled and seethed behind a locked gate in his mind. If he let one memory through, the rest would swarm behind. He would never be safe again. Inside the dark canopy of his bed, they would eat up all his other thoughts. They would hunt him into the daylight, throw a net of darkness over his head and entangle him for ever.

'Where's Lobb?' he asked brightly. 'May I go now? I want to find Lobb.'

George Beester sighed and released him to search for the dog.

For the orphaned heir to the Nightingale estates, there followed a constant shifting of households and a long succession of different beds. A few months on his own Tarleton estate, visits to his other three houses. A few months with his Uncle George at Hawkridge. A summer on another of his estates. Two months with an aunt in London. He remembered chiefly the pain of leaving cousins and newly-befriended pets.

In spite of adult prayers and a few charms cast in private by one particular aunt, he had hidden in blankness for the next seven years. His parents had left him, been set upon and killed in some terrible, unspecified way. He did not remember exactly how and no one was anxious to tell him. He had to make a new life without them, on the four estates that were now his and on sojourns with uncles, aunts, cousins, tutors and friends.

He paced the crest of Hawk Ridge toward the water meadows.

Memory had sparked before dying again. In his own kitchen at Tarleton Court, when he was ten, a kitchen groom had thrown a dead rat onto the fire.

'To the Devil with him,' the man had said, before he thought.

John had been alerted by the uneasy eyes the man then

turned on him. The man's quiver of embarrassment stood John's hair on end. John and the groom locked eyes.

The rat's fur flared as quickly as lightning. The flesh blistered, sizzled, blackened and drew back from the bones. The rat writhed as its sinews shrank and hardened in the fury of the heat.

'That's that!' said the servant with false heartiness. 'You'd hardly know, it was so quick.' He hooked a charred log-end from the side of the hearth into the central blaze. The ashy form of the rat crumpled as if it were hollow. It was gone except for the shriek of small sharp white teeth that rolled away to lodge against the leg of an iron trivet.

'Master John,' said the groom. 'Would you like a swig of the new cider? It's better than last season's. What do you think?'

John read correctly the attempt to distract him. He thought he would be sick. Then he saw that this was only an approximate idea. More precisely, he was a brittle shell around nothing, not even sickness. He was nothing, except for the swelling pressure of his eyeballs against the bony rings of their sockets.

If he touches me, I will crumble like the rat, John thought. His mind stopped there.

'I'm fine, Jack. Fine,' he said. 'Why are you fussing?'

Then, eleven years ago, when he was fourteen, memory had returned in a firelit room in a private London house. His uncle George Beester took John to a meeting of the directors of the South Java Trading Company. Beester greeted colleagues and introduced his wealthy nephew who might one day join them. There were a dozen men in the room. Then two newcomers arrived late.

In low voices, the men who knew explained to the men who did not. New investors. Francis and Edward Malise, from an old Catholic family which had survived King Henry by fleeing to the Netherlands. However, as the Malises were stubborn Catholics, the king had, by self-elected right, taken most of their money and all their lands. The Malise estates were sold or distributed to deserving supporters of Henry's expedient split from the Church of Rome. (One or two men had looked at John.) The parents had died abroad. Then, under James, the two Malise sons returned to England and crept slowly back into wealth and position. The new French queen of James's son Charles was said (by low voices into close-held ears) to be oiling their way upward, as she did for any man who could speak her alien tongue and was willing to make the sign of the Cross.

'A little over-concerned with being seen at court,' muttered Mr Henry Porter, owner of coastal ships that carried sea coal and dried cod.

Sir James Balkwell, owner of a large part of Buckinghamshire and local magistrate, replied, 'Who cares if a man cuts his hair long or short so long as he has money to invest?'

As he plunged through the meadows up towards the road, John startled sleepy sheep into bleating flight. At the top of the hill, he leaned his arms on a wall and lowered his head onto the hard damp stone.

The Malise brothers were wrapped in an expensively fashionable softness of lace and curling hair which contradicted their sharp-boned, beaked faces and dark, hungry eyes. They were as alike as a pair of hunting falcons.

The brothers set off a glimmer of fear in John, as faint as distant lightning in a summer sky. He stared, hunched into himself like a rabbit under the shadow of a hawk.

The newcomers turned sharp eyes on the assembled men. They were quiet in manner but shuffled a little on the perch, lifting and settling their feathers. They moved around the room, accepting introductions. Then they paused before the fireplace. Edward, the younger brother, turned his head to Sir James Balkwell. Firelight flickered on bones of his nose and cheek. Sir James said something. Edward Malise showed his teeth in a laugh and changed John's life for the second time.

Memory flared white-hot. John saw the things his uncle had begged him in vain to recall. He saw Edward Malise laugh in the orange light of the burning coach. His mother writhed in the brightness of her burning clothes. His father fell dead across his legs. John flew through the burning window frame. His hair flared. His heart was a red-hot coal. His arms and legs were flames.

He shrieked like a demon and flung himself through the bodies of the other men, across the room, shooting flames like thunderbolts, at that orange-lit, gleeful, beaked face of the Devil.

He knocked a cup of wine through the air and sent blood-red rain showering onto the hems of jackets and lace boot tops. A sheaf of papers fell from startled hands. The twin falcon faces snapped around. For a suspended moment, the time of an indrawn breath or the fall of an executioner's axe, John blazed across the room in the stillness of the men's disbelief and his own absolute intent.

The red-hot knives of his fingers seared Edward Malise's laughing face. Then the elder brother, Francis, seized him from behind. John twisted in the man's arms. The matching falcon face glared into his, contorted with effort, teeth bared. John tried to breathe, but the man's arms crushed his lungs. He wrenched free and, with all his force, knocked the face away. Francis Malise staggered two steps backward, then toppled. John sucked in air like a drowning man and threw himself once again at Edward.

Francis Malise's feet danced back another two steps, trying to catch up with his shoulders and head. His head smashed against the stone floor with the succulent thud of an overripe gourd. His lungs whooped like a collapsing bladder.

John didn't see him fall. He screamed and clawed at the

four men who tried to pull him off the other brother. Then slowly the stillness in the room chilled his fury. He looked where all the men were looking. Francis Malise lay on the stone flags, arms thrown wide at his sides, mouth ajar, jaw a little askew. All eyes in the room watched a small damp patch spread darkly out from his groin across the front of his pale blue silk and wool breeches.

John buried himself deep in the shadow of the Lady Tree. He leaned against her trunk and embraced her for steadiness. He had become a helpless conduit for the past.

The silence in the firelit room had continued for five more breaths, then everyone had shouted at once.

'Francis!' screamed Edward Malise. He jerked free of restraining hands and flung himself down beside his brother's body. 'Fetch a surgeon!'

Henry Porter lifted the head and examined the back of the skull. A man called Witty knelt to place his ear on Francis Malise's chest although the stained trousers had already announced death. 'It's too late.'

Sir James Balkwell sent a man to find an officer.

John stared down at the man on the floor. His anger alone had done that, without knife or sword or club. He had never dreamed he had such power. Now everyone shouted at him.

He looked blindly into their faces. His uncle pushed him across the room, down into a chair. From there, John could see only the soles of the dead man's shoes and a foreshortened peninsula of kneecap, ribcage, crooked jaw and nostrils.

Dead. He had done that. He had wanted to burn both of them to death in the heat of his rage. He had not thought that he had the power to succeed.

His uncle's face interposed itself intently between John and the foreshortened dead man. 'Why, John? Can you remember now? Was he the one?'

'Satan was shining from his eyes,' said another voice.

All the fire had left John. He shivered. He felt cold, and very young, and confused, burned to ash by his own fire. He had been right to keep memory behind the gate. Now, if he could only force it back again, the man on the floor might sit up again and demand that John be merely beaten.

Edward Malise raised his head and looked at John.

'Tell me!' his Uncle George begged. 'Why did you attack him?'

'I'm sure he didn't mean to kill him,' said another voice.

'He meant to kill *me*.'

John looked into the dark, prey-seeking eyes.

'He meant to kill me,' said Edward Malise. 'You all saw him!'

'You killed my parents,' said John.

John wept against the smooth grey bark. He shuddered and clung to the Lady Tree. He wept as he had not wept before.

So much loss, he thought. Mother! Father! The pain of loss! I can't bear it!

A hedgehog rustled unnoticed among the leaves. Later, a fox trotted past, unworried by the still figure that embraced the tree. The gamy smell of the fox pulled John back into the present night.

He felt the chill of his damp shirt-sleeve. He inhaled the night air and slid down to sit on his heels, braced against the tree, a little eased. Memory still flowed through him like the diverted Shir through its cellar pipes.

George Beester gave a great sigh of satisfaction, straightened and turned to Edward Malise. The other men's voices died like a wave pulling back. Silence curled tightly around John, his uncle and Malise.

Malise shook his head as if dazed. He laid one hand on

his brother's body. 'Forgive me, gentlemen, I can't get a grasp on this madness . . .'

'You stood beside their coach and laughed!' shouted John in fury. Surely all these wise older men could smell out the acting.

'When?' demanded Malise. 'What coach?'

'Your men blocked the door so they couldn't escape, my mother, father and nurse!'

Malise passed a hand across his eyes and drew a long breath. 'Can someone else take over this insane interrogation? Make sense . . . perhaps make this young man understand what he has done . . .' His eyes met John's again, briefly. 'Unless he is possessed. And then he is beyond any help.'

John quivered with fury at the note of forgiving compassion in the man's voice.

'He's not possessed by any devils,' said George Beester, 'but by memories no child should have.' He raised his voice to reach everyone in the room. 'When my nephew was seven, some of you will remember, my sister and her husband were burned to death in their coach. The boy was with them but survived. In spite of much time and expense, I never discovered their killers. I knew who might have wanted them dead . . .' Beester sighed again and studied Malise with gratified certainty. 'But I had no proof. The boy himself remembered nothing of that night until this evening, when he saw you and your brother.'

'Your implication is too monstrous and mad for me even to take offence.'

'Then it should be easy to answer,' said Beester.

Malise searched the surrounding faces for hostility or support. 'I swear that I am innocent. I did not kill this boy's parents, even though some of you must know that I had good reason to hate them, as my family have had for two generations before. The bones of my family were stripped by those vulture Nightingale upstarts. Or do you all choose to forget the plundering barbarities of King Henry? Do you shut his victims out of your thoughts as fast as the Star Chamber was able to forget the meaning of justice?'

'One barbarity never excuses another,' said Sir James. 'Nor do old stories of land disputes and exile answer the boy's accusation.' He looked severely at Malise. 'You should be careful, moreover, how you fling around that word "barbarity".'

'No doubt highwaymen killed his parents – it happens often enough. The Malises are being blamed for the guilty conscience of the Nightingales.'

'Where were you and your brother that summer?' asked Sir James. 'August, seven summers ago.'

'How can I answer that, at a time like this . . . ? But I don't even need to answer it. I've been falsely accused by a shocked and frightened boy, whose brain, as his uncle has just testified, was addled by his tragic experience.'

John opened his mouth but his uncle's hand closed hard on his wrist.

'Seven summers ago,' repeated Beester.

Malise stared into George Beester's face. 'It comes back to me now. I remember. My brother and I were both in the Low Countries . . . serving with a Flemish unit against Spain. We had just engaged the Count de Flores in a pointless skirmish.'

There was a murmur from one or two of the company members. Englishmen serving as mercenaries, in a foreign army. Former soldiers now playing at commerce with their blood money.

Malise felt the quiver of hostility. 'I will prove this to be true and when I have, I will expect reparation from you. As I trust the justice both of God and man to punish this youth for murdering my brother.'

Malise looked around in the silence and saw the assessing looks. 'It was seven years ago, and the boy was only seven at the time. Is this how you conduct the business of your company . . . wrestling truth and reason to the ground on the dusty memory of a fallible child? Sir James . . . ?' He turned in appeal to Sir James Balkwell.

'We are all as shocked as you,' said Balkwell to Malise. 'And we regret your monstrous introduction to our Company. As to our business dealings, sir, we examine all propositions calmly and without prejudice. No one here has yet laid a hand on either truth or reason.'

'Am I the one on trial, then?' demanded Malise. 'That man . . .' he pointed at George Beester '. . . has as good as accused me of murder when his Satan's whelp of a nephew has just killed my brother!' His eyes returned to the slack limbs and oddly angled jaw.

'The boy must be tried,' said Balkwell. 'It needs no examination to conclude . . .'

'It was an accident!' protested George Beester. 'It was surely an accident. He may have meant to attack – and with good reason – but not to kill!'

'We have more than enough witnesses to what happened,' said Balkwell. 'Intelligent men who have eyes and will report honourably what they saw.' He turned to Edward Malise. 'I'm sorry that you feel on trial at such a tragic moment. But the boy has also made a claim against you, and we must deal with it as judiciously as any other matter. Whatever my feelings, I cannot agree with his uncle that the death was an accident. Like you, I saw clear intent in his face. I wish, therefore, to examine why the boy is so enraged against you.'

I killed a man in rage, John thought. I should feel such a mortal sickness of my soul. But he still felt only the rage.

In prison, his newly acquired memory was still sharp as freshly broken glass. Time had had no chance to dull it. Seven years of rubbing and grinding took place in mere days. He lay on his cot, hearing, smelling, seeing, and feeling, again and again and again. Smoke, roasting meat, the screams of the horses and of his mother. His own hair on fire. Malise's beak. His father's groom who had saved him and almost certainly been killed while John slipped away through the bushes to fetch up at the farm. The thrust of his mother's hands as he flew through the window. They had saved him and died.

John hoped that rehearsing his memories might wear them out, but rage, grief and guilt wore him out first. Rage was the most bearable; he spun it into a case around himself like a silkworm. Then he raged that he had not paid heed in that firelit room to what Edward Malise had said – to the reason his life had been destroyed – instead of staring in a trance at Francis Malise's shoe soles. Then he sieved the memories again, for a detail, a phrase, a name, anything to give his uncle as evidence against the Malises.

Then he suddenly asked, why? Why did the Malises hate my family so desperately? That ambush had been a desperate act. He found the word 'vulture' lodged in his memory. He closed his eyes and saw again the flickering light on Francis Malise's body, and his brother's face. More words surfaced like dying fish. John curled tightly on his cot. Had the Nightingales truly been vultures?

After three weeks in prison, it finally occurred to John to become afraid, not of death but of how he would die. The rope – he had once watched friends of a condemned man hang on his feet beneath the Tyburn gibbet to speed the terrible slowness of strangulation. At best, he would be given a gentleman's way out on the block. He tried to tell himself that he would merely leap cleanly from this life into the next. He would never see the bloody mess and the strange turnip thing that had once held his soul.

He knew he would be judged guilty, because it was the truth. He had killed Francis Malise, in rage.

He knew that men had the right to punish him under

temporal law, but he had expected to suffer in spirit as well. On the contrary, he was still glad he had done it. This realization shook him profoundly. At fourteen, he began to suspect that Good and Evil, the works of God and the works of Satan, were not separated after all by a boundary as clearly marked as a river bank. As a child, you were good or you were bad. Usually you knew the difference, and if caught you were punished. If you didn't know the difference, you had merely failed to understand God's Will.

Now, at a time when he most needed his childish faith, he was most filled with wretched doubt. He called on God to explain the ambiguity that surrounded His Commandments. 'Thou shalt not kill.' If John felt unrepenting triumph, what about soldiers fighting in the King's name? And what about the soldiers fighting on the other side? There were long hours of opportunity, as John waited in his prison cell, for a Divine reply. The Lord did not seize the chance.

Is this one of the adult secrets, John wondered. That we walk as uncertainly as blind men? That to believe is merely to prescribe and to hope?

His uncle had bought John lodging in a room among the debtors of the Fleet Prison instead of a cell below ground. He also dropped the coins of his own suspicion into the pockets of gossip and influence. Sir James Balkwell had not been alone in feeling that John's accusation might be true. He and the others were easier in their minds when there seemed to be no hurry to bring the boy to trial.

'Bogus Englishmen as well as murderers,' George Beester said of the Malises wherever an ear would listen. 'Catholics ... French name. Whipped off to the Netherlands in King Henry's time and now they're slinking back again, encouraged by the marvel of a French Catholic queen on the throne of England and protected by her papist cronies.'

A successful, self-made man, Beester understood the close connection between principles and pockets and had the means to make this connection work for his nephew's cause. Even so, though he found many sympathetic ears, his efforts were not enough.

He visited the prison six weeks after John's arrest. John scrambled up from his cot.

'They're going to try you next week,' said Beester. 'The majority of those honourable men who witnessed Francis Malise's death have agreed, however reluctantly, that you intended harm. The plea of accident has been rejected. And Edward Malise is pressing his case among the Catholic faction that has the Queen's ear. It's her word against the other side's reluctance to act.'

Beester settled on a little stool and spread his legs wide to balance his bulk. 'I don't think I can save you in court unless we can find a strong enough case ourselves to bring against Malise. One last time – try to remember more! Even one detail . . . a name called out . . . livery.'

John shook his head. 'I'm sorry. I've been trying . . . Uncle, did the Malises have any right on their side?'

'Has the Devil been pissing in your brain?' George Beester flushed. 'You ignorant, evil young . . .' He stopped himself. 'I'm sorry. It's a fair question for a boy in your position.' He studied his sturdy knees. 'They had no right, only what they pretended was a reason. And Malise was canny enough to admit that straight off. His grandfather chose the wrong side, against King Henry while your own grandfather did not. The Malises tried every means to win their lands back. Your father had won a final lawsuit four months before he died.'

'Lands,' said John in wonder. 'My parents' lives for lands?'

'The Malises claimed injustice and persecution.'

'In a way, they were right.'

'Don't be a fool. The courts ruled that they were not. And that is the truth, as it stands, on this earth. The Malises are murderers. No law, Divine or temporal, gave them the right to play executioner.'

'I killed Francis Malise.'

'But with more right. And I still say it was an accident. And I have support on both counts. That's why you must not come to trial! Morally, your guilt is still a little slippery. All those official words and papers will set events rock solid. The logical sentence will be required. I must do something before then.'

'I did kill him.'

Beester leaned forward. 'Swear to me again that you saw Edward Malise beside my sister's coach!'

'I swear,' said John. 'By anything you like.'

His uncle studied the boy's eyes. Then he grunted. 'All right. There's no more to say. They won't have you as well.' He stood and rearranged the layers of his clothing for leavetaking. Beester saw no point yet in telling the boy that all four Nightingale estates, including Tarleton Court, had been confiscated by Crown agents to be held pending the verdict.

'If those two were guilty,' said Beester, 'then it may yet be proved. And what a shame, then, if you were already dead.'

He crossed to the unlocked door. 'Do you still keep handy that knife I gave you?'

John nodded.

'If rumour gets out that I'm trying to delay your trial, Malise or a helpful crony might just see fit to play God's role again. There aren't enough guards here. Take care.'

The heavy wooden door of the cell scraped across the floor. John woke. He listened. Heard the tiny barking of a far-away dog. Inside the cell, cloth rasped on cloth. The darkness was tight with the silence of held breath. John felt rather than saw the change in the darkness where the door would be. Someone had opened his door. He slid his right hand under the cotton bolster onto the handle of his uncle's dagger.

He waited, straining to hear over the clamour of his body.

Cloth scratched across cloth again, in the darkness near the door. Agile as an adder, John slid sideways off the bed. On the ice-cold floor, he listened again. Over the thumping of his heart, he heard a roughly drawn breath, and another. The intruder needed air badly and could keep quiet no longer.

How many were there?

Silently, John coiled himself near the foot of the bed. If he attacked now, he would have the brief advantage of surprise. He shifted his grip on the handle of the knife. The sound of breathing had not moved away from the door.

'John?' His name felt its way through the darkness on an urgent breath. 'Nephew John, it's Mistress Beester.'

Now he imagined a thicker darkness near the door.

'Your aunt . . . Uncle George's wife.'

His hand clamped even tighter onto the knife.

'John, are you there?'

The thicker darkness stirred. It seemed to retreat a step.

'Aunt Jane?'

'It was the right door! Thank God! Come at once!' The whisper was impatient and frightened. 'Come quickly. Your uncle is waiting in the street . . . Come!'

John stood with a surge of joy. He took a step and bumped into the table. He hesitated in the darkness. What if she weren't really there? It would be too terrible if she were a demon testing his soul's strength. She would vanish, and he would have to rebuild his courage again from scratch.

'Sweet Heaven, come now!' Fabric rustled. A cold but solid hand brushed his wrist, fumbled, gripped on.

John dived through the darkness after the hand.

'Close the door!' she whispered.

They cut diagonally across a short corridor to a second smaller wooden door. His aunt opened it and ducked into the shaft of a narrow stone staircase with John behind her. Steps spun down, down, down around a pole of stone into a well of darkness. John followed the hissing of his aunt's hems down the stone treads, his knees jerking in the rhythm of his descent. Slap, slap, shouted his feet. He tried to step more lightly as he followed his aunt's rustling shadow down into the well. Tap, tap. Tap, tap. The truth began to shake his numbness. Tap, tap. He kept one hand on the spiralling wall to steady himself. The pitted stone bit at his fingertips. The cold damp air had the rotting leather smell of bats. He was escaping. Alive.

A vestibule. A heavy door, slightly ajar. A porch. A passageway. John smelled the stench of offal and sewage as they crossed a bridge over the prison moat and passed through another gate. Then, a street. An unlit coach, and his uncle.

'In! In!'

Horses' hooves scraped on stone. Running water sluiced in a shadowed trench. Inside the coach, with the door slammed shut, John threw his arms around his uncle.

'You're not clear yet,' said Beester, patting the broad young shoulders. 'We must get you out of London tonight.'

'How did you do it?' demanded John. 'How did you unlock the doors and remove the gaolers?'

'Ahh,' said George Beester with satisfaction. 'It's a venal age.' He hesitated. He was pleased by his own foresight; he had extracted as much money as possible from the boy's estates in the twenty-four hours after Francis Malise's death, before the mill of the Star Chamber began to grind. John had bought his own freedom, at no cost to his uncle. It had been an elegant transaction. However, Beester was not sure that the boy would appreciate this elegance or understand his new estate in life.

'Are you aware, nephew, that the Star Chamber now holds the deeds to all your estates and assets? Your escape will make them doubly forfeit to the Crown. Your present freedom is the sole residue of your inheritance.'

'It's more than enough!' said John with passion. 'Thank you! And thank you, aunt!'

'I'm afraid it's far from enough,' replied Beester. 'As you will learn.' He studied the shadowy rectangles of darkened windows passing outside the coach. 'Now I must hide you in a safe burrow somewhere.'

His uncle took him upriver by boat from a dock near London Bridge. John perched in the prow. He watched the sleeping city slide past, then the great dark houses of the Strand, then the jumbled buildings that made up Whitehall. Later, Chelsea village, and much later, the palace at Richmond. Because he was only fourteen, he couldn't help thinking – now that he had escaped – that he was having the most amazing adventure.

'This is what life feels like,' he told himself, as the far, dark banks slid past and distant dogs barked. 'I am being tested.' Doubt still slept in his deserted prison cell. In John's euphoria at leaving behind the terror of the rope and block, he now knew that his clear sight would return. His tale would end as it should, after battles, voyages, and vindications, in his own reclaimed kingdom at the side of a blue-eyed princess.

He leaned against the Lady Tree, too tired to move. He listened for a few moments to the rustle of her mermaid tail above his head. Then he noticed the hedgehog crackling and snuffling in the leaves by his feet, the danger of the fox long past. His trousers were damp from the earth. His legs ached.

My aunt is right. I must leave at once. I won't let myself be arrested again. And to kill Malise here on Hawkridge Estate would be a shameful way to repay my uncle and his heirs. I'd spoil poor old Harry's chances at Court for ever.

He imagined going back to his chamber now and packing. Stealing away to Mill Meadow, saddling his horse and riding away.

In which direction? he asked himself. How do I choose?

He stood a little longer without moving. Malise had known him but said nothing. Why?

He's either playing with me or needs something. I should have paid more attention to what Hazelton was trying to say.

I won't run tonight, he decided a little later. I'm too tired, and there's too much to arrange. Unless I want to live as a vagabond outlaw, I must arrange my flight a little. If Malise hasn't raised the alarm yet, he may wait a little longer.

He was past thinking.

He laid his hand on the Lady Tree in farewell. You outlasted me after all, he thought.

Ask, ask, ask, she rustled.

I'd be a fool, thought John suddenly, to abandon everything before I know what Malise wants.

Four

May 25, 1636. Mild and still. No dew. Turtle doves
back in beech hanger. Apples in full blow at last.

Journal of John Nightingale, known as John Graffham.

Zeal woke cautiously, like a small animal sniffing the air
outside its burrow. She kept her eyes closed. In her experience
there was seldom anything on the other side of her eyelids to
hurry out to greet. She drew a resigned, waking breath. Then
she sniffed again in drowsy surprise. The linen sheet and
feather-filled quilt which covered her to her eyebrows smelled
of sunlight. A small, surprising goodness to credit to the day's
account.

She stretched slim, naked limbs. Her eyes opened abruptly.
Instead of plunging off the sudden edges of her narrow
London school trestle bed, her fingers and toes, though spread
as far as she could reach, lay still cradled in the softness of
a vast featherbed.

She propped herself on her elbows, breathing quickly. She
was on the deck of a ship-sized bed, in full sail across a strange
sea of polished wooden floor. The bed hangings, flapped and
draped, half-hid a distant horizon of diamond-paned
windows. The morning sun had transformed last night's
cavern of darkness and wavering shadows. The brown coverlet was really faded red silk. The hangings were rich midnight
blue. By torch- and firelight the night before, she had not

seen the fat bulges and gadrooning of the four bedposts, or the dusty tapestry above the fireplace of Hercules holding the giant Antaeus in the air above his head. The bulgy bedposts made Zeal think of plump women's legs wearing tight garters. Zeal imagined the legs beginning to dance.

Oh, yes! She breathed out a happy sigh.

A new, unexplored world. Another Indies, a new Virginia coast. At times in the past, she had felt exhausted by the need to learn yet another new terrain. But this one was different.

She heard an odd, distant, wavering noise which she would investigate later.

My own room for ever and ever! she thought. At last. This is it. She flung herself back onto her pillows to recover from the enormity of the idea. I shall wake up like this every morning from now on. No more shifting. I have finally begun the rest of my life.

Her new husband Harry lay in the next chamber in his own bed, where she meant him to stay for quite some time.

'Husband,' she repeated quietly to the embroidered blue silk of the canopy. 'Husband.' Testing it. She squeezed her eyes tightly shut and shook her head in pleased disbelief. What a difference that word made. She was exactly the same girl as before, but because she had a husband her life had changed around her more than she could yet imagine. People already treated her differently.

'My lady.'

Firmly, she set aside the memory of Mistress Margaret's tight eyes and bared teeth. And of Harry's glares across the dinner table.

I did it! she thought fiercely. I did it. Somehow, in spite of my uncle . . . I wanted it hard enough . . . All I had to do was want something hard enough and not care whether it was correct, or dutiful, or virtuous.

A spasm of anxiety curled her onto her side.

Selfish and wilful as it is, I mustn't care what my uncle and aunt think!

For fourteen years she had tried to please by being good, but had found that she could never be good enough, nor be good in all the different ways different people wanted. She had been dutiful and loving to her parents, but they had deserted her when she was eight for the superior joys of Heaven. She had then tried to please the assorted relatives who took her in. (An allowance from her inherited estate more than covered the expense of feeding and boarding her.)

She soon grew confused. No sooner had she figured out the rules in one household (both spoken and unspoken) than she was shifted to another where she had to begin again. One aunt (on the Puritan side of the family) had valued quiet, self-effacing children, another (a socially ambitious beauty) preferred spirit. One uncle insisted on prayers four times a day, while another ranted against self-congratulating piety and self-serving humbug. Several cousins had taunted her for being thin and pinched and ugly, while her cousin Chloe, whom she thought quite beautiful, was jealous of Zeal's red-gold wiry hair, blue eyes and fine pale skin.

As for Mistress Hazelton ... Zeal curled a little tighter. Mistress Hazelton watched her with a curious little distant smile, no matter what she did. In the four years since her uncle Samuel Hazelton had bought her wardship, Zeal had tried not to worry about what she might be doing wrong, and not to see that Mistress Hazelton pinched her lips every time she spoke to her.

Her uncle only made things worse when he defended her. He let his wife see that he was amused by Zeal's desire to learn Latin and by her questions about his business affairs (which were also her business affairs, as he had bought the use of her fortune along with her wardship). By the time, two years ago, that her uncle sent her to the boarding school in

Hackney to improve her deportment, dancing and needle-work, Zeal was worn out by trying.

I have anchored myself at last, she thought. When I have made myself the mistress, I will be able to choose my own way to be good or bad. Whether this place is good or bad, I shall make the best of it with a whole heart.

Outside the diamond-paned windows, the pale green tops of trees caught the morning sun. She uncurled and stretched again. The worn linen sheets slid smoothly against her skin. She spread her small pink toes like a cat stretching its paws and turned her head in the yielding welcome of the feather pillows. She now recognized the odd noise outside. It was the constant faint bleating of sheep.

Lady Beester. What a fuss everyone made about a title. It had even clamped a muzzle on Mistress Hazelton, for all her pious lip-curling at the lewd antics of the gentry. Again, Zeal smiled at the underside of the blue silk tester of her bed. What mattered was that Sir Harry Beester was her Harry.

He had appeared like a miracle, a very *gentil parfait knight*, and rescued her from the baying pack that had sniffed after her moderate fortune. Tall, handsome Harry, golden as Apollo, and kind. A little simple at times, but after six and a half years of being parcelled about, Zeal gave kindness its full weight in assaying the human soul.

Harry was also amusing. Though already twenty-two, he sometimes seemed her own age or younger. He did not scorn practical jokes or an occasional nostalgic game of hide-and-seek. He had never stuck his hand down her bodice to tweak her nipples, nor shoved his tongue into her mouth as other suitors had done. Most important of all, he had said that he quite understood how much having a child frightened her. He was in no rush for an heir. They could leave all that business until she was ready. He had sworn it in a solemn oath to her. In spite of her uncle's dark objections that Harry was a fortune-hunter like all the others, Zeal felt she had made a good trade for her money.

She lay in the shadows of the huge bed, breathing softly, warm with a child's first adult taste of the power of its own will. Harry would never regret his bargain either. She would be the most useful wife a man could want. She knew that he was disappointed in her as a social ornament, but she would startle him by how well she would manage Hawkridge House.

She eyed the unfamiliar objects of her chosen world and prepared to annex them. The pewter basin and jug on the table. A mirror. The end of a heavy carved oak coffer. The faded velvet-covered cushions on the bench fixed below the nearest window. The silvery-green trees outside.

She heard voices outside her windows as well as the bleating sheep. Her inventory of her new world suddenly leaped in length. Her peaceful warmth faded.

If I am going to be such a useful wife, I'd better make a start, she thought wryly.

She pushed down the quilted coverlet, slid across the acre of linen and lowered herself to the floor. Shivering, she looked around for a smock or robe. Her breath made a faint cloud in the chilly air. The rooms on the north side of the house were never warm in the morning until June.

Naked and on bare feet, she crossed to the window and peeked out. The paths of busy dairymaids, washing women, dogs, grooms, and chickens already criss-crossed the *basse-court* yard below. Harry's cousin John strode purposefully across one corner of the courtyard, head down like a dog on an exciting scent. Mistress Margaret's voice called through an open window.

A cold lump formed in Zeal's stomach. The weight of her new world landed hard on her chest. She put her right foot on top of her left, to try to warm it.

All those people expect me to tell them what to do.

She remembered Mistress Margaret's pinhole pupils and tight lips as she had welcomed Zeal to Hawkridge House.

She knows the house, knows exactly what to do and say here, and she'll be waiting for my mistakes.

Zeal lifted the lid of the carved oak coffer. It was nearly empty except for some linen scraps. No clothes. Goosepimples prickled her forearms, standing the fine gold down on end.

Do I have a maid to dress me here or do I dress myself, as at the school?

At the Hazeltons' her woman Rachel had slept on a truckle bed in her room. Here she was alone. She dropped the lid of the coffer.

Has everyone already breakfasted? Do they eat in the dining chamber or their own rooms? How can I go call Rachel when I'm stark naked?

She put her left foot on top of her right.

I'm cold. And Mistress Margaret hates me. And I irritated Harry at dinner last night, our first in our new home.

She had felt skewered by glares at the table – Harry's, Mistress Margaret's and her aunt's. There had been nowhere safe to look. Not even at Harry's cousin, John Graffham, who had seemed so friendly when the coaches first arrived but then ignored her all through dinner.

She wrapped her arms across her full pink-nippled breasts. Both feet were now numb.

How did I think last night that I could manage all these people? I shall pay for my presumption. I'll be punished for insisting on my own way. I'll never figure out what is right and wrong here. I'll never learn to run this place. Harry will be furious. His cousin will pity me. I'll be miserable for the rest of my life.

She climbed back up onto the bed, pulled the quilt tightly up around her neck and stared into the folds of the hangings at the end of the bed. She would not cry! Her predicament was no one's fault but her own. As so often before in her short life, she allowed herself a last brief moment of respite before she began to deal with whatever evil that life, the Good Lord and her own deserving might serve up next.

Her door opened.

'Where would you like to breakfast, madam?'

Zeal was unreasonably pleased to see her maid Rachel, an over-pious young woman of twenty-six selected by Mistress Hazelton. This morning, the sulky, pock-marked Rachel was Zeal's key to the newest set of unfamiliar rules. She could ask Rachel to bring what she could not find herself. Make *her* carry the weight of uncertainty. Zeal made her first decision as mistress of Hawkridge House.

'I shall eat here,' Zeal said firmly. 'I like this room. Don't you like this place, Rachel?'

Being in a strange house seemed to make Rachel, too, feel a greater warmth toward a familiar face. 'It's not as bad as I feared, madam.'

A little later, in smock, high-waisted jacket, stockings and mules, Zeal settled by the window with her bread, ale and cheese. She was feeling better. As Rachel helped her dress, Zeal had reminded herself that every new move had brought that same moment of helpless terror. Each time she shifted households she had wanted to die for the first day or two. Each time, she had pulled herself together and made the best of what was on offer. She had chosen this place and had no one but herself to blame if she failed here. She had Mistress Hazelton's household as a model. She had prepared herself by months of study. She would ride this panic into calm as she had ridden the other panics.

Rachel set a small chest at her side. While the maid put another log on the fire and shook out a loose day gown, bodice, petticoats and sleeves, Zeal lifted a book out of the chest. *A Good Huswife's Jewell* had been a school text. Beneath it lay *Of Domesticall Duties*, which Mistress

Hazelton had given her on her betrothal. Zeal herself had ordered *The Boke of Nurture* from a bookseller in St Paul's as soon as her marriage had been agreed. She had learned all three books by heart. The precepts that governed cheesemaking, distilling, the moral well-being of the servants, the counting of linens and ordering of beer swilled around in her head. Each day she studied a little more. One day she would be sure of it all. As she munched her bread and sipped the ale, she read, closed her eyes, murmured to herself, and read again.

A good wife must not let the serving grooms wipe their hands on the curtains nor permit any man to piss in the fireplaces, Zeal reminded herself. A good wife must set a constant example of industry and piety to the rest of the estate family. She must manage the household spending and prevent waste in the kitchen. She must oversee cleanliness both in the dairy and in the personal linen of her maids. She must obey her husband in all things, and know how to bind a wound. Here in the country, while she needn't know so much about buying clean water or choosing a freshly caught fish, she must know how to plant lettuces, pickle a cabbage and smoke a pig.

Zeal leaned back and blew out her flushed cheeks. She stood up decisively. She might as well begin carrying out her duties. Not on the curtains. Not in fireplaces. Watch out for moths, mice, dust. Count cheeses, turn linens . . . no, count linens and turn the cheeses. Her eyes closed with the effort of remembering and her lips moved as if she were at prayer . . . Dairy, no spitting at table, evening prayers, tinctures, eggs . . .

How can I count the linens or turn anything, she thought suddenly, until I know where they are?

'Rachel!' she called. 'Please shake out another loose gown, and an older bodice of black wool, with a plain collar and no poxy lace on the sleeves to catch on doorhandles and candlestands!'

She left her maid on her knees among a spewing of wool, buckram, silk and leather from the travelling chests. Outside the antechamber to her room, she heard Mistress Margaret's voice below, in the hall. Zeal ducked back through her own apartments. She would have to face her predecessor sooner or later, but not yet.

There was no answer behind the door on the far side which led into Harry's apartments. Zeal entered the empty room to begin her dutiful voyage on the high seas of being a good wife.

Before half an hour had passed, Zeal was having more fun than she had ever had in her life. From the first timid lifting of a coffer lid to examine the linens left at the bottom, she quickly arrived at the intense, wicked pleasure of licensed nosiness. There is no thrill so profound as that of flinging open strange chests, other people's cupboards, and closed doors. That it was her duty to snoop made the pleasure even greater.

Beyond Harry's apartment, she found a little parlour above the chapel at the east end of the house. She put her nose over the ledge of the internal window and peered happily down onto brightly-coloured tiles and carved pews. A half-naked female acrobat balanced on one of the pew finials. On others dolphins leaped and cheerful-looking cocks stretched to crow. A monkey in a hat sat on his curled tail. Not a skull or other *memento mori* in sight.

I knew I liked this place, she thought. Her delight was enhanced by the film of dust on the windowsill.

Mistress Margaret needs my help after all.

She doubled purposefully back through Harry's rooms and her own into the rest of the main wing.

'Good morning, my lady.' A housemaid curtseyed on the landing of the stairs.

'Isn't it!' replied a flushed and happy Zeal.

Zeal grew happier and happier as she pried and poked and

peeked her way through a series of other chambers. She buzzed with intent, her earlier fears forgotten.

Her breath came short as she fingered through musty treasures. Combs with hairs still caught in them, wooden teeth, rings without their stones. A squashed straw hat and yellowed silk stockings still humped and bubbled by absent toes. Caps, collars, and an entire silken garden embroidered on a single kid glove in faded chain stitch and French knots.

She sneezed from the dust in the chests and slapped at tiny moths which flew up on dusty grey wings. She would have lavender and wormwood tucked in among the clothes. Mistress Margaret was perhaps a little old to keep track of all the chests and coffers. Zeal's help might even be welcome.

She lifted out the crumpled muslin tiers of a distiller's sieve, slashed sleeves still curved to former elbows, the concentric circles of an old-fashioned iron farthingale, its ties still crumpled from the knots that marked the circumference of a once-living waist, perhaps that of a younger Mistress Margaret. Zeal stared at the farthingale. Mistress Margaret must once have been as young as Zeal was now.

In the base of a bench chest she found parts of an old suit of armour, awry as the broken shell of a dried-up beetle. It was like one her grandfather had worn, dented by fighting, a little rusty and dark in feel. Zeal imagined the man who had once worn it. Fierce, fast-moving in spite of the armour's weight, with intense eyes that glared out through the visor. Rather like Harry's cousin John. She put her hand into the hinged carapace of one glove and tried to close her fingers around an imagined sword hilt. The metal edges cut into her fingers.

To be such a one, who could wear that! And do those deeds. She felt a little queer and took her hand out again. But her imagined man joined the growing crowd of ghosts and present lives that Zeal pulled from chests and cupboards and clutched to herself. For the first time since her parents had died, she was writing a new history of the world with herself in the centre instead of on an edge.

Beyond a first-floor parlour and pair of sleeping chambers she turned left into the Long Gallery, which made up the entire first floor of the west wing of the house. The gallery would have held eight carriages end to end and was all of golden wood – waxed floor and panelled walls carved with bosses and folds – which creaked conversationally beneath her feet and hands. Sun poured in through windows down the long outer wall and across the south front. The gallery was warm and smelled of honey and beeswax polish.

'Ahh,' Zeal said aloud. She lifted her skirts and ran from the door to the window at the far end. The floor reverberated under her feet like a giant drum. Her footsteps echoed back from the panelled walls. She sat for a moment on the wooden seat beneath the window, panting happily.

There was a fireplace in the centre of the long, unwindowed inner wall. Zeal trotted over to it and wrinkled her nose. Sure enough, there was a problem there to be set right. This discovery made her even happier.

John rose early and listened for some time at his open door. Then, ignoring the silk breeches and padded doublet that Arthur had laid out for him, he put on his woollen work breeches, linen shirt and leather jerkin. He breakfasted in his room on a quick mug of ale and a slice of cold meat pie.

Without comment, Arthur folded John's good clothes and replaced them in a chest. Arthur was twenty-four, fair-haired and freckled. He had been born on an estate near Basingstoke and sent to work as a housegroom at Hawkridge House when he was ten. As boys, he and John had fished, swum, wrestled and talked whenever John visited his uncle's estate. At eleven,

Arthur had shown John the Lady Tree and dared him to put his hand on the meeting of her thighs.

When John had suddenly arrived for good at the age of fourteen, Arthur (then twelve), like most of the estate residents who knew John, had been fascinated by the mysterious drama in a far-off place that had changed John's name from Nightingale to Graffham and sent him into what was eventually understood to be hiding.

When the two boys first met again, Arthur was surly. He didn't want John to think that he presumed on childhood intimacy. John was preoccupied and seemed distant. They went on for several months with Arthur resentful and over-quick to snatch off his hat, John distracted but feeling yet another loss. Then John began to heal, to talk, to seek Arthur's opinions, and Arthur lowered his raised hackles.

As John slowly took over running the estate, he called more and more on Arthur's slightly edgy, challenging help. The two youths relaxed slowly back into respectful companionship without quite regaining the childish ease. In the end, Arthur moved formally from housegroom into the role of John's man. He gave John loyalty and an honesty that never flattered. In exchange, John stirred up Arthur's safe and humdrum life. Arthur felt that he never knew exactly what would happen next. He also had the more superficial but gratifying joy of being close to the man at the centre; everyone believed he knew what John thought, even if he didn't. Their connection was amiable, comfortable and trusting, but it had never been tested.

Now John watched Arthur thoughtfully, considered confiding in him, then decided to wait. He took his leather belt and dagger from the hook on the wall. He let himself through a side door into the little parlour above the chapel where he stood at the window and looked down into the *basse-court*.

The wet thump and sloshing of churns came from the open door of the dairy room. A boy was dreamily sweeping the brick pavement. A cat lay curled asleep in the sun on top of a barrel. Two washing women side-stepped out of the washroom, heads bent together over the heavy basket of wet linens they were carrying out onto the lawns to bleach in the sun. Nothing indicated the possible arrival of men-at-arms called by Malise.

Well, for certain, John thought wryly, I've not faced a day so filled with fascination for many years. I wonder if it will be my last one here. He used his wryness to mask from himself a puzzling sense of failure.

He went down into his office where he collected up a small bundle of papers, a bag of coins, and his pistol, all of which he locked into a cupboard set into the wall. He opened the doors and drawers of his collection, then closed them again. One of Malise's men was strolling in the forecourt. John watched him for a moment. Then he left the office to sharpen his knife on the whetstone in the lean-to outside the kitchen.

His uncle brought him safely to Hawkridge House and left again at once, a single horseman and groom, seen only by the family of house servants and two stable grooms.

Aunt Margaret had already been resident on the estate for fifteen years and resigned to spinsterhood. At first she had twitched and exclaimed, and cried out that they would all be ruined if John were discovered and retaken there. Then, still muttering disasters, she had applied poultices to his sores and rashes that prison had bred (even an above-ground apartment). She half-drowned him in tisanes, decoctions and nourishing broths. She doused him for lice and fleas. She prayed for him twice a day on her knees in the little chapel, on the tiles of tulips and royal Spanish pomegranates, her head bent between the female acrobat, the monkey, and a cockerel being swallowed by a fish.

'Poor, poor lamb. Poor doubly bereft little soul. My poor, dear nephew, so fierce, so unfortunate!'

'I'm well, aunt! I'm well! I don't need dosing!'

But she pursued him with mint and rosemary, with garlic and willow bark, and with the panic of suddenly acquired responsibility. Like his uncle, she understood better than John how the butterfly must now reverse nature and shrink back into a worm.

Two soldiers arrived a week after John did. They were making polite enquiries. No one who mattered had evidence to link Beester with his nephew's escape, however much some might suspect it. John saw nothing of his aunt's performance, of course, as he was hidden in the attics, but he picked up awestruck comments from the servants. The soldiers left later the same day, well-fed and unsuspecting.

John hid in the house for two more weeks while he caught up with himself. He curled up in his childhood thinking corners, the roof of the chapel or attics above the Long Gallery, to avoid his aunt and the curious house servants. Alone in the empty, open spaces above the drowsy activity of the house, he pondered what it meant to be an outlaw – outside the law, outside all normal daily structures that kept a man from floating out of the life of his fellow men like a fragment of ash up a chimney. He grasped the fact that he now had no home, no money. He depended for all his shelter, food, clothing, education and amusement on the generosity of his uncle, who had already spent and risked so much for him. He would never go back to Tarleton Court or any of the other three houses. The men and women who had called him 'master' from the time he was seven had another master now, as if he had never lived. He wept for his deerhound, Galen, in whose pen in the dog yard at Tarleton Court he had often slept when the beast grew too vast for the boy's bed.

After two weeks of thinking such thoughts, John decided that he must resolve either to die up there among the skeletons of mice and bats or to go back down into the world that had closed against him like a pair of curtains. He must force the curtains apart, or slice himself a way through. Otherwise, the actual wrenching apart of his body and soul in the act of dying would be a mere afterthought to the real death he had already suffered.

He came down from the attics and, in defiance of his aunt, bolted from his new prison and showed himself on the estate, to the relief and great satisfaction of all the workers and cottagers, who had talked about nothing but John ever since he had arrived. Some, like Arthur, knew John as one of Sir George's nephews. But if the master and Mistress Margaret wanted to make a mystery about the boy's arrival, they were delighted to conspire and speculate.

Breathing in the grassy air with an intense pleasure that brought him close to tears, fourteen-year-old John paced the overgrown fields with the long legs of a half-grown colt. He studied crumbling walls and fences, slipping roof tiles, sagging thatch and cracked beams.

Sir George was more merchant than farmer. In any case, he preferred his wool-producing Somerset estate and his London house to this tiny, isolated, unproductive puddle in Hampshire into which the news of Queen Elizabeth's death had taken three weeks to drip, and where many thought England was still at war with Spain.

John noted the missing roof on the octagonal dovecote, and the missing central wooden potence on which the ladder should be leaned when collecting eggs or birds for the pot. The power and prerogative to act had always been his, until very recently. Within the week, he had begun to put things right. If, while in hiding, he could not use his energies as a gentleman should, in hunting, study, dancing and politics, he would burn them up however he could.

He had the wit to start slowly. He learned that everyone on the estate knew without being told that he was third in line as Sir George's heir, after his cousins James and Harry, and this gave weight to his words. Nevertheless, he started small, mending walls, replacing roof tiles on the big house and having cottages repaired. At first, he consulted his uncle by letter. George Beester was content for his nephew to do as he pleased as long as it improved the estate and didn't cost in excess.

Growing bolder, John prowled over the hillsides, through overgrown assarts, where he designed coppices and cover for game. He judged the lines of overgrown field boundaries and placed new beehives according to the advice of Pliny and Columella. Next he hired a dowser, dug a well and built a pump over it to water the kitchen garden. By the end of his first year on the estate, he had begun to build walls to carve more gardens from the surrounding wilderness of beech and oak.

He was a little surprised by the complaisance of both his uncle and most of the estate residents. He did not begin to understand how grateful most people are to have someone else make decisions for them, especially if made with tact and grace.

His aunt had her hands more than full with feeding the house family of sixteen – servants, sojourners, parson and herself – who sat down at the Great Chamber table every noon and evening. As queen of stillroom and kitchen, she also ruled the gardens that supplied the pots. She happily handed over to her energetic nephew the insoluble problems of slugs, sparrows, worms, hail, too much rain, not enough rain, rust, frost, wilt, rabbits, thieves and selecting the right cabbage seed. John tackled it all. He sketched plans, made long lists, wrote letters in Latin (signing the new false name his uncle had devised) to London, Antwerp and Amsterdam, to ask for advice and saplings. What he didn't know and couldn't ask, he searched out in his growing library of Greek and Roman authorities.

A princeling does not happily decay into a beggar. Whether or not his uncle saw or cared, John repaid him, for the sake of his own self-respect, with immaculate walls, watertight roofs, and healthy livestock. He covered the walls and sweetened the air with fragrant offerings of Great Russetings, *Pommes de Rambure*, smelling costards, Billiborues, Keelings, Scarlet pears, Damasks, Chameleon cherries, Barbary apricots, Lion's peaches, and Nutmeg plums.

Sir George visited only twice. He was delighted with his nephew's unofficial stewardship, carried out for only the cost of the small annuity Beester gave the boy in any case. But half-way through John's third year, his uncle sent him a new parson as an ally and companion.

Dr Bowler had been tutor to the combined Beester and Nightingale families for many years and seen a whole generation from christening via first conjugation to marriage vows. He arrived on a muddy cart, anxious and surrounded by tied bundles of all of Caxton's herbals, Scribonius, Virgil, *Recettaria Fiorentina*, Pliny (complete), Cato, Varro, and Frampton's translation of the Spanish work *Joyful Newes out of the Newe Founded Worlde*. On his lap he held the cassowary's egg that was to become the first curiosity in John's collection.

Sir George's gesture was not pure generosity. Dr Bowler was a dreadful cleric. He lacked all sense of the moral absolute. The Lord's voice did not reach him clearly. When he did have strong feelings that inclined more one way than another, he doubted his right to insist on his own views more than another man's. Parishioners who wanted to be punished were as disappointed in him as the ones who craved absolution. Sir George felt that the Hawkridge parish would not only be kind to the old man but also permit his removal from a more demanding parish of wealthy wool merchants, near Exeter.

Bowler also questioned his own efficacy as a teacher. 'I fear that I will lead you astray,' he said to John more than once. 'Education is a most dangerous spur to the human soul. It leads to understanding, and understanding leads to sympathy. I am alarmed to find how persuasive and understandable I can sometimes find the words of proven heretics and even infidels. How do I know that one day, I might not go so far as to agree?'

But he suited John, and John suited him. John himself still suspected, as he had in prison, that man's belief might be born out of desperation. That faith in any Paradise, beyond that which he already had here in his little Eden, grew only from the absolute need for a world better than this one. In spite of Bowler's reservations about education, they shared the passion to know.

'Did you see here,' Dr Bowler would say, arriving in the door of John's office or bedchamber with a book, 'that soaking the seed in honey before planting makes melons sweeter? Do you think it likely that the sweet principle can be infused in such small quantity and still diffuse to any effect into half a dozen fruits?'

'Let us try,' said John. 'Half the seeds in honey, half not. Planted in the same bed, with the same aspect.'

'What pleasure it will be to test the results!'

And two labourers would be set to work immediately, preparing the melon bed.

Bowler's uncertainties drove John to prove the existence of inarguable truths – that a cutting from a bush, for example, always grew true and identical to its parent, while a seed quite often did not. John told himself that it was for the old man's sake, as well as for his uncle's, that he wrestled to quell nature's alarming disorder into an understandable complexity. For eleven years he had driven himself to maintain order and to prevent horror from ever again touching himself or those he loved.

While John waited to learn what Malise wanted, he flung himself from task to task with a ferocity that alarmed even his staff, who were used to his implacable enthusiasms. In the kitchen garden he spurred on the weeding women already busy on hands and knees among the fresh pale greens of young vegetables. He thinned and reset a late sowing of infant pot herbs. With the cooper, he checked the cracked wheel on Harry's coach.

As he was crossing the *basse-court* on the way to a storage shed, Lady Beester's small pale face had peeked from her window and vanished like a rabbit back into its hole. John saw no other sign of Harry or his guests.

When the bell in the brewhouse tower rang for dinner soon after midday, John hesitated. Then he decided that he could not sit through another meal with Edward Malise, not now that they knew each other. He excused himself to his aunt, took bread and cold meat from the kitchen and strode the length of the gardens into the fields beyond, above the mill, where his horse was billeted to make room in the stables for the London nags. John leaned briefly on the wall, chewing much too fast. He watched his horse graze and debated how best to arrange saddle, bridle and saddlebags, if need be. Then he climbed Hawk Ridge to study the road for horsemen. It was empty.

After dinner, John allowed himself twenty minutes with his back in the sun, standing with lengths of twine between his teeth, his mind cleared of everything but the struggle between symmetry and the untidy inclinations of nature while he tied the branches of a young peach tree against the warm south-facing brick wall. Blossoms had already opened on the short, grey-barked spurs.

I'm late with this task, he thought, but there was no time before. A flock of birds passed over his head with a rustle like a handful of spilling sand. In the corner of his eye, he saw another of Malise's men.

He set off towards the dovecote, which stood in a hazel copse above the highest pond, to see if there was enough dung for the new roses Sir Richard Balhatchet had promised to bring from London. Doves' dung was the finest, saved for his most precious plants. Poultry and pig served for the beans and cabbages. House soil went to fatten fallow land.

Malise's man followed him.

Oho, thought John. I'm not allowed to slip away, then. Why don't you go tell your master to come and explain himself?

As he crossed the *basse-court*, his aunt leaned from an upper window of the house.

'John! Wait! I must speak with you. I don't know what to do!'

John half-turned his head. Malise's man hovered in the alleyway between kitchen and gardens.

While his aunt came down, John opened the gate into the dog yard and squatted to stroke the heavy, rounded sides of Cassie, the pregnant bitch. Today she stood solidly on all four legs, enduring the weight she carried. She didn't try to lick John's ears as usual, though they were within easy reach, but merely pushed the top of her head against his shoulder and held it there. He found this gesture oddly touching.

'Are you frightened, old thing?' he asked her. 'Or do you imagine that I want comforting?'

'Why do you want comforting? Has Malise recognized you?' His aunt didn't wait for an answer. 'I hope he hasn't. Harry won't be able to do without you – he hasn't learned a thing since he was five.'

John stood up. His aunt always reminded him of certain herbs – tangled and woody with a halo of disorderly fluff. This afternoon she also looked as if she had been stepped on by a careless gardener. Her bearing was askew, fingers tensed, neck stiff. Her face was so flushed that it looked bruised. Her eyes were tightly undecided between rage or tears.

'I don't know what to do!' she said again.

'Come with me to the dovecote.'

Mistress Margaret set off so fast that John stretched his stride to keep up.

'I can't stay here, John!' she said suddenly. 'Not with that snippety little twig as my mistress. I told you she would drive me out! And I don't know where I can go!'

'Lady Beester?' asked John, nonplussed. 'That tongue-tied little girl is driving you out?'

'She's a monster!' cried his Aunt Margaret. 'And I've nowhere to go! Nowhere at all!'

John steered her towards the arch of the main gate out of the *basse-court* and nodded to the four women slapping clothes in the washhouse.

'You should have seen her at dinner! You'd think she'd been a lady all her life instead of for about five seconds.'

They waded through hens and guinea fowl on the narrow lawn between the wall and the middle pond.

'She sounds wondrously transformed from that white-faced, silent ghost of yesterday. What has she done?'

'She demanded the keys!' cried Mistress Margaret. 'And has turned out my chests and cupboards.'

'But surely that is what any new mistress would wish to do.'

'I've ruled this house for nearly thirty years,' said his aunt, her voice suddenly cold at his treachery. 'I am the real mistress of Hawkridge House.'

Cautiously, John said, 'Our lives have changed. Dear aunt, we have to accept . . .'

'She says that we have *moths*!'

John nearly laughed. 'And we don't?'

His aunt was silent while they crossed the bottom of the bowling lawn and passed through the hedge into the shrubby circle of the nuttery where the brick dovecote stood.

A cock fantail waddled on the grass of the clearing, puffed as the foresail of a galleon in a strong wind, cooing intensely after a snowy hen he had fixed on with his hard obsidian eye.

'Of course we have moths,' Mistress Margaret said at last in a voice so small that John could barely hear her. 'Everyone has moths! It's not possible to stop them no matter how much lavender and wormwood you stuff into the folds. And we also have mice, and beetles, and spiders and bats.' She breathed in and out deeply. 'But they're *my* moths and mice and beetles and whatever. I've been battling them for . . . twenty-six years . . . she hasn't!' She burst into tears so loudly that both doves snapped into flight.

John watched them land, improbably white on the roof of the dovecote. He felt as desolate as Noah when he saw the empty beak of his messenger. Beyond where you stand lie only endless wastes. It didn't matter whether Malise let him escape or not. There was nowhere else to go.

This truly was Eden here, John thought. I didn't stop to see it strongly enough. He embraced his aunt. 'I'm so sorry. I am truly so sorry.' Here was another he had failed to protect. 'You belong here. The girl is young and inexperienced. Just have a little patience.'

'I can't,' sobbed Mistress Margaret against her nephew's chest. 'I feel . . . I don't know . . .' She wept a little more. '. . . humiliated.' She pulled away and straightened her back, blotted her eyes with the back of her wrist and sniffed several times.

'We've been too many years without change,' said John. 'We're a little askew . . .'

'. . . I don't want to change!' Her voice was angry, but her eyes were frightened. 'Do something, John! Please!'

John gave a tight dry cough of a laugh. 'You should really speak to Harry.' He walked to the dovecote to test that its low door was securely locked. He must remember to leave Tuddenham the key.

'He'll just take her side, won't he? And say that she's the

mistress now. He won't understand. John, please talk to her, or to him, or something. Please, before you have to go.'

To soothe the fear in his aunt's pouched old eyes, he said, 'I'll try.' If he were given the time.

The girl was within her rights, of course, but might be persuaded to a little more gentleness with her predecessor's *amour propre*. If she were old enough for compassion.

As his aunt disappeared back towards the house, John suddenly could bear the waiting no longer.

He stalked quietly around the circle of the nuttery and slipped into the bowling lawn by the gap nearest the ponds. Malise's man waited just inside the gap to John's right, looking towards the dovecote. John pounced. The man yelped in startled terror.

'Tell your master to seek me himself,' said John to the unhappy groom. 'I'll stake myself out for him in the Knot Garden. Tell him it's time to stoop for the kill!'

Malise made John wait until nearly sunset.

He stepped on John's shadow where it fell across the brick walk of the Knot Garden. 'I almost missed you down there in the dirt,' he said. His falcon nose and steady eye followed John, a rabbit on the ground.

Without looking up, John shifted forward and removed his ghostly self from under Malise's elegant black rosetted shoes. He stretched out a brown forearm and cut off the head of a ragged white tulip. A petal fell and lay on the dirt like the bowl of an old spoon. John tossed the stem onto the pile in the elm-wood trug. Malise watched while he cut two more. The two men were alone in the small walled garden.

'Harry did well by his uncle's death.'

John looked up at that. 'No one does well by another's death. But some deaths are kinder than others – both to the dying and to the heirs.'

Malise's eyelids flickered. Then he raised his brows and

nodded as though ceding a point of debate. He watched John cut four more tulips.

'Do you enjoy the masquerade?' Malise finally asked. 'The former master of Tarleton Court, among others, and a courtier-to-be. Do you really like playing at being a rough labourer with no more ambition than a full stomach and a hot-lapped wife?'

John's hands hesitated a moment. Then he sliced and threw another stem onto the trug. His eyes watched his knife.

'I admire you,' said Malise. 'I wouldn't have the humility to tolerate it.'

John bent more fiercely to his work. Another cut, and another green, weeping ellipse of a stub left standing. Another ageing beauty tossed aside to make way for next year's flowering. The muscles under his brown skin bunched and relaxed with each stroke.

'How would you ever take orders from that ass Sir Harry?' Malise's tone was politely incredulous.

In the eye or throat, thought John. Messy, but so easy. His blood began to thump in his temples. 'You're in his house,' he said, 'accepting his hospitality.'

Malise shrugged away this trivial point of etiquette. 'Harry's made to be used. He's a social whore.'

He is deliberately provoking me, John thought. That's why he came here. He wants a new crime to hang me with!

Then reason told him that there was more to it than that.

With his head down, he looked around for Malise's men. He saw a flicker of serving blue just outside the gate, within quick calling distance. Well, he would not oblige!

'You may fool your cousin with your bows and scrapes and humble-servant manner,' said Malise. 'But to me you're as transparent as rain. No honest yeoman ever had your rage and hunger in his eyes. Even Hazelton, who is not the most subtle of men, feels something adrift in you.'

John moved to another pot. He felt curiously light. Anger had become a bubble under his breastbone.

Malise followed. His easy, conversational voice assumed shared knowledge. 'You no doubt saw that I didn't know you when I first arrived yesterday. You were still beardless and singing treble when you murdered my brother.'

'Harry didn't tell you?'

'Does he even know?' Malise sounded amused. 'Though we must agree that he hasn't got the sharpest of wits, I never dreamed he would drag *that* cousin centre stage with such a flourish of trumpets.'

John sat back on his boot heels and sighed, unreasonably happy to hear Harry's innocence confirmed.

'The scars on your jaw niggled at me. You had them . . . that day. The beard doesn't hide them. And then, after dinner last night, while you were annoying Hazelton.' Malise paused as if he expected John to speak, then continued, 'I suppose I must be grateful to Sir Harry. Until yesterday, I didn't know whether you were still in England, or even alive. I'd almost given up looking for you.'

'And now that you've found and know me, what do you want?'

Malise smiled pleasantly. 'The only thing I have ever wanted that you can give me – your life in exchange for my brother's.'

John held the golden-brown hawk eyes, then looked down at his hands. He turned the knife in his palm, almost absently, trying to steady his breathing. Then he looked up again. 'How alike we are then. That's all I want from you.'

'Your life?' Malise began to curl one end of his mouth.

'Yours.'

They were united in the intimate silence of perfect under-standing. At times in the last eleven years, John had questioned his seven-year-old memory of that falcon face beside the coach; now he was absolutely sure.

Malise knows more about my life than anyone on this estate. John felt dangerously off-centre, disturbed by their dark bond of understanding. 'Surely, we're squared. I've tried to let it go.'

'Of course you have. The wrong began and ended on your side. I'm still owed.'

Kill him now, John told himself. No matter what you thought you had decided. Before matters complicate themselves. He's daring you to take this moment. Go on, do it now! You could do it before his men could reach him.

He stood up, saw Malise tense. Then he bent and picked up the trug. 'I had already decided not to kill you here on my cousin's estate. I rather thought it might abuse the hospitality which you treat with such contempt.'

Malise manufactured a laugh. 'Your common sense has rusted away down here. You can't decide anything. I control your life now. I could call those two men you have spotted outside the gate and have them kill you, but I prefer the joy of watching the hangman go to work. Unfortunately, even that pleasure has to wait. I came here to recruit you before I knew who you were. You must, alas, do something for me first.'

'The same something that was choking Hazelton last night?'

'Necessity makes strange bedfellows, they do say.'

'Are you bargaining with me for my life?'

'Who knows if gratitude might soften me?'

'You want me to work for you,' asked John incredulously, 'while you twitch the rope around my neck tighter or looser, according to your whim?' Derision rang in his voice. 'Go back to Hell where you were born and bred.'

He turned away with the full trug, through the archway into the fruit garden and out through the side gate into the stable yard. It was empty of both horses and grooms.

John heard Malise's footsteps behind him. His hands slipped damply on the wooden handle of the trug. The day had become as intensely fascinating as he had expected it would.

He threw the tulip stems on the dungheap. Then he took a hayfork from against the wall. He threw a fork of fresh dung from a wooden cart onto the heap.

'I advise you to listen to me!' Malise's control was beginning to crack.

'You advise *me*?'

'Who else understands your dilemma better?'

Silently, John threw another forkful of dung onto the heap. He stopped work and leaned on the handle of the fork. 'But as you need me for some reason, it seems to me that the dilemma is yours, not mine.'

'My dilemma is merely distasteful,' said Malise. 'Yours is dangerous.'

John shook his head. 'Only if you imagine that I care any more.'

'You care, Mister Nightingale! You care.' Malise's voice was suddenly thick with unleashed fury. 'And if you think that you don't care now, you will come to care during the long cold hours in your prison cell. You will care when they cut your hair and loosen your collar to bare your neck. You will care when your eyes are popping out on their stalks and your friends hang weeping on your legs under the gallows to speed the awful slowness of the rope.'

John was seven years old again and looking into the Devil's eyes. A crumbling snakeskin under the branches of the Lady Tree. 'I'd like to finish my work.'

'*I* decide what you do,' said Malise. 'Not you! You scavengers' spawn . . . you . . .' He trembled; his fury pushed him close to tears. 'You insignificant *have-nothing*!'

John straightened and lifted the fork in both hands. Malise stepped back. Through thundering blood and blurred eyes, John measured the distance. He saw in Malise's eyes the thought that he was going to die.

'Help me!' shouted Malise.

Feet ran on the brick paths.

John's muscles tightened. His knuckles went white around the fork handle. He could not stop himself. Decisions or not. His arms began to move. The tines of the fork arched through the air. At the last second, he hauled the fork down, away from Malise's chest, into the dungheap. As Malise's two grooms erupted through the stable-yard gate with their swords drawn, John lifted the fork and flung a tangle of muck and straw into Malise's face. Then he stepped back and rested the tines of the fork on the ground.

The two grooms froze in confusion. With drawn swords and open mouths, they stared at their master. For several seconds, nothing moved in the yard except a gentle pattering of straws and clods from Malise's head and shoulders.

The grooms looked at John, who had welcomed them in silks as if he were the master, or at least chief steward, and now stood in wool breeches and leather jerkin like a field worker. 'Sir?' one of them asked Malise tentatively.

Malise ignored the groom. He brushed lumps of dung from the folds of his coat, his belt, the rosettes of his heeled shoes. He picked straws from the pleats of his lace collar and cuffs. His hand hesitated, shook a clot from behind his knife and let the sheath fall back against the top of his thigh. His skin had shrunk against his skull. The bony bridge of the falcon nose showed white. His eyes half-closed as if he were in pain.

'Sir?' repeated the groom.

Malise waved him to silence. He turned away, moving tightly, as if he were ill.

John recognized the agony of self-control. After the two grooms had followed their master out of the stable yard, he leaned the fork against the nearest wall. Then he leaned against the wall himself.

Oh Harry, he thought. What I have just done for your

sake! I should have done it. With his own men as witnesses, Malise will not forgive, no matter what favour I might do him.

A moment later he thought with triumph, I didn't let him push me off the path of my own will. It would seem that, for the moment at least, he had unimagined power over Malise.

I still must learn why.

The bubble of lightness expanded in his chest.

And Cousin Harry didn't betray me.

Malise ate supper in his room.

'Well?' Hazelton asked John as the rest of them took their seats around the long oak table.

'I'm sorry.'

Hazelton pinched his lips and looked away. His silent fury infected the others. Harry, John, Mistress and Master Hazelton, Mistress Margaret, Lady Beester and Dr Bowler sat in uneasy silence while their ale was poured. Rachel, Arthur and the other personal servants exchanged glances and kept their heads down. The evening sun gave a deceptive warmth to the dining chamber.

'Didn't Malise speak to you?' Harry asked John.

Aunt Margaret's eyes widened. She gave John a desperate questioning look.

'Didn't he report back?'

'I haven't seen him since . . .' Harry stopped.

'. . . Since you and Master Hazelton set him on me,' said John.

Hazelton banged his tankard down. He stood up. 'I have wasted a second precious day. Please excuse me if I go prepare to leave for London first thing tomorrow morning.' He stalked out of the dining chamber.

'Well, I will not make that dreadful journey again so soon,' declared his wife with finality.

'Of course not,' said Harry desperately. 'You must stay here as long as you like. We shall persuade him . . .' He looked after Hazelton. The Puritan merchant's bearing as he left had not suggested that he could be persuaded of anything. 'Should we have some food sent to his chamber? Aunt Margaret . . . ?'

Harry looked at the company around his table. The agents of his doom. Every one of them a hindrance to his hopes. And this wretched house! Every dream was now as good as dead. How unfair that such a wondrous prospect of the future should have turned so mouldy! He wanted to put his face in his hands and cry.

Mistress Margaret left the table to order food for Hazelton. Mistress Hazelton chewed with determination on a rabbit's thigh. Dr Bowler watched John with anxious eyes. Zeal observed everyone from under her eyelids. No one spoke for several minutes.

Harry stood up as abruptly as Hazelton. 'Will you all be kind enough to excuse my cousin and myself. We have urgent business in private.'

He dragged John up the main staircase, towards the privacy of his rooms. 'What the devil did you say to drive Edward from my table?'

John turned to close the carved wooden lacework of the dog gates across the stairs.

'He did speak with you?' demanded Harry.

'You already seem to know that he did. Why do you think he could sway me better than Hazelton?' John looked at his cousin with a vicious spasm of renewed distrust.

In the dusk of the stairwell, Harry suddenly looked as shifty as a poacher. He cleared his throat. 'I don't know . . . he seemed to feel . . .' He cleared his throat again. 'Anyway, he's a Chancery Warden. I thought maybe he understood the whole mess better than I do and could explain to you properly.'

'What mess?'

'Master Hazelton tried to tell you last night, but you wouldn't listen.'

'I'm listening now.'

'Not here.'

They mounted four steps in silence except for the creaking of oak timbers.

'If you're listening, does it mean that you might agree?' asked Harry finally.

'Probably not. But I've decided that I need to know what you want.'

'I don't understand you!' cried Harry in despair. 'I truly don't! It would be in your own interests as well as mine . . . !'

'Malise's interests will never be mine.'

'Why not?'

On the galleried landing a chamber groom was placing torches in the iron holders on the walls. Two other grooms hauled sleeping pallets out of a cupboard in the antechamber to the right. Harry's chambers beyond the landing were busy with grooms preparing for the night.

'Come to my room,' said John. At this point, Harry informed might be a little less dangerous than Harry ignorant.

'I know he's a Catholic,' protested Harry as he followed John into a short passage that led behind the Tower Chamber. They crossed a bedroom for male house staff and turned right into the suite of rooms in the east wing which were used by John.

'But his family are regaining influence,' he continued. 'Our little French queen is said to enjoy his company. You have no idea how hard I have wooed him . . . he can help me, coz . . . help all of us.'

'To become visible?'

'Exactly,' said Harry.

John's man Arthur was shaking out the daytime coverlet of the bed. John dismissed him.

When the door had closed, he asked Harry, 'Do you truly

not know that I must stay invisible? I have spent the last eleven years here in hiding, to avoid being seen.'

Harry looked uncertain, at a loss again for a slippery Latin verb. Then he frowned, as if he suspected he was being teased.

'I don't understand.'

'When I was fourteen, I killed Edward Malise's brother,' said John.

'Oh!' Harry croaked as if he had been winded. His blue eyes opened like oysters. 'No!' He opened and closed his mouth three times. 'It's not possible! It can't be!'

'I'm sorry to stand between you and glory, but I'm afraid it's true.'

'And he knows you?'

'Yes. Not when he first arrived, but he recognized me later last night, in the gardens.'

Harry's broad shoulders drooped. He gazed blindly at his ruined life. He shook his head minutely for several seconds. Then, to his credit, he thought of John.

'Oh, coz! Lord forgive me! I brought him here. Oh, cousin, I am an ass!' The wide blue eyes stared at John. 'No ... an Iscariot. I have sold my cousin ... my own kin ... for thirty pieces of silver. But I swear to you that I did not know ...' The noble pink forehead puckered as he searched his memory for traces of the thing he should have remembered. 'I don't *think* I knew.' His eyes closed as if the lids had grown too heavy to support. He swallowed. 'Forgive me. I swear, I didn't know.'

At the age Harry had been, John would have sniffed out such family dramas with the keen nose of a fox. But Harry was a different creature.

Harry circled away in confusion and guilt. Then he set like a hound on a new idea. 'So that's why he said last night that he might persuade ... !'

Light dawns at last, thought John.

'His brother?' repeated Harry. He seemed to be offering

John the chance to admit that he had got it wrong or was only joking.

'I was to be tried, but Uncle George spirited me out of prison. Opinions on the right and wrong of my case were divided. The pursuit was not over-keen.'

A ground mist of memory crept up on Harry. 'And Uncle George hid you away down here . . . ? I do remember now that you suddenly stopped coming with us to London . . . Mother said . . . Will Malise betray you?' Harry's eyes opened another notch wider. 'Will you . . . hang?'

'Malise lusts to kick the bench from under my feet.' John walked to the window and pushed it open to look down into the Knot Garden. The sharp, sweet smell of the freshly sheared lavender swept in. 'But he needs something from me first, and, dearest cousin, you must tell me what.'

Harry sat himself in the heavy oak chair-of-grace and began to reassemble his dignity. 'You make me nervous prowling about, sniffing the air like some animal.'

John leaned his hips against the edge of the high bed. 'Speak!'

Harry ran his fingers among the pleats of his lace cuff. 'You must swear to say nothing.'

John raised a laconic hand.

'A rumour could kill us. The Company is in terrible trouble . . .'

'The Company?'

'The South Java Company,' said Harry. 'The one Hazelton mentioned last night. I inherited Uncle George's interest in it . . . We have a Royal Charter. For the moment.'

When John did not respond, Harry continued. 'A Charter to trade between London and several East Indian islands . . . not the Moluccans, of course. The British East Indies Company is fighting it out with the Dutch for the main Spice Islands. But it's a rich world out there, John, and there are other islands for men adventurous enough to find them. You should smell our ships when they come back! I was once taken on board the *Boston Maid* – that's one of our three ships. She smelled of cinnamon and cloves!' For a moment, his face gleamed with visionary fervour.

'And the trouble you need to hide?'

Harry darkened again. 'We're going to lose our Charter, and without it we're all dead. The bloody Dutch sank two of our three ships this past year, and we need to lay hands on money before our last one – the same *Boston Maid* – returns to London. She's not due back for three or four months, and who knows whether *she'll* get back safely?'

'Can't your fellow shareholders among them scrape together whatever you need?'

'We don't have joint shares,' explained Harry. 'It's a regulated company. Members invest venture by venture, as they please. And we're small, not like the East India Company. And we don't have members from the Court. That's why Edward is so important . . . he would bring more in.' Harry abandoned his cuff and stared gloomily at his shoe tips. 'We must invest the little money we can raise in something that will bring a fast and safe return . . . I do wish you would let Samuel Hazelton explain.'

'Why do you need money so urgently?'

'To renew the Charter!' said Harry as if it were self-evident. 'And it's all the fault of the wretched, stiff-necked Scots!'

John laughed.

'It's not funny!' cried Harry. 'The King can't afford to feed his army on the Scottish border and, without a Parliament to help him, he's raising money any way he can. Direct pleas, threats, selling titles and charters. He insists that the South Java Company reconfirm its Charter with a large token of our gratitude and loyalty. And he has given us just five weeks to pay, or he'll revoke our Charter to sell to someone else. Then, even when we do have profits from the voyage of the *Boston Maid*, we won't be able to do anything with them.'

'You really need this Charter so badly?'

'Without it, our money will be frozen in our pockets. In London you can't trade in anything without a bloody charter or licence, not even mousetraps! Just as I'm learning how to make money grow! It's really not fair!' Harry glared at his feet. 'I won't sink back, John! I will not! I know now what my life could be! I need you to help!'

John studied his cousin. 'It's a sad tale,' he said, 'of a world as foreign to me as the East Indies.'

'But that's what is so perfect,' said Harry. 'We want you to go to Amsterdam to buy flowers. You know more about flowers than any one I know.'

'Flowers?' said John incredulously. Malise had suffered a face full of dung in order to buy flowers?

'Tulips. You may not know – there is an amazing market in tulip bulbs in the Low Countries just now. We sent an agent to see, and he tells us . . .'

'You want me to make the South Java Company an urgent fortune by buying tulip bulbs?'

'I do wish you would let Hazelton explain. I understand perfectly well, but somehow you make me confused.'

'I admit,' said John, 'that you've startled my interest awake. But much as I would like to satisfy my curiosity, there is no point in talking to Hazelton. I cannot work for Edward Malise.'

'Please, coz,' begged Harry. 'I understand your repugnance now, really I do! But you wouldn't be acting for Malise so much as for me . . . and Lady Beester. And yourself. To say nothing of our aunt and all the other piglings hanging onto the dugs of this estate!'

'How so?' asked John, his voice suddenly dangerous. 'Why is it now not for Malise or the Company but for myself and Aunt Margaret and all those other piglings?'

'If you won't be our agent to Amsterdam, I shall have to sell this estate.'

'*No!*'

'I don't want to,' said Harry weakly. 'But it's the only sensible thing to do. Our uncle left almost no cash. I have to keep the London house. The Somerset estate at least produces wool to sell and brings a little income. This place just sits here and moulders.'

'It costs little to live here,' said John. 'We produce enough to buy what few extras we need, like sugar and tobacco. Trim your ambition a little. Be a country gentleman – Sir Harry Beester of Hawkridge – there's no shame in that. I'm sure you could find ways to remain visible enough!'

'You still don't understand,' said Harry miserably. 'And anyway, I have debts.' He stood up and kicked a log back into the fire. 'Quite large ones, I'm afraid.'

'How large?'

'Well, there was the town-house to do up,' Harry mumbled. 'I must keep a London presence ... the new coach. Upholstery. Livery. Harness. Fringes for the harness, and a hammercloth for the coachman's seat. Two horses ... already had one pair. The shirts for the estate, and your own suit. A new bed for the town-house. And hangings, and plates, and all the other trappings.' He drew a deep breath and plunged on. 'Clothing for me, of course, and for my wife. Our wedding suits ... and diamond earrings for her on our betrothal. And a few other trinkets. And wooing gifts, and gifts to Master and Mistress Hazelton.'

John kept a rough tally in his head. 'Anything more?'

'I had to reconfirm Uncle George's title, and that wasn't free!' said Harry defensively. 'And there are annual dues. And of course, I had to give a banquet for my fellow Company members to celebrate my institution among them. And then there was the woman to hire for my wife, and all *her* wardrobe ... and two travelling chests. And I need attendants now I did not need before. And a new dresser for our London house ... And ...' He stopped in despair. 'I can't remember it all. I'm sure I have it written down somewhere. I'm not good at these things as you are.'

He sank his face into his hands. 'That's why I need you to help me,' he mumbled between his fingers. 'I need enough cash to help us keep our licence to trade, so I can hope to build my fortune back. And anyway, I've already borrowed against the estate.'

John felt physically ill. 'What about your wife's money?'

Harry raised his face indignantly. 'I paid for some of what I bought!'

'You owe a fortune,' said John. 'I cannot believe you spent another fortune as well.'

'Invested,' said Harry.

'In the two sunk ships?'

Harry nodded. 'And in the *Boston Maid*. I'm sure of good returns, once she arrives back in England ... if she returns. But by that time, it will be too late to satisfy the King.'

'How can you afford to invest in tulips?'

'I borrowed privately against the cargo of the *Boston Maid*,' said Harry. 'I can't pay the King with that money, because then I'd have nothing to invest to make more money to repay the loan. It's just too, too bad that the King won't wait until the ship returns!'

'Does Lady Beester keep control of any part of her portion?' John watched his cousin's eyes slide away evasively.

'She gave her permission for me ... for Hazelton ... to, er, invest.'

A mere formality, thought John. How could that child hold out against both uncle and husband? 'Does she know how things stand?'

'It's not her business to know!'

'She could be ruined. She might feel it was her business.'

'She'd manage,' said Harry sulkily. 'She's not used to luxury – first a court ward and then dependent on Mistress Hazelton and that boarding school. A cold, pinched life. She's already had more pleasure of her money with me than Hazelton ever let her sniff at . . .' He broke off. 'All that's beside the point, coz. The situation must be saved. Will you help?'

John went to his door and called Arthur to come light the torches. 'Go away, Harry. I have to think.'

'What can I tell Hazelton?'

'I don't know.' John crossed back to the window. 'No, tell him that I will at least hear him out.'

'Say you'll do it!'

'Harry, Harry, Harry. What makes you think I could even if I would? I'm a country yeoman, not a merchant. I don't want to be the instrument of your final ruin.'

'I'm sure Hazelton will satisfy you. You'll succeed. You always have . . .' Harry stopped dead on a new thought. 'Did you *mean* to kill Malise's brother?'

'Oh, yes,' said John. 'I meant to.' He followed Harry perfectly. 'I succeeded in that.'

Harry nodded as if reassured. 'I'll tell Hazelton now.' They both knew what he meant.

'There you are!' Harry said with relief. He stood beside his bed, arms spread above his servant's head while the man unhooked his breeches from the waistband of his doublet. Hazelton waited in the heavy oak chair-of-grace beside the fireplace. Malise sat with calculated, but not entirely convincing, ease in a smaller, leather-upholstered armchair. He looked away when John came into the room. Four pipes and a pot of Harry's Virginia tobacco lay untouched on a chest top.

'You decided to honour us, after all,' said Hazelton.

'It's no honour,' said John tersely. 'My cousin insisted.' He took the four-legged stool left for him. He wiped his hands on the thighs of his breeches. He had just finished his evening round with Tuddenham of stables, cow barn and sheep shed.

'Is there any point in this conversation?' asked Hazelton.

'I'm sorry again if I offended you last night,' said John. 'I took you at your word for a man who dislikes wasting time. I'm afraid I may have been overly direct in honouring your sense of economy.'

Hazelton nodded, half-mollified. 'Only one night lost if we come to an agreement now.' He glanced from John to Malise and back again.

'By all means, speak for us all, Samuel,' said Malise. 'The size of your investment merits it.' He leaned his head against the high chairback and began to study John with the fixed but distant eye of an anatomist approaching a dissection.

Hazelton flushed. He straightened a black silk fold along the top of his thigh and smoothed one side of his white linen collar. He stayed silent just long enough not to seem to obey the order given by Malise with such gracious arrogance.

'Mr Graffham, to match your own terseness, Master Malise and I are here, somewhat urgently, on behalf of the Court of Committees of the royally chartered South Java Company, of which your cousin is also a member. I am the Treasurer of the Company. Briefly, we ship woollen cloth, soap, and pins to those East Indian islands which are not in thrall to the British East Indies Company. Our ships return with nutmegs, cloves, copra and cinnamon which we then sell on through the properly licensed dealers.'

His raised brows queried John's understanding so far.

John nodded.

'Just now, the Company needs an agent to act for us in Amsterdam, at once. As I tried to explain last night, you would seem to be our man.'

'I have no business experience beyond the small affairs of this estate,' said John. 'I don't speak Dutch and I doubt that Latin and Greek are much spoken in the market place. From what my cousin told me earlier, you need a commercial man.'

'Did he explain exactly what we want you to do?'

'Yes,' said Harry eagerly. His man had helped him into a long, loose house coat. Now he sat on the edge of his bed and held out his left foot for its knitted silk stocking to be removed. 'Invest in tulips.'

'London commercial agents understand only money and markets,' said Hazelton. 'For this venture, we need botanical learning. Like yours.' Though he had accepted John's apology, his lips and tongue still twisted uncomfortably around this modest flattery.

'You don't need learning,' said John. 'Just write to dealers in Leiden or Amsterdam and say what you want. Any head gardener can tell you what to order. Your bulbs will arrive on the next ship.'

'Haven't all your Greek- and Latin-speaking correspondents told you that buying tulips in the Low Countries is no longer a simple matter for servants to arrange?'

'The Dutch have gone quite mad for tulips,' explained Harry. 'They're giving houses, coaches, the entire cargo of a merchantman for just one bulb!'

In silence and with raised brows, Hazelton watched the manservant untie Harry's second garter. Then he turned back to John.

'These are not normal times in Holland – we sent an agent to see for himself. Your head gardener would suffice if what we hoped to buy were only flowers like those I saw in your garden last night. But you must understand that the Dutch are no longer trading in mere flowers. Tulips have become a commodity, like saltpetre, or wood, or coal. Less useful, of course, but at the moment and in the right hands potentially more valuable.'

'The "right hands" still don't seem to be mine,' said John.

'Can you tell a tulip from an onion?' asked Malise abruptly.

John permitted himself a countryman's polite incredulity at city ignorance. 'Most likely, if neither tulip nor onion is a rare and unfamiliar sort.'

'Our agent who went to Amsterdam found the distinction more difficult,' said Hazelton. 'He said he could have eaten a fortune on a slice of bread and been none the wiser.'

'Tulip and onion are distinct enough,' said John firmly. 'I would be happy to inspect his bread. However, I would never swear to tell one tulip from another in the dry, any more than any other man.'

'In the dry?' asked Hazelton. 'What does that mean?'

'Without leaves or bloom, after lifting.'

'Then how can you tell the things one from another?'

'In the dry, as I said, you can't. When fresh, the leaves give clues, in their hue and texture,' said John. 'Some are pale green and lax, for example, others bluish and crisp. But for sure naming, you must see the flower itself.'

'Do you mean,' asked Hazelton, startled by this new thought, 'that you can only buy when the things are in flower?'

'If you want to be sure of what you buy.'

'Let me be clear,' said Hazelton unhappily. 'If it's not in bloom, you can't tell a bulb worth a thousand pounds from one worth a groat?'

'Not with certainty,' said John.

'There!' croaked Harry, chin pointed at the ceiling while the ribbons of his collar were untied. 'That's exactly why we need you, coz. To tell us things like that!'

Hazelton turned to Malise. 'That point seems to have escaped Timmons in his lather over onions.'

'Most tulips are finishing now,' said John. 'Or soon will. Bulbs are lifted in June. You're already late this year if you need to see them in bloom.'

Hazelton, Malise and Sir Harry exchanged looks of dismay.

'Are you sure you can't tell the difference between dry bulbs?' begged Harry.

'A more expert botanist might,' said John. 'Like Master Parkes who was apprenticed to the senior Tradescant, or

Doctor Hutchins, who has made such a noted bulb garden in Southwark.'

Hazelton stared down at his black lap. 'It must all be done within the next five weeks. Buying *and* selling.' He thought a little longer. 'Timmons did say that the Dutchmen seem to buy and sell all year round. We must assume that we can too.' He stopped studying his lap and turned assessing eyes on John. 'Do you begin to understand how you can help?'

'I understand your degree of risk, which strikes me as extremely high. I don't fully grasp your urgency.'

'I tried to explain earlier.' Harry fussed with his layers of linen shirt and coat. 'That we must pay to renew our Charter within five weeks.'

'The English Treasury is on its knees,' said Hazelton. 'Has been ever since the Glorious Bess emptied it to pay for the Irish Rebellion and war with Spain. Her short-lived predecessors had already traded Crown estates and sources of income for vows of loyalty. And then, the late King James. Joining the crowns of Scotland and England. Loyal English subjects didn't come cheap to a Scotsman with a royal trollop of a Catholic, French-speaking mother who thought he could rule England . . .'

'I protest!' said Malise. 'I won't allow treason . . .'

'Not treason!' snapped Hazelton. 'Just financial fact. As you very well know. I have no quarrel with His Majesty King Charles for screwing out every penny he can to help make up for his father's extravagance, and the expensive follies of his father's pet courtiers. That you and I are being screwed is merely our bad luck.'

Malise closed his mouth and leaned back again.

'In fact,' continued Hazelton with only the faintest glimmer of triumph, 'as a man of commerce, I have to commend His Majesty's ingenuity in devising more novel taxes and still more original schemes for wringing yet more money from his subjects' pockets. Need is his teacher, no doubt. Rumour says that his soldiers sent north to the Scottish border to hold back the rebellious hordes are now deserting for lack of food and wages. Our urgency merely reflects our King's. You're right, Mr Graffham. Our risk in not meeting His Majesty's needs, and in time, is extremely high.'

'My own ignorance will raise that risk,' said John. 'My cousin, at least, seems to have staked more than I would like to answer for.'

Malise made an impatient noise. 'Let me explain your suitability more clearly. We could never insult a Master Parkes or Doctor Hutchins with our commission.' He smiled pleasantly.

Harry gasped. But John merely inclined his head, like Cassie the staghound waiting for a command.

'The coupling of horticulture with speculation breeds a strange beast which needs a strange keeper,' continued Malise. 'We wish, for our sins, to deal with a rare madness in the commercial market of a foreign state which is our diplomatic ally but nevertheless takes every chance to blow our ships out of the sea.'

Hazelton tried to cut in. Harry stuttered in protest.

'In Holland,' said Malise, 'chimney sweeps and washerwomen rival merchants and landowners in the rush to gamble everything they have on the latest form of tulip. The Stadholder of Amsterdam and the heads of other provinces are trying, so far without success, to insert laws between men and their own insanity.'

Malise cut across both Harry and the authority of Hazelton's upraised hand. 'In short, no reputable agent knows the commodity. But no reputable scholar would risk making a fool of himself in such a questionable market. You serve us perfectly because you are neither reputable agent nor reputable scholar.'

A void of silence opened like the Red Sea. Harry's lashes beat against the top of his cheeks. Hazelton looked at the two pairs of eyes locked across the Turkey carpet and tried not to despair. He had seen hate before, but never so open.

Malise has scuppered us, he thought. Unless I can undo the damage. And he's a liar. I've never trusted the man, and I was right.

Stung on behalf of his recruit, Harry flung himself into the chasm. 'There's nothing disreputable . . .' he began.

'It's all right, Harry,' said John.

'You have a sweet line of persuasion, Edward,' said Hazelton acidly, at last. 'You'll turn the man's head before I can seduce him.'

'But it's not . . . !' said Harry.

John cut across both of them. 'Master Malise is merely being frank, like you and me, Master Hazelton. I can't take offence at honesty. On the contrary, he has finally made me understand my assets.' He straightened on his stool.

Quickly as a swift snatches a gnat from the air, he was touched by a flash of memory, of forgotten possibilities. A small boy, long gone, high on a horse's back, in the sunlight in the stable yard of Tarleton Court, a young Apollo curving through the heavens. Then it was gone. He let out a long slow breath. Why had that come to him now?

Harry plunged on doggedly. 'Edward, I must protest . . . ! There's nothing disreputable in trading with the Dutch. A Dutchman is court painter in Whitehall. I myself have seen his magnificent equestrian portrait of His Majesty.'

'Is the South Java Company licensed to trade in tulips?' John asked Hazelton.

'And as for architecture,' insisted Harry, 'Lord Hughes, with whom I had dinner only the day before we came down here, has a Dutch architect building a new house at this minute on his Suffolk estate.'

'Harry . . .' said John.

'And look at your own collar, Edward – is that English or Dutch lace?'

Malise glanced at Hazelton. You let your niece marry him. You allowed her money to fall into his hands. *You* deal with him!

Hazelton ignored both Harry and Malise. An ass and a liar. His colleagues had become more hobble than spur. 'A fair point, Mr Graffham. We do not have a charter to trade in tulips in Holland.'

'Would I be working outside the law?' The question seemed to amuse John.

Hazelton watched thoughts flicker in the grey eyes in the brown face, with its oddly feminine brows. I was right about him at our first meeting. There is more to this cousin's story than Harry knows or tells. I wish I knew more. Ignorance is always dangerous.

'Outside English law,' he said. 'But not against it. This present madness, as so often happens, grows from unbridled freedom – the tulip trade is not controlled by their guilds. Anyone it seems – even the most ignorant, the most debased – can speculate if he has the money. You will both buy and sell abroad. The Dutch will take our money happily enough. Do the job right and no one in England will ever even know.' Hazelton lobbed this final challenge with casual delicacy and leaned back against the carved oak of his chair.

Sharp. Sharp, that man, thought John. No wonder he's rich. He half-smiled. 'Do you trust me or are you merely desperate?'

Hazelton smiled back, although a frightening thought had just come to him. 'I was desperate when I arrived yesterday. Now that we have met and talked . . .' He smoothed the black silk over his knee once more. '. . . I accept the odds.'

'Then,' said John, 'I have run out of excuses to refuse.'

Harry let out a whoop. 'There!' he cried. 'I said he would do it!'

Malise looked at his hands.

I have escaped him again, thought John. From the coach,

from prison, and now, for the moment. How much longer can he bear it? He could almost pity Malise.

Hazelton merely nodded. 'You'll leave for London in the morning.'

'No,' said John. He had escaped Malise for the moment, but the man would never let him come back here. This life was over. No matter whether Harry had to sell the estate or not.

'But we must instruct you,' protested Hazelton. 'Make arrangements for your voyage, and for the money.'

'I need two more days here,' said John. His hand had shaped this estate for the last eleven years. His final footprints would not leave the helter-skelter scribble of a hasty run. He had to make everything safe for those piglings. 'Instruct me here.'

'I'll go to London,' said Malise suddenly. He sprang up as if ready on the spot to leap onto his horse.

'But . . . !' cried Harry. 'What about . . . ?' His spirits dived again. He had expected to lose his cousin and keep Malise, not the other way round.

Malise was already at the door, unable to stay in the room. 'We may be asking your cousin to perform the miracle of the loaves and fishes for us,' he said with his hand on the doorhandle. 'But even your precious cousin, Sir Harry, can't walk on water. He needs a boat. And the money, *bien entendu*, and a guard to watch the money. Someone has to arrange them. Please send my coach as soon as possible.'

'Wait!' Hazelton had suddenly lost control of this meeting, for reasons he did not understand. They seemed to have granted a delay which they could not afford. 'I must ask one question.' He turned to John.

'Please.'

'Do you swear as a God-fearing Christian soul that you have no reason whatsoever to wish our venture to fail?'

Malise paused, half-way out of the door.

'Oh,' said Harry in a very small voice.

'I swear,' said John without looking at Malise, 'that I will work only for your success.'

Hazelton, Harry and John listened in silence while Malise carefully closed the door.

'Then I suppose I must be content,' said Hazelton.

Five

May 26, 1636. No rain for five days. Mole cricket churred. Remind Tuddenham to stand in for me at Basingstoke market. I would like to see Cassie's pups before I go.

Journal of John Nightingale, known as John Graffham.

Malise set off for London on horseback with only one groom, first thing next morning.

Harry understood, of course. His future was as much in balance as everyone else's. But it still was not fair that Malise should be going instead of John. If only John had not been so stubborn about wanting to leave everything perfect on the estate, as if no one could manage without him. Harry tried to take comfort in having provided the agent so urgently needed by the South Java Company. But in truth, his cousin's new prominence made Harry want to cry like a left-out and disappointed child.

'You must come back immediately you've finished this business of ours,' he said, craning his head up at Malise in his saddle. 'I have such treats planned to amuse you, Edward! Hunts. Dinners. Concerts. You have no idea how well we can entertain ourselves here!'

John blew across the estate like a summer storm, trailing Tuddenham, Cope, his aunt, gardeners, and grooms like torn fragments of cloud. He checked and reminded. He wrote lists and directions for Dr Bowler to read to the majority who could not read for themselves. He sat Harry down and, with perhaps more urgency than tact, instructed him in annuities, widows' money, rents, the necessary repairs to the poorhouses in the village, and his role as unofficial head of the local churchwardens.

'Should I baptize that child when it's finally born?' asked Dr Bowler. 'I know I shouldn't, but I can't bear to think of infants in Hell . . . I'm sure He never meant . . . I mean, if you look at Christ's own words . . . And what about the leak in the vestry?'

'Let me get it straight,' said Tuddenham, with Cope at his elbow. 'You want the dove dung on them roses. Pig on the cabbages, lettuces, and kale. And *all* the cow turds in the yard dug into the fallow plot beside the long wall of the kitchen garden for next winter?'

'Not all,' said John. 'Don't forget the hot beds for melons. Cow dung there too, to keep the heat.'

'You won't forget, will you, John?' begged his aunt. 'What I asked you to do? The little snip grows worse every day. I found her in the dairy this morning disarranging the cheeses.'

Cassie the staghound bitch started to pace the length of her pen, stopping from time to time to lick beneath her tail.

'She'll whelp tonight,' said the young stable-groom to whose father John had promised one of the pups.

The seedling lilies had begun to wilt.

'You can't do it all, John,' said Dr Bowler that evening. 'It's not as if you're never coming back. We'll survive without you for a few weeks, months even.'

John drew a breath to tell the old man the truth about his future, but he didn't know what to say.

Bowler looked at him sideways. 'Come sit down somewhere, as we usually do after supper. It will reassure me.'

John agreed distractedly. As they walked, Dr Bowler began to hum, not happily but as cats purr when in pain.

'Fetch a rushlight,' John told the young stable groom. 'I'll watch with her. She's very close now.'

By the time the moon had slid across the corner of the *basse-court*, Cassie had delivered four pups. John stroked her flanks and wrapped the newly-licked pups in old scraps of flannel. Between the second and third births he remembered that he must explain to Harry that he was midway through settling a dispute between two tenants over a field boundary, which one man (the other claimed) had over-ploughed.

'Thank you, old girl,' he told the bitch. 'For finishing one thing at least.'

He woke the young groom who had curled up to sleep in the corner of the mastiffs' empty pen. 'Three bitches and a dog,' John said. 'Your father can have one of the bitches if he likes.'

The boy beamed and vanished.

The rushlight burned out. John sat on in the dark. Only one more day. I'll never leave everything right.

Then he sat up quite straight against the wall of Cassie's pen. As so often happens, darkness had allowed the quiet sneaking approach of thoughts which are frightened off by day like sparrows from a vegetable patch.

I don't want them to be all right without me! he thought. I want things to crumble in Harry's hands. I'm not leaving at all . . . I want my absence to be felt as acutely as my presence in the flesh.

He felt suddenly mortified, and at the same time strangely released. He sat a little longer in the dark court. Then, abruptly, went up to bed.

May 27, 1636. Still dry. House martins flying. The last
day.

Journal of John Nightingale, known as John Graffham.

The next morning, John sent Arthur to ask if Lady Beester
would speak with him after the midday meal.

'She's disappeared,' said Arthur a little later, with evident
satisfaction. 'Her woman Rachel's in a bad temper because
of it. That little girl's stirring things up, for sure.'

'Is that so?' asked John with interest. 'I haven't seen enough
of her to understand how. My cousin's new wife seems most
properly behaved when I'm around.'

'Our new lady's doing nothing improper,' said Arthur
quickly. 'That's not what I was saying, sir. Just doing what
she ought.' He grinned broadly.

'I see,' said John. 'Well, keep looking for her, and don't let
Rachel frighten you off.'

'It's not so much Rachel frightening me off as you dragging
me off to that mud puddle full of herring eaters.'

'Like that, is it?'

Arthur shrugged. 'You know. A new face is a rare treat.
Though she does pray in excess of good sense.'

'Definitely not for you, then, my boy,' said John good-
naturedly. 'Don't forget to pack us both some galoshes for
that mud puddle. And keep looking for our new lady. I'll be
in the stable yard.'

Finished in the stable yard, John said farewell to his gardens. What wickedness would it all get up to when he had
gone?

His handiwork lay neat and reassuring around him: the
pink walls with their tied-in fishbone trees, the squares of
well-behaved vegetables, the swagged vines trimmed as neatly
as Harry's moustache, the weedless paths, and tiny hedges of
box and germander drawn sharply around every shape like
the outlines of an etching plate. Witnesses to the fervour of

his battle against unreasoning disorder. Obedient subjects to his stewardship of a small part of God's earthly paradise which fell so terribly short of its heavenly model. Living answers to intolerable questions. Proof that he had been alive.

He imagined a lake of sullen green weeds flooding slowly across the tidy pools of vegetables and herbs. Armadas of ravenous finches sailed over the walls. Armies of slugs oozed from damp shadowy bivouacs. The general is away! The intelligence would spread from New Garden to orchard. Whispers would slide among the reeds of the ponds. The general is away. Attack now!

I must succeed in Amsterdam! he thought. I must not let this place be sold, even if I can't ever come back.

Then, suddenly, he wanted the parting to be over, to be gone and already to have begun whatever he must begin. His old life had died unnoticed among all the lists and orderings. He let himself out through the gate at the far end of the New Garden, crossed the weir bridge at the bottom of the third pond, and climbed the slope into the orchard for the last time.

A puff of pale pink cloud jiggled with a life of its own. Petals showered down. There was someone in one of the apple trees. John moved silently through the long, damp grass. If it was one of the estate boys, he would give him a fright. It was a game he often played with them. Children seemed to enjoy moments of safe terror. Then he would send the boy off to help Cope with the finches and sparrows in the New Garden. He stretched out his hand to grab the ankle.

The bare feet curved on the branch were white and fine-boned, with nails as iridescent as fish scales. They were very clean. The knobs of the ankles were smooth as snail shells, the shins delicate. Above them, firm creamy young legs disappeared into the blossom and the shadow of a tucked-up petticoat. John dropped his hand. He stared up at the shadow between the thighs. His breath and scrotum tightened.

Most definitely not a boy. A dairymaid? Another Cat? He had not meant to replace her. He was no trifler. But still . . .

A branch cracked.

'Hey!' he shouted, more roughly than he meant. 'Don't take the blossom! We'll have no fruit.'

One foot slipped. Regripped.

'Oh Lord!' said a girl's voice. A hand grasped a lower branch and a face appeared. 'Oh, no!' She bent down and gaped at him. Then she yanked her petticoat back down over her legs.

For a moment, still distracted by her inner thighs, he did not recognize her. Then her flush matured richly to the edges of her ears. Without the white powder and red lips she wore to meals, he was still not entirely sure of the face. But no dairymaid wore eardrops like that. Or, now that he thought, had feet so clean.

'Oh, it's you,' she said with an edge of relief.

'My lady . . .' he stammered, appalled and not sure for which of them it was.

'I thought you were one of the gardeners. Wait. I'll come down.' She began to climb down, still clutching her trophy of blossom.

He had no choice but to offer her his hand. She took it graciously, a prize dancing pupil leading a pavane, and jumped the last few feet, agile as a kitten.

'I'm sorry . . .' he began. Though he could perhaps be excused for not guessing that it was Harry's new wife up a tree.

'I didn't think about the apples,' she said. 'I won't drink cider for a week to make up.' She looked at him with wide eyes, for absolution.

'They're your own apples, my lady,' said John, searching for the correct tone in which to address his cousin's child wife who stood before him in naked feet, half-laced bodice, and petticoat. He did not quite trust those wide artless eyes.

'Harry's apples,' she corrected him with dry precision.

She seemed far more comfortable than he, but then he was shooing away the hopeful ghosts of Cat and her fleeting successor. And although he had finally found Zeal Beester, this was not how he had imagined raising the tricky question of his aunt's feelings.

Fully dressed and laced-in, his cousin's wife had looked skinny, as meagre as a kitten under its deceptive fur. Unlaced in petticoats, she seemed to expand. John decided he would be happier when she was dressed again.

'Do you always dress like that?' she asked him unexpectedly.

He laughed at the sheer effrontery. Then he realized that she had read his thoughts and was teasing him. 'Do you?'

Her mouth relaxed into a smile. 'As often as I can.'

'The same for me,' said John.

She nodded and laid her branch of blossom carefully on the ground as if she planned to sit beside it. But she remained standing, uncertain what to do next now that her hands were empty. She blew a loose strand of reddish-gold hair away from her mouth. When it fell back, she tucked it away with her fingers, following it with her eyes until she was nearly cross-eyed, like a small child trying to see its own forehead.

John watched her, amused and still a little off-balance. 'This is a lucky meeting, madam,' he said. 'I was looking for you earlier. I didn't think to search the trees.'

She half-smiled at that, pleased but wary. 'I have been thinking I would like to talk to you too before you go.'

'I'm flattered, my lady. Why?'

Now she smiled. 'Don't be flattered. I need to ask questions about this place. You're clearly the one to ask.'

His social ball batted firmly to the ground, John asked, 'What do you want to know?'

'Everything.'

'A modest request. But shouldn't you dress first?'

'Of course, if it worries you.'

Now John was sure he was being teased. Although, seen at ground level, she was perfectly modest, John looked at her overskirt and loose gown which lay in the grass under a nearby tree.

She smiled at the ground and picked up the tangle of silk, muslin and lace with dramatic distaste. 'Perhaps after all you're more like Harry than I thought.'

John started to deny hotly that he was like Harry in any way, then shut his mouth, amused at how nearly and neatly the girl had drawn him out of cover. Then he heard the hint of distance from Harry in her words. To ask more was irresistible.

'In what way alike, madam?'

'Well,' she said, 'when I first arrived here, I thought you were another of Harry's projects, like making a fine lady of me, and the house, but I thought maybe you liked it. Then I decided you didn't.'

John was now very amused. 'You're right. I don't. Harry will give up on me soon, if he hasn't already.'

'I wish he would give up on me!' She gave the bunched fabric in her hands a hopeless shake.

'Nevertheless, perhaps you should get dressed.' John turned his back politely. While he waited, he considered the unexpected composure and tastes of this former ward of those two Hazelton ravens. 'I thought all young girls like nothing more than fine gowns and jewellery,' he said.

'The ones at school do,' she agreed, her voice slightly muffled.

'But not you?'

'I *hate* fashion!' Her head must have reappeared. Her voice rang like King Harry's at Agincourt. 'I should have been a man.'

John grinned up into an apple tree. 'Harry's a man and he likes fashion.'

'Yes, but if I were a man, I could choose for myself whether I liked it or not!'

There was a pause filled with rustling.

Some dutiful wives would be delighted to be forced into finery, thought John. 'Did you choose Harry?' he asked suddenly, then wished he hadn't. It was a real question, and she seemed too young, or by nature unable, to deflect real questions off the shield of social chat.

'Yes,' she said firmly. 'You may turn around.'

She had done an approximate job with the layers, but a maid was still needed.

'Harry was my choice,' she repeated. Her eyes flicked to John's, saw his surprise and noted it as expected.

John felt predictable, grown-up, responsible. He looked for a safe path away from the ground he had impulsively chosen. To his surprise, she sat down under her apple tree.

'Harry wasn't forced on me, if that's what you thought. I chose him.'

John heard grim triumph in her tone. He hesitated, then sat in the grass facing her. 'Your uncle had someone else in mind?'

Her eyes flicked to his again. Predictability redeemed by understanding. She shuddered theatrically, as when she had picked up her overskirt. 'More than forty years old, with black teeth. Two wives had already died on him. He never saw me at all, even when I was sitting in front of him. He only saw my money. He didn't even pretend! He and my uncle sat and talked and planned how to use my portion for hours while I listened. And probably more hours when I didn't.'

'How did Hazelton ever let you meet Harry? It seems like a serious error.'

She liked that. She curled up the ends of her thin little mouth and stared down at the grass. 'They had got rid of me to boarding school . . . it suited us all. Harry was one of the Hackney Hunt.'

She saw John's blank look. 'The fortune hunters who hang around the schools in Hackney and Islington to sniff out the heiresses. Harry seemed the best of them.' She tried to untangle her left lace cuff from the ribbon ties of her oversleeve. 'One girl even got carried off by force . . . it was all right. She refused at the altar and the family had to give her back.'

John listened now with open delight, arms wrapped around his knees. His aunt's *amour propre* would have to wait.

'It had to happen to me sometime,' Mistress Zeal Beester explained. 'So I made the best of it. If I have to be under some man's rod, Harry is more amusing than my uncle or his friend.'

And more manageable, thought John, with enlightenment.

'Harry really is quite handsome, don't you think?' Zeal asked with possessive pride and anxious eyes.

'As handsome as golden-thighed Pythagoras,' John agreed. Then he felt himself begin to blush at the word 'thigh'.

The anxiety left her eyes. 'So now it's all settled. I know where I am,' she said firmly.

Harry would definitely be easier to manage than her uncle, thought John. Particularly when she grew just a little older and understood fully the power Satan gave to Eve. Even now, Harry had his hands full. John found himself grinning secretly again.

'And anyway,' added Lady Beester, 'I rather like this place . . . Hawkridge House. It's so peaceful that it makes me feel like either whispering or shouting, if you know what I mean.'

'Yes, I do.' John was warming more and more to this odd child. And amusement was far more comfortable than pity. He was sorry he would not get to know her better. He was also sorry that he must wrench their conversation around to her new role as mistress of this place, which she rather liked, and the worries of his aunt.

He watched her watch a bee as it circled her head.

'Don't fear,' he said. 'Just sit quite still. Bees don't sting unless they must. To attack is their last valiant act. They must save their weapons to defend the hive. One blow with their tiny spears and they die.'

The bee landed on her bare forearm. She lifted her arm to peer more closely at the heavy, plump body in the shimmer of wings. 'It has little hooks on its feet,' she said in wonder. Still gazing at the bee, she began to recite from memory, in Latin. '"Nature is so mighty a power that out of what is almost a tiny ghost of an animal she has created something incomparable."'

John looked at her in astonishment. Then he continued the quotation from Pliny, '"What sinews or muscles can we match with such efficacy and industry as that of the bees? What men, I protest, can we rank in rationality with these insects, which unquestionably excel mankind in this, that they recognize only the common interest? . . ." I forget the rest.'

'"Honey comes out of the air and is chiefly formed at the rising of the stars . . ."' she said. 'I think.'

'Do you read Latin?'

She nodded. 'My uncle taught me. I've read all of Pliny and Cato and Varro.'

'If you have Pliny and the other masters at your side, you won't need to ask me much after all. I will leave you the keys to my books if you like.'

The bee sprang away into the air. Zeal watched it go. 'It's so different when everything is real, not just in books. I think I'll need your help all the same.'

John looked away. He had already left. He was already bobbing on alien seas. He did not want the new grappling hooks of her need to stretch the end out past his enduring.

'The plants and animals themselves will teach you if you pay attention to them.'

She felt something cooler in his manner and quickly repaired her lapse in manners. 'Thank you for the use of your books while you're away. I really am more grateful than I sounded just now. But will you also help me when you come back from wherever you're going?'

'I'll do everything in my power,' said John mendaciously.

'Good. Harry will need all the help we can give him.' She locked John firmly into alliance.

The secret traitor looked down at his hands.

'This place will be my salvation,' she said.

'Not your glory?'

She gave him a puzzled look. 'What? Oh, like Harry, you mean?'

'I'm sorry,' said John. 'I knew better.'

'Don't apologize. It's complicated, learning to know strangers. I'll probably say far worse things to you.'

'Your salvation,' John reminded her gently. He must wrestle this odd conversation around to his aunt and be done.

'I shall work so hard that I might earn God's Grace again . . .'

'Again?'

She placed the tip of her forefinger into the matching pink bowl of an apple petal. John heard a great long, gusting, quavery sigh. She met his eyes in a direct look of panic and pride. 'I'm a lost soul,' she said.

He could not let himself laugh, so he frowned. 'Lost?'

'Damned,' she whispered. 'To eternal torment in Hell.' She pinched her lips tightly. She was in absolute earnest.

'Don't be a fool!' He nearly reached across the grass to stroke and soothe her as he did the horses and Cassie the staghound bitch. 'You haven't lived long enough! What can you know of wickedness?'

She shrugged. 'I am old enough to measure my heart against

the rule . . . I've always been wicked, ever since I was a baby. Everyone tells me.'

Mistress Hazelton, thought John murderously. And how many others I don't know? 'My poor dear child . . .'

'I was a disrespectful, disobedient child,' she said. 'I contradicted my aunt . . . I tried to run away from the school. And I defied my uncle to marry Harry, you know. He had to let me in the end, but he didn't like it. And that's on top of the natural and sinful infirmities of my sex!'

Lord have mercy on us, thought John. 'I see,' he said. 'As bad as that?' But at that moment she was oblivious to irony.

'So,' said Lady Beester. 'So . . .' Her tone brightened. 'When I was thirteen . . . last year . . . I measured my heart once more and saw again how short I came. And I made a decision.'

John held his breath.

'As I am almost sure to burn in Hell after I die,' she said, leaning forward, 'I shall do what I like when I am alive. As much as I can . . . as much as I am allowed. It makes life simpler now. I know where I am. Even knowing something dreadful is better than being confused. I thought that, just before I die, I shall appeal to God's Mercy. He might let me off, but probably not.'

John breathed out as if she had punched him beneath his ribs. 'You feel that?'

She nodded. 'I wish I didn't, but I do.'

'Have you banished hope?'

'Hope confuses me. I hoped my mother wouldn't die, but she did. I hoped that Mistress Hazelton would grow to love me, but she didn't. I hoped . . .' Her voice trailed away.

They sat in silence in the grass.

Her youth was real but misleading, thought John. 'Have you told Harry all this?'

He got a flash, not of panic but of unexpected irony.

'Do you think I'd tell *him*?' Then, 'Oh, Lord, you won't will you?'

180

'I swear eternal silence.'

She nodded. After a moment, she asked, 'Well?'

'I think you're brave but foolish.'

She relaxed back on her hands. 'I told Harry already that I don't like babies,' she said cheerfully.

'What did he say?'

'He laughed and said I'd come to it in time. And he promised . . .' She looked away. 'Anyway, I shall learn to make the potions and tinctures to keep barren.'

Poor Harry, thought John. My poor, amiable cousin. What have you tied yourself to?

'My sister died in childbirth,' said Zeal. 'So many . . .' She shivered. 'So there,' she said. 'See? Wickedness. I'm an unnatural woman.'

'You've scarcely become a woman,' said John carefully. 'You have time to change your mind about what kind you are.' Trying not to imagine her grown a little more, he heard himself become pompous.

She looked at him coldly for the first time. 'Now you're talking like an old man. I didn't think you would.'

'Is that last a compliment?'

'If you don't mind being a lost soul too.'

John's spine stiffened. The muscles of his face tightened. 'Why? What have I done, madam?' Who had told her?

'Don't look like that,' she said. 'I have no idea what you've done. But you're different, like a dog or horse. Not all wrapped up in layers and layers, like Harry or my aunt or that man Malise. Your middle shows.'

I've fooled a good many others, mistress, thought John. Made a life of it. Naked middle or not.

'Do you mind?' she asked. 'I've been watching you since we came . . . for the last three days. Maybe you don't know it yet . . .' Graciously, she offered him a way out. 'But I think you've decided as I have. And perhaps I'll do what you've done – redeem myself through labour.'

John drew a breath again. So that's what those downcast eyes had been doing! 'Some of us may have such decisions forced on us.'

'It's the same thing.'

The twenty-six-year-old man and the fourteen-year-old girl stared at each other across the orchard grass. John felt an absurd desire to burden her with the truth of his story.

'Do you believe in the Lord?' she asked.

'I think I'm a cautious heretic. Death seems to be a dark line drawn through man's knowledge, not a triumphal journey elsewhere. But I don't know.'

Behind John, the hen clucked gently in her bucket. 'Did you know there's another nest up here?' asked Zeal.

John shook his head. Unspoken words pressed against his teeth.

She grinned in triumph. 'Let me show you then, Mr Graffham. And I've only been here three days.' She began to rise.

He had no time to indulge himself, and it would not be fair to the child. He must wrestle their talk round to his mission for his aunt; there would not be another chance. He offered his hand and took her small cool one. 'A busy three days, I hear.'

She stopped in a confusion of lace and folds, half-way to her feet. 'From whom?'

'My aunt.'

Her triumph darkened like grass beneath a passing cloud. She looked away and pinched her lips.

John felt as if he had kicked Cassie or closed the door on a cat's tail.

'She hates me,' said Zeal. 'She wishes I had never come here.'

'On your feet, madam,' said John.

She rose, steadied herself and withdrew her hand sharply. 'My aunt is upset. She's old and used to living undisturbed like an ancient spider in the corner of a barn. She doesn't hate you, personally. She hates being dusted away, even though it might be necessary to get rid of the cobwebs. She's afraid, wonders where there's another safe corner.'

Zeal frowned. 'Am *I* dangerous?' She sounded incredulous.

'The most terrifying event of the last eleven years.'

'Oh, Lord!' said Zeal. 'Truly?'

'Truly.'

The flush began to rise again from her neck toward the lobes of her ears. 'I can't imagine . . .' She stood still, as if observing her inner being for symptoms of dangerousness. '*She's* afraid of *me*?'

John laughed aloud. 'Poor Aunt Margaret.'

Zeal's whole face glowed now with pleased disbelief. 'But she's *old*!'

'Exactly.'

Zeal stood thinking. She nodded.

John watched her begin to shift the axis of her known world. To draw a new piece of geography into her map, like a newly discovered ocean passage into a farther sea. Acquire yet another new horizon to sail for, and new perils.

'All right,' she said. 'I shall confess to her how ignorant I am. She can tell me everything she knows. That should make her feel better. Thank you for telling me. Shall I show you that nest now?' She dismissed all the world's problems with a spectacular smile full of small white teeth.

As he followed Zeal through the long grass of the orchard, John thought, Aunt Margaret doesn't stand a chance. Nor does Harry. And I'm sorry I won't be here to watch.

As Zeal bent over and parted a shaggy bright-green tuft of grass between the ice-grey roots of a pear tree, John took onto his shoulders the weight of absolute need. Harry must not sell Hawkridge estate.

Part Two

Six

June 1, 1636. Gulls I have never seen, with black beaks.
One rides our mast.

> *Journal* of John Nightingale, known as John Graffham.

On the deck of the London sailing barge, John braced his
legs against the swell and stared ahead at a world unlike any
he had seen before.

Is there more earth than water here, he wondered, or more
water than earth? How does a man know where to put his
feet?

Two flat sheets of dark grey iron mingled under a grey sky.
John could tell them apart only by the way they caught the
light. The glinting water leaned its massive shoulder against
the earth. The dull earth leaned back, forcing the water out
of its rightful place. The two elements braced like wrestling
Titans, kept apart only by tiny ridges of clay and sticks.

Above John's head the rust-coloured sail snapped and judd-
ered. After sailing east for a day and a half across the Oceanus
Germanicus, the barge now curved westward again around
the snail's coil of the Zuider Zee.

Straight ahead (according to the map that Simeon Timmons
had given John) at the mouth of the Amstel River, stood one
of the richest cities in Europe, richer than London, the *entre-
pôt* of the Baltic and East Indian trade, the heart of an alliance
of Dutch states which had England clinging on by her

fingernails to the fringes of both the East Indies and the Caribbean. Looking back to the west as the barge curved through the steely water, John could see nothing between him and England but a light grey mist.

He leaned forward against the spray, a Columbus or da Gama sailing full-tilt off the edge of his map. Amsterdam, Amsterdam Bourse, Cornelius Vrel, Justus Coymans – all those words and names that Hazelton had given him were as naked of substance as the skeletons of last year's dried grass. The rich, intricate details of life at Hawkridge House had given way to a future of grey mist.

Behind him along the rail leaned three armed men from the household of Sir George Tupper, Hazelton's stiff-kneed rose enthusiast who was also governor of the Court of Committees of the South Java Company. Below deck, Arthur and three more of Sir George's men, all armed with loaded pistols, guarded a chest filled with enough gold to buy Hawkridge estate and several fields of good grazing as well.

'I don't need to tell you . . .' Hazelton had said, his hands clenched. 'Don't take unnecessary risks.'

'Pirates,' Sir George Tupper had said suddenly. The South Java Company's headquarters were in his house. There John had met Simeon Timmons, the agent who could not tell a tulip from an onion. 'Deserting soldiers and sailors,' said Tupper. 'They like the short dashes and hiding places near the coast. Less dangerous for them than long-distance profits on larger seas. You'll need my men. Send them back when you land. Safer not to have an English-speaking army tramping around Amsterdam tickling curiosity. Go to safe ground and send 'em back.'

'You have only two and a half weeks,' said Hazelton. 'Trust no one. Cornelius Vrel was helpful to Timmons, but he'll be a rival investor now. Try to find that dealer Coymans without contacting Vrel.' His fists closed tighter on reins he no longer held. 'Only two and a half weeks! Don't be overwhelmed.

Trust your own good sense. Remember that you're dealing with jumped-up herring fishermen who happen to have a knack for commerce.'

He reminds me of myself leaving Hawkridge, with my lists and frantic instructions.

John's chief memory of leaving by dinghy from Tupper's private landing was how much noise the chest of money made when three servants swung it into the boat.

The barge slid past a small island that bristled with gibbets.

The skipper appeared at the rail beside John. 'Then they sink 'em,' he said with ghoulish pleasure. Showing this island to passengers was reliable entertainment. 'Sometimes don't hang 'em at all, just chuck 'em straight into the water all weighted down.'

Bodies hung thick as apples, ripened to different degrees.

'The Hollanders don't like criminals and sinners. Or Englishmen.' The captain spat into the water. 'Unless they've money to spend.'

John managed to lift one corner of his mouth. 'I'd best turn back now.' He watched the gibbet island fall behind them.

The bargeman laughed sceptically – he had counted the escort, seen their pistols, and weighed the chest with his eyes – and returned aft to take back the helm, shouting orders as he went.

Suddenly, a sharply drawn world leaped out of the damp grey air ahead. Ships loomed on the water. Masts bristled. Dogs barked into the soft damp air. A rooster crowed. John heard shouts and bells. He smelled cinnamon and tar. The barge slid below the soaring poop of an anchored East India merchantman.

John bent his neck back to look up at her name. The *Republiek*. Her stepped poop curved up like the haunches of a stretching cat, higher than the tower of St Paul's. She was bellied like an ox and swooped down to a low, mean, sharp bowsprit. The ship was heavy with red and gold paint, slapping with ropes, her sails lashed in like an earl's sleeves. Five decks of cannon poked reptilian snouts from her gun ports high over his head. As they passed the point where it angled into the water, her anchor chain was thicker than John's shoulders were wide.

She's twice the size of anything anchored in the Thames, thought John. Not even the King's own *Endeavour* matches her. An English trader with no more than forty guns wouldn't stand a chance alone against her in the Indian seas.

He watched her great wooden sides slide past. She could be the very one that sank the two South Java Company ships.

Four more East Indiamen lay at anchor in the deep water, two beyond the *Republiek* to the right, two to the left. They soared like cathedrals above the houses and huts of barges and lighters.

Those are not the boats of simple herring fishermen with a lucky knack for commerce, thought John. Mere trade does not need such arrogant excess. You can carry needles or nutmegs just as well without the gilt, the flags, the carved swags or the guns. They were built for war. These ships were designed to overwhelm and to conquer.

Briefly, he imagined that he was a savage waiting in terror and excitement, hidden with fragile spear and papery shield just above the beach as one of these beautiful monsters approached a Moluccan shore.

They picked up their pilot from another barge.

'We're going through the dolphins into the harbour!' shouted the bargeman.

The dolphins were a double palisade of wooden posts which protected both the mouth of the Amstel River and the city that lay along both its banks. The palisade stitched a double line through the water across their path and faded at either end into the low mist. Small craft were made fast to both sides of the double palisade. Inside, the masts of small ships grew thick as trees in a flooded forest. The great traders which were also warships had to lie outside.

Beyond the dolphins, John now saw the city itself – lines of low roofs as pointed as shark's teeth, the two great towers of the Old Church and the New Church on opposite banks of the Amstel. Other church towers, some slim and pointed, others rounded as a tapered stack of onions, punched up through the neat lines of red-tiled, steeply-pitched roofs. But even here, it was touch and go which element ruled, the land or the sea. Where London had streets, Amsterdam had water.

Old Church on the left, New Church on the right. John repeated to himself the geography lesson given him by Simeon Timmons. He took out the map Timmons had given him. Amsterdam curved tightly within parallel half-rings of defensive walls and moats.

'Like half a sliced onion,' Timmons had said. The man had onions on the brain.

The river was the arrow through the city's heart.

They overtook a ferry taking men in from one of the anchored ships and slipped through a break in the palisade. John edged aft along the narrow slice of deck that surrounded the opening of the cargo hold.

'I'll set you down on the Old Church side of the harbour at St Anthony's Gate,' said the bargeman. 'You can hire a small boat there.' He concentrated briefly on avoiding another ferry. 'I won't pay the Dutch toll to go through the dam into the Amstel. These cheese-eaters collect tolls even fiercer than the English!'

The low horizon of docks and sharp-gabled houses was divided exactly in half by a tall arched dam topped by the machinery of locks and sluices.

'River cuts the city in half like a knife through a pie,' said the bargeman. 'Past that dam, you can sail up the Amstel right on to the porch of the Town Hall. And dock your ship alongside your house, if you've the money for either. But it's the poor man's door for us.'

I can't do it after all, thought John. Wrecked on a pebble before I even reach the first cliff. He looked back blankly at the face of the Dutch boatman. If I can't even arrange for a boat, how can I begin all the rest? Find Coymans? Without using Cornelius Vrel?

Entering an alien geography changes the internal map of a man's thoughts and emotions. He needs to know that there will not be a wall across his door when he opens it, if there was not a wall there yesterday. Or that his bed has not shifted across the room unaided. Only when his body can move unthinking from landmark to landmark can his mind open to other cries for his attention.

John stood dazed on the damp, slippery cobbles of the foreign dockside street, in a country which was a flat maze of earth and sea, boxes and bundles around his feet, with Arthur poised pale and nervous on the money chest.

Three sailors propped on barrels and bollards were amusing themselves with open, if unintelligible, speculation about these foreign newcomers. John watched them eye Sir George's men.

'The sooner you're off back to London, the better,' he told them.

The air was thick with a harsh language which tantalized John's ear with flashes of near understanding. He could hardly distinguish the voice of the boatman from the surrounding racket. Rolled barrels thundered past on the stones, leaving the smell of tar and splintered wood.

'What in the name of heaven . . . ?' Arthur stared, his terrible responsibility briefly forgotten.

The three men walking toward them along the dock were unlike any John had ever seen except in paintings. Their skins were deep, rich brown. They wore turbans of silk, woven with silver threads, and gowns like ancient kings of Araby. Followed by eight servants in skirts, they passed almost unnoticed through the wool- and leather-clad sailors and dockers and trailed behind them the smell of sandalwood.

'The Magi,' said John in wonder. He followed the three men with his eyes. 'A little adrift from Bethlehem. Or else we're on an even stranger shore than I think.'

At last, with the help of acting, a little Latin, scraps of French, and silver, John conveyed to the boatman his need for lodgings and for transport there. Their boxes and the heavy, clanking money chest were tipped into a small rowing boat anchored in a bobbing fleet at the foot of some water steps. John and Arthur climbed in after.

'Another bloody boat,' said Arthur. 'I didn't like to say it before, sir, but I can't swim.'

'In these waters,' said John, 'who can?'

Their boat skimmed the seafront, to the left, away from the central river dam. It overtook the Magi and their retinue, then turned right into a channel barely wider than the boat. A low footbridge almost brushed John's hat into the canal. They slid along below street level, between wet stone walls. John tipped his head back to look up at high pointed gables, cranes and winches, warehouses and sluice gates.

They floated into the sudden spaciousness of a large rectangular basin edged by market stalls and backed by the steeples of two more churches. A lighter lay tied close against the cliff-like wall of a house, beside the open double doors of a water-level warehouse room. The smell of nutmegs came from the sacks on its deck. A procession of black-clad children, graduated in size like a set of carved toys, marched along the basin's rim.

Their boat turned into another narrow channel, past a nunnery, under more bridges. They brushed close against other craft, sometimes with their heads only a few inches from the boots and shoes on the streets above the canals.

John noted how tightly Arthur was holding his pistol. The farthest Arthur had ever been from Hawkridge House was the market at Basingstoke.

And I'm as lost as he is, thought John.

The boat turned again into a wide canal lined with houses. '*Singel*,' said one of the boatmen. He waved an arm at the large canal. They bumped gently alongside a set of water steps.

The lodging house leaned its tall, narrow face a little towards the canal as if admiring its reflection. It was two windows wide and five windows high, capped by a sharply-peaked gable. Just below the peak, an iron bar jutted out above a solid wooden door, trailing a double rope and pulley instead of a flag.

John climbed the steep stone steps up from the canal to the cobbled street, then another even steeper flight from the street to the *stoep* of the house.

Mevrouw Padtbrugge, the householder, reminded John of a peony bud, round and tightly packed into her black silk dress. She spoke no English but seemed satisfied by what the boatman told her. She smiled guardedly.

'*Klaar*,' she said. She drew John inside and shut the door firmly.

John hauled himself behind her up four floors of a corkscrew wooden stairs by a rope which dangled down the centre. The stairs were so narrow that the woman's skirts brushed hard against both walls.

How the devil would they get the money chest up here?

In the room, John peered down from the open window to the quayside far below.

Mevrouw Padtbrugge reeled in the rope on the hook at the end of the iron bar. She lowered one end of the rope to the street. John peered down again. Far below in the street, Arthur and a man from the house bundled the chest into a net. The net was hooked onto the rope. Then they hauled on the other end of the rope; the last negotiable assets of the South Java Company rose slowly into the air, swinging wildly, towards the fifth-floor window. A waterseller, an eel vendor, a small boy and two passing boatmen watched and shouted advice as the widow grappled for the net. She hauled it into the room where it landed with an alarming metallic crash.

John was reasonably satisfied with where arm-waving, silver and luck had brought them. Sir George's safe ground. They were at the top of a tower. Mevrouw Padtbrugge seemed unlikely to tolerate such things as thieves in her immaculate domain. The mere idea made John smile.

He was called down to the ground floor to sup in the late sunlight in the front room that opened off the street. Mevrouw Padtbrugge, in Dutch, introduced five well-washed, well-mannered children – Jacob, Jan, Mary, Joseph . . . John lost track.

Two other lodgers appeared, less washed than the Padtbrugge children but equally polite.

'An English!' cried one. 'Welcome to Amsterdam. I am Hein Snijder. I make books in Zaandam. The finest leather and vellum is in Amsterdam.'

The second lodger, Pieter Zwellen, spoke no English and smelled of fish. There seemed to be no Mynheer Padtbrugge. Snijder explained under his breath to John that the *mevrouw* was a widow.

They arranged themselves around the long table in the late afternoon sun. The widow's white-capped head bowed beneath a painting of Abraham sacrificing Isaac; conversation paused. She prayed at length. Then she treated her guests to a breast of veal, venison in pastry, salad, stuffed cabbages, boiled spinach chopped with currants and butter, pickled herrings, cheeses, pretzels, bread, apples, pears, nuts and a good Rhenish wine.

The widow herself ate little of this abundance but rejoiced

in her guests' appetites with a generosity which surprised John after the set of her lips and the severity of her prayers.

'Please eat,' she begged him, explaining with gesture when her words failed. She called back the serving maid to put another morsel on his plate.

'She says that waste is a sin,' explained Snijder, the book-binder.

The maid poured more wine into John's green glass *roemer*.

'I'm a botanical scholar,' he said, in answer to Snijder's questions. 'Come to consult the great botanical men of Leiden and Amsterdam.'

Snijder passed this on.

John saw all three pairs of adult eyes measure him for an academic gown and find an ill-fit. The widow looked at his rough brown hands, the two male guests at his scarred jaw.

John chewed innocently on his stuffed cabbage. 'And to buy a few bulbs,' he amended. 'For the garden on the estate where I work in England.' He ached for his tale to be the simple truth.

He saw the three pairs of eyes now revise him into a head gardener with a little education and ideas above his station. The widow and Snijder seemed satisfied, the fishmonger not.

'You want to go to Leiden or Haarlem,' said the book-binder. 'The best growers are there. I go every year with my wife only to look at their fields in full blow. What a shame you've just missed them.'

John was so close to those scraps of Paradise fallen to earth. But he was not his own man; he had urgent masters and no time for private lusts.

'I was told to look for a dealer here in Amsterdam,' said John. He drew a mental breath and plunged. 'Justus Coymans?'

The bookbinder shook his head and translated for the widow and Zwellen. 'Coymans?'

Mevrouw Padtbrugge also shook her head.

The fish merchant said something. Snijder translated. 'Not a grower he's heard of.'

The fish merchant's suspicion of John was clearly deepening. He looked at John's hands again.

'He's not one of the greats on everyone's tongue,' said Snijder. 'The Bols, and Quackels, the Catoleyns and van Damms. Here in Amsterdam, you said?'

The fish merchant watched John steadily over his masticating jaw. He asked a question.

'What kind of bulb?' repeated Snijder.

'Tulips.'

Aha. The fish merchant suddenly smiled, satisfied at last. 'Just be careful,' he said, via Snijder. 'Personally, I don't like what's going on. Too many new faces in Amsterdam. Too many people taking stupid risks. It's not natural. You can't eat the things, or wear them, or get any other real good out of them at all!'

'But I disagree!' cried Snijder with passion, after translating. 'There is good in tulips. Consider beauty! *Pulchritudo*!'

'I'm on your side,' said John.

The fish merchant said something more and Snijder answered angrily.

'What did he say?' asked John.

'He said, "Forget beauty at those prices!"' Snijder cut viciously at a rubbery herring. 'The man inhabits a different world than I.'

The widow said something placating, then turned to John. He understood the word 'boers'.

'The Bourse?'

'She says that if Coymans is not a grower, he might be a dealer. And if he's a dealer, he might be found at the Bourse on the Dam.'

'*Twaalf*.' The widow held up all ten fingers and then two more. Then two again.

'Go tomorrow between twelve noon and two o'clock. Ask

for your man there. Who knows, you might find him.'

As he hauled himself back up the tight spiral of wooden stairs to his treetop room, John suddenly remembered his long, spinning descent from prison, begun as John Nightingale and ended as John Graffham. He arrived on the top floor, breathing hard.

He took Arthur's gun and sent him down to his supper in a courtyard at the back of the house. Then he bolted the stairway door and leaned on the edge of the hatch. He looked out into the tops of the canal-side trees.

These houses needed roots like molars to grip deep into the sand and mud. As with the *Republiek*, John felt chastened. He must never underestimate, as Hazelton and other Englishmen clearly did, a people who had wrestled a city out of the sea.

After Arthur returned and folded his cloak against the money chest as a pillow, John pulled his own low bed across the door. He tried to sleep, but the tall, narrow, creaking house seemed to sway like a ship at sea, with his bed in the crow's nest. I'm too high, he thought drowsily. That's why I can't hear the sheep.

ꩰ

When Zeal entered the kitchen, silence slammed down across the chatter. Spoons dropped against the sides of bowls. A knife-blade clinked.

'Good morning,' she said brightly.

'Good morning, my lady. Morning. Morning. My lady.' The cooks and kitchen grooms stood frozen, as if struck by an evil spell, in poses of scouring, slicing, and stirring, except for a woman who shook a pan of fingerling fish over a small charcoal fire in a brick stove in one corner, her arm jerking back and forth while her eyes locked on Zeal.

This smoky, odorous cavern still confused Zeal. Its details

still eluded her after nearly a week. It felt huge after Mistress Hazelton's small neat London cubby hole, where one needed only to warm meats and pies bought already cooked, or heat milk for possets. The fireplace was a small house in itself, fronted with hanging ladles, forks and drying cloths, its arched cave filled with looped chains, ratchets, cranks, cranes, spits, hooks, trivets, and pots that dangled or balanced thick as ripe fruit on a tree.

Zeal's eyes skated in nascent panic over carved wooden utensils whose purpose she still did not understand, baskets of vegetables that she might have recognized in a calmer moment, bowls of unidentifiable mess.

A dead pig lay full length on the long central wooden table. He seemed to squint at her through pink swollen lids. Six doves slung limp heads over the table edge and stared at her upside down with dull black eyes.

Too many eyes in this room. Too many strange things she knew nothing of.

'Is everything all right, my lady?' asked the woman who seemed to be the chief cook.

'Yes.' Zeal drew another breath. 'Thank you.'

If she turned and left now, her retreat would be unmistakable.

'Would someone be kind enough to come with me to the New Garden?' she asked.

'Peter,' said the cook to a boy who had been slicing onions. 'You'll be helping our lady with the pot herbs. Here's your chance to shine. You'll want clogs, my lady.'

Zeal followed the blushing Peter out of a further door towards the gardens with her dignity relatively intact. She would study her books again that night, paying special attention to kitchen matters.

'I really do know how to do it,' Zeal reassured Mistress Margaret, later that morning. They were in the cheese room, next to the milk house in the *basse-court*. 'You must let me try!' She knew from her books but had never actually tried. In London, the mistress bought cheeses. She didn't make them.

Mistress Margaret pinched her lips and stepped back. Her hands dived down the sides of her apron, collided in mid-hem. Then one hand leaped up and fastened on her apron waistband, where her keys had hung before she had to give them to this little chit who called herself the mistress of the house. The fingers of her other hand felt blindly into space at her side.

Zeal cut a piece of curd from the snowy bank just visible through the misty sea of whey in the curd trough. The sharpness of Mistress Margaret's eye made Zeal's hand want to shake. Carefully, the girl lifted the fragile, wobbling curd on the end of her knife and laid it on the table. Then she heated the end of a poker in the little fire that kept the cheese room just warm enough but not too warm. She muttered a silent prayer, touched the poker to the curd and pulled it quickly away. The curd hissed, stank and clung briefly to the poker.

Zeal examined the broken thread of melted curd. 'Too short. We must leave the curd to pitch a little longer.'

'It's long enough,' said Mistress Margaret sharply. 'The thread must be half an inch. That's half an inch.'

'Not quite.'

They eyed each other across the wooden curd trough. Mistress Margaret's face was bright red. Zeal's was white. Two dairy women watched, pink with excitement.

'I shouldn't think London gentlewomen have much experience with cheesemaking,' said Mistress Margaret. 'If you leave it too long, not even the pigs will eat the cheese.' She drew a breath. Zeal reminded herself of her last conversation with Harry's cousin John.

Misinterpreting Zeal's silence as retreat, the older woman struck again. 'Anyone can make cheese. But cheese you can eat ... that's a different matter!'

Zeal felt the eyes of the dairy women hot on the back of her neck. She heard their amusement racing through the estate. By bedtime even the frogs in the ponds would know that she had been beaten in the Battle of the Trough. On the other hand, John had asked her to be kind to the old woman.

'You don't learn it from books!' said Mistress Margaret triumphantly.

'All the more reason for me to learn from experience,' snapped Zeal in spite of her good intentions.

Mistress Margaret pinched her mouth and looked away. The dairy women exchanged glances.

'With you as my tutor, of course,' Zeal added kindly.

'Anything you say, my lady,' said Mistress Margaret dully. 'Do as you will with the cheese. Leave the curd till it's ruined. It's for you to say. If you will excuse me . . . There might be something I can do in the stillroom.'

Zeal left the two dairy women to strain and break up the curds. She promised to return later to help wrap the curds in cloth and put them into cheese vats to drain and harden. She nodded graciously at the deep curtseys dropped by the women and left the *basse-court* to find somewhere to sit and tremble for a few minutes in private. Victory brought its own price.

She followed a trail of smells – lemon, lavender, fox, leaf mould, grass – to the top of Hawk Ridge. She had been eyeing the ridge all week. The wind was light but firm. The sky moved quickly from black cloud to sun and back to cloud again. Even when the sun was out, the blue of the sky was as thick and dark as paint, a tent laid close above the earth.

Zeal sank down into the grass, straightbacked and sniffing for more messages in the heavy air. The grass blades were soft swords that brushed away their own injuries. Bees hummed. A sudden blast of sun hammered her into the ground like a peg.

The house looked smug to her, shadowed in the odd shifting light. A pretty girl, all pink brick and fancy patterns. Then the sun hit it again, and it looked simply contented, stretched along its flat terrace of land between sloping drive and ponds, with the diverted stream tickling its belly. From here Zeal could see how it had grown this way and that, with jogs and unexpected corners.

No wonder it still confuses me, she thought. It's not the neat square chest I imagined packing my new life into.

She leaned back on her hands. She liked this backside house better than the more formal one she had first seen from the front, with its central porch and symmetrical projecting wings. This house lacked the order and discipline that Harry extolled in architecture and which Zeal found a little too male and Roman. This house kept disappearing around unexpected corners. It dangled secrets. It did not aspire to grandeur. If she kept it clean and polished, it would ask no more of her.

A bee landed on the tip of her knee. She watched its tail quiver and thought she could hear the minute scratching of its hooked feet on her apron. The trembling feeling of her fight with Mistress Margaret had been blown away. A deep calm filled her.

I'll find a way to reassure your aunt, she promised the absent John.

The sky turned the colour of slate. Zeal was suddenly chilled by a cloud shadow although sunlight still touched the top of the hill beyond the house. She was too cold to sit any longer but not yet ready to go back. I've not gone to the limits of the estate, she thought. And I don't want to wait till John comes back to show me.

She looked back down at the house.

Mistress Margaret will welcome my absence for a little longer.

Half-sure that she acted only from compassion for the old woman, she set off over the crest of Hawk Ridge through a hazel copse away from the house.

* * *

'Oh!' Zeal peered along the faint path in disbelief touched with fear. She looked to make sure that she was not observed before she climbed the slope of the beech hanger closer to the tree. She blushed and looked around again. Then she reached out and touched the ribcage, just below the closest grey, sharp-nippled breast. It was hard beneath her fingers as she had known it would be. Why had she expected otherwise? Still blushing, she looked quickly up into the tree's branches.

Its leaves were a pale green lace stitched against the darker green of an oak. Zeal's eyes slid down the calves, past the knees and along the thighs to the Mound of Venus. She put both hands behind her back. She felt wicked looking at such indecency. She imagined that the leaves and clicking twigs whispered 'wickedness, wickedness'. But she was also fascinated.

Her eyes ricocheted from *pudendum* to breasts and back again. Beside that displayed female amplitude she felt like a sapling, an arrow shaft.

Had John seen her? Touched her the way Zeal had just touched her? She knew that Harry would never have clambered this far up the steep slope of the hanger. She suddenly imagined John sitting on his heels with his back braced against the tree, his head thrown back to rest on the grey bare shoulder. The conjunction of John and tree confused her further.

Then she saw the mounds of fresh earth at her feet, between the knobby grey roots. With a thumping heart, she knelt and dug. A message on a scrap of paper, mouldering, blotched, barely legible. 'Deliver us fro . . . vil.' Deliver us from evil.

Someone thought this tree creature was a delivering force, on the side of Good.

Zeal wished the creature had a head. It might be less frightening with a head.

The imagined John lifted his head with a slightly distant, considering look in his pale grey eyes, as the real one had done in the orchard before he left, as if he wanted to say something to her.

Zeal reburied the spell.

There's nothing to be so frightened about.

She ran back to the house as if into the embrace of an old friend.

'There are too many women!' said Harry with passion.

Zeal and Mistress Margaret raised their heads from their needlework, Dr Bowler and Tuddenham, the estate manager, from their after-supper game of angel-beast.

'The cooks are women. The kitchen grooms are mostly women . . . kitchen maids! None of the good London houses have maids! You'd think we were at war and the men all gone for soldiers!'

'We use the labour we have,' said Mistress Margaret, looking up askew, eyes wide with alarm. 'John needs the men for the heavy work in the fields and stables.' She ducked back down to her tapestry stool-cover.

'I'm surprised he doesn't have women working as stable grooms! I can't imagine what Malise and the Hazeltons thought.' Harry kicked a coal back into the fireplace of the small parlour where they sat after supper. 'Actually, I can imagine only too well! And why they all left so soon.' He crossed to one of the windows. 'Lord, why won't that wind stop?'

Zeal turned her head to listen. The wind sang above the notes of the fire. Ooosh, oossh.

'I'm going to start them digging out the banks between the ponds tomorrow,' said Harry. 'If I can find any men to do it.' He looked around for acknowledgement of his bitter joke. None came. 'Make some kind of a start putting this damned place right.' He glanced sharply at Bowler and Tuddenham to catch any disloyal exchange of looks.

Mistress Margaret laid her needlework on her knees and nibbled a fingernail with concentration.

'Shouldn't you wait until John returns?' asked Zeal recklessly.

'It's none of John's business!'

'He may be able to advise you on things you ought to know before you start.'

'I doubt it.' Harry glared at his wife. 'Why are you so concerned with his opinion? I thought you understood how he has held this place back.'

'We've only just arrived,' said Zeal mildly. 'We should make our acquaintance with the place before we start to change it too much.'

'You sound just like my cousin ... don't want a thing changed.'

'I do like the place as it is.'

Mistress Margaret gave Zeal a look of ironic surprise.

'Well, you'd better get over that, because things are going to change!' Harry slammed back down into his chair beside the fire.

Zeal rose and went to the window. Outside dark tree creatures bent and waved in the wind. They seemed to shift their roots in short, ponderous dance steps. Closer and closer to her window, they shook their dark, ragged witchlocks. They quivered and convulsed.

Zeal pretended fear, like a child. The dark women lay flat on the wind, streamed with wind as if rising from a wave. Closer and closer, then they retreated again.

I'm safe in here, thought Zeal. The trees lurched, not unhappily, and danced away.

Seven

June 2, 1636. Summer more advanced than in Hampshire. Many roses in full blow. There are more strange beasts in the streets of Amsterdam than in all of England's menageries.

Journal of John Nightingale, known as John Graffham.

'The Bourse?'

'*Boers*?' The boatman seemed to understand. John stared up at the street above his head, trying to keep track of their way as they slapped and splashed through a maze of dark green canals.

He had left Arthur munching bread and cheese with his back braced against the money chest and his pistol in his lap.

'Did you see them all watch us arrive last night?' Arthur had asked. 'Weighing this box with their eyes as we hoiked it up. I don't like it.'

'Seize your chance, man! Hawkridge doesn't give us many such chances to be heroes. And I want to be done with that chest even more than you.' John checked the heavy bar across the door of the pulley hatch and lowered himself down the corkscrew stairs.

The boat slid out into the large rectangular basin of the day before, crossed it, slipped under bridges, waited to enter locks, and was suddenly among the forest of masts John had seen from a distance poking up through the rooftops in the middle of the city where no ships should be. The boatman stopped by a flight of water steps tucked under the bow of a docked three-master. As John climbed the steps, barrels rolled along a plank over his head from the stern of the ship onto the high quayside.

A vast market place lay beside the Amstel River. Close to the quay edge crouched a customs building of some kind. At opposite ends of its sharply-peaked roof, weather vanes of Fortune and Neptune leaned into the gentle breeze. Beyond it stood an official building bright with flags and guards.

'*Boers*!' called the boatman from below. He pointed onward, through shoppers, vendors, beggars, dogs, dockers and porters pushing wheelbarrows, to a third building that spanned the Amstel River like a massive bridge.

The new Amsterdam Bourse had been built in 1608, on the Rokin near the Town Hall and the city Weigh House, which John had already noted. From the outside, it looked to John like a walled city, complete with the cathedral spire of a clock tower. Long straight walls marked at intervals by flat pilasters enclosed a field-sized chunk of precious Amsterdam soil.

But it was a walled city with the bridge up. Outside the locked central doors, under the tall clock tower, men had gathered like chickens around a farmer with a basket of corn.

John set his back against the railing of the arched bridge that spanned the water in front of the Bourse and studied the men. The wealthy wore silks, the lesser sorts fustian. Almost all were in black according to the strictures of the city *predikanten*. Glowing onion shapes rose here and there among the dark hats and feathers – the turbans of Moors and Ethiops in bright gowns, like the three Magi on the harbour dock. John also saw a few full beards and fur hats of Muscovites.

Two hundred or more. If Justus Coymans were there, how the devil to find him?

A carriage rolled into the square and stopped. John watched a man in black silk rush out of the crowd and climb into the coach. A few moments later, the man climbed down again, writing notes, and flung himself back into the jostling, wittering flock in front of the Bourse. The carriage left. John watched four more carriages and four other eager brokers repeat this pantomime.

This Bourse is clearly a place, thought John, where some gentlemen will trust their purses but not their persons.

As he watched, the outlying bodies were sucked abruptly inward. The flock compacted and flowed towards the main doors of the Bourse like water into a drain. The great clock began to strike noon. The square emptied itself into the great walled citadel. John left his bridge and followed.

'*U mag niet naar binnen.*'

The man's meaning was clear enough. Frustrated, John peered past the guard into the great arcaded court of the Bourse.

'I must go in,' he said pleasantly, in English. 'I'm looking for a friend.'

The guard on the door said something else. He was polite but regretfully firm.

John blew out a frustrated breath. 'Justus Coymans. Is Justus Coymans in there?' He tried again in Latin.

The guard rolled his eyes at the denseness of foreigners. John reached for his purse to try a different tack.

'He's trying to tell you that to go inside, you must be a member.' It was an old man's voice. He spoke English but was not an Englishman. Strong 'r's and a soft breathy leakage of air around the sibilants. 'The Dutch are very hospitable, but to get inside where things happen, you must always be a member.'

His face was as brown as a ploughman's but soft-skinned and daintily wrinkled like a well-oiled kid boot. Small alert black eyes perched on either side of his knife-blade nose, under a currently fashionable beaver hat and above a precise trinity of goatee and moustaches.

John felt a rush of gratitude for understanding and being understood. 'I hadn't thought how devilish it would be to speak a foreign tongue.'

The old man laughed. 'It is, and I can tell you, for I've led a most devilish life.' He laid a hand lightly on John's elbow. His head came just to the bottom of John's ear. 'Come. I will translate you.' He led John back toward the door of the Bourse.

He spoke quickly to the guard. 'You are my guest,' he said to John.

The guard accepted a fistful of coins. They passed under an arch into a vast open colonnaded court.

'So,' said the old man. 'Here you are in the court of Queen Money. Now what?'

John stood stunned. The court seethed. Were these the stern, humourless cheese merchants Hazelton and his colleagues had led John to expect?

These men shouted and pushed. They leaped into the air, embraced, snatched at each other's sleeves, pounded backs, slapped hands. They scratched their heads, rolled their eyes, cracked their knuckles. They paced and turned. Hallooed across twenty yards and leaned close to breathe into each other's ears. They formed and re-formed pairs and groups faster than a drunken May dance. Here and there a solitary, motionless figure hovered, intent as a hawk.

'What do you want to do here?' repeated the old man. 'Are you buying or selling?' He looked delighted at John's astonishment.

Still staring, John said, 'Neither. I'm looking for a man and foolishly believed I could find him.' He looked more closely. 'There are no goods for sale here.'

'You're mistaken,' said the old man. 'Everything in the world is for sale here – saltpetre, grain, Japanese lacquers and

Ming porcelains, Malacca pepper, Turkish carpets, pickled ginger, diamonds, pearls, rubies . . .' His black eyes examined John with intense interest.

'I see none of them.'

'All carried on the hot winds of their breath. Look!' The old man pointed into the air with a clean, soft-skinned, wrinkled hand. 'Quickly, look, by that pillar! There go two hundred bales of raw Chinese silk!' He sketched a wide arc in the air with his hand. 'And there by that pillar, a ton and a half of Baltic grain. And there . . . !' He swung like a man following a kite. '. . . Ah, there, just settling now . . . seven hundred pounds of English soap.'

Two men, one in black silk, one in indigo, punished each other's palm with schoolmasterly slaps.

'*In blanco*, my friend. On paper. The Dutch come here to go mad so they can remain so sweetly sane in all other things.'

'Do you spy any tulip bulbs flying through the air like acrobats?' asked John.

The old man did not answer for a minute. 'Hmmm,' he said finally. 'You won't find tulips here. They have their own *collegii*. Where you must also be a member. I think we should go back outside.'

'Senhor Francisco Gomez de Fernandez,' said the old man, bowing slightly. 'Portuguese by birth but little else.' Under his hat, Gomez's hair was silvery white, though his beard and waxed horizontal moustaches were coal black.

John hesitated only a second. 'John Nightingale, plain mister.' The name tasted sweet as a sun-warmed apricot. Why not? He was a mere agent here, the substantive of the verb 'to act'. His name did not matter, except to himself. He had not spoken his real one aloud for years. He said it again. 'John Nightingale.'

They replaced their hats on their heads.

'Thank you, sir,' said John. 'For your kindness just now.'

Gomez shook his head dismissively. 'It's a pleasure to speak English again. I left London ten years ago . . . You said you were looking for someone.'

I can't trust the man just because he speaks English! thought John. But, *pace* Hazelton, I have to start somewhere.

'Justus Coymans,' he said.

'Coymans,' repeated Gomez with comical flatness. 'Coymans.' He began to walk along the water's edge away from the Bourse. 'Well, you won't find him in there. Come, you may buy me a drink and talk to me in another language than Dutch.'

Half-amused, half-wary, John allowed himself to be taken in tow. At least Gomez knew Coymans, though he didn't seem to like him much.

'Wine, ale or milk?' asked Gomez. 'Milk for me. My stomach is crabbed with age.' He smoothed his hat against his jacket cuff and laid it on his neatly folded cloak. He was even older than John had thought when he had first taken off his hat. Mentally, John lifted his hand from his sword.

'Pains at night.' Gomez waved for the serving woman. 'So you've come to Amsterdam to become rich.'

'Why do you say that?'

Gomez merely tilted his head enigmatically.

'I'm a botanical enthusiast,' said John. 'I want to enlarge my knowledge. And buy a few bulbs.'

'To Flora!' Gomez raised his tankard of milk and his eyebrows. 'Goddess of Blossom and mother of fortunes.'

'So we hear in England, though, as I said, fortune is not my purpose.'

Gomez shook his silver head. 'Naah, Senhor Nightingale. Don't lie to me. You don't come to look at pretty flowers armed with the name of Justus Coymans.'

'I must have been misled in London,' said John.

'I should think not,' said Gomez. 'If you're looking for Coymans, you're looking for Coymans.'

John smiled his defeat. I can still work through Cornelius Vrel, he thought. Send word to him at his house today. Meet tomorrow. I'll only lose one day.

'I will take you to Coymans's house tonight,' said Gomez, 'if you wish.' His eyes were bright with eagerness.

John tipped his head back and drained his *roemer*. Why would Vrel be any less risky than the elegantly fragile old Gomez with his dyed moustaches and beard? He may be over-eager, but I could cut his throat as fast as he'd cut mine. And I have only two and a half weeks.

John's body was tight from too much caution. 'That would be most kind,' he said. 'Coymans's house, tonight.' As soon as he had said the words, he felt better. Then he reflected on the eagerness in Gomez's eyes.

'Do you . . . ?' He hesitated. What did the old man expect from John? Or would he be insulted?

Gomez understood. He smiled briefly, dismissing an awkward subject. 'Don't worry. If it comes to anything, Coymans pays me.' Then he leaned closer, as if anxious that John not misunderstand. 'I would take you there without reward, but Coymans doesn't trust anyone he doesn't pay.'

'Stop! Right where you are!' The man spoke English.

John froze, except for his right hand which slid toward his dagger.

The man sat with his feet on the table, one arm thrown over the back of his chair, the hand out of sight. 'Don't move a muscle!'

The room was hot and bright with torch- and candlelight, the table disordered with a rich meal just ended. Tumbled napkins, spilt wine. Fruit peelings, bones, spoons sticking out of glasses. Smell of beer, flowers and tobacco smoke rising from white clay pipes. Seven men stared at John, in their shirtsleeves, stockings and belts slackened. Their feathered hats hung over chairs; one lay on the floor like a rooster run over by a cart.

John kept his hand on his knife and moved another step into the room. Layers of fine smoke lay on the air.

The man who had spoken left his feet on the table but raised the hand that hung behind his chair. In his large fist was a pistol. He pointed it at John.

'Be so kind as to step back to just where you were before.'

In the silence, a maid came into the room and began to clear away the plates.

'Your right hand was a little closer to your hip, I think,' said the man with the pistol. 'Another step back, I said.'

John felt Gomez pull at his sleeve. He stepped back and half-turned. 'Senhor Gomez, this doesn't feel like a market place. Could you have mistaken the address?'

'Look at me,' bellowed the man with the pistol.

John turned, pulse pounding and a little puzzled. He saw a large man, face red, shiny with grease and hilarity. Light tawny hair sprang up from a wide forehead. His eyes were small, crinkled at the corners with laughter and as cold as a canal in winter.

'That's right.' The man swung his feet to the floor and levelled the pistol in both hands, elbows on the table in front of him. He cocked his head and peered along the barrel.

Two of the other men suddenly slapped the tabletop with their palms. '*Een!*' they shouted. They slapped the table again. '*Twee!*' The smack of their palms on polished wood echoed like a pistol shot. '*Drie!*'

The man cocked the pistol.

'*Vier!*' The men's voices grew louder.

Against his will, John's body clenched itself for the impact of the lead shot. Someone laughed loudly.

'Steady,' said Gomez softly. His hand still rested lightly on John's right elbow.

'*Vyf!*'

'How much longer, Saski?' the man with the pistol asked in Dutch.

A thin man sitting behind the table grunted. His left hand darted and pounced, hovered, swooped, jabbed, stroked a piece of paper before him. 'One minute . . . one minute . . .'

'*Zes!*' The men now slapped both palms on the table.

'This one is not so co-operative,' said the man with the pistol. 'I don't think I can hold him long.'

'What the devil are you playing at?' exploded John. 'Is this the way you people welcome strangers? My purse isn't worth much, if that's what you want.'

'*Klaar!*' cried the man with the paper.

'One minute and forty-five seconds,' said a deep voice in Dutch from the shadowed end of the table. John caught the sense of time-keeping.

The man with the pistol stood up. 'Welcome, Francisco and friend!' He laid the gun beside the carcass of a chicken and came around the table. Behind him, the other men clustered around Saski.

'To the life!' exclaimed one. 'Raised eyebrows and all. A perfect Englishman!'

John understood well enough that he was a source of great amusement.

'Come in,' said Coymans. He flung an arm around Gomez. 'Do come in!' he said to John in English. 'Your life is out of danger now. But you must see that I couldn't risk letting you upset Saski.'

John breathed down hard on the anger that rose in his throat. The men were openly laughing at him now.

'Come see yourself as a stranger sees you,' ordered Coymans. 'Before his eyes are fogged by your first word or act. See yourself, absolute and pure. At a beginning. In the moment before our friendship has begun to transform us both, as it must, like the sea and a stone, each working on the other.' He leaned and plucked the paper from Saski's hands.

John had been caught on the page, in loose energetic lines. Without detail, but real as a bird in flight. Poised, both alarmed and puzzled. Black eyebrows raised in a startled inverted 'v'. Hand on knife, ready to fight but weighing the need. Gomez shadowy at his back. He might have been baited for sport, but it was an impressive trick.

He laughed. 'Is Saski always so honest?'

The thin man behind the table passed over another drawing. Coymans showed it to John. It was of Coymans proffering the first drawing, leaning forward, his face reaching eagerly for John's attention, hair wild with drink and the late hour, mock supplication in the quick lines which captured his wide shoulders and arms.

'One minute and thirteen seconds,' said the deep voice from the far end of the table.

'Forgiven?' asked Coymans.

'I forgive the fright,' said John. 'Your manners need a little more in the way of apology.'

'A glass of beer? A song? A verse?' asked Coymans. 'Francisco, what does this new young man of yours need to make him content? The maid, by the way, is mine.'

'Wait!' cried Saski. His left hand made a fierce short scribble. 'Done!' He held up Gomez. The still watcher. Body hardly there, just a few vertical lines, everything in the eyes and the hard little moustaches.

'One minute and ten seconds! His best time of the night!' cried the time-keeper.

'But it's not complete!' complained another man. 'He never finishes!'

'What's left out that anyone needs?' demanded Coymans. 'Find some Flemish wine for Saski!'

John and Gomez seated themselves in the chaos of picture passing, incomprehensible jokes, beer and wine pouring,

Coymans bellowing, and a rush of serving women in from the kitchen with castles of dried fruit and rounded drums of black, yellow and orange cheeses. At the centre of the mêlée sat Saski, still and intent. Only his eyes moved, and his left hand, which darted, pecked, slid and caught life on the wing like a swift plucking a gnat from the air.

'You haven't answered me, young man,' said Coymans. 'What do you lack? *Que voulez vous?*'

'His name is John Nightingale,' said Gomez. 'You must speak politely to him for a while, Justus. You're still atoning.'

'So, what do you want then, Mister Englishman John Nightingale?' repeated Coymans. He leaned forward on the table. The fine linen of his puffed shirtsleeves bunched up around his ears and the candlelight shone red through the halo of his curling hair.

John's brown hand shot across the linen cloth and closed on the pistol that lay beside the chicken bones. He picked it up and cocked it. He leaned both elbows on the table and pointed the gun directly into Coymans's face. His grey eyes were as flat and steely as the water of the Zuider Zee.

'I want you to make me very rich, Mister Dutchman Coymans.'

This time, the maid froze with a jug in her hand, half-way to pouring.

The muscles of Coymans's face clamped themselves tight to his large, square skull. His eyes were two reflected candle flames.

'Please don't move,' said John. He listened for the telltale rustle of cloth behind him but heard only the silence of men holding their breath.

'I don't have my purse on me,' said Coymans. He raised his voice. 'Do any of you, my friends, happen to have yours here to satisfy this gentleman?'

'No one moves,' said John. 'Translate, Senhor Gomez!' He risked a quick, malevolent look over his shoulder at the others seated around the table. Then he looked at the artist. 'Saski?'

'*Klaar*.' With an impassive face, the thin artist shoved a paper across the table between Coymans and John. Drawn in swift, fleeting line, Coymans stared into the barrel of the pistol. Among the untidy rucks, springing hair, wide shining cheeks and moustaches, Saski had planted two small, astonished eyes darkened by fear.

'One minute and thirty seconds,' said the time-keeper. He held up one finger and the stump of another cut off at the first joint, for John to count. Laughter and relief exploded around the table. Only Coymans and Gomez did not join in.

John uncocked the pistol, turned it and handed it back to Coymans. 'Forgiven?' he asked.

Coymans took the pistol. He looked down at it reflectively for a moment. 'Of course. I already know the worst about myself. I have for years, or I would never have let friend Saski into my house.'

'Only a very brave man invites reminders,' said John. 'I salute you.'

Coymans put the pistol out of sight. He shook himself. Brushed his moustaches one after the other with quick swipes of his broad hand. He raised his voice to its former raucous level. 'What graciousness the English have, don't you think? As smooth with their words as their weapons! If one only knew which it was going to be! Let's have beer down at this end, please! Beer for the entertainers! *Bier*! We don't perform for free. My glass is empty and Mr Englishman John Nightingale has never had his filled. For shame!'

The conversation swelled again. Glasses rose and fell. Pipe smoke climbed into the shadows of the ceiling like tiny fakirs' ropes. Saski watched and drew with his little stylus of black lead wrapped in string.

English antimony, or *grafio piombino*, from the blackness of the lines, noted John in passing interest. He himself had and treasured such a pencil, less cumbersome than pen and ink for drawing live specimens in a field or thicket. He sat alert, sifting for meaning in the confusion of alien sounds. He tried to judge what kind of men these were, but wine and relaxation had blurred them. He watched Gomez speak. The old man was known to these men but was clearly not of them. But how does one judge foreigners? The pistol was still there even if not visible. He felt Coymans touch his arm.

'You want to become rich?' asked Coymans quietly. 'Even without my purse, I'm the right man.'

'I *need* to become rich,' replied John.

'Need relative or need absolute?'

'Need absolute.'

'I see.' Coymans leaned back in his chair. 'How much do you have to work with?'

'Enough.'

'Now, now, Mr Nightingale. That's no help. Are you here to buy ships or pies? If I am to build your fortune, I must know whether I'm using straw or Baltic oak.'

John considered the vulnerability of Arthur, under the eaves of the widow's house on the Singel, perched on the chest with his pistol clutched to his chest. 'Your skills don't run to straw?'

'Maybe, if you're willing to risk all your straws.'

'I can't risk any. There is no room for risk.'

Coymans snorted. 'You want riches without risk?'

'That's right.'

Coymans's derision became open. 'There's no such thing, my friend.'

'Then I must create it for the first time.'

'Oh,' cried Coymans to the ceiling, palms upward, imploring the deities. 'Wonderful! Listen to the Englishman! He has descended on my little country to bring forth miracles. A new Creation. Riches without risk – a "first time" which has eluded even me all these years.'

'Is this the first time your countrymen have gone collectively mad?' asked John. 'Or do they do it with frequency?'

Coymans stilled again. 'I take your point ... Are you a law-abiding man?'

John did not falter. 'Of course.'

'That's a pity,' said Coymans. 'I thought for a moment I saw one way out of your dilemma.' He studied John, working his mouth reflectively so that his moustaches see-sawed back and forth like a rower's oars. 'Never mind. Why don't you come with me up into my parlour. We can talk without all this noise from my ruffian friends.'

'How rich is rich?' Coymans squatted on his heels in front of the fire that burned more for light than for heat. Above his head, a carved wooden Neptune flung a carved wooden net across the mantelpiece at three wooden seahorses. 'It's time for candour.'

John looked around curiously.

They were in a panelled room with shutters pulled tight. The windows, when open, would give a view over the main street in front of the house and along the narrow canal beside it. Across the main street, Coymans would have a fair view up the large canal of any boats coming into the city from St Anthony's Gate. He would also be able to see which small side channel they might slip into. Apart from one heavy oak table, an inlaid cabinet on a stand and two chairs, the room was bleak. No clues to its owner. No tulips. No flowers of any kind.

There were pictures in heavy gilded frames, more than a hundred, but instead of decorating the walls, they leaned in stacks on the floor, naked canvas and board backs turned to the visitor's eye. A large leather-bound portfolio leaked sliding sheets onto the oak tabletop without giving away more than the odd sketched hand or etched cloud top.

'Come,' said Coymans. 'Away from the dangerous brigands

downstairs, you can safely tell me how much straw you have tucked into your bags.'

'I need to make four thousand pounds into twenty thousand.'

'In how long?'

'Two weeks.'

Coymans stood up. 'You want to multiply your money five times, in two weeks, without breaking any laws? Stop wasting my time.'

'Fine.' John turned to leave.

'Where are you going?' asked Coymans.

'To ask Senhor Gomez for another introduction.'

'Nah . . . nah, don't leap off like a startled toad,' said Coymans. 'Sit down.' He pointed to one of the two chairs. 'I lied. You're not wasting my time. I was merely softening you up before I tell you my rate of commission.'

John laughed and sat. 'If it's that high, I can't afford you.'

'Twenty per cent,' said Coymans, 'but only of profits. There are knaves and trimmers here in Amsterdam who would try to take commission on the entire sum invested, win or lose.' He stood with his arms thrown wide, inviting possibility into his smiling embrace.

'You make me my twenty thousand,' said John, 'And you can have anything more that my four thousand breeds.'

'You are either very ignorant or very dangerous,' said Coymans. 'I must find out which – your stone to my sea, friend. The grinding begins.'

John recrossed his elegant legs. Next to Coymans, he looked sleek and very still. Red lights from the fire quivered on his hair. 'I thought I was merely asking to buy and sell some tulip bulbs. You are a tulip dealer? You sound more like a diamond cutter and appear to deal in art.' He glanced toward a leaning rick of paintings.

'I'm not a tulip breeder like Bols, Barent Cardoes or Jan van Damme,' said Coymans. 'I don't grow the things, just buy and sell. That's why I live comfortably here in the shadow of Amsterdam's wall, while they still splash around out on their reclaimed mudflats near Haarlem.'

'Cardoes was the first to breed the "Princes" range of fringed tulips,' said John. 'Can't he afford a palace yet?'

Coymans suddenly looked angry. 'If you want a connoisseur, go somewhere else. But Cardoes and van Damme won't make you any bricks from your straw, my friend. They just grow tulips; I make the money!'

John cocked his head like Cassie the staghound. Coymans's type was new to him. Habits and behaviour unknown. Venom undetermined. But he heard sharp fierce teeth snap in the blur of geniality. 'Money will do for the moment,' he said.

'When can you bring me your four thousand pounds? The sooner I start, the sooner you'll have your bricks.'

John shook his head. With a silent thanks to Samuel Hazelton, he said, 'I can speculate without specie. I'll have it for you by the time any payment is due.'

Coymans nodded in vigorous approval. 'Well refused! There are those in Amsterdam who would have run away with your money, if you had been silly enough to hand it over. Meet me here tomorrow night to hear how we fared. Dine with me.' It was a cheerful order.

'I would like to come with you tomorrow,' said John firmly.

Coymans's eyes blinked and chilled another degree.

'As a disciple,' said John. 'To learn about breeding gold – my experience is sadly limited to sheep and cabbages.'

The moustaches see-sawed in consideration. 'Meet me tomorrow morning on the Dam, then, just before noon. Beside the Weigh House. You will need enough in your purse for wine and meat for several friends – think generously. As you insist, I'll teach you to go trading in the wind.'

'Can't you instruct me a little tonight?' It would be hard enough trying to follow matters in a foreign language.

Coymans stood unusually still for a few seconds. The small,

chilly eyes wandered over John's face. Then he threw open the door.

'MARIKA!' he bellowed into the stairwell. 'Mr Nightingale thirsts for enlightenment. Bring him our sample book. At once! He's a man in a hurry!'

John heard a young woman's voice, sharp and unrushed, downstairs in the tiled hall. He wondered if she was the maid who had cleared the table so placidly while Coymans pointed a pistol at one of his guests.

Light footsteps climbed the creaking oak staircase. The young woman who came into the room was nearly as tall as John. She clutched in her arms a leather-covered box which hid her upper body. For a second, John thought she had two heads. One face visible above the leather box was long, strong, smiling, blue-eyed and built of seductive curves. It was surrounded by a springing confusion of hair like Coymans's, but light gold rather than tawny. The other face was small and grey with a pale centre, in the middle of which sat two bright, malevolent black eyes.

'My sister, Marika,' said Coymans. 'Dearest, Mr Nightingale is English; he is also a new client. I want you to seduce him, befuddle his senses, and generally make him putty in my hands.'

John bowed. The young woman smiled, asking John's understanding for her brother. She put the box on the table. 'I can't imagine why Justus still takes my obedience for granted,' she said in only slightly accented English. 'You and I will decide, Mr Nightingale, whether or not, and how far, I am to carry out his instructions.'

On her shoulder, the monkey bared its teeth at John.

After his first shock, John hardly noticed the monkey. Marika Coymans was two women in one, both beautiful but totally opposed, woman and baby, open and closed, wide meadow and exquisite walled garden.

Her high, wide forehead and firm chin were noble. Their

generous spaces and open seas would have sat well on the goddess Athena. In contrast, the centre of her face was a delicate, slightly crowded landscape of curves. Her arched nostrils (with the faintest suggestion of extra flesh on the tip of her long straight nose) hovered close above the tight sweet curves of a small, soft mouth. The top arch of her rounded chin hugged the ripeness of her lower lip. The centre of her face was not even Venus, but Cupid as a very young child. Her large heavy-lidded eyes, both knowing and amused, told him that she knew very well how much she had disconcerted him.

John tried to calculate her age. She had the self-possession and dignity of an older woman, much older than Cat who was probably eight years her senior, but her skin was as fresh as new leaves. She might be no more than twenty.

When she had placed the leather box on the single table, he saw the shoulders of a youth and a waist shamelessly loose in its girdle. But her hands were softly delicate like her mouth and nostrils. She rested them, and their tapered fingers, against her tall body as if offering them refuge. Then one hand moved to the hollow below her throat while the other found safety in the monkey's grey fur.

John's fingertips itched to explore the luxurious softness of her flesh. Even its slight excess, as under the curve of her jawbone, seduced, like the exposed quarter-globes of her breasts that were cut by the hard line of her bodice top. He thrust his hands behind his back lest they unwittingly betray him. A treacherous warmth grew in his thighs and groin.

Silently, he cursed. The odds on getting his throat cut in the next two weeks were high enough as it was. The worst of it was, Marika Coymans knew of the itch in his hands and the warmth in his groin. He saw the knowledge in her assessing gaze, as steady as her brother's but less chilly.

'I must go see that my guests haven't stolen their plates,' said Coymans. 'Poets and artists believe they have a right to be sustained on this earth by clods like myself. Bring him down, dearest, when you have finished.'

John heard his heavy footsteps creak down the wooden staircase to the ground floor.

The monkey braced its haunches and flew through the air onto Neptune's wooden crown, above the burning fire. Marika Coymans opened the leather box and lifted out a large watercolour painting.

'Some of the bulbs my brother handles ... *The Prince of Denmark*.' She laid the painting out for John to see.

'*The Prince*?' His voice rose. Flowers at last, but not as he had expected.

A half-naked woman stared boldly from the paper, one foot a little forward as if she wanted to step out of the flat plane. With one hand, she offered the viewer her right breast. In her other hand, she held a white and wine-coloured tulip.

'A rose, feathered variety,' Marika said demurely. 'A pure white body with burgundy flames. Appreciating rapidly in value. I believe that Justus sold five yesterday for eight thousand florins.'

She lifted another painting from the box. 'And now a rose, flamed tulip. *Diana*.'

Tulips replaced arrows in the quiver of the goddess, who carried a bow and wore only a wisp of veil.

'You will see that *Diana* differs from the *Prince* only in having a smaller proportion of white. And, although you can't tell without touching a real bloom, the petals are a little crisper.'

'A very fine texture,' said John gravely. He kept his hands clasped tightly behind his back.

'And next, the *Yellow Crown*,' said Marika, equally gravely. 'A bizarre, flamed.' A single red and gold bloom lay across the full, rounded belly of a reclining houri. 'Not so rare as *Semper Augustus*, but with more potential to rise.'

Like myself, thought John. And the minx knows it perfectly

well. He had to swallow before he could speak. 'They are all most persuasive, but I was in the net, mistress, before you began. Your brother and I had agreed. Why all this *parabola*?'

Marika looked at him with wide, blue-eyed astonishment only faintly tinged with mockery. 'For fun! Why else? Aren't you enjoying yourself?'

John swallowed again and met her eyes assessingly. If she had shown him these pictures at Hawkridge House, he would have concluded that she was a whore. Here, he was unsure. She was from what seemed, by the house and clothes, a solid commercial family. Perhaps Dutch women were much freer by nature . . . not all . . . there was also Mevrouw Padtbrugge.

Marika's blue eyes darkened with apparent concern. 'Is fun not allowed in England? Perhaps your king keeps it all for himself and his French wife?'

John felt a tug at his left knee. He looked down. The monkey had descended unseen from the overmantel and untied his left garter. Its fingers picked at his boot top. Then it pulled out the top of his stocking and scrabbled among the hairs on his calf.

John shouted with more irritation than he had intended. The monkey leaped in great arcs from floor to table to window ledge to a chairback, and into Marika's arms. It lay against her breast, long thin arms wrapped around her, glaring over its shoulder at John like a jealous child.

'A few crumbs of fun fall to the lower levels now and then,' he said. 'Even our cottagers are allowed to smile on alternate Saturdays and to guffaw on saints' days in the summer.'

Marika stroked the monkey's furry skull while it gazed up at her through its long lashes. She gazed at John through hers. 'Do those guffawing cottagers like being teased any more than you do?'

I will tear that damned monkey out of her arms and kiss her, thought John. He saw her eyes read the thought.

Or I must retreat. I've been made a fool of twice already

tonight. And I want her brother to deal for me, not run me through with his sword.

'I came to the Low Countries to do business with your brother, madam. As you are clearly aware, I find you most charming. But, if you will forgive me, you are unfortunately also beside the point.'

She bent her neck and kissed the monkey's furry skull. Tendrils of gold hair bounced and slid gently on the long sweet curve of her strong neck. John watched her press her lips against the monkey's head. She raised her eyes and caught him watching.

Marika smiled, a blow to his chest. The corners of her mouth pulled back into the abundance of her cheeks. The central point of her upper lip tightened against her white teeth. She stood smiling and gently stroking the monkey's back. She ran a creamy hand down the creature's spine and drew the coiled tail between the knuckles of her hand.

'You must make friends with Erasmus first,' she said. 'Or you'll get nowhere with my brother.'

John stood stubbornly in place. Lord help me, he thought.

She held his eyes. 'Come.'

John crossed to her slowly and ran his forefinger gently down the monkey's back.

'That's nice,' she said, still smiling, still holding his eyes. 'He likes it like that.'

Her ease and arrogance suddenly enraged John. Protected by her family and position, she was acting like a harlot. 'Must I take Erasmus to bed before I can get anywhere?'

'Oh no, he just comes along.'

Why?

John marched ferociously along the reflecting strip of the canal back to the widow's house. She wasn't struck by a bolt of love, not within a quarter-hour of uncomfortable talk. Why all those theatricals from both sister and brother? Why

226

does Coymans want me humiliated, dazed, befuddled, and puttified?

He glanced behind to see if he was being followed.

Take warning, you country bumpkin. Even if that's only their natural humour and means nothing more, you're among strange beasts here, for sure!

He checked behind again, but the thick darkness of the narrow side alleys could have hidden a battalion of Coymans's spies. And there was still life in the streets though the midnight had been called long ago. On Hawkridge estate, John would have distinguished instantly and finely between noises that belonged and those that did not.

He leaned for a while in a shadow, to watch the street. If Coymans learned where he was lodging, that would be four thousand easy pounds, with no dealing needed.

I must move Arthur and the money in the morning. But where?

He walked on. A cloaked shape passed behind him through a slice of yellow light from a window. He leaned against the railing of an arched bridge until the shape vanished into a house.

And that sister! That self-satisfied little witch!

His fingertips still itched to stroke her throat and lips. He had thought to escape by turning his rage into icy politeness and ironic gallantry, but Marika had seemed to enjoy his incivility, knowing perfectly well what had caused it. She had just smiled and stroked that damned animal and invited him to dine the next night.

Just for fun.

If you distrust the brother, which you do, John told himself, then you must fear the sister just as much.

The street rose and fell like sea waves beneath his feet, up over the arches of bridges high enough for folded masts to pass beneath, then down to quayside level again. John swam back through a darkness thick with shoals of alien fish and hauled himself up around the mast at the centre of the widow's corkscrew stairs. He was delighted, at the top, to find himself looking up into the barrel of Arthur's gun.

Eight

June 3, 1636. Much use here of plants as pure ornament.
Monkeys kept as ladies' pets. Most produce in market
of familiar sorts.

Journal of John Nightingale, known as John Graffham.

'Hell's teeth!' said John the next morning. 'We'd as well try
to move a herd of sheep in secret!'

Even broken down into separate bundles, the money rattled
and clinked like prison chains. And he couldn't think where
better to take it. That snap of teeth in the midst of Coymans's
geniality had set him zig-zagging like a frightened hare.

Arthur said, 'I felt safe enough up here with the rope pulled
in and only those stairs to watch.'

John nodded. He didn't like it, but for the moment he
couldn't think of better. Mevrouw Padtbrugge seemed an
unlikely confederate for thieves. But then, how could he be
sure? In England, he would have trusted his sense of her.

Arthur frowned as he studied his employer.

'What's wrong, man?' snapped John.

'It's not like you to shilly-shally. If you're that worried, I'm
terrified!'

'I'm fine!' Too many little piglings back at Hawkridge
depend on it.

He left Arthur settled in for a long, boring day on guard.

Coymans was waiting in the open space of the Dam, with

the Bourse at its top, the mast-filled water of the Damrak at its bottom, and the pale grey tower of the New Church rising above the cluster of red-roofed houses on the right. Between the church and the side of the Damrak stood the chunky, porticoed Weigh House, where the swelling wealth of Holland was weighed and assayed before it rolled onward in a golden wave from the ships into the pockets of the merchants and the laps of their wives. Neptune and Fortune twirled idly on their iron spikes at either end of the Weigh House roof.

Far below Neptune's trident, on the stone quayside, Coymans leaned against a bollard full-bellied with coiled, tarry ropes. The masts of anchored ships marked languorous time in gentle arcs behind the two red feathers of his vast wide-brimmed hat.

'Are you still law-abiding this morning?' Coymans looked over John's shoulder into the middle distance before finding his eyes.

'Yes,' said John shortly.

'Too bad. I've been sitting here thinking about how to make you rich without risk to your four thousand. The easiest way, of course, with no financial risk at all, is simply to sell bulbs you don't have and never intend to have.'

'That doesn't sound risk-free.' John's eyes were drawn down to the deck of the ship below him where crates were being swung up on to the quay with a surprising delicacy.

'That's porcelain from China. *Kraacke-ware*.' Coymans raised his arm and shouted a greeting across the heads of the stevedores to a black-dressed man on the deck. '. . . I didn't say it would be risk-free. I thought you were only worried about risk to your money. You didn't seem that concerned last night about your neck.'

'It comes close after the money,' said John.

'You'll never make a fraudster, then!' Coymans set off briskly across the crowded square, dodging porters stooped over low-slung wheelbarrows. 'Perhaps just as well. That plan of mine would need a quick exit back to England and prevent your return for quite some time. Which would be a pity, as I like you more and more each minute.' Coymans flashed his white teeth in John's direction. 'And, of course, with such a trick, I couldn't introduce you to a *collegium* myself – I must continue to live here. Still, it's worth thinking about . . . no investment, except in wine money and a little politic good fellowship.'

'Dutch buyers would trust an Englishman?' asked John drily.

They followed the side of the Bourse away from the sea front, towards the toe of the Amsterdam sock.

'Of course not! You'd have to work through a broker. But I could find one or two willing to take advantage, or so they would think, of an ignorant foreigner. They'd slaver over you until you had slipped away, and it was too late.'

'How lucky I am to have met a different breed!'

Coymans was merely amused by this exchange. 'You're lucky you ran into Gomez who knew where to bring you to find what you need!'

They turned and twisted through alleys, crossed four canals, and passed through a flower market where the cobbles bloomed like a spring field. Coymans stopped.

'Here we are. At the *emporium mundi*. The heart of the world's market. The White Cat.'

John peered from the bright morning into the brown shadows of a tavern. Tobacco smoke coiled, rose and spread into a haze against a beamed ceiling. Glasses clattered and clinked. Voices muttered and rumbled amid hawking, spitting and coughs. Cloaks and hats slid from chairs. Women leaned on men's shoulders with a bright, false interest.

'In there, it's still last night.'

'No, no!' cried Coymans. 'In there, it's already tomorrow night! Forget the past. At the heart of the world's market, the future is about to arrive!'

Coymans swept through the shadows of the White Cat, cape aswirl, arms and voice raised in greetings. John slipped after him. As he listened to the answering shouts and met curious eyes, he thought that he might as well have hired a trumpeter to herald his arrival in the Dutch tulip trade.

He lifted a woman's enquiring hand from his shoulder, kissed it gallantly and gave it back to its owner with a grimace of regret. At the Bourse on the Rokin he had recognized at least the hubbub of a market. In the lunatic darting and hand-slapping he had seen the energy of transactions. These men in the White Cat lolled like happy frogs, in a thick brew of smoke and beer. But Coymans did not stop in the large front room. He led John at amazing speed, given the number of dear friends he encountered, through a heavy panelled door on one side of the great fireplace at the back of the room.

The room behind was as large as the front room but had its shutters closed. Here the night still ruled entirely. John wanted to flee. Men were packed almost shoulder to shoulder – no women back here. Their noise racketed off the dark walls. The bones of their faces gleamed orange in the light of dozens of candles in sconces on the walls, on the tables, on stands that grew from the floor like fiery trees. As he and Coymans poised briefly in the door, John sensed the fractional pause that follows the plop of a fat grub onto the water above a school of hungry fish. Then the furore resumed.

Coymans was mobbed.

'What are you buying today, Justus? What is it today? *The Widow*? Is it *The Widow*?' they implored him. 'Noble or common, Coymans . . . how do you stand today?' Men pulled at his sleeves, tried to stop him with a hand on his massive chest.

'Wait and watch,' said Coymans. 'And have your florins ready.'

John watched and tried to understand. A man breathed nonsense into his ear.

'In English or Latin,' said John. 'I don't speak Dutch.'

'Switzers,' murmured the man in a warm gust. 'Tell Coymans. Ortiz and Jacobs, both buying in secret at the Petticoat. Tell no one else. I'm in for three thousand florins.'

'Switzers?' John twisted his head to see the man's eyes. 'But those are some of the most ordinary! I planted two bushels in my own garden this spring, for a few pounds!'

The man looked amused, tapped his nose and repeated, 'Tell Coymans. He understands.' He left John abruptly.

Coymans's hand found John's arm and reeled him through the crowd like a recalcitrant fish. 'Your purse, my friend!'

'What am I buying? You've explained nothing yet.'

'You're buying your name on the slate. As a paid-up member of the *collegium*. It's the only way you're allowed to deal. Quickly!' Coymans stopped a small, neatly-bearded man in black silk and a white cap tied under his chin. He switched back to Dutch. 'A new member for you, Snoeck. A generous Englishman!'

John caught the word 'Englishman'.

'A new member,' Coymans repeated in Latin, for John's benefit. He counted out florins from John's purse.

The small man in black nodded politely at John and asked Coymans in Dutch, 'Do you vouch for him? What surety do we have?'

'I'll do all his dealing,' said Coymans. 'He just pays.'

The man laughed. It was friendly enough, but John flexed his fingers and worked to keep his face both honest and enthusiastic. He could not control the flush of annoyance which crept higher and higher above his white lace collar.

I wish I spoke the bloody language! he thought. It's like being a child with the adults making knowing remarks over your head.

The small man pushed between chairs and tables to a slate six feet high that was fastened to the back wall. He wrote John's name with a flourish and pointed him out to the rest.

Three boys in aprons passed out tankards of ale. John's health was drunk.

'Now what?' John asked Coymans.

'Now you deal.'

There was not one tulip bulb in sight.

'How?' asked John.

'Leave it to me.'

Reluctantly, John left it to Coymans. For the moment. He wondered whether Hazelton and the others had overestimated himself or underestimated the difficulties.

Coymans abandoned him. John watched the two red feathers bob and sway through the candlelight. Once they disappeared. Then John located Coymans deep in a huddle in a corner beside the fireplace with the man who was three thousand florins into Switzers.

'Ten florins for wine and food, please,' said the small man in black politely.

'I paid before.'

'No, no. That was for membership. This is wine money.'

John handed it over. A sickening thought which he had been resisting suddenly grew insistent. What if Coymans were a straightforward cheat? He and his colleagues might continue to cozen John as long as he was simple enough to keep handing over his cash. Coymans would have to make nineteen thousand pounds before it would no longer be easier for him simply to steal John's four thousand.

He studied Coymans across the room. The man was known here. If this place really was a bourse (but how could he tell for sure?) then Coymans appeared to be a dealer. John was happier with his logic than with the suppositions on which it balanced.

Coymans slapped hands with a large man in gold and blue who invaded space almost as much as he did. Three other men rushed up with eager questions.

John's stomach unclenched slightly. Coymans was a rogue,

without doubt, but not on the scale of wine and slate money. His house, his paintings, his table surrounded by toadying guests, his sister's self-satisfaction, were fruits of wickedness on a far grander scale.

'All right, let's go.' Coymans suddenly reappeared. 'Once you've signed this for the notary upstairs. Business is over for the day.' He pressed his way out through a mob of questioners like a king through a crowd of beggars.

'Switzers,' he said to their eager faces. 'Switzers. Yes, it's true. I bought Switzers. As many as I could.'

John heard the word 'Switzers' fall like negligently tossed coins.

'You'll dine with me tonight? My sister's invitation is even more fervent than my own!' Coymans doffed his hat with mock civility. 'Come at six o'clock. And now, please excuse me. The Dam is that way . . . just follow the canal.'

'Wait!' John seized Coymans firmly by the arm. 'I have a condition for being your new toy – and your sister's. You must tell me what the devil is going on! What happened in the White Cat?'

Irritation flashed in and out of Coymans's eyes. 'You bought six thousand florins' worth of Switzers. Two hundred bushels.'

'Switzers!' John exploded. His stomach filled with ice. 'The most ordinary garden type after the plain yellow and red Goudas! What happened to your fabulously valuable *Diana* and *Yellow Crown* with such potential to rise, as your sister assured me last night? Why did you waste my money on the cheapest sort?'

Coymans sighed. 'The type we buy is irrelevant. Our only concern is what happens to their price between the time we buy and the time we sell. Switzers can rise as well as Imperials and Bizarres. By the bulb, perhaps not so much. But, my cynical friend, you own two hundred bushels of the things!'

'How much did you pay?'

The irritation returned. 'Work the total out for yourself. Thirty pounds per bushel, due in five days.'

'That's much more than I paid last autumn.'

'Of course. That is the whole point, which you so far fail to grasp.'

'I'm trying,' said John. 'Most honestly, I am trying.'

Coymans beamed again. Then he laughed. 'You look like a bullock expecting to be slaughtered. Don't worry. Come to dinner. Drink too much. Wait for tomorrow. Then you will understand. Try to relish the delicious suspense.' He leaned his tawny whiskers close to John's darker curly head. 'Let go of what you think is valuable, my scholarly friend. You're in this with me for only two things – florins and fun. Neither is worth much without the other. Together, they're worth more than all the rest.'

It was the first thing Coymans had said that John believed. 'Until six o'clock?'

John nodded. He watched the broad shoulders and bobbing red feathers vanish around the corner of a narrow street. Florins and fun. It made sense of all the rest – the theatricals, the energy, the noise. The man was in it for fun as well as money.

I must keep my eye on my purse, my hand on my sword and endeavour to be as much fun as possible.

John climbed the stone steps to the high *stoep* that raised the front door of Coymans's house above flood level. The door stood open to let in the evening sun. John peered through bright motes of dust caught in shafts of sunlight. From the far wall of the large entrance hall paved in squares of black and white marble, a life-sized portrait of a man who was not quite Justus Coymans gazed sternly back. In one large fur-cuffed hand he held a full purse, in the other a skull. A globe stood on the painted table beside him. John heard the fragile, watery notes of a virginal. As he stepped inside the house, the music stopped.

Marika framed herself in a doorway with the monkey in her arms. It hung on her like a heavy grey girdle, strapped on by its long arms with knife-edges of fur along the bones. Behind her, in the wood-panelled room, the virginal's lid was up. A chair had been hastily pushed back and abandoned. A skirt flicked in the corner of John's eye as the maid who had been watching out for him slipped away to the back of the house.

When he looked at Marika, John was relieved. She was pretty enough, but no witch, just a young woman with unnaturally soft skin and a strange contradiction in the lines of her face.

She greeted him cordially.

A sufficiently hungry fish can imagine a worm dangling where there isn't one, John rebuked himself. I was over-nervous last night. Misled by foreign manners. He felt a twitch of disappointment.

'Come into my music room,' said Marika. 'I am going to keep you for myself a little, so we can talk when Justus isn't telling us what to do. I like to practise my English. It isn't so good as my French, but then I have spoken that since I was a baby.'

John noted the casual riches of the room – the paintings, the porcelain, the Turkey rugs, Venetian mirrors, a fine globe (the same one that was in the portrait in the hall), and a marble boar. There were no flowers except in frames.

'Please sit down.' She pointed him to a chair beside a table covered with a Turkey rug. 'My brother is still talking business. He is always talking business!' She folded her tall, strong-shouldered body gracefully onto another chair and looked at John expectantly. The wide forehead was serene as an evening sky, but her baby's mouth curved with wicked delight.

John said how glad he was to be there, how gracious the invitation. He complimented her English – it needed no practice to improve its manifest perfection. He assured himself that he felt nothing more today than curiosity. Why that smile of wicked delight?

John looked away from her mouth, at the sheet music on the rug-covered table, at a chitarrone with two broken strings that leaned against the virginal. He glanced again at the paintings on the walls. Why that expectancy? What was the girl waiting for? Was there something he was supposed to say? He began to feel a little cross.

The monkey unclasped itself from Marika's neck and picked at the lace edging of her sleeve, its face closed and intent. Then the small black fingers turned with equal intensity to the pursuit of a flea on its own grey furry thigh. John was reminded briefly of Aunt Margaret's restlessly moving fingers. Then he saw what Marika was waiting for him to see.

She had seated herself directly below a large painting. Above her golden head, a naked blonde Pomona, the Roman goddess of fruit and fruiting trees, poured a cascade of apples, cherries, oranges, plums, grapes and peaches into the arms of an amazed and grateful shepherd (or farmer) in vaguely classical, rustic dress. A mountain of fruit tumbled from a cart that was just visible behind her in a landscape of rocks and hazy columns of broken temples, more Italian than Dutch.

The goddess, a little larger than life, wore only an intricately detailed necklace, pearl eardrops and a wisp of gossamer that floated up from her shoulder like a wing. She had wide shoulders and long, firm arms strong enough to carry the earth's bounty. Her flesh was as warm and juicy as her fruit, and the painter had dotted her nipples with the exact same red as the cherries. Both her hair and her face were Marika's.

In spite of himself, John read the goddess's body and imag-

238

ined the flesh that sat across from him hidden inside layers of buckram, wadding and silk.

This young Dutchwoman was outrageous. And he did not believe that it was simply for sudden love of himself. She was toying with him, like her brother. He did not like it. He also thanked the Lord that the thick fabric of his doublet hid his stiffening member.

'Do you like it?' Her eyes gleamed.

'A very fine work,' said John solemnly. 'Can you explain the allegory? The goddess I recognize.'

The monkey leaped from Marika's lap onto the table and began to spin the globe.

'You will note, then,' said Marika, smoothing her skirts, 'that the man to whom the goddess gives her gifts is dressed in simple clothes. He is an ordinary man, a humble farmer, not a prince or nobleman. We have no princes in Holland. The richness of the earth is for everyone. That is the moral of the painting.'

Were her nipples really that colour of fresh pale red, or were they merely the painter's device?

'Are you shocked?' she asked.

'Would yes or no amuse you most?'

The delicate pink mouth tightened.

I've spoiled her fun, John thought. I'm supposed to blush and stammer and cross my legs.

'I had hoped to amuse you,' she said.

'Oh, you do amuse me, please have no fear.'

'*Merde* to that!' she said clearly. She stretched out an arm to the monkey. 'Let's go find my brother. You were quite charming last night when you had had a little wine.'

I'm for gobbling up, thought John at dinner. As surely as the chickens, cheeses and pies. They're both toying with me. I should need no clearer warning to get out now with my skin still in one piece.

He glared down the long table across the debris of the meal, through the fog of tobacco and wood smoke. At the far end, Marika turned away from the man with whom she had been talking and gave an order to the maid. Tiny sparks from the golden light of fire and candles burned along the curves of her hair. Then she leaned forward again, stretching one white arm along the table. John could not hear her words but he felt the force which animated her. He watched her mouth curve around the words she was pouring out to a man of about his own age.

Any of us will do as well as the next, John thought sourly. He watched her drinking in the man's words to her. She shook her head impatiently, laughed in protest, barely able to keep silent until he had finished speaking.

Suddenly, she looked past her companion straight at John. Caught, he refused to look away. With a sense of unexplained terror, he saw her go still. Her blue eyes grew thoughtful. Her wide smooth brow tightened slightly into a small frown. John was an object under deep consideration.

What was she thinking, inside that stillness? He had to know.

Then she acknowledged him as another living creature. The curves of her cheeks rounded. Her upper lip lifted away from the neat white teeth. Her eyes gleamed. Her energy rolled down the table at him like a blast of cannon fire.

The calculation of that smile freed John from the terror stirred in him by her stillness. He nodded curtly. He decided that he could handle a professional flirt. Even one with a brother who had seemed to be acting as her pimp. As long as he remembered that it was all in the name of business.

'Do so many always dine at your table?' John asked Coymans, at the head of the table on his left. Saski sat across from John, as silent as ever, left hand darting and scraping across his paper.

'Sometimes more. I like to scatter corn for the flock to peck at.' Coymans had grown red-eyed with drink. His great head sank down heavily between his shoulders. 'Some think me a fool for my largesse.' He glanced at Saski. 'But that suits me. Never seem too sharp, Englishman. Never let your true edge show. I don't know anything about you, but I already know you too well for your own sake.'

Another warning, thought John.

Voices shouted at the other end of the table. The monkey, Erasmus, uncurled from whatever perch he had been lurking on, flew through the air like a familiar. He landed, plop, on shoulders, hats, unwary laps. He coiled and leaped, chittering and rattling his teeth in excitement. From one shoulder he reached down and snatched the white clay pipe from the smoker's mouth.

John heard Marika's laugh like a clear bird call above the roar of the men.

The monkey coiled and uncoiled in great delicate leaps down the table among the glasses and knives. He dropped the white clay pipe among pieces of broken bread and reached out a black naked palm to untie one of the points that held John's right sleeve to his doublet.

Even her bloody pet takes liberties with me, thought John. The animal regarded him with clear dislike. When it reached out again, he lightly slapped its paw away. It bared its teeth.

One of the Dutch guests called out something which made the others howl with laughter.

'Said that the ape's getting you ready for my sister,' said Coymans. 'You shouldn't discourage it.' He seemed amused.

'And you're not slitting your corn back out of his gizzard?'

'It's all in fun,' said Coymans. He lowered his eyes and drank deeply from his glass.

Get out! John told himself. There's more than money at risk here.

Saski passed him a drawing across the table. It was Marika's moment of stillness.

After dinner, the cards and dice came out. Marika leaned on John's shoulder while he played. He lost a handful of *stuyvers*.

'Come,' she whispered in his ear. 'I want to talk again.'

'Careful,' said Coymans. 'You'll make the rest jealous.'

John pushed back his chair with good grace, in the midst of a bawdy clamour. Saski drew but kept the paper to himself. Marika took a candle and led John back into the music parlour. The room felt very silent after the dining-room.

'Why does it make you so angry if I do the wooing?' asked Marika.

'It's your reasons for wooing, madam.'

'It's what you *imagine* my reasons to be.'

'And what are they, then?'

She curved her lips deliciously. 'Erasmus likes you.'

'That's an obvious lie.'

'He hates you then.'

'Agreed. Why does that make you woo me?'

'Because he knows me better than any other creature. We have no secrets, he and I. And he can feel your thoughts. And he hates you. He's more jealous than I've seen him for years. That tells me what is the truth between us.'

She looked up the small distance between their heights. 'Do you really not feel it?'

He felt it. Heat and weakness like a mortal fever. Death, when it came, would more resistible. He raised his hands helplessly in submission. 'Of course I do.'

'Then why not take everything you can get?' said Marika. 'Even your English poets tell you that!'

She was apricots, peaches, pears, and nipples red as pomegranate seeds. John stroked downy peach skin and bit on earlobes as soft and crisp as new leaves. Her belly curved like a melon. Pomona rolled from her basket in a torrent of ripe fruits, tumbled at his feet, moistened his fingers and dazed his eyes with plenty.

'Taste me, peel me,' the goddess cried. 'Nibble me down to my core. Lick up my juices. Plant yourself in me.'

Drunk with surfeit, he pressed her like an apple.

He lay on her with the sweat chilling on his back. He raised his head just far enough to kiss the almonds of her closed eyelids. Then that wide cloud-like brow. And then, very tenderly, the soft, vulnerable baby mouth. He felt her smile beneath his lips. Her arms tightened around his neck. He felt absolutely happy and absolutely terrified.

'I must go,' he whispered.

'More,' she said. 'No! Don't go!' Her arms closed tighter. 'I'll be so cold! Stay with me!'

He relaxed his weight onto her again. How many others had lain like this? Oddly, it didn't matter. The whisper of taint stirred him.

He felt fur brush against his thigh, then a weight on his bare back, which was not Marika's hand or leg.

'Has that damned animal been here all this time?'

'Of course,' laughed Marika. 'I told you he would.'

John tried to turn his head. Erasmus was a ghost in the corner of his eye, smiling lips bared over sharp, pointed teeth and eyes like a leprechaun.

The next morning, John found Coymans leaning on the same bollard beside the Damrak. The porcelain ship below them was deserted except for one bored sailor on watch on the bow. 'Today we go to the Petticoat,' said Coymans. He showed no sign of knowing that John had left his sister's bed only a little before Matins.

They set off in the opposite direction from the day before, down a narrow street of pointed gables between the arched Bourse and the pale grey New Church.

'There's another *collegium* there,' said Coymans. 'Where

they've been stewing since yesterday like eels in ginger.'

John heard a particularly self-satisfied note in his voice. 'Did you by any chance add the ginger?'

Coymans looked startled, then delighted. 'A large fistful and a good stir!'

'Are you a master cook?'

'*Sans pareil.*' Coymans smirked in mock modesty.

John realized that he liked the man because of his open roguery, not in spite of it. The world was too full of admirable Samuel Hazeltons. He suppressed a yawn and a smile. He felt less urgent than he should about finishing his business in Amsterdam.

He wanted the day to be over, but only so that the night might come sooner.

'Explain to your apprentice, please.'

'Watch me first,' said Coymans. 'Let's see how quick you are.'

The Petticoat was grander than the White Cat, with less smoke in the front public room. Fewer women leaned their breasts against men's ears, and more of the men here wore black silk and fine wool.

'Justus!' A pink-cheeked man of about thirty years leaped up from one of the tables. He was not fat but suggested it. His soft face seemed to have bones only at the forehead and chin. John had noticed many like him on the streets. Wisps of moustache perched without conviction at the corners of his full mouth; his pink chin was without beard. His mid-brown hair, coat and collar were all simply cut. His linen shirtsleeves were merely gathered onto a band, without lace. He pushed between stools and shoulders, desperate to reach Coymans.

'Dirck Koopman,' said Coymans under his breath. 'More ambition than wit. Mynheer Koopman!' he cried.

Koopman spoke low and urgently.

The three men went back outside into the tree-lined avenue

that ran along a wide, deep canal just off the harbour. Koopman looked over his shoulder, then poured out a stream of urgent Dutch.

Coymans listened, pursed his lips and see-sawed his moustaches.

'Koopman wants to buy your Switzers,' Coymans translated for John. 'Refuse the offer.'

'How much is he offering? We want to get rid of the blasted things!'

'Just refuse!'

'Not unless you tell me what's going on. I thought we had to deal in the *collegii*.'

'That is indeed the issue.' Coymans turned to Koopman with regret. 'There's another dealer across the canal, watching us, at this moment,' he added.

The man talked with two old women and a man in a porter's apron, trying not to make too obvious his interest in Coymans and Koopman.

Koopman directed a storm of words straight at John.

'You can't afford to jeopardize your position as a reputable dealer,' interrupted Coymans.

John glanced back at him. 'Absolutely not!' he said. 'My reputation is more precious to me than my gold, etcetera.'

'Exactly!' Coymans's teeth flashed. The regret he relayed to Koopman was infinite but tinged with a sanctimony that sat ill on his wide, drink-reddened face.

Koopman continued to plead with John.

'Switzers began to rise yesterday,' explained Coymans. 'Today, the climb continues. But as you correctly pointed out yesterday, Switzers are common and many people can offer them for sale. Koopman is working on a corner. He plans to buy the rest of us out, then put up the price without a rival undercutting him.'

'Excellent. Sell him the damned things!'

Coymans shook his head unhappily, a man torn by a painful decision.

'May I suggest on your behalf that you would do better to go inside the Petticoat? Not only because you should, but because you could invite a higher offer.'

'How much higher?'

Coymans narrowed his eyes. 'You. Prefer. To go. Inside!'

'Absolutely,' said John. 'I really should go inside!'

There was intent consultation in Dutch.

'He offers a premium of ten florins per bushel to pay for the risk you would take in dealing outside the *collegium*,' said Coymans. 'We progress. Consider it, please.'

John nodded. Coymans watched Koopman.

Koopman nodded to the man across the canal. The man nodded back.

'Ah,' breathed Coymans in English, 'so it's that way. Good. We can safely proceed.'

Again, John listened to the unintelligible rush of words. Koopman had become cannier. Hot pink spots flared on his round cheeks. And now Coymans seemed to be making proposals. Koopman nodded.

'He'll pay a further fifteen florins per bushel,' announced Coymans. 'We're nearly there.'

John strained his ears as if effort could penetrate an alien tongue.

Suddenly Koopman and Coymans both nodded.

'It's done!' said Coymans. 'In your money, thirty-nine pounds per bushel, including the premium for risk for the first two hundred bushels.'

John gasped. The year before, he had paid £3 per bushel for the Switzers he planted on Hawkridge estate. Coymans had bought John's 200 bushels at only £30 the day before.

'And in addition,' said Coymans, 'he has agreed to pay . . . let me see . . . ten pounds more per bushel to allow for the price to rise – for your remaining two hundred bushels.'

'I don't have . . .' John started to say. How could he sell what he didn't own? But he swallowed. 'Whatever you advise.'

'We will meet Koopman again in two hours to sign and notarize the papers. Also to collect the money. In view of the movement in the market, Koopman has agreed to settle immediately, for all four hundred bushels. Even more . . .' the satisfaction crept into Coymans's voice again '. . . he will also waive his right to a discount for delayed delivery of the second two hundred bushels. You have ten days, free of interest charges. Accept!'

John did. But Justus Coymans had some explaining to do!

After glancing up and down the street, Koopman held out his hand. John slapped it, a little sheepishly.

When they looked back, Koopman had already approached the dealer on the other side of the canal.

'Koopman is an amateur,' said Coymans happily. 'You must never try to corner a market as wide as that. Switzers!' He snorted his disbelief. 'It seems so easy these days that every discontented fool thinks he can make his fortune. Street-sweepers, washerwomen. Koopman is a tapster!' Coymans whooped with laughter. 'Some are doing it, mind you. I've known streetsweepers cannier than judges.' He flung a friendly arm across John's shoulder. 'Wealth is the only true democracy, Englishman. Once he has it, any man is a king.'

'And now,' said John, 'unless you've urgent business, we have two whole hours in which you can explain what you have just done with my money.'

'Does it matter so long as you get your profit?'

'We're sharing the profit. I would also like to share the fun.'

Coymans stopped in the street. 'Ahhh!' he said happily. 'My friend. My true companion. I knew when you pointed my own gun at me across my own table that we were fated to be friends.' He embraced John in a great flapping of cloak.

'How can I deny such a request, from one such as you?'

'Enough, enough,' said John drily. 'Start with the ginger.'

Coymans shrugged modestly. 'I bought Switzers, too, yesterday and the day before. Big purchases. As did one or two of my friends. To start the price up. And you gave another shove yesterday. It takes only a few buyers and a lot of rumours. The beauty of this particular case is that far more people can afford to buy Switzers than the more valuable bulbs. And many small buyers push the price up just as surely as a few larger ones. The rush for Switzers is on. As Koopman has noticed.'

'And those other two hundred bushels,' said John, 'that I have promised to deliver but don't own . . . ?'

'You don't own them yet,' agreed Coymans. 'You will wait to buy them until I've pulled the ginger back out of the pot. They'll cost you much less than Koopman is paying today. Probably less than yesterday. Even more profit to meet your absolute need.'

'Is that lawful?'

'Why ever not?' Coymans sounded indignant. 'You weren't to know that I am going to dump my stock back on the market in a day or two, at less than the going price at the time. Prices will then begin to drop. But, as I lack your urgent financial need, I'll be perfectly satisfied, considering that I bought at the very bottom. I'll be rid of all my Switzers before prices drop to what I originally paid – to what you no doubt paid last autumn for yours for your garden. You just happened to arrive at the right time to buy Switzers. Another time, it might have been *Yellow Crowns* or some new form growing in secret in some back garden or hidden field.'

John became thoughtful. 'That will be a little hard on Koopman. He'll have to sell for less than he paid me today.'

'If he has any sense, he'll forget about his corner and start unloading as soon as the prices rise a little more. You saw him talking to that dealer across the canal? He might have been selling again before we were even out of sight. I may have maligned him – his wit may yet triumph over his greed.'

But what about the streetsweepers and washerwomen? wondered John. Would they find it fun when the price of Switzers fell below what they had paid?

'Of course,' added Coymans, 'while it's all quite lawful, it wouldn't do to let too many others know. My gold is worth as much as my reputation, etcetera.'

John laughed. 'You've nothing to fear from me on the subject of reputation.'

'No,' said Coymans. 'I shouldn't think so. In spite of the Latin.'

'Is it so clear that I'm a rogue?'

'You could be one of the family.'

John's growing enjoyment of his strange new temporary life suddenly chilled. After a moment he said, 'It must be done faster. This is already my third day here. I've worked it out that I've made about eleven thousand pounds. We have to move faster.'

'Faster, and without risk?' Coymans was briefly serious. 'And clean as a housewife's apron on Sunday morning? You're asking too much.'

'Am I?' John stopped in the street and fixed Coymans with the full force of his gaze. 'In truth?'

He had never asked whether his task was impossible. Impossible for him, yes. But not whether he was flinging himself without point into the bottomless sea of impossibility.

'Yes,' said Coymans. 'I'm enjoying the challenge of your rules for the game. Fighting with a hand tied, if you like. Makes good sport. But if you are truly asking what odds I give on our success – so much money, in that time – they're bad. Not ones I'd stake my own money on. Will you give it up?'

John turned to look down into the grey-green water of the canal. 'The amount and time are fixed. I have no choice in either.' He thought of Koopman, and the streetsweeper and washerwoman. 'And it must be clean.'

'That leaves risk,' said Coymans.

If John tried and failed, Hawkridge House was lost. Zeal Beester, Aunt Margaret, Dr Bowler and the rest of them would be dispossessed. On the other hand, if he did nothing, the estate was still lost. If he tried, he might succeed.

'You're not a gambler,' said Coymans, 'or you'd know how enjoyable risk can be.'

John thought a moment longer. 'I'll prove you wrong by making you a wager. My hat for yours that you can't make me enjoy the risk I'm about to take.'

'But your hat has only one feather; mine has two!' protested Coymans.

'Then you'll work harder to win.'

Under their banter, Coymans's eyes became speculative and then purposeful. 'You'll do what I say without all that protest and argument?'

'No,' said John. 'With more at stake, I shall question more, and protest more if I disagree with what I understand. Is that clear?'

Now Coymans's eyes were cold. 'Disagreeably clear. But I must point out that the risk is not yours alone. If things go wrong, you can scuttle back to England with your tail between your legs, but I must live here. I won't let a hesitation or mistake of yours bring me down. Do you understand that?'

'Do you know,' said John, 'we are speaking more honestly now than ever before. If you swear always to be this honest with me, I'll wager my money and my hat with a light heart.'

It was a necessary lie.

'It would be better if you just gave me your money and kept out of it altogether,' said Coymans.

'No.'

'You're a brother . . . a true friend. But you're also a novice. A danger to me and to yourself.'

'Then instruct me,' said John. 'Wouldn't that be fun?'

Coymans sucked his upper lip between his teeth so that the tips of his moustaches pointed almost straight up. His eyes grew no warmer. 'All right. My hat for yours. And pray we both keep our heads to wear them.'

Marika seated John on her right hand at supper that night. He could hardly pretend to eat. She made no attempt but just sat, silent in the rowdiness, looking at him and stroking the fur on Erasmus's head while the monkey drowsed in her warmth. Half of her was bright in the firelight, half in shadow.

Be careful. Be careful. Even as he exhorted himself, John's blood buzzed. He was tired of being careful. Eleven years of being careful began to slip from him like a badly-fastened cloak.

Marika leaned over and whispered, 'I'm watching your mouth, and remembering.'

'Remembering isn't enough.' He could not pull back now even if he decided he must. There seemed no need to pull back, not yet.

At the far end of the table, Justus Coymans was deep in loud conversation. From time to time, he glanced down at his sister and his new protégé. John could detect no anger in him. Coymans seemed more interested in the drawings Saski passed him from time to time.

Two guests stood to sing a part song of meltingly sweet melody and obviously filthy words. Another man began to drum the dancing, skipping beat on the table with his spoon.

'Come,' said Marika. 'Make more memories.'

Her bed was soft with feathers and creaked like a ship.

'Here,' she said. She spread long, strong thighs, and pushed his head down to taste petals of flesh, smoothly glazed like a morello cherry.

While yielding, she commanded.

'Come this way, this way, my love. Feel. Follow. Closer.'

A perverse erotic anger possessed him and he contradicted her. As he forced her away from her own will into the path of his own, he saw a secret glint of satisfaction in her half-closed eyes. John, the victor, cut himself against the sharp white teeth of the vanquished. He tasted the salt of his own blood with the salt of her sweat.

Finished, he lay panting, beached like a whale. Marika's warm leg lay across his belly, her breath on his shoulder tip.

I want to stay like this, he thought.

'Let's not ever move,' said Marika. 'Not one muscle.'

I'm sailing blind, off the map. Whirlpools and monsters on the horizon. And I want to sail straight ahead with eyes wide open.

༜

June 5, 1636. Rain. Tulip trade is chiefly in sorts with broken colours. Breeders outdo each other discovering novel breaks. In season, the women are said to wear these flamed and fringed tulips instead of jewels. My poor humble Goudas would not dare lift their heads in such exalted company.

Journal of John Nightingale, known as John Graffham.

The next morning, John returned to Coymans's house, which he had left only in order to relieve Arthur for a few hours of freedom.

'This tulip business is more demanding than cows,' Arthur had said. 'Don't wear yourself out, sir.'

John had had trouble meeting his man's eye.

'I propose,' said Coymans, 'that you invest everything in one or two bulbs of a single rarity, one whose price is rising fast and looks likely to keep on doing so. We'll see how it moves. Hang on for the peak, or your departure, whichever is earlier. That way, you bend no laws and just might make your twenty thousand.'

The shutters were open in Coymans's first-floor parlour this morning. John looked out of the window at the boats skating across the basin.

'All on just one or two bulbs?' The idea gave John a curious empty feeling.

'That's right. It's possible, of course, to sell if the price seems to peak, and then sink everything into another rarity.'

'And if the price doesn't rise enough, in time?' Another thought occurred. 'What if the price falls?'

'That, my friend, is the risk you have elected to take.'

'There's no other way?'

Coymans laughed. 'Is every man in Amsterdam a millionaire? Didn't you learn anything yesterday and the day before?'

No choice. Leap!

'Go ahead,' said John. 'Which tavern sells such precious flowers?' Quiver of chill or thrill. A little short of breath. All those thousands. For a flower or two. After the careful ponderings of Hawkridge House.

'I'm off to the Petticoat,' said Coymans. 'To stick my ear in the wind.'

'For how long?'

'Today. Leave it to me. We will deal tomorrow.'

'Too long!' said John. 'I have only ten days left, allowing two days to deliver the money from here . . . and that's with a good wind back to England.'

'Since when are you a glutton for risk? You ask the impossible of me. I provide it. But I can't do that blind, without information. My pride is tied up in this, you know, quite apart from my commission. I won't let you throw your money into the sea. If you don't allow me this one day, I resign as your broker.'

John glared at him. 'Take today. But I come with you.'

'You'll get in my way, and understand nothing.'

'You may make the money, but I grow the things. Like your mere breeders on their mudflats, I do it with curiosity and attention. How do you know if what you pay for is what you get?'

'I don't,' said Coymans. 'At this time of year, I must trust the seller, as my buyer must trust me. But by reputation, I am not friendly to cheats. And, on the other hand, I have never been foolish enough to sell a Switzer for a *Semper Augustus*.'

'Would you know if you had?'

Now Coymans glared at John. 'No. Would you?'

'Not with certainty,' said John. 'But more than you. If I am to trust all my money to one or two bulbs, I'm coming with you to see what's on offer.' He had a further thought. 'What might cause the price to drop? Besides the chance that someone might undersell us, as you plan to do with Switzers?'

'Controlling legislation,' said Coymans. 'Like that which the stadholders are debating at the moment. Or general panic among buyers, which would ruin all prices, not just that of your rarity. Or the introduction of a new bulb which is very similar in flower. Any of those. Or even just plain lousy luck.'

'What is he saying?' demanded John.

They were in the back room of the Petticoat.

'*The Widow*. To be auctioned. Selling yesterday for seven florins per ace.'

'Ace?'

'About two grains.'

'For a *tulip*?' John was stunned. In his moments of greatest lust after a flower or plant, he had never dreamed that such a sum might be spent. 'Impossible. Insane.' He could not do it, could not physically part with so much money for so little.

Coymans shook his head impatiently. 'Not for the bulb

itself. For the right to sell on. You must stop thinking of flowers. Think of gold, or fine porcelain, or a bargeload of straight-grained oak. *The Widow* is a possibility.' He uncrumpled a drawing of Saski's from his pocket and studied some notes he had written on the back.

'What does *The Widow* look like?' asked John. He might just stake on her for the sake of the devout generosity of the full-budded, tight-lipped Mevrouw Padtbrugge.

'How the hell should I know? And what difference does it make?'

'Find out.'

Coymans lowered his head between his shoulders and scowled.

'Ask!' John's voice was quiet but sharp. His body rooted itself with an implacability that his estate workers would have recognized.

Coymans swirled away into the sea of gesticulating bodies. John watched him approach one man after another, and watched their heads shake in perplexity. Finally Coymans found his man. He returned. 'Red base, gold flames, finely feathered.'

'She's not for me,' said John. So much for the Mevrouw.

'It's not your decision,' said Coymans, 'my meddling friend.'

'Red and gold are a common break.'

'That hasn't hurt the price, as you can see for yourself.'

'The chances that a similar break might appear are too high. I've seen it happen more than once among my own Goudas,' said John. 'I refuse to woo *The Widow*.'

'Who then?' demanded Coymans in exasperation. But his eyes weighed John with a new and growing interest.

'Introduce me,' said John. 'I will tell you after meeting.'

'Ask!' said John again, in the White Doublet. 'How is *Prunelle* coloured?'

Still glowering, Coymans did so. 'White streaked with wine. Feathered.'

'Mere streaks are not uncommon, even in those colours,' said John. 'But perhaps.'

'No,' said Coymans. 'I have heard rumour that a breeder called Bols will have offshoots ready for sale in September. The rumour is enough to sink us, if it spreads.'

'Agreed,' said John. 'Forget *Prunelle*.'

In the Little Hen, Coymans went to seek information without being asked. The rain had stopped. John waited outside and watched water from the heavens drip down from the eaves to join forces with the sea water that swelled the canals. Coymans reappeared from the mêlée in the back room.

'Two on offer here. *Royal Agate*, flamed. Wine on white. Two florins an ace yesterday. Up twenty-five per cent today, so far. And *The King of Kandy*. Very new on the market, so his performance is still hard to predict, price not yet as promising as *The Widow* or *Royal Agate*. Maroon flames on white base. Touched with green. Named in honour of the recent Dutch treaty with the said king.'

'Touched with green?' asked John. He felt a sudden spiking of lust nearly as violent as that provoked by Marika. White base, maroon flames, touched with green. He had never seen a tulip like that. 'Who's selling it?'

Coymans pointed.

'Introduce me,' said John.

'You can buy only through me,' said the dealer, translated by Coymans. 'Old Bols doesn't like to speculate. He won't use other dealers. Old-fashioned breeder . . . hasn't realized what's really happening.' He smirked.

'Breeder's son-in-law,' Coymans added.

Bols again. 'Is he selling any other tulips at the moment?' asked John.

Coymans translated.

'Not yet.' The dealer winked. 'Come see me in two months.'

'What is he working on?' asked John.

The dealer winked again. 'Can you imagine *The King of Kandy* with a deeper Ethiop tinge to his complexion?'

John swallowed. He could. He could see *The King of Kandy*, or his Ethiop cousin, embroidered in rows into the long bed of the Knot Garden. The warm pink brick would set off the dark warmth of the flower's wine-stained petals. He would stitch white tulips into the design to echo the white of the King's white base. That faint tinge of green would link the tulip's stern clarity of form to the controlled green texture of its boxwood frame.

Coymans pulled John away. 'Are you thinking of the *King*?' he demanded quietly.

'It's a rare combination,' said John. 'At least in my experience. Have you heard of many like it?'

'No.'

'We need to know how many more Bols may have in the cradle,' said John.

Coymans see-sawed his moustaches as he pursed and unpursed his lips. 'I can try to find out.'

'Can I visit him?'

Coymans looked alarmed. 'Why?'

'I'd like to,' said John. 'And I can ask him about offsets.'

'Just like that?' Coymans now sounded both amused and incredulous.

'Why not?'

'Why not, indeed?' Coymans lifted his hat to John with an ironic flourish. 'Perhaps he'll recognize another innocent. Let babes speak with babes while the elders stand by and learn from their mouths.'

'And all those . . .' Bols spread his arms to a field where a flock of stooped, scratching boys heaved yellowing leaves out of the ground into baskets. The earth stretched away on all sides to an infinitely distant horizon, interrupted only by the small wrinkles of canal dikes. Far in the distance, John could make out the shoulder of a large dike holding back the sea.

'All those came from one single parent bulb of *Minerva* seven years ago,' said Bols in possessive wonder. 'Truly the Lord's lilies of the field. I wish you could have seen them in bloom!'

'Astounding! I would have liked the sight.' John inhaled the wind that rolled across the vast flatness. It was heavy with salt even here out of sight of the sea. Coymans hovered impatiently on the side, translating.

'If you don't mind a little walk, I have one field of late tulips still in full blow. Would you like to see it?'

'Please!'

Coymans raised quizzical brows, but John cocked his head and grinned back. He would snatch a little personal pleasure from this afternoon, business or not.

Bols led off along a muddy track with John at his side and Coymans tucked close in their wake.

'And do you ever dung your bulbs?' asked John through Coymans.

'Never dung!' cried Bols in horror. 'It brings on rot and putrefactions. You want seawrack . . . collected from the shore, rinsed well and dried in the sun. Then chopped fine.'

Coymans passed on this information in a flat voice, but John and Bols exchanged complicitous glances of a passion shared.

'But you must rinse it in sweet water,' added Bols.

Bols's bald head was as brown and shiny as one of his own bulbs. His eighty years showed only in mottled, wrinkled hands with fingers calloused like the pads of a dog's paw, and in his nearly toothless mouth. Fifty-five years before, he had turned from being an apprentice gardener on an estate to growing flowers for sale in the markets in Amsterdam and Leiden. Now his rolled-up shirtsleeves were silk, and his wooden clogs protected fine leather shoes.

He led through the closed court between two large barns and a fringe of sheds, back out into the flat space with the infinitely far horizon.

'There!' he cried. 'Self-coloured breeders. Nearly finished, but they're still something to see.'

On cue, the afternoon sun sliced through the bank of grey cloud and laid a strip of brilliance across the tulip field.

Coymans poised to translate, but John could not speak. Bols stood silent beside him.

Two acres of muddy earth glowed a rich translucent yellow. Sunlight and petals shimmered together in the faint breeze. Molten gold spilled across the earth. A sudden current of air pressed the tulips into a bow which travelled through the ranks like a departing wave. Gold-dust flakes of petals quivered to the ground.

Bols and John both sighed with pleasure.

'The breath of their soul,' said Bols.

'Constantly reborn,' said John.

Coymans raised his eyebrows at them both as he translated.

'I have never seen so many flowers at once,' said John. 'Cabbages, yes, and other useful plants, but not this divine fingerprint from God's hand, for joy of the soul alone.'

His body felt lightened and his spirit a little giddy with the possibility of something else, as he felt in the presence of all other immensities – cathedrals, open hilltops, the sea.

Coymans rolled his eyes comically as he passed all this on. Bols looked pleased. John still stood bemused and filled with longing.

'You are a young man. You can have a field like that before you even need a walking stick,' said Bols. 'They will multiply themselves for you. Just give them proximity and the freedom to choose their own mates. Wanton creatures that they are!' Bols gleamed at John with the knowing wickedness of a naughty boy and waited for Coymans's translation to catch up. 'All you have to do is choose the best and nurture their offsets or seed. Last year I got more than a dozen new breaks from that lot. Some may be valuable.' Bols turned a quarter circle and pointed to another field of blue-green leaves. 'Those are four years old from seed. They'll bloom in just three more years.'

'More of your treasures like *Prunelle* or *The King of Kandy*?' asked John.

'No, no!' Bols looked shocked. 'Not out here! Not yet! Come back to the sheds. I'll show you. Hein!' He bellowed for his assistant, who appeared eagerly from one of the barns.

'This is my pet – she's a good parent.' Delicately, Bols pulled the peaty soil from around a bulb growing in a pot to show John the crown of tear-shaped offsets around the bulb's base. 'These are ready to be broken off and potted-up to mature.' He stroked the bulb with his horny thumb as if it were a bird or kitten's head and handed it back to the boy Hein to repot. 'She produced six offsets the year before last – four that are ready to sell this summer and two more that I've kept for breeding stock. As far as I know, even old van Damme hasn't come up with one quite like this one.'

'Is it *Prunelle*?' asked John.

'*Prunelle*'s over there,' said Bols, nodding across the shed. 'This one is *The King of Kandy*. My son-in-law's idea, that name. Up-to-date, he said. A tribute to our national diplomacy in the East Indies. Not like my usual gods and goddesses.'

John and Coymans did not look at each other.

'How many parent bulbs do you have left?' asked John.

'Three. This one and the two new breeders I just mentioned. And eighteen offsets, isn't it, Hein? And of course there are the other four that son-in-law Jan persuaded me to sell.'

The boy nodded.

'I want to live to see a field full of His Majesty.'

'I'm sure you shall,' said John.

'How long?' asked Coymans suddenly.

'Eight years,' said Bols cheerfully. 'No longer.'

'So why are you selling four this summer?' asked John. Time was against Bols. 'You'd have your field faster if you kept them all to breed.' He avoided Coymans's eye.

Hein looked up from his pots. This appeared to be a question he himself had asked.

'My son-in-law talked me into it,' said Bols, with a slight darkening of his humour. 'My daughter's expecting their fifth child. Jan – that's my son-in-law – asked if he could sell those four bulbs for the child's portion. What can I say? It's a grandchild, after all.' Bols showed his gums, cheerful again. 'Sacrifice one fair flower for another, eh? Well, what's the harm in that? I may not live to see that field, but the child will.'

'I can think of no better legacy,' said John.

Bols studied the sky and then his mud-caked clogs. Then he asked Hein to give him back *The King of Kandy*'s pot. 'Here,' he said. He dug out the bulb again and snapped off one of the offsets. 'Take this with my compliments. Start a royal line in England.' He put the small, succulent tooth on John's palm. John protested, suddenly hot with guilt. He had come here as a spy and did not deserve this generosity.

Bols closed John's fingers on the treasure. 'Just send me a bulb back if you get a further colour break. I'm hoping for more green. Van Damme says it won't happen. Let's prove him wrong.' He showed his toothless gums in anticipatory glee.

'Done!' John glanced at Coymans. 'This is a private treasure.'

'How much is it worth compared to a full-sized bulb?'

'You tell me.'

Coymans thought briefly. 'Hide it. The fewer known to be in existence, the better for us. Take the damned thing home with you and nurse it for the next fifty years, if you like.'

'Come back in the spring, young man,' Bols ordered John.

'Then we'll show you sights that will make you fall to your knees in wonder, won't we, Hein? And I wouldn't mind a bag or so of English chalk while you're at it.'

Promising chalk and pursued by repeated invitations, John climbed back into Coymans's small canal barge with the infant *King of Kandy* wrapped safe in his handkerchief inside his shirt and, in his head, the information he and Coymans had come for.

'You must buy all four from his son-in-law,' said Coymans quietly. He glanced back at their boatman. Their voices were trapped between the high banks of the canal that cut straight across the fields towards the concentric curves of Amsterdam. 'Then we've cornered the market. There's no one left to unsettle our price!' He took off his hat and absently replaced it. 'I think we might have done it!' He blew out a sharp, shallow breath. 'Doesn't it stir your innards, my English friend? If the stadholders don't legalize us out of business, I'm going to enjoy the next ten days!'

They found Bols's son-in-law next day in the Little Hen. Coymans took him aside. Jan wanted three thousand pounds each for his four *Kings*.

'Beat him down!' said John. 'I don't have that much.'

'I've tried.' Coymans's face was already red with anger.

John felt a passing spasm of madness. He could not possibly be even discussing such a price for four tulip bulbs.

Madness spreads like the plague, he thought. I've contracted it. As that first spy for the South Java Company – Timmons – clearly contracted it. Together, we will carry this new plague to England. Hazelton, Harry and Malise are already infected though they don't yet know it.

'Try again,' said John. This is the one, if any one is, he thought. 'Get him down! You must!'

Coymans tried. He begged. He charmed. He shouted.

'He knows the value of what he has, curse his eyes,' said

Coymans. 'As well as I do.' He took off his hat and began to spin it fiercely between his hands. 'He wants to go to auction. Says the *King* is already entered on tomorrow's list.'

'Is this another impossible game?' asked John.

Coymans smoothed the feather between his fingers. Put his hat back on. Pulled his beard. Crossed his arms. Belched. Scratched his ear. 'It's so nearly possible it makes me sick!'

The son-in-law raised his eyebrows and made regretful noises.

'Auction it is,' said Coymans. 'Blast these novices. If he were a proper dealer, he'd have more respect for me and my reputation. The newcomers think all they have to do is make as much money as they can and run. They don't think about the coming years, the bad years, the times they will want a little give in the game.' He watched the dealer working his way through the crowd. 'He'll try to start where we finished.' His tone was vicious. 'We don't stand a chance.'

He shocked John by suddenly lunging after the dealer. With a broad smile at the surrounding men, Coymans grabbed Jan by the arm and swung him back to where they had been standing. He spoke fast and low, in Dutch.

John watched Bols's son-in-law pass from outraged dignity, to cautious interest, then to a gleam in the eye.

'He's withdrawing three of the *Kings* from tomorrow's auction,' Coymans told John. 'Because we now own them, at three thousand pounds each. I made up the difference. He's putting up only one for sale tomorrow.'

'ALLELUIA!' Coymans threw his head back and bellowed with joy. 'Praise be to me and to the E-e-e-e-englishman!' He waved his large hand and other voices rose in obedient chorus.

'ALLELUIA!'

'What are we celebrating?' asked Marika.

'A secret,' Coymans said. 'I'll tell when we collect our fortunes.' He raised his mug to John at the far end of the table.

'We?' asked Marika. 'I thought only Mr Nightingale was paying.' She smelled of roses and sandalwood and her knee was warm against John's thigh, even through her skirts and petticoats. His hair was rumpled and his cheeks hot. He was drunk as an abbot on one cup of wine and total disbelief. One week before, he had been hunting snails in the Knot Garden at Hawkridge House, dragging his heart like a bullock's hobble. He fumbled on the floor for his hat and skimmed it the length of the table.

Coymans caught the hat, saluted John with it and slapped it askew on top of his unruly hair. 'Your Mr Nightingale, my dearest, is such a wise and clever man that your brother has taken leave of his senses and invested in a client's affair.'

'You invested?' Marika widened her eyes and parted her pink curved lips in theatrical amazement. 'Why are you wearing his hat?'

'I didn't have enough money,' said John. 'Justus stepped in with the difference.'

The widened eyes turned on him. 'You must be even more clever than I already know, to seduce my brother into such a thing!'

'O, Fortuna . . . !' sang Coymans, off-key. 'Come, someone who knows that tune . . . sing it for me!'

There was more to the deal, John was quite sure, but Coymans would not say.

'O Fortuna . . .' The guests' voices rose in praise of Fortune, changeable as the moon . . .

Coymans lay back in his chair, mug half-empty in his hand, curls springing around his face and from under John's hat. Saski drew, Marika's knee lay like a hot coal against John's thigh, and Erasmus searched the salad with quick black fingers.

Nine

The screams came from the *basse-court*. Zeal picked up her skirts and raced out of the New Garden, around the fiddly paths of the Knot Garden, along the alley and into the rear court. A young kitchen groom sprawled against the dog yard wall. It was Peter, who carried vegetables to the kitchen for her. Another groom and a dairy woman bent over him, knocking bees from his skin. His face had already begun to swell under the red lumps where he had been stung.

A kitchen maid jumped up and down, waving her hands in the air and screaming. Other maids and grooms flapped aprons and clothes at the air, yelling and screaming a little less loudly. One of the dairy women tried to calm them all. Children appeared at gates and windows as news of excitement spread.

The air hummed with the quick dark shapes of bees. They zig-zagged over the heads of the maids and grooms, dived and circled. Zeal heard their fizzy rage through the other voices in the *basse-court*.

'Peter's been stung terrible!' cried a maid. 'And one's got up Hester's sleeve!'

'There's a swarm in that churn,' another voice offered.

'Get back!' cried Zeal. Couldn't they see that the more they flapped and screamed, the more alarmed the bees became?

'Peter tried to shift them,' said the maid. 'Look what they done!'

Zeal circled through the mêlée to the groom. He had gone

chalk white in between the red lumps that deformed his face and neck. His mouth was blue.

'Where's Tuddenham?' someone called. 'Where is he?'

'Sowing beans in the Far,' said someone else.

Mistress Margaret arrived in the door of the house. 'Simon, go fetch Tuddenham . . . If only John were here!'

'Mistress Margaret!' Zeal called urgently.

'Oh Lord!' said the old woman in hushed despair when she saw Peter. 'Get him inside at once. I'll go start making poultices, though I don't know if it's not already too late.'

'You two . . .' Zeal pointed at two grooms. 'Take Peter into the house for Mistress Margaret.'

The churn vibrated with a single angry voice, magnified by the drum of the churn. Zeal moved closer.

'My lady, get back. You'll get stung like Peter!'

The bees boiled up in the churn and nearly overflowed.

'Throw a sheet over them!' said a groom.

'We need smoke . . .'

'There's no need . . .' the dairy woman kept trying to say.

Zeal heard terror inside the buzzing churn. 'WILL YOU ALL GET BACK! AND BE QUIET!' She hadn't known that her voice could be so loud.

In the startled silence, everyone retreated against the walls and into doorways.

Zeal turned to the dairy woman who seemed the only other sane person there. 'How long does it take to get to the Far and back?'

'Not that long,' said the woman. 'But Tuddenham doesn't like to handle the bees. Mr John usually does that, when they swarm. And he always takes the honey himself.'

'Here's fire for smoke.' A kitchen groom offered an iron pot of coals.

Zeal had no idea how to get the small rising tendrils of smoke down into the churn. It certainly wouldn't be enough to send the bees to sleep, as she had read. The edge of panic seemed to have left the hum in the churn, so she went closer. The flying bees also seemed fewer and quieter than before.

'There's one in your hair, my lady!' a maid cried.

Zeal sat on her haunches in a billow of skirts, beside the churn. The pitch of the hum had definitely dropped. The churn no longer whined. A bee landed on the elbow of her sleeve. Zeal watched it prod the fabric, trying to decide where it was. Then it launched itself into the air again, in what she imagined to be panic.

Poor things, thought Zeal. I'd be terrified too.

She laid her hand on the churn. The wood felt alive under her palm. She put her other hand on the other side. The churn vibrated between her hands.

'My lady, don't!' someone called. 'You could get killed.'

'We can't leave them here,' she said.

'Put a sheet over them, like I said. And then squash them all to death!'

Zeal made sure that there were no bees crawling on the sides of the churn. Then she embraced it with both arms and stood up. In absolute silence, she staggered with the heavy wood and iron vessel toward the *basse-court* gate. She moved slowly, careful not to jolt her passengers. A halo of bees shimmered around her head and shoulders.

I don't know why you were stupid enough to fly in there in the first place, she told them.

A procession followed her out of the *basse-court*, along the ponds, across the weir bridge and up into the orchard. The grooms, the maids, three dairy women, and nine children. Dr Bowler stood up from his seat under a tree and dropped in behind Zeal with his book under his arm. Tuddenham darted out from the New Garden gate.

'Go tell him to find an empty skep,' murmured Zeal over her shoulder to Dr Bowler. 'And bring it to the orchard. Quickly.' She felt for each step before she trusted it and prayed that she wouldn't trip over a sagging petticoat. She drifted cloud-like up the bumpy slope of rough orchard grass. At the same time, she scanned desperately through her memory of Pliny, Columella, *The Good Huswife*, for the precise details that she needed next.

I hope you're all as full of honey and sleepy as you're supposed to be, she said to the buzzing churn.

Tuddenham waited for her in the orchard with an empty wicker skep, held upside down like a cup.

'Who will help me turn the churn?' she asked.

After a pause, Dr Bowler said, 'I will.'

Tuddenham held the skep out at arm's length.

I saved you from being smoked or squashed, Zeal told the bees. Please return the favour now. Do what you're supposed to.

With Dr Bowler's help, she upended the churn over the empty skep. For two seconds, nothing happened. Zeal gave the churn a little shake. A seething ball of bees rolled out of the churn and landed plop in the skep. Zeal dropped the churn, took the skep from the white-faced Tuddenham, and quickly turned it right-side up onto a wooden fair-standing that was empty from the year before. She stepped back.

Stay there! she ordered them.

The hysterical cheer shocked her. She had not noticed how many people had followed her from the *basse-court*. The crowd in the orchard cheered again. Zeal was a little confused by the noise, as if she had woken up from a sleep. One or two bees crawled out of the little arched opening and felt their way around the wooden porch.

'They need only one thing more to make them stay,' said Dr Bowler. He called six of the children forward to sing the bees a song of welcome to their new home. They circled the skep three times, trailing six high sopranos and a baritone.

As the others began to drift back to work, Zeal sat on the grass and watched her bees fly in and out of the skep.

She felt disaster as soon as she trotted in through the *basse-court* gate. Peter had died before the bees were even in the skep. Zeal cried herself to sleep for a week over this dreadful breach in her new world.

It amazed and upset her that the groom's death seemed to increase the sudden adoration and awe that some of the estate residents now felt for her. They seemed to think that she had done something wonderful – though it was really straightfor-ward enough if you kept your head – while in fact she had allowed something terrible to happen.

I shouldn't have sent him off like that, for someone else to care for. And it wasn't fair to Mistress Margaret, at her age, to feel she should take the blame.

Zeal wondered if John had ever failed like this. She wanted desperately to talk to him about the complexities of death and bees. She couldn't talk to Harry. He had been absolutely furious that she had taken such an idiotic risk and had taken to calling her, with an unfriendly twist to his lip, 'Our Lady of the Bees'.

🌷

June 7, 1636. Rain. I wonder that the Hollanders don't all build themselves arks.

   Journal of John Nightingale, known as John Graffham.

'Only ten days remain before I must sail back to England,' said John to Coymans.

'With deep regrets, I can only tell you to eat, drink and enjoy yourself.'

'As an accused man enjoys himself waiting for the verdict of pardon or death.'

'I'm glad my sister didn't hear you say that.'

John flushed. 'I apologize. It's a dark vigil lightened by the company of an angel.'

Coymans shouted with laughter. 'An angel! Marika, an angel? Oh dear, Nightingale, I lose faith in your wisdom. My sister's a lovely, spoiled brat. With only me as her guide in the world since she was six, what can you expect?' He abruptly stopped laughing. 'Only Marika rules Marika's life. But don't mistake the freedom I give her; she's very dear to me. My closest friend. The only woman I can trust. She chooses her own sweetmeats. I make sure they're not poisoned ones.'

'Or so strange that they disagree with her digestion?'

'I have purges for those,' said Coymans with a wide, frank smile. 'Go find her.'

'I'm coming with you.'

'Not today. You played your part, and very well too. Leave it to me now. You'll suffer too much at the auction and get in my way. I'm off to put ginger in several pots.'

To distract him, Marika took John to an exhibition of paintings in a private house near the Damrak. Canvases covered the walls of the room from floor to ceiling. The householder and patron leaped up from intense conversation by the window with two other men to kiss Marika. He greeted John cordially enough but as if he did not expect to meet again.

Marika pulled John quickly past several landscapes and stopped below a formal flower piece, meticulously rendered in every detail down to an ant on the petal of a peony. She looked up at the canvas.

'That's by Saski.'

'It's hard to believe,' said John. 'It's nothing like his drawings.' A pair of eyeglasses glinted on the white damask tablecloth on which the jug of flowers sat. Saski had shown the precise brown edges of a worm hole in one bud. His flowers sat smug, plump and a little glassy in their Delft jug, far less alive than the swift-like swooping lines in his sketches.

Admirable but less lovely than the reality they strained to surpass.

'Oh, this is his bread and cheese work,' said Marika defensively. 'Not all his patrons are as brave and generous as Justus . . .'

John moved on and stared up at a vase of sleekly succulent tulips.

Marika looked at John. 'You're not paying attention.'

'What news of *The King of Kandy*?' asked John that evening with a dry mouth.

Coymans seemed slightly restrained, his gestures smaller. John heard caution and cunning in his voice. 'He moved ahead of *The Widow* today. Doubled his price in the auction, then the buyer sold again. Doubled *his* purchase price. The *King* is sizzling!'

John sat with Marika's arm around his neck, giddy and terrified at same time. 'When do we offer ours?' Even the warmth of Marika's arm felt unreal.

Coymans winked. 'I had a quiet word today, with two rich enthusiasts. And let each of them know that the other is interested.'

With eight days left, the man who had last bought the single bulb of *The King of Kandy* sold it for a profit of a further fifty per cent.

'Good for one day, but not enough,' said Coymans. 'We wait.'

That afternoon, Marika entertained John in the small geometric walled garden behind the house. John had never seen such globular precision of box nor such military roses.

'You do have living blossoms, after all,' he said.

'But not so interesting as Justus's painted ones, do you think?'

'On the contrary, I find these much more interesting. Perhaps you mean to say that they are less fun.'

'I can't imagine what you find so interesting,' said Marika. 'These mean nothing. You can't eat or drink them or sell them or flirt with them. They have nothing to feed my dreams.'

John and Marika looked at each other across four feet of scrubbed paving stones, intrigued by the possibility of their first quarrel since they had become lovers. Then that merest glimpse of the chasm flung them towards each other, all the more intensely because of the slight frisson of loss.

The next day there was a meeting of the stadholders, rumoured to concern further legislation to control the dealing in tulips.

'All deals from the end of April will be nullified,' said one man at the White Doublet.

'From the end of next month . . .'

The King of Kandy did nothing that day.

Nor the next day.

'I don't like it,' muttered Coymans. 'Need to keep the movement.'

He was absent from supper that night.

We won't make it, thought John. A profit of nearly ten times what we started with. It's not possible. Even without a new controlling law.

Marika took John on the country canals for the day, in her brother's small sailing barge. She left the bargeman behind and sailed the boat herself. They slid along the straight gleaming ditches all the way to the horizon, which suddenly hesitated and rearranged itself into an infinity of grey choppy sea. They ate ham and cold meat pies on the dike top, balanced on the exact front line of the war between earth and water.

With six days left before he had to return to England, the single bulb changed hands once more.

John calculated. At the day's price, his bulbs would fetch a little more than half what he needed. 'What do you think, Coymans? Is the game still possible?'

'The stadholders are still arguing,' said Coymans. He frowned at nothing for a very long time. 'The statute passed last year was observed by some and not by others. We may have nothing to fear. In any case, you must come with me today. I need you to explain to possible buyers why a new bulb similar to the *King* is so unlikely to arrive suddenly on the market.'

At midday John found himself in the Petticoat, speaking through tendrils of tobacco smoke to a circle of intent faces, explaining the odds for and against different colour breaks in tulips.

'And now we auction our three *Kings*,' said Coymans. 'In open cry.'

'Seven thousand florins each bulb.'

'Seven thousand and ten.' The bidder had been in the circle of intent faces listening to John's discourse on colour breaks in tulips.

'One of my rich enthusiasts,' murmured Coymans.

'And fifty.'

'Eight thousand.'

Dear Lord, thought John. For a flower. How much is that now, in pounds? How many more? His brain scrambled among unruly numbers.

Coymans leaned forward, sharp-eyed and sweating.

'Eight thousand five hundred.' A hush pressed down on the men's voices.

'Getting there,' whispered Coymans.

'Eight thousand and six hundred.'

The back room of the Petticoat was totally silent. The sounds of laughter came faintly through the closed door from the front room of the inn.

'And seven fifty.' Not Coymans's rich enthusiast.

'Will someone give nine thousand?' asked the auctioneer.

The silence grew deeper. The enthusiast had his arms

273

wrapped around himself, rocking in an agony of indecision and desire.

'Nine thousand?' the auctioneer asked again.

A drop of sweat ran down the side of Coymans's nose and into his moustache.

'Take it!' whispered John with sudden decisiveness. The price had already risen past the limit of reason. A panic seized him. Get the money out! 'It doesn't matter if it's not quite enough. We'll do something else. *Take it*!'

Coymans ignored him. 'Withdraw the bulbs,' he said.

In the silence that followed, John heard his own voice cry 'No!'

Then other voices crashed into the silence on top of his.

'The owner doesn't want to withdraw,' shouted the last man to bid. 'The sale is valid. The *Kings* are mine at eight thousand, seven hundred and fifty!'

The rich enthusiast still rocked himself as if in pain.

Coymans turned viciously on John. 'Keep your mouth shut! You chose the bulb. This is my part.'

'I feel it!' said John. 'We should sell now.'

'It's not your decision!' said Coymans. 'Don't forget that my money made your own purchase possible! You'll not ruin me along with yourself!' He turned back to the auctioneer. 'Withdraw the bulbs!'

The auctioneer turned to appeal to John.

'He wants to know if you agree to withdraw,' said Coymans tightly. 'What are you going to do?'

Ice water flowed in John's veins. His mouth dried. The panic to pull his money out was still with him. But Coymans had made a fair point of honour. If he had not risked his own money, John would not be here now, considering whether to refuse a price of 8,750 florins. But if John pulled out now, he would be close to his target. There must be another way to make up the difference. Or perhaps what he had now

274

might be enough to satisfy the King until the *Boston Maid* returned to London. He swallowed.

'And if a law is passed?' he asked Coymans. 'Before we can try again?'

'Withdraw!' said Coymans between his teeth. His face was as red as the feather in his hat. 'Or I swear I'll kill you!'

Withdraw from the sale and maybe lose it all. Lose Hawk-ridge House for Aunt Margaret, young Zeal Beester, Dr Bowler . . . Coymans means his threat. It matters so much to him. And there is doubtless something he hasn't told me.

'For the sake of your earlier help and not your present threat,' said John. To the auctioneer, he nodded. 'Withdraw the bulbs.'

Still in a rage, Coymans swirled and boiled along the canalside beside John's controlled stride. 'You idiot! I should never have let you come.'

He isn't sure yet himself, thought John. I wish he were! 'Explain,' he said tersely. 'I need convincing! You may have money at stake, but I carry responsibility for more lives than my own. I don't like wagering my future on your greed. Or has the game sucked you in past the control of reason?'

'I've nearly achieved the impossible for you, and you want *convincing*!' Coymans slapped viciously at a tree trunk with his gloved hand.

'What game are you really playing?'

Coymans's eyes gleamed piggishly, like an enraged boar. 'You don't want to know.'

'I must know.'

'Must!' echoed Coymans in derision. 'The meddling apprentice *must* know!'

'Or I withdraw altogether.'

'You can't!'

'Why not? Ruin is ruin. I'll choose for myself what form it takes.'

Coymans said nothing for six angry paces. 'The man who bid 8,750 florins could not have paid,' he said abruptly. 'He's a mercenary soldier, back from Spain. Hasn't ten stuyvers to his name.'

'Then why was he bidding?' John already saw the answer.

'Because I ordered him to.'

John stopped Coymans with an iron hand. 'You said it would be clean! I accepted risk on those terms only! You say you don't like cheats. Well, I care even less for cheats and liars!' Now the rage was John's. 'If I understand you, your mercenary pushed the price up, for my bulbs. Not only are you a cheat, but you have made me into one as well!'

'If we had sold the bulbs at the inflated auction price, you might have reason. But we withdrew. What harm did we do? Whatever intention you might think you see, tell me, where did we in fact transgress?'

'Then why?'

Coymans was recovering his balance. 'Did you see my rich friend at the end? He could hardly contain himself when he thought he had lost the bulbs. Now he will have a second chance, and a little time to get used to the prices mentioned today. And if he, of his own free will and after reflection, offers to pay us nine thousand florins per bulb, surely no blame falls to either you or me.'

'It stinks,' said John.

'To a delicate beginner's nose, perhaps. But believe me, your conscience can rest easy.'

'Why will he buy tomorrow what he refused today?'

'He won't buy tomorrow. He'll buy the day after. Tomorrow, he will buy that other single bulb whose progress we have been tracing. Then his thirst to own all four will be too strong to resist.'

'He's not fool enough to pay that price.'

'You might not be. I might not be. But part of this game

is understanding your fellows. I understand him. He's fool enough.'

'Why will he buy the single bulb?'

'Because he will hear tonight that you withdrew your three because you plan to buy it. To own all known *Kings*. And then to raise the price for all four to twenty thousand florins each.' Coymans was smiling again. 'A good Hollander like him won't tolerate the idea that a mere Englishman might control the market for a supreme achievement of Dutch horticultural skill.'

The following day was intolerable. John stayed at the Widow Padtbrugge's boarding house in the morning to allow Arthur a few hours of liberty. Coymans went to tickle the greed of his rich enthusiast. Just before sundown, John went to dine yet again at Coymans's house.

There were only twelve at dinner. Marika and John, Justus Coymans and his secretary, Saski, a sea captain, two actors, a spice merchant, and two musicians. John, Marika and Coymans formed a subdued hub around which hilarity surged and ebbed uncertainly.

'We have him on our hook,' said Coymans with determination. 'Spiegel. He's frightened, but hungry. He bought the single bulb, as I predicted. Nine thousand florins. We meet him tomorrow evening to conclude for our three. A private deal on our terms.'

'Will he agree?'

'If he meets us, he'll agree. And I'll take a notary to prevent a change of mind. We'll sign on the spot.'

And if Spiegel doesn't meet us, then what? John did not care to voice the question any more than Coymans wanted to hear it.

John held Marika's hand against his mouth. Her fingers smelled of peach juice and lemon. He wanted Marika's presence, her warmth, her attention, absently, as he had often enjoyed Cassie's presence, but for the first time since meeting, he did not want to make love to her.

He and Coymans could not yet do what they most needed to do. But they couldn't think what else to do in the meantime.

The entire company sat on at the table in an aimless tension caught from Coymans and John. Saski drew slack shoulders and hands tight around mugs. His quick lines caught off-balance bodies, unresolved movements, and half-hearted gestures. And Coymans, subdued as a rain-soaked chicken.

The monkey's small black fingers picked endlessly, at fleas, at ribbons. His entire being focused on searching his armpit and groin. His air of rage was subdued, all of his anger in his probing fingertips. Saski drew unfocused eyes half-watching the animal's self-absorbed intensity.

The actors and the sea captain threw their knives at a knot on a beam; the misses clattered onto the tiled floor until Coymans shouted in irritation. Later, Marika played the virginal until she ran out of music she knew.

John returned very late to the widow's house to sleep, more drunk than he had intended or realized. A messenger from Coymans woke him at six o'clock the next morning.

'Come at once!' said the messenger.

'Has Spiegel pulled out?' asked John, still out of breath. He tossed his cloak onto a bench beneath the stern skull-holding portrait of Coymans *père*. His head ached from inaction and last night's wine.

Coymans took his elbow and marched him up the wooden stairs to the private, shuttered parlour on the first floor. There, he released John and threw open the shutters of one window to look out over the rectangle of water in front of the house.

'It's worse!' he said. 'We could always find another rich man ready at any price to defend Dutch property from the English.' He turned from the window and flung himself into a circle around the room. 'Old Bols is going to sell those breeder bulbs he showed us. That bastard son of the devil, his son-in-law, must have persuaded him to cash in on the price we have achieved.'

'Isn't that Bols's right?' asked John reasonably. 'Are we so petty that we grudge him that? What harm does it do to us?'

'What harm?' Coymans stopped dead in disbelief. 'What harm?' he repeated. 'God preserve me from novices! Don't you see what this could do to the price of all the bulbs? We're no longer selling three of the only four in the world, but three of seven, and who knows how many more, perhaps? Exactness doesn't matter. The idea and the rumours are what will count. At the very best, my friend Spiegel won't buy our three tonight. Not at our proposed price. He'll wait and see, try to bargain a little with Bols. Bols need only undersell us by a little and we're finished. I've built a magnificent pyramid of cards. Pull out just one, even wiggle it a little and, whoosh, the whole thing's flat!'

'Can't you offer to lower the price a little?' asked John. 'Make the best deal you can with Spiegel, and let us try some other way to earn the balance I still need?'

'I must persuade Bols to wait. It needs only a few days.'

'From tomorrow, I have three days.'

'I KNOW how many days you have!'

That afternoon, Coymans found John pacing the gravel paths between knee-high, sharp-edged box hedges in the little walled garden behind the house.

Coymans was radiant with fury and frustration. 'Spiegel wants us all to meet tomorrow night. Bols, you, me and Spiegel. Face-to-face combat. The price can only sink.'

'What did you tell him?'

'That I'd let him know tonight whether we agree.'

The following evening, Spiegel, Coymans, John, and a notary named Waard waited in a corner of the Golden Cockerel. Spiegel was over-bright and a little shifty with nerves. Coymans had calmed and acquired a renewed glint. They talked politics, gossip, anything but bulbs.

John lifted his beer mug and set it down untouched. His stomach was too tight for drinking. His head had not stopped aching since the morning before.

Bols didn't come.

The four men, surrounded by noise, grew more and more silent.

'It's not a long journey,' said Spiegel. 'He can sail all the way.'

Spiegel, Coymans and Waard, the notary, tapped tobacco into long-stemmed white clay pipes, fussed with the lighting coals, sucked, brushed tobacco from their clothes, blew tight nervous jets of smoke into the thick, beery air. Coymans called for more drink.

One hour. Still no Bols.

The four men sank into silence. The noise around them rose as the men around them grew drunker.

'Mynheer Bols is not coming,' said Spiegel.

Coymans nodded. 'Shall we carry on without him? We've given him more than enough time if he is serious about selling to you.'

Spiegel relit his pipe. 'I propose that we meet again tomorrow night. It's not like old Bols to go back on an arrangement without a good reason.'

John looked at Coymans, appalled at losing another day.

'I might have another buyer by tomorrow night,' said Coymans.

'Not on the open market, you won't,' said Spiegel. 'Not at that price, when no one knows what Bols is going to do. And I don't like to think that you are already dabbling behind my back in another "privileged" private deal, *ex collegio*. I'll take the risk.' He smiled with a touch of malice. 'I know that patience doesn't come easily to you, Justus.'

The effort visible behind Coymans's answering smile

was terrifying. 'Of course, my friend. I must obey your wishes.'

Two days, thought John. Two days left! I can't do it! I was a fool to withdraw from the auction! His mind began to rehearse words to tell Harry, Hazelton and Sir George that he had failed.

Aunt Margaret, I am so sorry! And Dr Bowler and little Zeal . . . How will Malise react? John suddenly wondered. Will his pleasure at my failure override the pain in his pocket? What public punishment will he prescribe for me? I should have left Hawkridge House that first night, after Harry and Malise arrived. Before I knew what was at stake and agreed to do the impossible.

'Tomorrow evening, then,' Spiegel was saying. 'Here. I will send word to Bols myself to make sure he's coming. Even if he has decided not to sell just now, I need to know what he intends to do with his *Kings of Kandy*. Rather affects what I do, you understand.'

'Indeed, I do understand,' said Coymans.

After they left the Golden Cockerel, Coymans burrowed deep as a badger into his own thoughts. When John began to speak, he raised a hand. 'I'm thinking. Don't bother me.'

John was choked with rage at himself for giving in to Coymans and withdrawing from the auction.

'We must auction again tomorrow,' he said. 'And take what price we can get. That still leaves a day for one last desperate gamble.'

'I don't know,' said Coymans. 'I just don't know. We'll decide in the morning. Go home and sleep if you can. Meet me on the Damrak at eight o'clock. Good night.' He swung away abruptly and vanished into a small alley above which the house peaks leaned together until they nearly closed out the sky.

Next morning on the Damrak, John saw Coymans on the far side of the water through a palisade of masts, in excited conversation. Coymans came to meet John. He was in full flash and swirl again.

'It's a miracle, my friend. We must go into the church now and give thanks. A miracle!'

'What has happened?'

Coymans's face sobered. 'A shadowed miracle, I should have said. Bols went keel up early yesterday morning, in his sheds. No one knows exactly why, but rumour has it that his heart gave out. Probably with too much excitement. The old man hadn't left his mudflats much in the last years . . .'

'Bols is dead?' The world quivered and hesitated in its spin. For the same beat of time, John felt his own being falter.

'Yesterday morning,' said Coymans, looking more closely at John. 'That's why he didn't come.'

'You call that a miracle?' John's voice was level but very, very chilly.

'It's more than ordinary chance,' said Coymans. 'My friend . . .' He flung an arm across John's shoulder. 'I diagnose a griping of honour. A flux of principles. A fever of conscience. But let me purge you of an unnecessary illness . . .'

'It is indeed more than ordinary chance,' said John. He stepped aside, out of Coymans's embrace. 'And I marvel at your joy.'

'All right. Let's speak directly.' Coymans stopped and faced John squarely. 'I regret the death of a fellow human creature. But the man had lived his allotted time . . . more than many. He died in the prospect of enormous wealth, probably burst a vein with surmise and greed. I hope to die so happily. So, I regret in principle, but I will not be a hypocrite and say that his death is not the best turn Providence could have done you and me. And if you're half as honest as you like to pretend, you'll admit your own sneaking, secret pleasure. Ruin and failure have been deflected.'

'Because Bols is dead, Spiegel will now pay your price?

What of the son-in-law? Why won't he proceed with the sale?'

'This,' said Coymans, 'is the heart of the miracle. Bols had gone to his sheds to prepare his *Kings* for the journey into Amsterdam. Unfortunately for the son-in-law, and fortunately for us, he had not yet done so. It seems that, with Bols dead, there is uncertainty about which bulbs are the *King* and which are other sorts.'

'And to be sure, the heirs must wait until next spring to see the blooms.'

Coymans beamed. 'The nub, my friend, the nub! For us now, the old man's bulbs might as well not exist!'

'What about his assistant . . . Hein? Doesn't that boy know which bulbs are which?'

'It seems not,' said Coymans. 'At least, they say he couldn't find them.'

'Do we meet Spiegel again this evening, then?'

'Spiegel can go to the devil,' said Coymans. 'We are going back to auction this afternoon. Spiegel can bid *in collegio* if he doesn't mind the competition!'

They were mobbed at the door to the back room of the Petticoat. Hands pulled at their coat-sleeves. John shook his head at the babble of questions. Coymans threw his inquisitors off like a shower of nuts.

'*Drei*!' he shouted. He held up three fingers and spun in the centre of the room. 'Three *Kings*! Who would like to be the lord of three kings? There are only four known to the world now!' He paced around the small clear space in the centre of the room, fixing each man in the packed circle with his eye. 'Who will be the King of Kings?'

The auctioneer called for order. 'Three *Kings of Kandy*,' he announced. He wrote the words on his slate. 'Bidding is open. Who will start for nine thousand?'

At first John wanted only to flatten himself to the ground and bury his head under his paws like a terrified dog. The shouts in the dark back room of the Petticoat were nonsense, the cries of madmen, the elusively significant omens of dreams. Then came a hush as voices fell out of the bidding.

Spiegel had joined in. He looked helpless and frightened, as if he didn't know whose voice had borrowed his breath and tongue to shout out those numbers.

The other chief bidder was the man who had rocked in silent pain at the previous auction. Coymans's other rich enthusiast. Now he had decided. His voice slammed down over Spiegel's, again and again. His eyes were as intent and implacable as a determined child's.

A third voice called out, high-pitched with emotion. Then Spiegel. Then the other man. The auctioneer looked at the first man, with the high-pitched voice. He closed his eyes, shook his head.

Spiegel shouted.

The other man knocked Spiegel's offer out of the air before it had even taken flight.

The crowd moaned.

Spiegel hesitated, then shouted again.

The voices of the two bidders grew softer and softer. The hush in the room wound tighter and tighter.

John quivered and drove his nails into his palms. Though he could not understand a word, he felt enormity begin to grow in the thick air that smelled of beer, tobacco smoke, damp wool and animal fear. Something outside ordinary life was taking place.

One look at Coymans confirmed this enormity. He seemed poised in the air a little above the floor. His eyes gleamed. His lips were drawn back in a breathless snarl. The white Brussels lace of his collar jumped with the force of his pulse. Otherwise, not a hair or muscle of his body moved.

Afterwards, John could remember only the sense of an event happening. The event itself was drowned in the thundering of his blood in his ears and the strange inability of his eyes to see clearly. He smelled the event more clearly than he saw it. A sharp, feral tang cut through the familiar musk of excited human bodies.

The auctioneer asked a question. Repeated the question. Then said something in a flat, disbelieving voice.

'Forty thousand!' whispered Coymans. 'Forty thousand florins for each bulb!'

The hush gripped the room for a moment more. Then the crowd exploded.

John had his back pounded and his palm slapped until it was purple. Above the heads of the crowd he saw Coymans, flushed, sparkling, with a deep satisfaction in his small cold blue eyes. Coymans took John and the buyer upstairs into a small private chamber, with the notary, to sign the papers immediately. John would collect the money the following day and Coymans would deliver the bulbs on the next.

I must arrange immediate passage back to England, thought John. Leave the second the money's in my hands.

'Your brains and my balls, my friend!' said Coymans to John under his breath as they went back down the stairs. 'We should work together again! Come back with your commission when you've delivered the money to England. We'll make you rich yourself next time, not just those other bastards! It's even more fun working for yourself!'

John laughed. He felt weak with relief and disbelief. 'I confess that the sense of fun escaped me from time to time.'

'Terror is fun,' said Coymans. 'And to seduce you further into returning, I have decided that I won't take everything over the target. I'll take only my original commission of twenty-five per cent. That leaves you the balance to invest next time, with me as your broker.'

'Exceedingly generous,' said John. 'As your original commission was only twenty per cent.'

Coymans was delighted. 'With every day, you seem less

stupid. I could come to like you as much as my sister does.'

And I must get clear of you as fast as I can, thought John. Our good luck, in which you so rejoice, stems from an old man's well-timed death.

John's face felt hot; his head swam. He drank more wine and tried to imitate the expected euphoria. He ached to feel perfect satisfaction, disbelief, happy madness, but could not.

He smiled across the terrace at his host in the honeysuckle bower and felt a pang of guilt at his own discomfort in the face of the man's unflagging hospitality. Apart from Bols's death, he was also weighed down by the physical problem of all that money. Coymans, and half of Amsterdam, knew how much he had.

They had all moved out into the garden for fruit and sweet-meats after the celebration supper, pulled of one accord by the warm rays of a setting sun after a week of grey sullen days. The guests sat on benches around the small flagged terrace or lolled on their elbows on the stone. John sat on the terrace with his back against a stone obelisk, one of a pair that marked the entrance to the convoluted garden walks and their cannon balls of box. A lilac dripped its honey scent over their shoulders. The buds of a blush white rose which John did not recognize were just relaxing into bloom behind him. One of the two women guests that evening invited John with her eyes to admire the noisette roses tucked between her breasts.

Marika passed a basket of fruit. Pomona in action. Over her shoulder, she gave John a wicked glance.

He acknowledged the joke and continued to think badly of her brother. Coymans might have other friends with swift boats and swifter knives, who would weight an Englishman and sink him as happily as the executioners sank criminals off the gibbet island.

John watched Marika peel an apple. The apple commanded

her entire being. Her full lower lip was tucked under her white, neat upper teeth. Her creamy hand, which had touched him in so many different ways and in so many different places, now existed only to guide the small sharp knife between flesh and skin of the fruit. She carved away a long crisp red coil of peel. Unaware of his gaze, she sighed in visible satisfaction when the peel came away in one unbroken ribbon. She cut a slice from the apple and handed it to Erasmus. Then she cut another slice and slid it between the exquisite curves of her lips. She chewed, savoured and swallowed. Then she laid down both fruit and knife on the stone bench beside her. A strange, slightly forlorn expression came into her eyes.

Now what? they asked. What is there next?

Let me show you! John felt a rush of intense lust for her forlornness stronger than any that her provocation and strength had ever stirred. The two other women there that evening were shadows beside Marika's rich glow.

He hauled himself back to business. Need a boat . . . passage. Need someone to trust. Not Marika, alas, the only woman whom Coymans trusted. The devout and immaculate Mevrouw Padtbrugge, whose house nevertheless suggested a worldly financial mind at work? Gomez? Perhaps.

He remembered the tone of Gomez's voice. 'If you're looking for Coymans, you're looking for Coymans.'

'Where can I find Gomez?' he asked Coymans.

Suspicion flared in Coymans's wine-reddened eyes.

'I owe him tangible gratitude for introducing us.' John raised his glass.

Coymans returned the toast. 'Ah, well, the old man could use it. His best days are over. He has rooms in Warmoesstraat, above the baker, backing onto the Amstel.'

Saski got up from his bench to give John a drawing of Marika peeling the apple. He waved his hand to indicate that John should keep it. John raised his glass again in thanks.

Two men went into the house and brought out their fiddle and pipe.

'A jig! A jig!' cried one of the women. Marika pulled a guest up from the stone terrace and began to dance, with Erasmus swaying unsteadily on her shoulder. Someone began to drum on a bench with a spoon, and a drunken voice bawled 'lalalala la! diddle diddlediddle dee!'

'Dance with me!' cried Marika to John as she slid past in a sideways gallop. He climbed to his feet, unsteady with wine. She tossed Erasmus to her first partner and whirled into John's arms.

'Spin me off my feet!'

He held her around the waist and spun in place. Her arms tightened around his neck. Her weight dragged and then lightened as he turned. She wheeled around his hub, skirts and feet flying off the floor. John saw a blur of other wheeling petticoats and feet. The garden dissolved and spun around him, lit by flashes of the low, revolving sun. They moved too fast for sound to catch up with them. John leaned back against her weight until they were perfectly balanced in a centre of stillness. Marika's feet whirled high above the floor. Dimly the sound of clapping reached him. It grew faster and faster. He spun faster. Marika's weight pulled harder. John leaned further into their balance.

If I stop, we will both fall, he thought. I must keep spinning for ever. He held her tighter and they flew. The sun flashed faster. The clapping raced. The heels of his boots drummed. Then she began to slip.

Sweat greased his hands. His muscles ached from the tightness of his grip. He seemed to hold her only by her fingertips. He eased his spin. Slowly, slowly, he lowered her like a sail. John heard her toes scrape on the floor and saw the billows of her skirts collapse around her legs. At last, they stood still, locked together and panting while the garden continued to spin around them.

'Don't go!' said Marika fiercely into John's neck. 'Oh God! Please don't go!'

How can I leave all this? John asked himself later in her bed.

Finality made them both reckless. She made a last unstinting offer of herself. He felt her throwing herself before him like evidence in a trial.

He gave himself to giddiness again. Tonight he was unbothered by the dark witch-widow eyes of the monkey which had perched on the bedhead. They rolled and curled together like snails, slipping tighter and tighter into a graceless, ecstatic lump.

Then he opened out like a galleon's sails, hollowed with wind and hot in the salty sun. Bruised but nevertheless filled with well-being.

'I must go back to England tomorrow. I don't see how I can leave you, but I must.'

'I know,' said Marika. 'But you must come back here when you've finished your business. I order you.' She bit his left nipple gently. 'Justus will make you rich, and I will make you happy.'

'And we will all have such fun,' said John with a touch of dryness. But he twisted his hands into her bright curling hair and savoured her mouth one more time.

I could come back, he thought. This does not have to be the last time. If Malise means his threats, Amsterdam is a place I could come. I may be wrong about her brother. I could come back and do all this again.

He kissed her again, then held her face away so he could look into her eyes.

I wonder what truth Saski would draw now.

Ten

June 17, 1636. Dutch gardens are as immaculate as
Dutch houses. I believe the *mevrouws* must scrub each
leaf as hard as they scrub their floors. No weed dares
grow in all Amsterdam. I have not been such a diligent
gardener of my soul.

Journal of John Nightingale, known as John Graffham.

'Come tell me when you know what time you will sail!'
Marika begged the next morning. 'I want to come and wave
you off, veiled in black.'

And did your brother ask you to find out? John gave his
boot a sharp yank before he answered.

Marika's eyes sharpened. 'I won't say goodbye yet. I
couldn't bear to say goodbye, knowing that you were still in
Amsterdam for another seven or eight hours! Promise you'll
at least send a messenger. Promise me!'

'I promise,' he said reluctantly.

'But I shall kiss you goodbye now.' Marika held tightly to
his neck with both arms. Then she pulled back and engaged
his eyes. 'Please come back.'

John stopped abruptly and leaned on a canalside railing. His
heart titupped like a frightened horse. He pretended to look
down onto the greasy hat of a passing boatman. He was

being followed. He had not been conjuring up demons from unfamiliar shadows in an alien land.

The man behind him stopped as if to watch a canalside dentist trying to calm a terrified customer. He had a square, bare forehead, blackcurrant eyes sunk into the puffy dough of nose and cheeks, untrimmed hedge of salt-and-pepper beard. Shapeless, black felt, featherless hat and short breeches tied in above saggy grey knitted stockings. A cheerful background figure in an inn, an edge-of-a-crowd man. Harmless-looking enough, except that John had now seen him too many times. He remembered the forehead, a startling expanse of naked flesh between hat and hedge. There was another face too, on the edge of John's memory. A more stooped figure with a stick and no centre teeth, who carried a basket of eggs.

John turned his head a little toward the small crowd gathered around the dentist. Those baggy clothes could hide either flab or brawn. The unpadded shoulders were wide enough to give trouble.

The man on the dentist's small wooden chair shrieked. A man in the crowd caught his flailing arms and pinned them. John's man laughed with the others and looked sideways toward his mark. John stared down at a mysterious shape wavering on the bottom of the canal. Of course I've been followed, he thought, cursing himself. Why didn't I listen to myself when I was still myself, before I was drunk on foreign liquors that were too strong for my stupid, arrogant head? I couldn't have been more visible than I have been, going about with Coymans. Or more careless than with Marika.

Coymans? But Coymans would hardly need to have him followed. John had rushed daily of his own free will to thrust his head into the mouth of that particular lion.

All Amsterdam must know I have that money.

I'm so close! Nothing must happen now!

A tidy mountain range of early cabbages, carrots and kohlrabi slid below him, then a boat full of black-clad children. A dog sniffed at his left ankle.

John bent, offered his hand for approval. He scratched first the black ear and then the white. Scratching the dog made him feel better. He thought hard while he progressed to the wrinkled, scalloped jowls. Then he gave the flat head a final pat and set off in urgent purpose for the Warmoesstraat.

The baker pointed up a tiny flight of stairs that led first to a sleeping platform above the shop and then up into a stairwell that looked to John no larger than a hollow tree. He began to think he had come to the wrong place for the help he needed. But as he was already here, he climbed to the platform and inserted himself into the hollow tree. The ladder-like stairs stopped on a tiny landing outside a disproportionately heavy wooden door. John knocked.

A man's voice called out in Dutch.

'Senhor Gomez? It's John Nightingale.'

John listened to silence, then to slow footsteps on a wooden floor, and then to scraping bolts. He could pretend that he had merely come to say farewell and to leave a token of his gratitude.

Gomez wore a brocade dressing-gown. 'What's wrong?' he asked intensely. 'What's wrong? So, come in!' A delicate old hand reached out and reeled John through the door with surprising force.

'I'm sorry to disturb you . . .' John began. Then he saw the room he had entered.

Gomez watched John look. 'Surprised? You won't offend me if you say that you are surprised.'

'After the bakery, and those stairs . . . Forgive me, yes, I am.'

'Not much comes in here by way of the stairs.' Gomez undid the belt of his dressing-gown and retied it more neatly.

Under the gown he wore a shirt of white cotton finer than any linen John had ever seen. His moustaches, not yet waxed, hung like small, fluffy squirrels' tails below the strong, tanned nose. 'Most of it flies up here.' He pointed to the open window, outside which dangled a rope and pulley on a beam. 'This was the warehouse room for flour until the baker bought the house beside this one and used the water-level room there instead.'

'It's a very different warehouse now,' said John with awe and revised expectations of the old man. Clearly, Coymans had never seen this place. 'You would never know from below.' He gazed in amazement at the stacked paintings, the vibrant hummocks of Moorish carpet, the silver candelabra, the books. Though there was little furniture, the vast room was as densely packed as his own Knot Garden in high summer, with similar pathways and small clearings in which to move. It smelled of honey, musty leather, and the cinnamon which seeped everywhere near the docks. Gomez himself left a trail of sandalwood.

'It doesn't do to let the world know what you have,' said Gomez. 'The invisible live longest.'

'That's why I've come to you. I've become too visible.'

'I *knew* something was wrong when I heard your voice in this place,' said Gomez. 'So sit down and tell me.' He led John between a spinet stacked with blue and white Chinese *kraacke-ware* plates, along a gulley between cliffs of books, under an acre of knotted carpet hanging from a beam, to a pair of ivory-inlaid stools on either side of a small table. On the table sat an interrupted game of chess between ebony and ivory pieces. The black king was within two moves of being in check.

'I cheat,' said Gomez. 'I decide who I want to win and make it happen. It reassures me on bad days.'

'Then you're the very man I need to advise me on my own next moves!' said John with relief. He explained.

'Who would have thought tulips could be so dangerous,' said Gomez. 'Poor Bols. I had heard.'

'An auction could stop any man's heart . . .' John's pale grey eyes looked sharply at Gomez. 'You're not saying more than that?'

Gomez shook his head. 'No. I don't know anything worth saying. At his age, in any case, Bols was simply waiting his turn.' He stood up. 'Stay here. I won't be long. Read something while I am gone. Enlarge your mind and lift your soul!' He waved at a cliff-face of stacked books. 'Over there you will find Pliny, *Naturalis Historia*, all thirty-seven books. I would hope to be back before you finish them.'

He replaced dressing-gown with silk coat and left, moustaches still as fluffy as squirrels' tails.

A few moments later, John heard a knock. He unbolted the heavy door to see Gomez again.

'Here,' said Gomez. 'I apologize for having forgotten. Some breakfast.' He handed John a loaf of bread, still almost too hot to touch. 'There's cheese under the spinet.' He vanished down the hollow tree again.

The bread was barely cold when Gomez returned.

'You can sail tonight, just after dusk. From St Anthony's Gate, where you say you arrived. Can you find your own way there? I will meet you at the barge. You must look for it among the others. The *Sneek*.'

John laughed aloud. 'Thank you,' he said, still smiling.

'What?' Gomez was puzzled for a minute. Then he smiled. 'Oh, yes, I see. *Sneek*. It's the name of a Dutch town. Yes, ha, ha. Rather amusing.' His fingers discovered the softness of his right moustache. 'Anyway, it's cash before boarding. Now, we have a lot to do in the meantime. As soon as you get back to your lodgings, send your man here to me with three strong sacks.' He bent out of sight behind a leather chest studded with copper nails. 'I must array myself as a member.'

'Of what?' asked John.

Gomez stood up with his dressing chest and a fur hat. 'Of the very small, select club of men who can be trusted.'

John hesitated in the Warmoesstraat. Which way? Now his feet would tell him what he truly believed about Marika Coymans. Then he turned toward his lodgings with the Widow Padtbrugge. There was no time to see Marika now. She must be content with her farewell kiss. But the truth was, he did not want to risk testing her.

Just after the midday meal, John opened the door of his room at the top of the Widow Padtbrugge's house to a very large, bona fide member of Gomez's trustable club. A distant relative by marriage, Gomez had said. The man was evidently not used to such humble surroundings.

'Mynheer Nightingale . . . ?' The widow's voice, slightly breathless, leaked up around the dark bulk above her at the top of the spiral stairs. 'Wine?'

'*Nee dank u mevrouw*,' said the bulk.

Business only, thought John. No frivolous consorting with suspect foreigners. Strictly business. He stood aside to let the man in, then dropped the bar across the door.

'Arthur,' said John.

His servant, already back from his errand to Gomez, stood stiffly to attention to cover his nervous delight in these excitements after so many days of imprisonment. He knelt beside his bed, cut open the mattress and pulled out rattling bags of coins. Then he operated on John's bed. Their visitor began to sort the coins into neat gold and silver columns. Meanwhile, John lifted their cloaks from a stack of gold and silver plates. He unbuckled three large leather bags. Last, he unlocked the chest and lifted back the lid.

'Ah,' said the visitor. 'Yes.' He stared down into the chest. Then he bent, exhaling audibly as a bellows, and picked up a gold ingot. He examined it, handed it to John, bent again, turned over a silver spoon, and asked for pen, paper and ink.

'Will you sign a letter to say that you authorize the Marrano as your legitimate agent?'

John raised his black brows, puzzled. 'Who?'

'The Portuguese Marrano,' said the man. 'The old man, Gomez.'

'With a good will.' John wrote and signed as asked. Gomez, Portuguese, a Marrano (whatever that was). More layers that John had missed in his foreign ignorance. He was almost sorry to be leaving with so much still left to learn in this place. And with teachers as varied as Coymans and Gomez. And Marika.

His visitor began to count the money and list the other items. By the time he had finished the accounting, two hours later, John had thought wistfully more than once of Mevrouw Padtbrugge's rejected wine.

In mid-afternoon, a carter delivered four heavy wooden chests from Gomez. Once they had been reeled up the pulley, John sent Arthur for a walk along the canal. Arthur came back alight with satisfaction. A man with four middle teeth missing, and a stick, was selling eggs on the far bank, just across an arched bridge.

'And that walking stick could stop a charging bull,' said Arthur. 'The man himself's no more than thirty.'

'Do you still hanker to be a hero?' John asked him.

Arthur nodded.

John fixed him with his most impressive glare. 'Well, shed that ambition at once! I don't want to lose you this side of the Oceanus Germanicus, or that Rachel of yours might pray me into Hell. Swear to me that you won't suffer a fit of valour and rise to the occasion!'

'If you say so.' Arthur paused diplomatically. 'I hope I can count on you, too, sir.' He coughed. 'To watch your temper, I mean.'

Later, The Forehead replaced The Eggseller outside the widow's house. But neither was in sight at dusk, when the five chests were lowered heavily, one after another, by rope and pulley from the fifth-floor room among the treetops onto a cart.

I don't like it, thought John. I had expected to see at least one of them. I like to keep my enemies in view. Any of those bodies swilling along the cobbles could be the ones to fear. I hope I'm wrong to be afraid, but I'm sure I'm not.

The widow kissed him on both cheeks and gave him a long list of unintelligible instructions.

'I'll send you . . .' John began, then stopped. He could not think what to send from England that they did not already have here in Holland. And he didn't know where he would be sending from. If he had been returning to Hawkridge House, he could at least have sent her some honey flavoured with English flowers. 'A letter,' he finally said. Even from prison, he could send a letter.

She waved as the cart bumped and rumbled away over the stones, a bud that had opened as far as it ever would. John waved back, but he was already watching the dark openings of alleys and the deepening shadows under the canalside trees.

They trundled noisily under the pale stone side of the New Church toward the harbour, then across a bridge over the Damrak, below the market place and the Weigh House, onto the Old Side. John strained his ears to listen through the creaking of the cart, the metallic rasping of the horse's shoes against stone, and the usual evening noises . . . what were the normal noises here? Above the cart and horses' shoes on the cobbles, he heard knife blades rasp and wolves breathe.

They clanked and rattled safely through an empty market place.

By the time they turned left into Warmoesstraat, John felt foolish. So much trouble because he had suddenly become afraid. When he saw the dark fortified tower of St Anthony's Gate loom at the end of an alley, above the toothy line of roofs and candlelit windows, he began to compose an apology to Gomez for putting him to so much trouble.

The cart stopped. The carter explained in Dutch.

The alley ahead was too narrow, it seemed.

John pointed back along Warmoesstraat to a wider way through to the docks. The carter shook his head and lifted down one of the boxes.

John swore to himself. He looked ahead and behind. A quiet street. Two figures a long way down. A cat. Nothing else to be seen. Everyone had gone into the houses, for pea soup with ham, and cheese, and those mountains of carrots, cabbages and kohlrabi.

John swore again but got off the cart. He swung a second box to the ground. Arthur followed suit.

Arthur can't hold the gun while he's unloading boxes, thought John in sudden alarm. Then his forehead slammed against the floor of the cart. He lay for a second with the cart floor hard and cold under the shifting mist in his head. His head thundered. Pain both front and back.

I didn't fall.

Groggily, he turned and slid down to sit on the ground with his back against the rear wheel. A draw cord of pain pulled his eyes tightly shut.

I was hit.

He forced one eye to open a crack and saw a dark leg. A heavy boot. A joggling scabbard tip.

Hell and damnation! I was right after all.

'Arthur?' he whispered.

The boot and scabbard spiralled away. John became violently seasick. He retched and tried to stand. Was shoved down again. His sword jammed under his legs. He retched again, then levered his eyelids to half-mast. Shadows swirled around the cart. The cart itself seemed to be moving, but the wheel was braced hard and cold against his shoulder.

'Arthur?' he said, more urgently.

Voices spoke in that accursed language that he felt he could almost understand. Low and fast. As urgent as his own.

'ARTHUR!'

'Here.' Behind him.

The boot returned to the back of the cart with its fellow. The attackers were unloading the chests. Sword still under his legs.

John put his hand on his knife. Then, with effort, lifted it away again. He saw hats and cloaks, very high above him. Hats pulled too low to see if The Forehead were one of them. He tried to raise himself a little, to see better.

One of the boots kicked him hard in the side. A bear clamped its jaws below his ribs. He rolled away, lay trying to breathe, then hauled himself onto his knees. He crawled two paces. Cobbles sharp under his knees. He hauled himself up the front cartwheel to his feet.

The hats now bent in the shadows along the alley wall. The docks were beyond the hats. Why didn't the thieves just take the chests and go? John had not expected them to stop to open the chests on the spot. Don't open the chests!

He heard an angry oath. Their boat to England lay at the other end of that alley.

'Arthur?'

A shadow hauled itself upright alongside him. They clung to the side of the cart for a moment like sailors on a spar spewed up by a sinking ship.

John drew a careful breath. The bear's jaw in his side opened a little. He took a deeper breath. His head merely rumbled now, instead of thundering. 'Can you walk?'

'I'll kill the bastard sons of Satan,' muttered Arthur.

John looked back for another way through. Too far. No safer. The hats would catch them either way if they wanted to. He drew his sword. 'I'm sorry, Arthur. I didn't think they'd open the chests on the spot. I believe there are three of them. You may need to be a hero after all.'

'Thank God!' muttered Arthur. 'Or else I'll choke with rage.'

John let go of the cart, balanced, and walked towards the alley where the hats were bent over the chests, and at the end of which lay his boat for England.

The shadows were too thick for them to see the hats. Slowly, slowly, he and Arthur eased themselves forward, ears aquiver for the slightest rasping of fabric or grating of boot on stone. John crouched. He saw the faint shape of lighter sky at the end of the alley, uncarved by the shapes of hats. He crouched lower and peered along the alley at knee level. Some squared shapes. No hats.

They advanced a little farther. The chests stood open. No shadows beyond them.

'I think they've gone,' said Arthur.

Still carefully, they edged to the end of the alley. It was empty.

'We're lucky they'd no taste for revenge,' said John. 'Do you feel as much of a fool as I do?'

'Heroic, thank you,' said Arthur.

The *Sneek* lay at the bottom of some water steps about a hundred feet to their right. By the time they found her, John wanted nothing more than to lie down on something soft and close his eyes.

Gomez was waiting at the top of the steps with the captain of the barge and two sailors. 'What happened?' he cried. 'We thought we heard something but couldn't tell where! Are you all right? Your forehead is bleeding!'

'It's nothing,' said John. 'We were right, you and I, to be suspicious. And Arthur's porterage this afternoon was rewarded. I don't know who those men were, but they don't have literary tastes. Your books are back there in that alley.'

'And here's your wealth,' said Gomez. He handed John a small flat leather pouch. 'Metamorphosed.'

John took the pouch and opened it. Inside was a single folded piece of vellum. 'All?' he asked in disbelief and a sudden violent terror. He tried to read the Latin written on the vellum, addressed to a Jacov Fernandez. The bump on his forehead began to thud again like a drum. Gold coins, ingots and plates, with silver spoons and gilt candlesticks had dematerialized. Nothing was left of the unwieldy fortune but a fine, spidery web of words he could balance on two fingers. The old man had diddled him elegantly and absolutely. 'All?'

'All. We cleared your hoard safely as soon as you and your trackers left the widow's house. Not a soul followed me here. The decoy worked.'

John weighed the pouch and parchment in his hand. He thought he had trusted Gomez. He thought he still did, though the drumming in his head made it hard to think anything. 'How silent it is,' he said. 'And light. And nearly invisible. A magical transformation.'

'Not magic,' said Gomez. 'Business. That's your bond of exchange. The big merchants can't keep heaving boxes of money from one to another, so we make understandings.' He watched John with amusement. 'It's all there. Don't keep hefting it as if you expect it to gain weight.

'And listen . . .' He guided John a little away from the other men on the edge of the dock. 'If your money instead of my books had been in those chests, and it had been stolen, you would now be penniless. You must understand that if that parchment is stolen, you are also penniless. My cousin Jacov will only pay out for that document. Not for you . . . for whoever holds that document in his hand. That strip of dried sheep's belly skin is money – nothing more, nothing less. Keep it safe.' He looked at John's face again and sighed. 'You'll believe me when you get to Cousin Jacov.'

'I believe you now,' protested John, a little too warmly. 'You're a magician, sir, and I am your bemused but grateful apprentice.' John tucked the pouch inside his shirt next to his skin and clasped the old man's warm, dry hand. He hoped his own hand was not chilled by distrust.

'I'll see you when you return,' said Gomez. '*Até à vista.*'

'I'm sorry to say that I'm unlikely to come back.'

'*Até à vista, adeus,*' repeated Gomez. 'Now get down onto your boat before our trick is understood and your friends from the alley try again. Give my respects to Cousin Jacov. Do something about that head. Go, go. Go! I'm an old man and I'm getting cold.'

A day and a half later, a little after dawn, as the *Sneek* eased into the wide embrace of the Thames estuary, John made a decision.

'Arthur.'

'Sir?' His man levered himself off the barge rail where he had been enjoying his freedom from the terrible tether of all that wealth and rehearsing how he would tell Rachel (among others) the extraordinary tale of his last few exciting hours in Amsterdam. They had made up for the tedium of the rest. He had forgotten that he could not swim.

John gave Arthur a heavy purse.

'What's that for?' At that moment, Arthur almost resented wages. Being paid diminished the glow of those tense shared moments on the cart, of clinging wounded side by side, of entering the alley shoulder to shoulder into possible ambush and the grasping arms of hungry death.

'That's to guard your future. I don't know my own.'

'Do you mean, if Mr Gomez has diddled you?' Arthur was sure that the magical transformation from gold to vellum was complete sham, but it had not been his place to question.

John shook his head. 'I must trust that he hasn't. I mean, your best future may not lie with me.'

Arthur drew back as if John had hit him. His freckled face went white. 'Are you letting me go? Is that what you're say-

ing? What the devil have I done, except fight by your side?'
His voice was incredulous.

'No, of course not . . . I mean to say, yes, but for your own good.'

'Since when has being turned out of his position been for any man's good? Where can I go?'

'Arthur, I'm doing this badly. It's your position that I'm trying to protect. I may not go back to Hawkridge House. I want you to be able to go back if you choose.'

'Sir?' Arthur stood stiff and unbelieving.

'I can't return to Hawkridge House.'

Arthur laughed from shock. 'Sorry . . . sir! I didn't mean . . . Don't joke, sir!' John *was* Hawkridge House, Sir Harry or no Sir Harry.

'I may not have another chance to tell you . . .' John swallowed. This was harder than he had thought. 'It's no joke. There may be soldiers waiting for me in London. And if not today, there will be as soon as my return is known.'

'Soldiers . . . ?'

'An old crime. Before I came to Hawkridge House. My past sniffed me out when I had almost forgotten it.'

'What crime? If you don't mind me asking.'

'Murder.'

Arthur sucked in his upper lip and stared at John, blinking hard. 'He deserved it,' he said firmly. 'I've no doubt.'

'Nor have I. But I'm less sure now of my right to have been his executioner.'

'How old were you?'

'Fourteen.'

The fair young man hefted his new purse and thought. 'With respect, sir, if that's the case, why have you come back at all?'

John looked away over the rumpled pewter water. They were passing anchored merchantmen. Lighters and ferries stitched one shore to the other in a web that grew denser the farther upstream they went. John patted the breast of his doublet over Gomez's pouch. 'I have to return these lives to their owners.'

Like John, Arthur was quick. It was part of their unexamined bond. And he had been listening to Gomez on the dock by St Anthony's Gate. 'Let me take those lives back for you, wherever they need to go. You set down somewhere in Southwark, vanish and, if you like, send me word later where to come join you.'

It was a sensible suggestion.

'Thank you,' said John. It was sensible, and he trusted Arthur's honesty utterly. With a good story about John's mysterious flight, his man would come to no harm. Hazelton would probably reward him. So long as Gomez hadn't swindled him. 'Thank you, but I can't!'

Arthur's freckled face set stubbornly. 'You can trust me.'

'I know that, you fool!' John looked away again. But if Gomez has swindled me, I must be there. Arthur can't bear the message of ruin. 'I think perhaps that I want a flash of glory before I'm forced to run.'

This Arthur understood. He held the purse out to John again. 'Then I'll take my chance with you. And you'll need this more than me.'

'Compromise like a sensible fellow. At least keep the money. I don't know when I can pay you next.'

'Enough said,' said Arthur. He would regret not seeing Rachel again, if it came to that. But beating the dust out of sleeping pallets and laying the fire was tame employment for a man who had helped beat off foreign assassins. More or less, he amended honestly. He thought he might enjoy becoming the squire of an outlaw adventurer. If he hadn't had the misfortune to be born near Basingstoke, he might even have run away to sea as a boy.

They had sailed on a cargo barge which braved the treacherous sand bars of the estuary to land its cargo at the London docks, rather than set down passengers more safely on the coast. Merchantmen lay in mid-river, placid as toys, while the ferries, wherries, sailing barges, and dinghies cut across each other's trails in the early light, upstream and down, from shore to shore, heavy with people, vegetables, timber, coal, horses, sheep, cattle, coaches and carts. Houses crowded the north bank, the city side. Just upstream from the gardens of a large beerhouse, the fields of the southern bank began to fill with houses as well.

St Katherine's Stairs. Iron Gate Stairs. Green hills swelled behind the drying fields of St Mary Grace's Abbey, a little blurred by a mantle of coal smoke. Traitor's Gate and the Tower and they were into the city itself.

Samuel Hazelton had resisted the growing fashion for living in the country, out of London's fog of coal smoke and black dust. Many of his colleagues and acquaintances rode by horse each morning from Covent Garden, Charing Cross and beyond. He preferred to live near the centre of the business world.

John and Arthur disembarked at the water stairs at Customs Wharf, paid a man to watch their belongings, took a wherry to Old Swan Stairs above London Bridge, and climbed Old Swan Lane to Thames Street. When they arrived at Hazelton's large town-house on St Laurence Hill, John hesitated slightly. This was the first of the burrows where Malise might wait.

Hazelton had been awake for the last five nights. His corrugated tree-bark face was grey. When John was shown into the first-floor parlour, Hazelton was sitting by the fire in a heavy chair-of-grace with a cover around his legs. He did not stand.

'Sit down, sir. Please sit down. Pleasant voyage? Prefer carriages to boats myself. When did you arrive?'

John sat, was served a mug of ale. Hazelton asked about

the smoothness of the sea, commented on the continuing lack of rain and how it would influence English crops. Then he began to complain that he was exhausted by constant, inexplicable pain in his legs.

John realized that the man was terrified.

'It's done, sir,' John said.

'Done or undone?' Hazelton's tongue clicked in his dry mouth.

'Done! Forty thousand pounds worth of done!'

'Forty thousand? Lost, you mean? Or brought back?' Hazelton blinked and looked past John as if for bags or chests. 'Where? Who's watching it?'

'With me here safely, in this room.' John pulled out Gomez's pouch and stood up to hand Hazelton the bond of exchange.

The bond rattled in the older man's hands. 'Who is this Jacov Fernandez?'

'A diamond merchant of Lombard Street.'

'Can he be trusted?'

'I trust his cousin in Amsterdam.'

There was a touch of defiance in John's tone. Hazelton licked his thin, dry lips and smoothed the piece of vellum on his knees. 'Forty thousand,' he repeated blankly. He looked up at John. 'Did you have the money in your hands? Or was it always on paper?'

'It was around my neck throttling me. I wish someone had told me how unwieldy a fortune is.'

Hazelton hardly listened. He pushed himself to his feet and stepped over the coverlet which fell to the floor. 'James!' he shouted through the parlour door. 'My cloak.' He turned on John. 'Where does this Fernandez live?' To his servant he said, 'Send for Sir George Tupper to meet us at . . .'

'The Fenchurch Street well,' said John.

'We'd better go test your trust!'

Jacov Fernandez lived above the dark narrow cavern of his

diamond shop, behind heavy doors, locks, bolts, bars and shutters.

Sir George, Hazelton, John and a small flock of serving men waited through a lengthy trope of clicks, rattles, metallic squeaks and wooden moans. A servant finally peered through the half-open door into the street. He looked terrified at their numbers.

John gave him the letter Gomez had sent for his cousin. The servant shut the door again. Again they listened to the clicks and rattles. A little later, he returned, played a shorter version of the unlocking trope and let them in.

Fernandez greeted them in a heavy silk robe and tight-fitting old-fashioned cap. He was a little younger, paler and plumper than his cousin Gomez. His moustaches had never aspired to the horizontal but sagged comfortably into his salt-and-pepper beard. 'Which of you brought the letter from my cousin? Did he look healthy? You can't trust what people tell you in letters, they never like to say what's wrong.'

'He's in good health,' said John, 'and sends you a Dutch cheese. I have it here.'

Fernandez laughed and looked quickly at Tupper and Hazelton. 'Thank you for your trouble. If I had known, I could have sent him an English one in return.'

'He also sends this,' said Hazelton hoarsely. 'Can you honour it?' He handed over the bond.

Fernandez put down the cheese. He read the bond. When he looked up, his tinge of diffidence had gone.

'Of course,' he said. 'Give me the day to gather it for you.' He returned the bond to Hazelton's hovering hands.

Tupper and Hazelton searched the anonymous little parlour for omens, but the room had been designed to keep all its secrets to itself. As Fernandez politely showed them out, he gave John a familiar departing clap on the back. He had these three sorted out.

Back in the street, with the day to get through, Tupper said, 'I'll ask . . .'

'So will I,' agreed Hazelton.

But it's too late to change anything, thought John. Whatever you may learn about Fernandez.

'Will you come back with us tonight?' asked Hazelton.

Or will I skip town before my confederate Fernandez disappoints you, do you mean? thought John. 'Of course,' he said. After a moment, he asked, 'Is there any word of my cousin?'

'No,' said Hazelton abruptly. 'He hasn't been to London since you left for Amsterdam. No doubt too busy taking up the reins at Hawkridge House.' He limped a few more painful strides. 'Edward Malise has been lying low, too. Someone told me he had gone abroad again.' He looked at John, who avoided his eyes.

Sir George said goodbye and agreed to meet them again at the well at half-past four that afternoon, with two armed men and a carriage.

As soon as John and Hazelton were alone, the older man dropped his voice below their servants' hearing and asked, 'What is the trouble between you and Malise?'

'I can't say.'

'You have the gift of irritating me,' said Hazelton with reasonable cordiality. 'I'm not playing a nursery game.'

'Nor am I. I'm sorry. I haven't wanted to irritate you.'

'I need to know why Malise thought he could swing you round, and why he then failed. It wasn't Malise who changed your mind for you, was it? In spite of that fine speech you made about preferring honesty and finally understanding your true value to us?'

'You're right.'

'I usually am,' said Hazelton as a statement of simple fact. 'Here we are. Will you join me for breakfast?'

John accepted and followed Hazelton's laborious climb to the first-floor parlour.

'Tell me!' ordered Hazelton, when they were alone. 'Your relationship with Malise bears on both our futures.'

'My secrecy protects my future. My neck's at stake.'

'If Fernandez is a man of his word,' said Hazelton, 'and we conclude in triumph, as I'm just beginning to let myself hope we shall, it happens that we . . . the Company . . . might want to use you again. Without knowing more, I would not be happy to do so.'

John teetered close to unloading onto Hazelton's black lap the ring of fire, the screams, the laughing face in the firelight, and the last eleven years. But it was too soon. Hazelton might become an ally in time, but now he was discussing business, not making an offer of friendship.

'If you do have the occasion to employ me again, I won't let you work in the dark.'

Hazelton was irritated again, but there was nothing more he could say.

At a little after half-past four, the three men once again listened to the diamond merchant's locks. Fernandez was now fully dressed in black, like Hazelton, and ready for them.

A miracle of metamorphosis, thought John, as he watched the dried sheep's belly change back into gold. Even more miraculous, it was no longer his responsibility.

'I told your cousin that he was a magician,' said John to Fernandez. 'And so are you.'

'It's a matter of convenience,' said Fernandez. 'As you must agree. Only the magic of keeping one's word. How could we accomplish anything if men didn't keep their word?'

Hazelton and Tupper took a sharp, polite interest as Fernandez's assistant made stacks of coins, bars, and plates. The sky over London was nearly dark by the time everything had been counted, weighed, assayed and loaded into the chests brought by Hazelton. The chests were then moved under guard into Sir George's carriage which had been left fifty yards away from Fernandez's house in a street wide enough to take it.

Sir George, Hazelton and John were silent with nerves for the two hours it took to reach Sir George's house on the river, just outside the city. A boat upriver would have been faster, but then attention would have been called to the cargo.

At last, Sir George locked the money safely away in the offices of the South Java Company. The three men stood in front of the fire in his private parlour.

'Praise the Lord!' said Hazelton suddenly and intensely. A red spot burned on each thin grey cheek.

'Well done, sir! Well done!' Tupper slapped John on the arm, then slapped Hazelton. They grinned and took deep breaths, and slapped arms again.

'I'm almost past thanksgiving,' said Tupper. 'Awed, if you like. And I've never seen a rogue who looked less like a rescuing angel ... well done again, sir! Drink. Drink! The grape was invented to bolster our mortal insufficiency at times like these. I must get drunk, or I'll burst!'

'The man might prefer to have his commission.' Hazelton raised his brows at Tupper.

'Of course. Of course.' Tupper unlocked his wall cupboard again and took out three leather pouches. 'Well earned. There's recognition there of the surplus you brought back. You'll be off back to Hawkridge now, I expect, to take Sir Harry the good news.'

'Back?' John took the pouches from Tupper. Lord, how heavy they were!

'A messenger with your news is bound to be welcome. Why shouldn't you go back?' Tupper's boisterous voice carried on while his eyes sharpened. He and Hazelton exchanged a glance.

Malise is abroad, thought John. I could go back. Briefly. Joy began to take him over, painful and thorough as a mortal illness.

I can see it all again. Its people. And beasts.

But can I then bear to leave it all a second time?

It didn't matter. The joy was as fierce as lust. He would go, whether he could bear it or not. His known life would go on a little longer. He could step back, however briefly, into his old familiar skin.

He addressed the ghost of Bols. I'll take your infant *King* back after all to start that dynasty. If my arrival in Amsterdam led by chance to your death, I'll see to it at least that your field blooms.

Part Three

Eleven

June 25, 1636. England. In hedgerows, wild briar, Great Purple Monkshood (*aconitum pur.*), small mallow and common mallow, burnet rose all in full blow. Titlarks and blackcaps sing. Apples begin to blush. How such abundance delights my heart.

Journal of John Nightingale, known as John Graffham.

'John! I would have had music, John!' said Dr Bowler. 'I wanted to play you back to Hawkridge House, but Harry ... Sir Harry ... said that ... too much time ... it wasn't possible.'

Bowler had been waiting outside the forecourt gate near the top of the beech avenue. John dismounted and embraced his old tutor amid jumping dogs and cheering, jostling children. The bell in the brewhouse tower still pealed his arrival. A boy leaped for the reins of John's horse.

'Your greeting is music enough,' said John. 'How has everyone fared while I was gone?'

'Well enough that you won't despair and ill enough that you needn't fear.' Bowler's small eyes glinted. Then he looked away, embarrassed by his own wickedness.

Cassie the staghound bitch broke from between two beeches, galloped up the drive and flung her forelegs across John's shoulders. He laughed and embraced her, turning a little from her hot, happy, doggy breath.

315

'Pa says her pup can sleep with me and my brother!' The boy whose father had taken the pup bounced at John's right side, waving for his attention. 'Shall I show it to you?'

A small girl pulled at John's left sleeve.

'. . . Yes, yes!' John said to her. Then he nodded his agreement to the boy with Cassie's pup. '. . . Get down girl,' he said to Cassie. To the child at his sleeve, he continued, '. . . I brought enough Dutch honey waffles for all of you, if you ask politely and don't dance all over my feet.'

He walked down the drive to the forecourt gate, surrounded. A boy proudly led his horse. Arthur followed, still mounted, his eyes seeking someone not yet there. The yellow cur took up position beside John's left leg and would not be edged out, even by Cassie.

'"Praise God from whom all blessings flow . . ."' sang Bowler suddenly in his high true baritone. He raised his hands and brought in a ragged chorus of children for the next line. '"Praise him all creatures here below . . ."'

'John!' called the excited voice of his aunt from the forecourt gate. 'Oh, John! You're back!' She picked up her skirts and began to roll with her arthritic gait up the sloping drive.

'How could I not?' John called back.

'John . . .' Bowler suddenly stopped both singing and conducting. 'A word before you're hauled away.' He crossed his arms and tucked his hands into his armpits as if warming them on a cold day. The children's voices trailed off uncertainly.

'Speak, *magister*.'

Bowler licked his lips unhappily. 'I wouldn't want to take the gleam off a sterling day . . .'

'You couldn't dim its lustre if you tried,' said John, with apprehension. 'Out with it!'

'Did you do it?' asked Bowler, low and fearfully. 'What you went to do, you know, the money . . .' Bowler suddenly lost faith in what he thought he knew. 'Harry let slip . . .' He

316

blushed, uncrossed his arms, and hid his hands behind his back. 'The estate at risk . . .'

John took pity on him. 'Yes, my dear doctor, I did it. All is well.'

How sweet to tell someone who cared for him and to share good news with those who would profit from it!

'I must keep a suitably modest face on it, but – just privately between us – I am most monstrously overjoyed and relieved!'

'Ah,' said Dr Bowler with quiet satisfaction. 'We've been terribly worried . . . not that any of us doubted you, you understand.' Colour returned to his cheeks. 'But Harry has been in such a flibber. None of us was quite sure what was happening, or going to happen. It was like waiting for the millennium. Unsettling. I did persuade the churchwardens to dun the parish for a new roof.' He looked sideways at John. 'Am I right to suppose then that the church roof is still our concern?'

'You are.'

'The Lord be praised!' Bowler's voice was fervent.

'I'm not sure how much He had to do with it,' said John. 'I'll tell you more sometime . . . Mistress Margaret!'

Aunt Margaret dropped her skirts and flung her arms around John.

'My dear aunt!' John looked down at the small head with white wisps escaping from under its cap. 'I trust those are tears of joy . . . Cassie, down, I say!'

The little procession passed through the gate. Three geese lowered their heads, raised their wings and hissed at the dogs. 'Harry's gone hunting,' said Aunt Margaret. A hint of censure leaked through her joy. 'Went out this morning, before the lad from Bedgebury estate ran over the fields with the news you were sighted. Said his nerves couldn't stand the waiting.' She blinked up at John with watery eyes.

'He did it!' Bowler told her in a voice aquiver with emotion. 'All will be well.'

'I wish someone would tell me what's going on,' said Aunt Margaret. 'No one ever explains to an old woman. But good news is good news.' She found a handkerchief in her sleeve and wiped her eyes. 'Let me get you some bread and ale. I don't know where her ladyship is, either. How long have you been riding without a meal? I should never have let you go off like that!' Tucking away her handkerchief, and the loose strands of hair, she wheeled away up the steps onto the porch and into the house. 'Agatha! Agatha!' Her voice faded away toward the buttery.

John paused on the top step of the porch. How rumpled and furled the countryside looked. How friendly, enclosing, welcoming and intelligible.

'Who else is here?' he asked Bowler.

'Just family.'

So, for the moment, it was also safe. No men-at-arms or constable. Edward Malise was abroad. John could draw a quick breath.

The children dispersed after promises of honey waffles. Cassie trotted into the house where her nails could be heard clicking on the tiled floor. The yellow cur wrapped himself round and round until he had made a shallow nest in the gravel at the bottom of the steps just below one of the stone eagles. The bell on the brewhouse tower still clanged.

Back. He's back. Back. He's back.

Officially rung in. Against all odds, and not for long, but back.

'I would have liked to hand the bonds of exchange over to Hazelton myself,' said Harry. 'But well done, cousin, all the same.' He smelled of horse. His hunting boots left a spoor behind him on the Turkey carpet. 'I'll leave for London straightaway in the morning, on horseback – you can send my things after me by cart. There will be important Company work to be done now. But first, of course, we must think how to celebrate your triumph without having to explain too much to the others.'

The others have deduced far more than you imagine, thought John. And if you ache to be a major player in this drama, you should have been in London waiting for me, as Hazelton was.

He bit ravenously into the bread and cheese his aunt had brought here to the Small Parlour.

Harry's extreme relief betrayed his earlier certainty that John would fail. He had not been waiting in London, because he could not endure the shame of facing Hazelton and the rest when his cousin came back empty-handed.

'Why don't you and I just raise our glasses in secret to the future of Hawkridge estate with Sir Harry Beester at the helm?'

Harry nodded with relief. 'I suppose secrecy is best. What are you going to do now? Does Malise know you're back here?'

'Hazelton says he's abroad. I'm safe for the time. Then, I don't know. I must change my name yet again. Perhaps sign on for a voyage with Tradescant to the Americas. Or steal away, far, far from London and look for a small piece of land to buy with my commission from the Company.'

'You'll set all in order here first?'

'As much as I'm given time for.'

'And then I can help with your escape,' said Harry eagerly. 'I'll arrange for a secret transfer of your stipend from Uncle George . . .' Harry lit up with the joys of conspiring.

'Cousin John!' A girl's happy voice interrupted them.

'Lady Beester!' John stood hastily and bowed, still holding his bread and cheese.

Zeal poised uncertainly, half-ready to embrace him as Aunt Margaret had done, half accepting the courtesy due to her new position. Her face beamed unwitting joy. John glanced at Harry.

She had put on a good gown that morning. Then at some point she had removed the sleeves and tucked up the overskirt into the waist. Dried grass had caught in the lace of the undersleeves which she had shoved half-way up her arms. The hem of her brocade petticoat was rimmed with dirt. Her bare forearms were turning an unladylike brown.

'I was prepared to greet you, but then I went up to the orchard with the bees. Then I heard the bell.' Zeal crossed to him and seized his free hand with both of hers. 'We are so pleased that you're back, aren't we, Harry? And I have so many questions to ask you.' She dropped his hand. 'And are you redeemed by your labour abroad?'

'Redeemed?' asked Harry sharply.

'More than I dared to hope, madam,' replied John.

She beamed at him, flushed and pleased, poised to say more. Then she said, 'And is that how you're rewarded? With just bread and cheese? I have meat pies waiting for you in the kitchen!'

'I can manage it all,' said John. 'I've been weeks on foreign vittles. Bring it on, my lady!'

Zeal allowed him to humour her. She grinned. 'You have such good manners when you want. Better than some at court.' She shot a look at Harry.

Don't do that! thought John. You may be too young to know what you're doing, but the damage is still real enough.

'I'll go fetch it,' said Zeal with vigour.

When the door had closed behind her, John asked, 'How are she and our aunt rubbing along together?'

'I'd like to thrash the pair of them,' said Harry ferociously. 'Women, children and animals! What sane man would want to deal with any of them? At least you can sort those two now that you're back.'

'The ignorance, John!' exclaimed Aunt Margaret later, over bedtime posset and cold meat. 'It's hard to believe that a fancy London education can leave a girl so woefully pig-ignorant. I'm not saying that she isn't trying. And she has had some luck ... You've no doubt already heard about the bees. And she took poor Peter's death touchingly hard ... But honestly, John, if I didn't watch all the time, I can't tell you the dreadful mess she might make of things. At least, she sometimes admits that, old as I am, I might have something to teach her. But she still leans too much on those wretched books of hers.' Mistress Margaret wiped her mouth delicately with her handkerchief, then explored its lace edging with her crooked fingers.

'When I was a girl, we listened to our elders, didn't trust for our instruction to the deceptions of *words*! All these new ideas ... innovation, that's what they are! And we all know that innovation seduces the soul toward novelty, and then to frivolity.' She frowned at the fire, tucked her handkerchief back into her sleeve and smoothed her skirts firmly. 'I'm glad you're back to help keep the child from going astray.'

John fell into his bed late, dazed with too much celebratory beer, unexpected shows of affection, and the whole woodpile of concerns that had fallen upon him as he passed through the forecourt gates.

How can I ever leave all this again? Alcohol blurred the jagged edges of the thought.

As he had never been absent since he had first taken refuge on the estate, no one had ever missed him before. It was pleasant, being missed. He gave a comfortable beery belch. He sniffed the well-known sharpness of the leather headboard and the faint mustiness of the wool curtains. He turned over and enjoyed the perfect fit between his stone-like head and its own familiar pillow. For one night, he would pretend that he had come home to stay.

He turned again restlessly. He imagined that he could smell cinnamon. A few nights before, Marika's bright head had rested beside his, on the brocade pillows of her gilded wood bed in Amsterdam, with Erasmus weighing down the cover over their feet. John opened his eyes and stared into the darkness. He was filled with a sudden coldness as absolute as death. He would not see her again.

Dear God! He rolled onto his side and curled tightly in pain, fists clenched against his mouth, elbows pressed together into his waist. He wanted her. He would never have her again. Other grateful supplicants would feast on the goddess's bounty.

I want. My God, I want!

Close that door, he told himself. Or you will go mad. This is your real life again, however briefly. A man should be master of his mind, and body.

But that bed in Amsterdam felt more real than this bed, that remembered body more alive than this fleshly one. This life felt more fragile than the one he had left for ever in Amsterdam.

His old life hadn't known that it was supposed to have ended; it had carried on and waited for him to return. Not one person here seemed to see how close that life had come to ending for them all. Even the people who knew seemed to forget before he had been back one day.

Harry had scowled and said he supposed that John could find a new churchwarden to replace one who had inconveniently died the week before. Aunt Margaret had enlisted his help with her terrier's cough. Zeal had dragged him off to see the shelves of cheeses maturing in the cheese room and a new bee skep in the orchard. (She didn't tell him the tale of the bee swarm, but he had already heard it three times.) Cope had made him admire the new hot beds. Together they had pondered the continuing drought.

I am needed here, John told himself. I helped to make this world. Lying in the dark, he built a wall of details, to lean against that other world and Marika like a dike against the sea.

Tuddenham had found mice in the small grain store, in spite of the new saddle stones. Cassie's pups had been paraded before him. John had inspected the church roof that wanted mending and the broken leg of a labourer who would be badly needed at harvest time. The field boundary dispute had been held over by the disputants until his return.

'You must speak to Sir Harry,' said John sternly.

'Yes, sir. We'll do that. But we'd like you to be present, sir, if you will.'

I must tell them all the truth when I leave again. At least the piglets have all moved happily from the stable yard sty up to Pig Acre. Firmly, he held in his mind the image of the piglet that bolted in excitement to the far end of the enclosure, froze when it suddenly saw how far behind it had left the others, and then raced back in terror.

At last a blurred, releasing sleep rolled in over him.

'It's too bad you must leave again for London so soon,' he had said to Harry at supper. 'I'm out of touch, need you to instruct me. And I'm sure there are many things I forgot to tell you before I left.'

'Indeed there were!' said Harry, spurning the offered diplomacy. 'But there's no help for it. I want to be in at the kill in London. I need to be seen there, as an architect of the renewed Company. Problems here will just have to wait until I get back.'

Behind Harry's ill-temper lay the half-admitted truth that if he were in London, it would seem less obvious that John had taken over again. And also, Harry could evade the problem of the still-separate ponds.

John will take over anyway, thought Harry, whether I'm here or not. He half-wished that Malise would come back to England and remove his cousin for good.

He watched John laugh with Mistress Margaret and then call jovially to Dr Bowler about some obscurity of estate life.

Officious as always. Made worse by this last success among those Dutch herring-eaters.

Harry had noticed John's tact, but felt it as patronage.

'. . . thinks Iphigenia might have to be put down,' said Dr Bowler, leaning across the table to John, 'but he waited for your return. You must have a look at her in the morning.'

Harry glared at the parson over the rim of his tankard. Another patronizer. All Latin verbs and ground bass! *Pizzicato* blah, blah, and blah, blah *nobis pacem*! Fat good all that would do Dr Bowler in Whitehall! Not that he'd ever get near the place. Nor would his precious John, for that matter.

He couldn't deny that he owed his cousin a lot for what he had done in Amsterdam – though John had really only done what he had been instructed to do. Harry managed to smile when Bowler proposed a toast of welcome to John.

I really am grateful! thought Harry. I really am. 'I second that toast, coz,' he said, waving his glass to include all his dependants around the table. 'Welcome back!'

His cousin had done well enough, off over there among foreigners and such, Harry would be first to admit. But John would find London and Whitehall a different challenge. It was just as well that he would never have to face it. Escaped criminals don't go to the royal court.

Harry drank more beer, feeling better. He drank some more. The night was warm, the estate beer fresh from the stream-cooled cellars.

And they're my cellars, thought Harry. My ale. Why am I bothering myself anyway? John'll have to skulk off soon enough, as soon as Malise gets back. I'm still the owner. I can throw him off the estate any time I like. In the meantime, I choose to keep him here. I need him here just now, so I can go to London with a clear mind.

'. . . you'll tell me, then, if I get it right?' Zeal was asking Mistress Margaret.

Harry had missed the subject under discussion.

'You may pickle me with ginger if anyone ever tells you anything, my lady,' replied Mistress Margaret tartly.

Everyone laughed, including Zeal.

And then there's her. Harry watched his wife's slim face turn, laughing, in the slanting rays of the late sun that fell through the window. Sunburned like a dairymaid! He sighed. And that wild hair. I despair.

'John,' cried Zeal across the laughter. 'Please tell your aunt . . .'

'"You may pickle me with ginger if anyone ever . . ."' John mimicked in a high quavering voice, and ducked a mock blow from his aunt.

I'd best take the little chit with me to London, I suppose, thought Harry, feeling suddenly alone. Before she gets any fonder of country manners.

'I order you to come.'

'Don't be silly.' Harry looks like a child about to have a tantrum, thought Zeal. 'I mean, be sensible. How long will you be in London?'

'I'm not sure.'

She had wondered why he followed her to her chamber after supper instead of staying in the Little Parlour to smoke and play a few hands of angel-beast.

'Then send for me when you do know. Anyway, I can't pack all my trunks and boxes by the time you leave tomorrow.'

I can't leave! she thought in panic. I won't leave! I'm never going to leave, ever! And there's so much I must do now that Cousin John's back to help.

She called up a craftiness forged and honed during the last six years of dealing with indifferent strangers. 'Do you really want me there while you're in the midst of important matters? I'll need teaching before I can meet all your important friends.'

'I thought you found better manners here than in Whitehall.'

'I was only teasing. I don't know anything about Whitehall. It terrifies me. I'll probably stand and gape and gawk and make one *faux pas* after another.'

Arms akimbo, hair radiating in a bright wiry halo, half-undressed, she looked to Harry like a young fishwife, lacking only the bloody apron and the smell. In the right circumstances, he didn't mind a fishwife or two.

'I couldn't bear to damage your standing!'

His lips unclamped a little.

That's better, she thought.

'It might be better,' said Harry, with the solemn air of a man consulting inner voices, 'to keep my mind on business for the next few weeks. When everything's under control on that front, I can send for you, take you in hand and lick you into shape. Give you my full attention . . . no time when we were married. Too much else to be readied. No time for the bride, eh?' He laughed.

Zeal laughed back cautiously. Something in Harry's eye made her cross her arms in front of her.

'. . . take you in hand,' Harry repeated, listening to his own words with interest.

Zeal kept her smile, but became as alert as a rabbit.

'What there is of you,' said Harry, speculatively. 'In hand . . .'

Oh, no! thought Zeal.

She stepped back as Harry stepped forward, but his reach was longer than her stride. His mouth hit the corner of hers as she turned her head. Her upper lip snagged on the corner of one of her teeth. She tasted salt.

'You promised! You promised not to!' She twisted and wriggled with the panic-stricken force of a terrified kitten.

'It's only a kiss!' He released her so suddenly that she staggered back and stumbled over the hem of her petticoat.

Zeal glared as she untangled her feet. 'You promised!'

'Only a friendly kiss!' said Harry indignantly. 'What can I do? Say, am I allowed to take your hand, madam? May I help you down from a carriage? Up the stairs? Tell me, so I don't misunderstand. How closely may I approach your sacred presence? Eh? Wife!'

Damn it! thought Harry. How can I want the little chit at a moment like this when she's making a fool of me and looks no better than a slut herself?

'Don't be cross!' begged Zeal. A deep, deep instinct told her to become very still, very small. Invisible. She pulled back into herself and watched her husband from cover, like a moth pretending to be a piece of tree bark or a hen pheasant turned into a stand of dried fern.

There was a pause.

'Oh, Lord!' cried Harry once more, 'I despair. Don't worry! I'll leave you alone to suck your dummy and play with your dolls!'

He slammed the door of her room behind him. After a diplomatic pause while his footsteps retreated, Zeal slid the bolt home.

June 26, 1636. Onions whose seeds I soaked in honey water look exactly like those denied the sweet pleasure. All pot herbs are slack with dryness . . .

Journal of John Nightingale, known as John Graffham.

The next morning was taken up getting Harry off to London. Saddlebags had to be packed with enough clothing to last until a cart could arrive. Harry had to direct one of the housegrooms what to send after him in chests and trunks.

His best hackney was lame; the second best had to be caught and brought in from pasture. His groom had lost a riding boot. Harry's knife-box needed to be polished and his best gloves perfumed. He wanted to send a letter to his distant neighbour Sir Richard Balhatchet. The travellers needed bread and cold meats and ale to take. It was midday before Harry, groom and manservant clopped up the beech avenue and vanished into the green sea of summer leaves. John felt the entire estate give a collective sigh of relief and settle back on its haunches.

For John the day then continued very much like the day before. Warm greetings and waiting problems showered down like grain spilled from a brimming apron. Zeal tracked him as relentlessly as Cassie and the yellow cur, asking questions. He answered them all, warmed by her interest. By teaching he also discovered the selfish joy of rediscovering how much he himself had learned.

John could now see why young Lady Beester frightened his aunt. The girl had clearly taken a grip on the estate with those brown little hands. Her relish could be mistaken for ferocity by someone who was already afraid. John had been accused of as much himself.

However, young Cope didn't seemed alarmed. He gawped and blushed and smiled and leaped to fetch whatever Zeal asked. From the head gardener's slightly sulky deference as John instructed Zeal, John surmised the role that Cope had played while he was in Amsterdam. What man could resist such interest in the things he knew and loved best?

'You've grown!' John told her.

'Do you think? My skirts are still long enough.'

She did seem to take up more space than before. John watched her as they discussed where to plant the winter cole-worts and debated with Tuddenham and Cope how to keep the seedlings watered if the dry spell continued. When she arrived, she had been a splinter insinuated into events, had watched other people as if she weren't really there in the same space with them. Now she entered rooms like a drumbeat and gusted across the lawns.

'I think you have decided to be here,' he said to her suddenly.

She looked startled. Then she laughed. 'The place made me decide. It's so lovely. I shall be here for ever . . . or until I die.' She turned her face in the light breeze like a deer reading news of sweet meadows and distant dogs. Her hair burned with tiny lights in the sun. John smiled with pleasure at the sight of this healthy, happy young animal.

If I did nothing else in Amsterdam, thought John, I saved Hawkridge House for her to love. Harry's lakes and porticos and fifty-nine statues are gnat bites. When I go, as I must, she will love the place for me. I think even old Bols might feel that his sacrifice had some value.

John stretched his arm to the nearest fruiting wall to test the hard green knob of an infant apricot. Then he abruptly pulled it back.

'What did you really do over there?' Zeal suddenly asked. 'In Amsterdam?'

John felt a jolt of guilt and pushed Marika out of his mind. 'I met the new alchemists.'

'That was a serious question.' Zeal put her hands on her hips and frowned with mock severity.

'And I gave a serious answer. I dealt with men who transmute living matter into gold.'

'How?' She was suspicious and amused.

John dug into a pocket and pulled out a small cloth-wrapped packet. He unwrapped the offset from *The King of Kandy* and held out the pearly fang on his open palm.

'What's that?'

'The seed of a gold tree.' He widened his eyes at her.

Zeal frowned and leaned closer to his palm.

'An unnatural wonder.'

She caught something in his tone and looked up. 'You didn't like those alchemists?'

'I liked them,' said John carefully. 'And wonder if I shouldn't. As with their magic. I can't quite see the wickedness in their tricks, but I'm uneasy.'

They both stared at his palm.

'The man who gave that to me is dead, and his death helped bring all our good fortune . . .' John cut himself off abruptly. He hadn't meant to say so much. 'In truth, this thing in my hand will grow in three short years into wondrous beauty . . . if it survives the slugs and snails.' He avoided her assessing eye. 'It's an infant tulip, my lady.'

'That little tooth?' She helped him lighten the mood again.

'A tulip more lovely than you or I have ever seen: white and purple, I'm told, tinged with the freshest green, fringed like a glove but finer than man could ever make. Petals crisp and soft at the same time. You will want to sit and stare for hours in awe.'

'At that funny little thing?' Her voice teased but her eyes still assessed. She had heard clearly all that he had said, meant or not.

'Don't you believe me?'

'I'd like to.'

He pricked his ears now to the tiny sigh. 'Then for three years, Cope here shall be Saint George and guard it fiercely against all those slimy dragons in order to encourage your faith.' He smiled at her. 'Come, let's put him to bed.'

As soon as he spoke, he thought that an unfortunate choice of phrase. But Zeal seemed not to notice his discomfort. They went to the shed that stood braced against the north-facing wall of the New Garden.

With Cope hovering, still uneasy when John did the work himself, John prepared a pot to set in the shade of one of the Knot Garden walls.

'May I look after it?' asked Zeal intensely.

'"That funny little tooth?"' John mocked. 'For three whole years?'

She ignored his frivolity. 'I've never watched something grow for so long and seen it happen.'

Poor child, he thought. Bundled about like that. 'No puppy or kitten either?' Or monkey.

She shook her head. Then grabbed at the knot on her nape which loosened with the shake and threatened to uncoil.

'Then . . .' John looked away from her hand on her hair and drew himself up magisterially. 'I appoint you official steward to *The King of Kandy* . . . when His Majesty is fully grown. In the meantime, you must be his nurse.'

He knelt and put the pot on the ground. Tenderly, he tucked the offset into the peaty soil in the pot.

Zeal stooped beside him in a billow of skirts and stared into the pot as if she expected to see a blue-green shoot emerge before her eyes.

John looked sideways at the intent set of her slim white neck, the small bump of bone just below her nape, and the sliding coil of red-blond wiry hair. He looked back at that tiny, white, vulnerable hill on her nape. A second bump lay a little lower, in the shadow of her collar. The delicate line of her spine curved under her tight bodice-back down into the mysteries of her skirts. Below the waist, as unreal and incorporeal as an angel. John suddenly wondered whether her nipples were the same cherry pink as Marika's or brown like Cat's. He stood up abruptly and stepped back, horrified.

'Is there still a litter of kittens in the hay barn?' he asked Cope. 'Lady Beester might want to nurse us another mouse-catcher or two while she waits for her King.'

'Oh, yes!' She stood and turned so fast that her skirts caught on the box hedge. 'Please! What do I have to do? Do they need milk? What fun! Do you know, I definitely saw a mouse in my room two nights ago . . .'

At least he had distracted her successfully. Without the

kitten diversion, she would surely have read his wicked thoughts as quickly as she had read his earlier tone. She had heard more in his casual flippancy about alchemists than he had admitted to himself. And she was right.

John left Zeal in the hay barn with Cope, sitting in the hay trying to coax four half-wild kittens onto her lap. He needed to be alone and examine himself. Surely his spasm of lust had been aimed at Marika. In her absence, it had merely fallen on the nearest object.

He cut through the New Garden again, crossed the weir bridge and climbed through the orchard to the top of Hawk Ridge. Even on the crest, he felt crowded by trees and thickets. He took a deep breath and thought of the flat, wet, distant, grey horizons of Holland.

My eyeballs have been stretched, he thought wryly, by all those distances. As well as my morals.

His nose still remembered the salt and fishiness of the sea, even back here among the sweetness of crushed grass, sweet woodruff, and wild mints. Traces of the nutmeg, cinnamon and cloves that perfumed the Amsterdam docks still lurked in the folds of his clothes, along with Marika's musk and rosewater.

He stretched out full-length in the yellowing grass and looked up at the sky.

I'm back. Successfully. Safely. For the moment, my worst enemies are my own thoughts.

He ran his hands through the grass. The sharp, silky blades slid gently but dangerously across the soft skin between his fingers. His ears were filled with rustlings and chitterings and squeaks. A lark plunged and soared and plunged again above his head. Much, much higher, the still point of a hawk balanced on the air.

The sky was opaque. There was afternoon sun but it was diffused, like a lantern behind a screen. Grey clouds bulged treelike behind the crowns of a stand of oaks and beech, but too high to bring rain.

Everyone seemed happy to see him. He was happy to see them. Too happy in one case, it seemed. He was back on known ground, confident of what needed to be done. Malise was temporarily abroad.

He sat up again and leaned his forearms across his knees.

So, why do I half-want the worst to hurry up and happen?

That night, John took out Saski's drawing of Marika, made after she had eaten the apple. He wished the artist had captured another moment, not this oddly vulnerable, empty stillness which filled him with a dangerous protective yearning. But the double curve of those full lips was there for his appetite to admire, and the line of her throat, and the fragile delicacy of nostrils and mouth between the noble continents of her forehead and chin.

The air inside the hangings of his bed was dusty and hot. The hangings crowded him. He wanted Marika there, now, naked, arms spread, cherry-nippled and sly with lust. His member stiffened as he imagined her.

Well, you can't have her, my lad! That wicked adventure is over. And there's no one here for you either!

He remembered the line of Zeal's spine under the taut fabric of her bodice-back, and the billow of skirts around those slim, creamy thighs up which he had ignorantly gazed with budding appetite. Her bare toes had been as smooth and pink as apple buds.

He sighed and rolled onto his other side. Two and a half years of Cat had not taught him how to deal with a Marika. After a moment, he rose and padded naked to the window overlooking the herbier and Knot Garden, preceded by his nodding, wilful imp of Satan.

If Adam had been so easily corrupted in his innocence, how

did the Lord imagine he would fare with this small devil permanently attached?

John could just make out the deep black interlocking lines of box and germander against the dark shadows of the walk and beds. Moon under cloud. Everything was a shadow among other shadows. The house was sunk deep in a sea of shadows. He closed his eyes and saw the wide, flat, wet Dutch horizon.

What would have happened if Malise had not been a member of the South Java Company, had never found him, and John could have brought Marika here? She deserved better than her brother's *demi-monde*. But what would those ironic blue eyes make of Hawkridge House? How soon would they ask 'What now? What's next?'

He imagined Erasmus among the chickens. That was more entertaining. Perhaps a pike might catch him. Or a hawk. Excellent thought!

As it was, Malise would not stay abroad for ever. John's own time here was undoubtedly short.

Satan temporarily subdued, John wandered across the room to look out into the forecourt. A shadowy dog trotted across the gravel, shorter in leg than Cassie, darker and thicker than the yellow cur. Bellman or Ranter, one of the patrolling mastiffs. The big gates were shut and locked. Once wolves and outlaws and maurauding knights from other domains had raided sleeping manors. Now it was beggars, dispossessed farm workers made landless by field enclosures, and deserting soldiers.

John sighed again and turned on his bare feet. Then he swung back to the window. He couldn't sleep. He no longer had a Cat. He dare not visit the Lady Tree in this mood; she seemed to unsettle him. He watched the shadowy dog zig towards the porch of the house then zag away as if it had suddenly thought of something better to do. Then John saw the shadow on the porch.

The mastiff would have been tearing the night apart if the shadow on the porch were a stranger. Still, it didn't hurt to check.

His mood soared on the wings of purpose. He flung on a linen shirt and pair of breeches, shoved his bare feet into a pair of slippers, and let himself down the small staircase in the east wing into the office and kitchen block below. He left both sword and gun in his office. From the side alley door between kitchen and herbier, John went silently through the arched gateway into the forecourt. The gravel betrayed him.

'Who's that?' A young woman's voice, startled but not afraid.

'My lady,' said John, almost equally startled. 'I keep finding you in the most unexpected places.' His footsteps grated in the night.

'Isn't that rather fun?'

John heard Marika's voice speaking from the shadows. 'For you, perhaps,' he said.

There was a wounded silence.

'Forgive me,' said John.

'I like it here.' Zeal sounded defensive. 'I often come out here at night.'

'What does Harry think about that?'

'He doesn't know.'

'I see,' said John. After his thoughts in the garden that afternoon, he kept a safe distance between them.

'Anyway, he's gone to London.'

She sat on the top step, level with the heads of the two eagles, with her arms wrapped around her knees. 'Are you going to scold me?' she asked.

'Should I?'

After a moment, she said, 'Sorry. I'm just feeling pity for myself. Sometimes I feel that everyone else scolds me.'

'Who is everyone?' He remained standing on the gravel in his slippers. She moved her hands to her lap. John saw the dark shadow of a kitten curled in the hammock of her night smock.

'Harry, I suppose. And Mistress Margaret. She scolds the most when I am most definitely right. John, I have really tried to be gentle to her, like you said. I really have . . . I'm so glad that you're back!'

'So I can scold Harry and Aunt Margaret for you?'

'Yes, please.' Her dark profile stared out toward the humps of the beech avenue barely visible beyond the wall. 'Although you're different since you came back.'

'Is that so?' he asked neutrally. 'For that matter, so are you. But I mean it as a compliment. From the sound of it, you don't.'

'You've been terribly kind, to answer all my questions, and give me *The King of Kandy*, and this kitten . . .' She bent her shadowy head and stroked it. 'But you make me uneasy.'

The kitten diversion failed, thought John unhappily.

'You're not so quiet inside.' She huddled over the kitten. 'For example, with you hovering like that, I feel I must keep saying something instead of just sitting here peacefully, as we did that time in the orchard.'

The Devil moved his tongue. 'Would it be better if I sat down?'

'Maybe.' She shifted her hips along the worn stone step.

As soon as he sat, John wished he hadn't. There was only the thin fabric of his shirt and her smock between their bare skins. He wrapped his arms around his knees and withdrew behind the palisade.

They sat silently. The shadowy mastiff trotted back across the gravel from around the west wing and vanished toward the gardens. An owl hooted in the orchard. Frogs, ducks and insects creaked and muttered in the darkness around them. A bat streaked across the night.

'Is it better?' asked John finally.

'Worse!' Her voice despaired. 'I feel that we're both waiting for something.' She turned her dark face toward him. 'I don't know what it is.'

John knew. He leaned against her warm arm. The shadow of her face lifted to his. She had stopped breathing.

There was a dreadful pause. Her face continued to hover in the darkness. John groaned and pulled back sharply. He fumbled for her hand, found it, and kissed that instead. She sank back into herself.

'Oh Lord, Zeal, please forgive me! I don't want to make you unhappy in any way.'

What was I doing just now? he asked himself ferociously.

His tongue rolled on like a runaway cart. 'Can you try to forgive me? You're right – I have changed, and I don't know how. I think I am a little confused . . .' His tongue kept babbling.

Evil, evil man! he raged at himself. Admit that you half-knew she wouldn't pull back! Thank the Lord, reason had arrived in time. Sinning with Marika, however delightful, had left its taint on his soul.

It's going to be hard enough for Zeal, he thought. Making a life with Harry.

Zeal pulled her hand out of his.

'I can't believe you really need protection against Harry and my aunt,' he said. 'But I'll give what I can while I'm still here.'

'Thank you,' she said in a tiny voice. She didn't ask for how long that would be.

'Dew is falling. We should go back into the house.'

'I suppose so,' she said. She continued to sit.

'Shall I take you back?'

She stood up, holding the kitten against her breast with one hand. She brushed the front of her smock with the other. 'I wish you *had* kissed me, just now.' Her voice was just tinged with anger. 'I wanted to know how it's done before I start all that with Harry. I mean, not just all squashed against your teeth like the Hackney Hunt!'

'You would do best to practise with Harry,' said John hoarsely.

The sooner he left, the better. No need to wait for Malise to move him on.

He delivered a silent Zeal to the bottom of the big staircase, closed the dog gate behind her and went back out into the gardens.

I'm a danger to both her and myself. And to Harry, for that matter.

He found himself pacing the *allée* of pleached hornbeams that ran along the west wing. That kiss had surely been aimed at Marika's ghost. It grew out of last night's lustful fever. The taint of sin spread like the plague.

By the third time he had walked the length of the *allée*, he had admitted to himself that he wanted to bed his cousin's virgin wife.

John was as relieved as Zeal was miserable when a messenger arrived on horseback the following afternoon. John was to dine one week later at the London house of Sir George Tupper, director and shareholder in the South Java Company.

338

Twelve

July 3, 1636. London. Sir George's damascene roses very fine. Have begged cuttings, though where I will plant them only the Lord knows.

> *Journal* of John Nightingale, known as John Graffham.

'I didn't know you'd be here!' exclaimed Harry with open dismay. 'What are you doing here? Why aren't you at Hawk-ridge House? Is it safe for you?'

'Sir George invited me,' said John.

'Sir *George*?' Harry's scarlet face looked brown in the torchlight. 'Where are you staying?'

'Here.'

'In *this* house? Did Sir George . . . ?' Harry rallied fairly well. 'What an honour for our family,' he said, still short of breath with shock. 'Decidedly.' He was blinking very fast. 'In time, I might even hope to get my hoyden wife accepted. Though perhaps not for the night and breakfast as well.'

'Your country cousin will do his best not to disgrace you,' said John with only a slight edge on his voice. Poor Harry. Mainly for his cousin's sake, he had already tamed his hair, trimmed his beard and crammed himself into a suit of sea-green silk with a rose-silk lining which matched the rose-silk frills of the tops of cream kidskin high-heeled shoes which left his ankles feeling cold.

'How extraordinary,' Harry was saying to himself. 'I

wonder why . . .' Then he caught up with John's words. 'Oh, you look quite fine, coz. Perfectly fine. Don't worry.'

Indeed, the slimmer line of the new breeches showed off John's long, strong legs better than the fullness of the old-fashioned trunk hose had done.

'But you should wear at least one glove,' said Harry. 'Your hands are far too brown for a London gentleman.'

'You're the London gentleman,' said John. 'I'm not.'

Just as well, thought Harry, with those farmer's shoulders exposed by the narrower cut of the new London doublets.

'And is this your famous London, Harry?' asked John gently. 'Explain me its wonders.'

The noise of Sir George's guests rumbled and sputtered around them like a river over rocks. Though it was night, the garden in which they stood was bright with torches.

Not a garden at all, thought John with the hint of a mental sniff. More a pleasure court. Too much stone.

The corners of the walks and parterres were marked with starry flags and golden fishnets flecked with gilded wooden fish. Cages of finches and larks hung from poles, their cries inaudible among the hundred raised laughing voices of the guests and the rasps of catgut being tuned by the string consort on the raised terrace that overlooked the Thames. Half-visible behind a fallen canvas wall stood a cart bearing an enormous cage. Waiting behind the bars stood three women in pearl ropes and phoenix feathers.

And little else, it seemed.

'The performers,' said Harry, following John's eye. 'Don't let them make you blush. It's common enough for women to perform privately in London now. But only uncommon women.' He laughed at his own joke. 'Dr Bowler would no doubt blush, but the music to be played later would make him die of envy. Real written music . . . not his pious hymns and country rumpty-tump!' Harry began to look happy again. 'It *is* wonderful, isn't it, coz!'

John nodded agreeably. The perfumes of the guests mingled with the roses, the torches, rotting vegetation and sewage.

'Look! That's the Queen's dancing master. And one of her waiting women! French, of course. Three ladies, any of whom I'd gladly bed . . .' Harry dropped his voice only a little. 'The ones wearing classical dress. Naiads, or nymphs, or something.' Harry leaned close, confidentially. 'I climb, John. Slowly, I climb!' He watched the crowd with barely contained glee. 'There's an earl, in dark grey and pearls . . . and *he's* a knight. And him, in green. And him.' He watched the last two gentlemen stroll past deep in discussion of a clearly weighty matter.

'Don't let the frivolity mislead you, coz,' Harry said. 'These people rule the world . . . That's a duke, by the way, there, by the fountain . . . Or they're friends of the ones who do. The Hazeltons of the world have their place, of course, but these people don't let their effort show so much. Now you can see what I was trying to explain to you when I first came to Hawkridge House. I want to become one of these men!'

'But you weren't born to it.'

Harry flushed even darker. 'I'm not enough of an ass to yearn for an earldom or a dukedom. Sir George Tupper, our host, bought his baronetcy five years after our Uncle George bought his. I'm not the complete fool you think me. What I want is possible. Fifty years ago, a man like Sir George could never have moved so fast from flogging tanned hides to entertaining noble ones.'

The burnt sugar tones of the largest viol led the rest of the consort into a pavane.

'And now the dancing!' said Harry. 'Coz, just watch these city women! Please excuse me.' Harry plunged away.

John edged back into the shadow of a yew hedge from which he thoughtfully watched his cousin swoop on a partner for the pavane. Sir George, the former hide flogger, led out one of the titled naiads. Harry was right that he lacked knowledge of the world after hiding for so many years. At least Justus Coymans had been an education of a kind. Perhaps Harry seemed a fool only when he occupied the wrong world.

'Handsome stranger with such knitted black brows, will you dance with me?'

Startled, John turned. The woman wore classical drapery like the three naiads, one white shoulder quite bare. He bowed. 'John Graffham, madam.'

'And I am Allegory.' A strong cool hand slid into his. 'I prefer to call you Enigma. Why haven't you been to London before?'

'How do you know that I haven't?' He was amused.

'If you had *really* been to London, I'd have seen you,' she said. 'Do you speak French?'

Over her shoulder John saw Edward Malise. At the same moment, Malise saw him. The next triple beat carried them past each other and out of view.

'Be careful!' said Allegory sharply. 'I'm wearing sandals.'

'Forgive me, madam,' said John with a dry mouth. 'I lost the rhythm.'

When he and Allegory turned at the top of the terrace, Malise had disappeared. Fool! You should have asked about him the minute you got to London, John raged at himself. You were as seduced as Harry by all the London wonders.

As soon as the dance finished he would make his excuses to Sir George and disappear. Malise had no doubt gone to fetch his men-at-arms.

I had a chance to prepare my flight but was too careless to take it.

For the next three minutes, he gave himself totally to planning his next move and avoiding Allegory's nearly naked feet.

At the end of the pavane, she was carried off by a tall, extremely thin blond man in pale blue and gold. 'You remain to be solved,' she called back to him over her departing bare shoulder. 'From the colour of your hands, I think you might be a Moor. Don't leave London yet.'

'Her sister is married to a French count!' Harry appeared, patting his cheeks with his lace-trimmed handkerchief. 'However did you meet her?'

'Sir Harry Beester! Mr Graffham.'

They turned. 'Sir George.' They spoke in accidental unison.

'Sir George, I . . .' John began.

'Welcome, both,' said Sir George. 'Sir Harry, my wife is agog to hear how your bride is taking to country life. Would you be gracious enough to lift her from her tenter-hooks?'

Harry wavered uncertainly between feeling flattered by Lady Tupper's interest (Sir George had married upward into a landed Norfolk family) and the strong suspicion that he was being got out of the way. He looked back twice, as he retreated towards Lady Tupper, at his cousin still standing by Sir George's side.

'Sir George . . .' John began again. With a thump of fear he looked into his host's placid face. Malise had told Sir George to bring him here. Men-at-arms waited in the house.

'Inside,' ordered Sir George, with a broad guiding hand firmly lodged on John's back. 'Out of this din . . . and it'll get worse in a moment when those three caged females start to caterwaul. I have someone who wishes to meet you. Came specially for that tonight, in fact. Thank you for struggling up from Hampshire on such short notice. But I think you may be interested in what my guest and I have to say.'

This doesn't feel like the prelude to arrest, thought John, as he passed through an arch cut in the yew hedge. From opposite sides of the terrace, Harry and Edward Malise watched him leave the party with Sir George Tupper's arm across his shoulders.

* * *

The stranger seated in Sir George's parlour raised a long-fingered, gracious hand to John. There were no soldiers in the room.

'Mallender,' he said. 'You must be Mr Graffham. Please to sit down. And you, Sir George.'

A man servant poured three glasses of red wine and retired.

'A good Flemish red, if I remember your last dinner, Sir George,' said Mallender.

'The same one, my lord.'

'A job well done in the Low Countries, I hear,' said Mallender to John. 'We'd like you to go back.'

In disbelief, John looked from Tupper's box-like head with its bargee's face to the attenuated grooves and knife-edge bones of Mallender. He still half-expected arrest.

'To do what, my lord?'

Mallender leaned back and lowered his nose to his wine glass. Sir George leaned forward on cue and took over.

'You told Hazelton that tulip prices were still climbing when you left Holland. In my experience, there is a pattern in such matters. Excitement builds to a peak. There is a crisis of speculation. Then prices fall. The best time to invest is while the excitement is still building, before the crisis is reached. Now, in fact.'

'You may already be too late,' said John. He screwed his mind around to the topic. 'When I left, the stadholders were already trying to control the market with legislation. Some men heeded the laws, others didn't. There is no reasonable pattern to depend on. Rumours change daily. Even in my ignorance of markets, I cannot see such madness rolling on for ever. It must break like a wave, perhaps over a tiny, unnoticed pebble.'

'Go to Amsterdam and judge how the mood of the speculators is swinging,' said Tupper. 'You will have complete discretion. If it is indeed too late, just eat a few of those herrings and come home.'

'Is there no absolute necessity this time, then?'

'Is anything absolute?' asked Mallender. 'The need is certainly great.'

'Do you speak for the Company, sir?' asked John, suddenly alert in a new direction.

'The King's army in the North still needs feeding,' said Mallender. 'And England needs more ships.'

John turned his head and looked into the fire. The King's army again. Not through the South Java Company, but direct. The King's army on the Scottish border, still hungry and still deserting, and ships to fight those great Dutch East Indiamen. How did I come to be here? he wondered. Listening to such propositions? This is even more unreal than a monkey named Erasmus undressing me for a wealthy Dutch whore.

'I am authorized to invest forty thousand pounds,' said Mallender. 'A good-sized loaf, but too small to feed the multitudes for long enough. Does it frighten you?'

John gripped the sides of his chair for balance. 'It's a fearful weight for a simple country man.'

'Who better than a simple country man to help his country?' replied Mallender lightly.

'If he can.'

Mallender brushed away this modesty. 'Sir George has been quite frank with me about the former difficulties of the South Java Company. You dealt impressively with a difficult and delicate matter. Nevertheless, I'll be frank and tell you, if there were a safer way to multiply our loaves we would long since have taken it. Our once-loyal subjects seem to have forgotten the support they owe their King when he is in need.'

'Duty . . .' said Sir George. 'Don't forget duty, Mr Graffham.'

'And suitable payment, of course,' said Mallender. 'Duty and reward – a seductive pair!'

I'm being trussed and spitted between the two of them, John thought. Neatly as a capon.

Then he saw why he had to accept. A condemned man can't lose when he tosses a coin for his life.

'I wouldn't drain one more farthing from the hard-pressed Treasury,' he said. 'My King's gratitude would be enough reward.'

Mallender tilted his head back and looked down his nose. 'If only more Englishmen felt as you do.' He studied John with a half-smile. 'Is there any particular form this non-pecuniary gratitude might take?'

'Time enough to say, my lord. But nothing, I swear, that should keep His Majesty awake at night.' Unless Malise fought back through the Queen.

Mallender looked amused. 'It's a reasonable counter-offer. Does that mean you agree?'

'May I have time to think, sir?' asked John.

'Not if the request is a polite prelude to a refusal.'

'Then I don't need to think, but I would like time to sort a few matters on my cousin's estate.'

'One week.' Mallender stood abruptly and put his unemptied glass on a table.

John and Sir George leaped to their feet.

'Sir George, you'll arrange another meeting immediately Mr Graffham has attended to his cousin's pigs and sheep?'

'Stay a moment,' said Sir George, when Mallender had left. 'I imagine your head is racketing like a tennis ball, but there's more I'd like to put to you.'

'I'm past amazing.'

Sir George bent to scratch the head of a greyhound which had just clicked into the room. 'Samuel Hazelton thinks that you're ambitious.'

'Then he sees more clearly than I do.'

'Not uncommon for strangers to do that.' Sir George watched the hound settle, grunting and sighing, in front of the fire. 'I am also a stranger. I see hunger.'

'For what, sir?'

'Don't know. I'm too much of a stranger for that.' Sir George turned to face John. 'Damn it, man, you tell me!'

'Why expose my cravings to a stranger . . . however hospitable and gracious he may be?'

'To have them filled.'

John took a deep breath and shook his head, smiling. 'Oh, Sir George. There's a sulphurous ring to those words of temptation.'

'You can have what you want.'

Ask, ask, ask, the Lady Tree had said.

John closed his eyes. He shouldn't have touched the wine tonight.

'You disbelieve me.' Sir George's voice was flat but amiable. He stood solidly balanced on both stocky legs, arms behind his back, at ease.

'The world is not designed by God to give each man what he wants. The design is ours only to interpret, and accept.'

'What makes you so sure of that?'

My whole life, John wanted to say. 'What I see.'

'And what did you see in Amsterdam?'

'I beg your pardon, sir? I don't follow your drift.'

'In Amsterdam you saw a nation without princes,' said Tupper. 'A successful, thriving nation. Where every man could make himself into a prince, with wit, hard labour and the help of God. Some men would say that such a princeless state is contrary to nature. If I were to believe those men, I would undo myself.'

John's black brows met. A band tightened around his chest. 'Where are you leading, sir?'

'Not to treason, Mr Graffham. You're not being embroiled in anything but finance. I'm merely leading you to the freedom of possibility.'

Tupper looked nothing at all like the Devil. He resembled, rather, a large Salisbury ram. Squared forehead and slightly protruding eyes. Tight cap of blond curled hair cut short and

347

now turning grey. Wide muzzle, narrow nostrils and long upper lip, thick neck and shoulders that suggested the smooth bulk of an unsheared fleece.

'Do you discuss such things with him?' John glanced after Mallender.

'Just because we're linked in business, it doesn't mean I like or trust the man.' Tupper refilled John's glass. 'Don't misunderstand,' he said. 'I have no dislike for princes. I merely find them irrelevant to my own life, except in their ability to exact taxes. Mr Graffham, my father lived in a hutch leaning against the London Wall. You can see for yourself what I have now. You arise at least from the middling sort. Why pull back your hand from the world's riches?'

'Not by choice!' The words escaped.

'I only half believe that,' said Tupper. 'Would you pull back from buying your own estate instead of propping up Sir Harry's fortunes? Would you pull back from a place in the South Java Company?'

John now stared, wordless.

'Will you talk again, in fuller company?'

'You know nothing of who I am, or was.'

'My father was a knacker,' said Sir George. 'Though I don't make a point of it to Lord Mallender.'

A knacker is not a criminal. But John nodded.

'I know what you can do,' said Tupper. 'And that is what matters to men like myself. And Hazelton.'

'You conjure up visions more amazing than golden fish and caterwauling phoenix, Sir George.'

'There's a light in your eye, Graffham, one I recognize.'

Why not? thought John. Why not?

He sat silent for a long time. 'Does my cousin know what you intend toward me?'

'He was there making a lot of noise when we debated whether or not to invest again. When the time comes, he'll have his legal voice in voting you in.'

'And Malise?'

'Ah, yes . . .' Sir George's ram's eyes regarded John thoughtfully. 'Hazelton warned me.'

'Is Malise part of this venture?'

Sir George shook his head. 'He was abroad when we planned it. As you know, members invest venture by venture. I don't think Hazelton would have allowed him to invest in this one. He said he wouldn't tolerate a second impudent refusal from you.'

'I promised him a confession before I undertook any more Company business. It might change both your minds.'

'Then you shall confess to Hazelton tomorrow.'

'I had hoped to leave for Hawkridge House at once . . .'

'Tonight? Don't be a fool! One step at a time. You stay here. We'll breakfast with Samuel. You make your confession. Then I'll send you upriver on one of my own boats. Now come back outside and learn to enjoy the fruits of labour.' Sir George slung a heavy arm across John's shoulders and propelled him back among the lanterns and golden fish.

John leaned on the stone balustrade above the Thames, in the farthest, most shadowed corner of the terrace. He tried to steady himself with the stinks and open darkness of the water. Wherry lanterns cut from shore to shore.

Excitement uncoiled in his gut, as cold and alarming as a snake waking in the spring sun.

Ask, ask, ask, said the slipstream of a wherry against the stone of Sir George's river wall.

Ask for a place in the South Java Company. Money to buy his own estate. A pardon from a grateful king for the death of Francis Malise. And why not?

And if I go back to Amsterdam, thought John, I can see Marika again.

A shadow leaned beside him on the balustrade. 'O meteor-gleam of ambition,' said Malise's voice. 'Lighting a little second or two, before the darkness returns.'

John pushed himself up from the balustrade.

'Don't leave so soon,' said Malise pleasantly.

'With regret, I must.'

'With equal regret, I say that you must not. Now that you've saved the Company's bacon, I want what you owe me.'

John turned to walk away.

'I have a constable waiting outside.'

John stopped.

Why didn't I ask if Malise had returned? I have been insanely careless. Wished myself into thinking I was safe.

'It would be gracious of you to allow yourself to come outside rather than embarrass your host by being taken here among his guests.'

Malise moved close in the candlelit darkness. He was only a few insubstantial wavering patches of light – his cheekbone, the bridge of his nose and left shoulder. His voice trembled. John's hand eased toward his knife.

'There is an armed man behind you.'

There was no one else near the balustrade. Harry was not in sight among the crowd.

'As I told you once, I prefer to watch you hang, but if forced, I might rush my pleasures.'

John lifted his hands away from his body. '*Concedo*.' I agree the logic, not I submit. He remained poised.

Leap the wall? Tide in or out? Were there rocks below the wall? Why didn't I take heed a few moments ago?

'Let's go,' said Malise. 'I'm not in a party mood, not yet.'

'Nor am I, of a sudden,' said John. If I shout for help, he thought, in all that garden full of people who can I trust to take my part?

He now saw Harry, leaning like a flower towards the sun

of the man he had said was an earl. Would he take John's side against an aspiring favourite of the Queen, here among the men who were all that he most yearned to become? Or would Harry be glad to be rid of a thorn? He was better not put to the test.

'As you're hell-bent on preserving the courtesies,' said John, 'let me say goodnight to Sir George.'

Malise hesitated.

'Or do you need a have-nothing like me to teach you manners?' asked John.

'I'll pay the hangman for a sticking knot,' said Malise tightly. 'Or bribe the swordsman to bungle the first six strokes.'

'He's over there.' John turned to the man behind him. 'With your permission . . .' He slid away through the press towards the multicoloured silks that surrounded Sir George, with Malise's man at his shoulder.

'Sir George, I've come to say farewell. Master Malise is pressing me hotly to take alternative lodging tonight.'

'Eh?' Tupper looked confused, then annoyed, then the heavy lids blinked. 'One moment, sirs. Not so fast. Excuse me, my dears . . .' He disengaged himself from the clustered silks.

'Spurning me already for an arse-licking courtier?' he asked John. 'Has ambition shot to your head so fast?'

'Sir George,' said Malise, arriving through the crowd. 'Let's go in. I'd best explain privately.'

Sir George turned cool eyes on Malise. 'Well, if you *suggest*, I propose that we all obey.'

Once again, John found himself in Sir George's parlour.

'I am arresting this man for murder,' said Malise.

Tupper turned his large ram's head toward John with an air of unsurprised enlightenment. 'You are?' he enquired with cordial interest. 'Who's been murdered? Not one of my guests, I hope. That would spoil the evening for sure!'

Malise hesitated briefly to weigh this unexpected challenge from a jumped-up butcher's son.

'John Nightingale, known for the last eleven years as John Graffham, killed my brother Francis, in the South Java Company's own offices. At least two of your guests here tonight saw him do it.'

'I do remember, as it happens, though I wasn't there at the time.' Sir George turned his square-cornered ram's face to John again. 'That was how many years ago?'

'Eleven,' said John, with resignation. 'It was to have been my confession to Hazelton.'

Tupper nodded with the satisfaction of having had things explained. 'Then you're that nephew of old Beester's, said to have fled abroad with all those Catholics and debtors and such. The boy who made all those accusations . . .' Tupper looked at Malise. 'I also happen to remember that Sir James Balkwell more than half believed him.'

Both John and Malise now stared at Tupper with astonishment.

'His accusations were crazed . . . unfounded,' protested Malise.

'True in every word,' said John fiercely.

'We need a higher authority than my humble self to deal with this,' said Tupper. 'Go fetch Lord Mallender again,' he ordered Malise's man. 'Urgent.'

'There's not one shred of evidence that my brother and I were anywhere near the coach when it burned!' Malise could hardly contain himself, even for Mallender. 'We weren't even in England when Nightingale claims we murdered his parents, and the Flemish military rolls will prove it. Twenty wealthy, considerable men saw him kill my brother! How can you balance the word of those gentlemen against that of a crazed child?'

Mallender studied John. 'An unresolved case. Clear guilt

on one hand, possible reason to forgive on the other. One man's word against another's. Or was the death an accident after all? I'm not a legal man but I remember the debates.' He turned to Malise. 'Can you be patient?'

'I have been patient, my lord, for eleven years!'

'Then what is a few more weeks to spleen so long contained already?'

'*Spleen*, sir?' Malise nearly exploded. Then his acute political sense picked up Mallender's tone. He shifted his grip on the conversation like a man rehefting his knife as he circled a foe. 'With good enough reason, I will try to be even more patient. So long as you promise me an eventual trial.'

'Take it from me, that there is reason, of the very highest sort.'

Malise flinched. 'And do you promise the trial?'

'Don't presume, sir!' Mallender turned icy.

Once again, as in the stable yard, John watched the agony of self-control cramp the sinews of Malise's body. Two knobs of bone showed white through the bridge of the falcon beak. 'I must be advised by you, my lord.'

'Excellent. And pray don't feel that it would be helpful to plead your case meanwhile to a higher authority, in French.'

'In French, sir?' Malise's eyes went as blank as a dead coal. 'I would not, as you say, presume.'

'Excellent,' said Mallender again. 'Good evening, sir.'

'And now, our gaolbird,' he went on, turning to John when Malise and his man had left. He clicked his tongue several times against long, yellow teeth. 'Are you guilty?'

'Yes, my lord.'

Mallender sighed. 'I can't condone taking the law into your own hands. We are all subject to the hierarchy of authority. If one man balks, he threatens the whole structure.' He raised his eyebrows in the direction of Sir George. 'We would be fools, would we not, to send him abroad, with forty thousand of Treasury money – a man who might want nothing more than to vanish into another life? What a gift!'

'Indeed,' said Tupper. His large fists were clenched in his lap.

'And he'd be a fool not to take the chance if you gave it to him,' said John. 'So where are you leading us, my lord?'

Mallender gazed briefly at the door through which Malise had left.

'Towards an appeal to the highest authority, as it shines through onto mortal man in the person of His Majesty, King Charles.'

'You'll apply for a pardon?' said Tupper.

'How else can we safely send Mr Nightingale back to Amsterdam?'

Sir George unclenched his fists. John sat shakily on the nearest stool, past thinking of protocol.

'Was that by chance the reward you had hoped to claim?' asked Mallender.

John nodded.

'However, Nightingale,' said Mallender. 'I would hate to be left looking like an ass when it's all over. You'll get your pardon – if indeed I can persuade the King – when you return, with the multiplied money.'

'Of course, my lord,' said John through a dry, tight throat. To be Nightingale again, here in his own country, speaking his own tongue, not merely to play at his old self for a brief snatched time on foreign soil.

John bowed distractedly as Mallender left the room. He could reclaim the first half of his life, when he had been the master of Tarleton Court. He would have brought the money back, whatever Mallender might think, but this promise would make him godlike in resolve and implacable in purpose.

Sir George interrupted John's thoughts. 'I'll pass on your

confession to Hazelton in the morning and doubt if he'll be much surprised. You must leave London at once, after all. And I'm sending two armed grooms with you as far as Windsor, in case Malise's impatience overcomes his good sense.' He thought for a moment. 'And I want one of my men to come to Amsterdam. One man of your own at your back is not enough.'

John looked up and nodded. 'Does Malise know I'm going?'

'Not yet, most likely. He's just back from abroad. But he'll learn soon enough if he wants. I can't muzzle all the Company mouths against gossip.'

'What on earth are you doing?' asked Harry from the door of John's chamber in Sir George's house. 'You missed those women, and the songs.'

'Packing to go back to Hawkridge,' said John. He tossed his riding boots to Arthur. 'For a week. Then I'm off again to Amsterdam.'

'Sir George asked you, then?' Harry leaned against the door frame and watched Arthur buckle a saddlebag. 'Do you need me to come with you?'

'No,' said John sharply, distracted by a missing glove. 'Arthur, have a look among the bed covers . . .'

'Perhaps I should,' said Harry.

'Please yourself.' John straightened and looked closely at his cousin. 'You've only just returned here. Won't you miss all your London wonders?'

If John had begged him to return to Hawkridge, Harry would have made his excuses and stayed in London. As it was, he decided that it was essential for him to go back to oversee John's departure from the estate.

They left by boat up the Thames at two o'clock that morning, with their horses. Sir George sent his two armed grooms in addition to Arthur and Harry's two grooms and personal servants, as far as Windsor. John did not believe that Malise would follow him out of London but he accepted the escort all the same. Malise had already lost patience with the legal process at least once.

John told Zeal two days later as they strolled rather formally in the Knot Garden, making notes of what needed to be done while he was away.

Zeal went white. 'Back to your alchemists?' she whispered. She looked at him directly for the first time since the night he found her sitting on the porch. 'Oh John, be careful of their tricks!'

'There's nothing to fear.'

'Then why are you afraid of them?'

'What are you talking about?' demanded Harry from the alley gate.

'Amsterdam,' said Zeal unhappily.

'Oh, yes. Cousin John is off again on one of his missions to the Great Swamp of Europe,' said Harry bitterly. 'However will we manage without him this time?'

That night John woke to the sound of screams. Faint and thin like the end of a dream, but they went on and on. He yanked back the hangings of his bed. The screams became clearer and more distinct. A woman's voice screamed like an animal hung up for the butcher's knife.

John swung off the bed and pushed open the nearest window to listen, his head cocked. Not outside, from inside the house. He snatched up the gown which lay on the chest at the end of his bed, covered himself, stepped over his man Arthur on a trundle bed in the connecting tiring room, and ran onto the galleried landing at the top of the stairs.

Here the screams were even louder. Arthur followed him onto the landing, with a drawn dagger. A blurred, anxious face appeared in the hall at the bottom of the stairs. Aunt

Margaret was already there with her maid, Pris. Agatha Stookey came running up the stairs.

'John!' cried Aunt Margaret. 'Harry's killing her! He won't open the door!'

The screams grew long and regular.

In Zeal's anteroom, Rachel was hugging herself in tears.

'He won't open the door!' she cried. 'What's he doing?'

The door of Zeal's bedchamber was barred on the inside. John banged with his fists.

The screams stopped.

'Go to Hell!' bellowed Harry's voice inside the room. 'Get out of here.'

'Harry! For the love of God, what is happening?'

'LEAVE US ALONE!'

John's hands fell to his sides. He and Aunt Margaret looked at each other.

'My lady?' called John. 'Is all well?'

There was a long silence. John put his head against the carved wood panel of the door. Nothing.

'Go back to bed!' Harry's voice now shouted from just the other side of the door. 'This is none of your bloody affair!'

'My lady?' repeated John.

'Go away.' After Harry's bellows, her voice sounded very small, like the mew of a new-born kitten. She paused as if to draw breath. 'Please!'

John turned to the crowd behind him in the anteroom. 'A marital dispute, it seems,' he said calmly. 'We're all too used to the tranquillity of bachelor life ... and rural manners. Back to bed.'

Rachel settled back onto her cot, still sniffing uncertainly and glaring at the locked door. Arthur moved a step in her direction, then changed his mind. He and Agatha excused themselves pinkly, with mumbles and much ducking of their heads.

'Go back to bed, Pris,' Aunt Margaret said to her own

woman. 'Some ale, John? Or *eau de vie* to help you off again?'

'No thank you,' said John distractedly. She hadn't screamed like that for a joke. He wondered if he should use the door in the panelling, the narrow private passageway between the walls, to break into Zeal's bedchamber.

'I told you she didn't know anything about anything,' said Aunt Margaret, who knew even less about such matters herself. 'Poor thing,' she said. 'Poor silly little thing.'

When John returned for his breakfast of bread and ale after inspecting the stables, there was no sign of either Sir Harry or Lady Beester.

'Both ate in their rooms this morning,' said Aunt Margaret. 'Separately.'

John hesitated at the bottom of the stairs, started up, came down again, and went to his office where he tried to read his books.

A little later, as he was making final amendments to the estate inventory, Harry crunched across the forecourt towards the stables, dressed for riding, head down and walking fast. John stood up to call from the window, then drew back. Harry shouted for a groom to saddle his bay gelding and vanished around the corner of the east wing.

Just before the noon bell, Aunt Margaret put her head through the office door. 'Rachel can't find her ladyship anywhere,' she said. 'She's not been hanging around here with you by any chance?'

John shook his head. He wished she had been.

Aunt Margaret stayed where she was. The fingers of one hand explored the cuticle of the thumb on the other.

'Are you concerned?' John asked.

Mistress Margaret pushed her lips out in a tight little pucker, disclaiming full responsibility for any sentiments voiced. 'I thought she might still be a little upset after last night . . .'

She puckered her lips again and scratched the side of her nose. 'She's been a nuisance. From the first moment . . . I hate to bother you.'

John stood up. 'Did Rachel look in the gardens?'

'And the outbuildings. And I've been all over the house. Even the cellars.' Her ever-moving fingers picked up her skirt to explore a greasy spot, and dropped it again. 'I got nothing else done this morning.'

She'll be in the orchard, thought John.

He peered up into the thick, heavy green leaves and shiny green knobs of the apple trees and called. But she wasn't roosting anywhere. No heaped overskirts marked her climb.

'Lady Beester . . . Zeal! It's John.'

He searched the pears and the plums. He climbed the ridge and searched the hazelnut coppice just over the top. Becoming alarmed, he scrambled up the beech hanger to the Lady Tree. The Hawkridge dryad wore a fresh rowan wreath around one thigh, just above the knee, but Zeal was not in her branches nor huddled among her roots.

John cut back downhill and through the kitchen gardens to the stables, alert for her small shape on the paths among the lettuces, onions and red-blossomed tripods of beans. None of the weeding women had seen her that morning.

Zeal's mare chewed quietly in its stall. None of the grooms or stable boys had seen Lady Beester. John ran back to the *basse-court*. Lady Beester was not visiting Cassie and her four pups in the dog yard. Nor had she been seen by the women in the brewhouse or dairy. The cheeseroom was empty.

John peered through the hedge at the flat green empty space of the bowling lawn. He visited the dovecote. Then he returned through the front forecourt, past the twin eagles, to the gardens at the other end of the house. The girl was not in the herbier, the Knot Garden, the New Garden, the arbour on top of the Mount, or on any of the stone benches tucked into the hedges.

Now terrified, John crossed back to the far side of the ponds and followed the valley of the Shir down to the mill. The mill itself was still locked and quiet, until the harvest.

As he climbed back to the house along the track that followed the millrace, he glanced down unwillingly into the swift green twisting strands of water. No glints of red-gold.

I should have asked whether she has taken any belongings from her rooms, he thought. I should have broken in last night.

He nearly walked past her.

Five semi-tame wild geese made dark lumps in the shadows of the large willow that overhung the weir between the bottom pond and the top of the race. Four other geese pottered gracefully on the water near the edge of the pond. One of them hooked a large triangular black foot over the edge, tried to heave itself ashore, fell back with a splash, tried again, thumped loudly up onto the bank, and waddled off swinging its tail violently from side to side. John paused to watch, briefly distracted by this transition from watery grace to earth-bound clumsiness. One of the small dark lumps under the willow was Zeal.

She sat with her back to the path, arms locked tight around her skirts which puffed out over her drawn-up legs. Chin buried between her kneecaps, she stared at the wooden palings John had had driven in to reinforce the crumbling bank. As John approached, the seated geese honked in alarm and deserted. He squatted down on his haunches. Zeal closed her eyes as if that would make him disappear. Her face and eyelids were red and swollen.

After a long silence, John began to throw pebbles into the pond. At the first splash, she opened her eyes. John could hardly bear to look at the change in her. His hands were cold. He was terrified of saying the wrong thing. Why couldn't he think how to console her?

'Don't worry, Mr Graffham,' she said thickly. 'I'll be well enough.' She turned her head away. 'Don't look at me, please, or you'll make me even more miserable!'

'You can't be miserable and well at the same time,' said John.

'Oh yes you can! You wouldn't understand,' she said. '*You're* not married.'

He inhaled sharply.

'I shall kill myself,' she said. 'Then Harry can get himself another wife and all will be well.' She reached out to a mallard drake which had swum up to the edge of the bank. 'No, I won't,' she decided suddenly. 'I will stay alive for ever instead and get my revenge on Harry that way!'

'Why revenge?' asked John carefully. He knew the answer and wondered why he was making her say it.

'He broke his promise!' She drew two quick hiccuping breaths like a child trying to stop crying. 'He swore to me. Then he broke his promise!' She turned cool eyes on John. 'Please go away now and let me think. I have much to think about.'

'I don't want to leave you here alone.'

'I promise I really won't kill myself,' she said. 'And *I* don't break my promises.'

Still he hesitated. He felt nearly as guilty as Harry.

'Please!' She was clinging to the fringes of her dignity.

'Will you promise to come to evening chapel?'

She shut her eyes and compressed her lips into their old thin line. Then she nodded. 'Promise.'

He could barely hear the word. As he returned to the house, along the path beside the ponds, his legs trembled.

Harry shot him a red-eyed beam of animosity as they passed in the great hall. Harry smelled of horse and ale. He had been away from the estate all day.

361

Just before sundown, while John was settling a dispute over a pair of boots between one of Harry's London grooms and a houseboy, he heard thudding in the Long Gallery overhead.

Harry was smashing tennis balls against the wood panelling of the gallery.

'Did she run to cry on your shoulder then?' he demanded, as John appeared in the doorway. 'Bitch! I did nothing that wasn't my right . . . !' He turned and smashed a ball into the wall on John's left. The carved panel reverberated like a drum.

John bent and picked up a dead ball that lay at his feet. 'You raped her.'

'God's testicles!' shouted Harry. 'I'm her *husband*! How can I bloody *rape* her?' Another ball hit the panel and flew back to Harry. He scooped it up and smashed it against the wall just to the right of the door, a little closer to John.

'I thought you told me you had promised not to force her until she was ready,' said John. His voice obliged him by remaining reasonably steady. '"Contract marriage only, coz" . . . "I can amuse myself elsewhere."'

'I've already done that! Today. And *she* at least was happy to have me. There are real women in the world, thank God, not just puling, screaming, scrawny, half-plucked, Puritan, God-save-me virgins!' Harry bounced his ball twice on the floor and served it straight over John's head through the door into the neighbouring chamber. Porcelain crashed behind John but he did not turn to look.

'I shall thrash her,' said Harry ferociously. 'She can't humiliate me like last night! The whole estate was sniggering behind their hands today. I'll teach her that I rule in my own house! When they hear her screaming again tonight, you tell them why!'

The next ball hit John's shoulder as he crossed the floor from the door. He found himself holding Harry by his jacket front.

'If you touch her again, I'll shove that ball so far down

your gullet that it comes out your arse!' He lifted Harry and threw him against the wall, like a mastiff finished with a rat.

Harry, bounced, staggered, and found his balance. He stood, clutching his racquet, shocked into total stillness. John was just as shocked. They stared at each other for several seconds.

'I'm sorry, coz,' said John quietly. 'I didn't mean to hurt you. I just don't want you to damage that child any further.'

Harry swished the racquet back and forth, like the tail of an angry cat. He took a step away from the wall, head lowered between his shoulders, hot pink spots glowing on cheekbones and forehead.

'I won't fight you, Harry,' John warned. 'I didn't mean to hurt you before.'

Harry swished his racquet again. 'Shall I tell you, Cousin John, the real reason I bedded my wife last night?'

John retreated one instinctive step.

'That's right, coz,' said Harry. 'I had to protect myself against you! A contract marriage is only a contract, as you well know. Not a marriage until consummated. Do you think I can't see how you've insinuated yourself into my wife's favours? Do you think I can't figure out by myself how useful her estate would be to a man who has nothing, like yourself ... you could afford to leave England, become someone again, make a life somewhere you aren't an escaped felon. It would be so easy for you ... trustworthy, safe old Cousin John ... to climb into my saddle before me. A few legal formalities. Then goodbye, husband Harry. Greetings, husband John!'

Harry stood panting.

John stood looking back at his cousin. Then he leaned down and rolled the tennis ball gently to him across the floor. 'Goodbye, Harry.'

'What!'

John turned to the door of the Long Gallery.

'John! Where are you going?'

John turned back. As if speaking to a very slow-witted child he said, 'I am leaving Hawkridge House immediately, not five days from now. After Amsterdam, I won't return. I shall try to leave things in good order.'

'Leave for good?'

'Yes.'

'You can't!' cried Harry. 'I need you here, when you get back, to run the place!'

'I won't stay here to make trouble between you and Zeal.'

'But we've fought that out now!' cried Harry. 'We understand each other.' He went even redder in the face. 'And the problem is now solved in any case. There's no more danger in your staying.'

'I think there is,' said John. 'I don't ever again want to risk killing you.'

Arthur was less pleased than John had expected at the news that they would leave for London in the morning.

'It's Rachel,' he said. 'She thinks I'm avoiding her.'

'Are you?'

'On the contrary, the closer the better. But it needs time.'

'Go find Rachel,' said John. 'Tell her to ask her mistress to come speak with me in Hall Place. Then you're free for an hour or so to lay the blame wherever you like.'

Zeal entered Hall Place warily. 'Is it just you?' Then she stood with her hands clasped on the front of her skirt. The pose reminded John of the stiff-armed terror of her arrival.

'Zeal, I have to tell you something difficult.' He hesitated. 'Will you come to my office to talk?'

She shrugged.

Jealousy might now have been exorcized from Harry, but the dislodged demon nudged John for houseroom. He wished he had shaken Harry until his neck broke. And then thrown him against the wall.

Zeal had come to evening chapel as she had promised but supped alone in her room. She followed John now out of Hall Place, through the oratory next to the chapel and the hall that led past Dr Bowler's chambers into the east wing. The kitchen was already quiet and dark. A single groom tended the fire. They walked along the cheesy, beery corridor past the locked housekeeper's room and, finally, into John's office at the front of the wing. There she again stood, not quite as non-present as when she arrived, but refusing to lend her life to whatever was going on.

John unlocked his cabinets and opened drawers one after another for Zeal to see what lay inside. Eggs, shells, birds' beaks, elephant's pizzle, stone fish. From his book coffers he lifted out Pliny, Cato and Columella and laid them before her on his table as an offering. He touched the blowfish on the sill and the elephant's tusk on the wall. Then he put the table between them.

'Here you see as much of the greater world as I could shrink to fit within the boundaries of Hawkridge estate. I pass it to you.'

'To console me?'

'If you need consolation.'

'I don't!' She turned her back on the office and looked out into the thick dusk in the forecourt. 'I chose my bed and now I must lie on it. At least the bed's on Hawkridge estate.' She swallowed. 'What is that difficult thing you must tell me?'

'I must leave again tomorrow.'

'Why?' She whirled around to face him. 'Not because of what I said that night on the porch? I'm sorry. I was being wicked . . . I don't know what was wrong with me. Or is it because of the scene I made last night? Please! I don't want you to leave because of me!'

'Oh, Zeal . . .' He shook his head. 'You're not to blame. I

must prepare earlier than I thought to go back to Amsterdam . . . meet with some men in London first . . .' He heard how falsely his voice fell across the air of the little office. 'But that's not it, entirely . . .'

'You're not coming back!' She stated it with certainty and despair.

He could see only the pale oval of her face. The growing darkness made it easier to speak. 'A deed of mine at fourteen has come back for vengeance. When I went to Amsterdam last time, I thought then I would never return here. This return was a gift. Now there's a chance that I can settle the past. If I can do that, I must start my own life again, as myself not as Harry's cousin. I couldn't bear to leave again without telling you the truth.' Or at least part of it.

'Do you want to leave Hawkridge?'

'I don't want to leave what it has been to me for the last eleven years . . .'

'But now it's become Harry's Hawkridge, not yours.'

'And I don't want to leave you.' He allowed himself a quick, pleasurable surge of truth before he clouded it with evasions. 'Not with so much to do, while you're still learning.'

'But you must.' The same flat certainty. The same despair.

'I'm sorry, sir . . .' A housegroom interrupted them. 'I didn't know you were still working here. Would you like a torch, or a rushlight?'

'Rushlight.'

They waited while the youth lit a tallow-soaked rush from the kitchen fire, brought it into the office and clipped it into the upright iron stand on the table. The tiny flame threw their shadows huge across the upper walls and ceiling. Dim lights glowed in their hair but their eyes were dark under their brows.

'I can only leave at all because I leave the estate in your hands,' said John. 'I have loved this place more than anyone but you can imagine. I wanted to see you tonight to ask you to keep on loving and tending it. Harry and I and all the rest

366

are far luckier than we deserve that you happened to choose him and fetched up here as mistress.'

'You want me to be you?'

'Take my place.'

'You believe I can?' She turned away, so that the rushlight sparked only on the tendrils at the back of her neck.

There was a long silence. Then John heard a tiny squeak. 'Are you all right?' he asked.

'I'm crying.' Her tone left his question unanswered.

John went around the table and put his arms around her gently. She leaned against his chest. Then she leaned away, but didn't pull free of his arms. She found a shadowy handkerchief in her shadowy sleeve.

'It's funny . . .' She sniffed, then wiped her nose with the handkerchief. '. . . I wished you were here to talk to the day I moved the bee swarm and Peter died . . . About how life is mixed up, good with bad. It doesn't let you feel one thing at a time: happy or sad, ashamed or proud. Right now, for example, I feel both miserable and all right.' She sniffed again. 'Guilty and sad and pleased with myself at the same time.'

'I think that applies better to me,' said John. Her hair smelled of lemon balm and rosemary.

Don't make one false move, he warned himself. This is more than you expected or deserve. She felt easy in his arms. Miraculously, she had broken through the awkwardness triggered by his lust and intensified by Harry's jealousy. Against all odds, it was a comfortable, thirst-quenching moment.

'Thank you,' she said. 'For the books, and all those wonders . . .' She gestured with the lump of handkerchief at the open drawers of his cabinets. 'I shall study them.'

'Make notes,' he said. 'Keep a journal of what you do on the estate, and when. And things you notice. You'll find it helpful from year to year. I've left you the last eleven years in that chest there.'

'Do you really think I can do it?' she asked.

'Zeal Beester can do whatever she sets her mind to.'

There was another, very long pause.

'Can she kiss you goodbye?'

John's arms tightened involuntarily. His breath caught in his throat. He forced himself to relax his hold. 'She can do anything.'

'All right, then.' She leaned against him and held up her face. 'Don't squash my teeth.'

He kissed her as delicately as he would lift a seedling or newly hatched chick. Her mouth was warm and soft. Interested. His control cramped his muscles and stopped his breath. Nevertheless it was an easy kiss that made its own rules. He breathed in the ghost of the sun on her skin and moved his mouth gently on hers. Ferocity tapped on his shoulder, but this was not its time. They parted on a shared impulse, at exactly the last moment of peace. She stepped back out of his arms.

I should have snuffed out the rushlight, thought John, too late. Who knows who might have crossed the forecourt just now? I didn't protect her even there.

'Will you let me know where you start your own life?' she asked. 'If you manage to settle your past.'

'Of course. I might even become a neighbour.'

'And what if I need to write you some question about the estate?' He heard a desperate craftiness in her voice that he remembered from her first days at Hawkridge. 'Can I write to you in Amsterdam?'

He quite liked that idea. It made their parting feel less absolute. 'I don't see why not.' He searched the shadowy table for a scrap of paper and his pen.

Coymans or the Widow Padtbrugge? It felt indecent to let Zeal write to the house where Marika lived. But then he reconsidered. A letter from Zeal would not be Zeal herself. Marika didn't come into it. And the widow might not have rooms free.

He wrote down Justus Coymans's name and where he lived on the Old Side of Amsterdam. As he handed the paper to Zeal, he felt as if he were giving her one end of a very, very long cord, of which he held the other end.

She held it up in the rushlight. 'A real place! Now you won't just disappear.'

Thirteen

'Marika!' bellowed Coymans up the stairs. 'Your Englishman is back!' He turned to the maid who had let John in. 'Go tell her.' Then he shouted to the back of the house for beer.

The maid picked up her skirts and scampered up the creaking stairs in search of her mistress.

The sound of Marika's name shocked John. Brazen and reverberatory as a bell after its silent life in his thoughts for the last month, it stirred both lust and terror.

Coymans flung an arm like a merchantman's anchor around John's shoulders and steered him out of the painted gaze of Coymans *père* into the music parlour. 'Didn't I say you'd be back?' he demanded. 'And I'll wager you're richer than when you last arrived.' The sharp, cool eyes swept down John's frame to his boots and back up again. 'Certainly better dressed. Sit, my English friend. Sit!'

He returned to the door to demand, at a bellow, where the refreshment for his guest might be. He did not sit himself, but stood with his hands on his hips examining John as if he were a particularly satisfying purchase. 'Well, well, Nightingale. Back again. Helpless against the siren song of gold.'

John stretched his long legs across the black and white floor. He gave the lazy smile of a man beyond petty baiting. 'A longing for wet feet, Justus. The puny puddles of England can't compete.' Even while he spoke, the painted Pomona drew John's eyes.

Coymans followed his eyes and laughed. 'Naa. You're back for tulips and my sister. Don't lie.'

'You're right. And with even more scope for fun.'

'Well, you've picked an exciting time!'

'Why is that?' John heard the hint of warning, but the picture distracted him.

How strange her nakedness looked, even though he could have mapped it by heart. Now, for the first time, he noticed the eagerness on the goddess's face as she tried to read the exact degree of the farmer's gratitude. The shadowy figure in background, John now saw clearly, was next in line for his share of the largesse. The portrait was less flattering than he had thought on his last visit.

Coymans walked restlessly around the room. 'The market's in full spate. A non-swimmer could drown.'

'Unless, of course, he has you to buoy him up like a Grecian porpoise,' said John, still smiling but listening hard again. His grey eyes searched the once-familiar room for other marks time might have made, either on the place or on his vision of it.

'You were never a shipwrecked sailor,' retorted Coymans. 'But you're right. You'd be a fool to venture very deep without me at your side.'

John's ears quivered for the sound of Marika's feet on the stairs.

'She's coming, man! She's coming.' The small eyes regarded John with amused speculation. 'Tell the truth! Perhaps I'm wrong, after all. Which of us have you come back for? Are you going to dash my spirits now and tell me that you've only come for true love's sake?'

'I still need you to pimp for me with the Goddess Fortune,' said John in a reassuring tone.

Coymans blinked once.

In the small beat of silence, John forgot for a second to listen for Marika's footsteps. Two months ago, Coymans would have expected nothing less than the friendly insult.

Then Coymans laughed. 'Then welcome back, my brother-in-fun! The business will test both of us to the limits . . .' He crossed back to the door leading into the hall. 'Where is my sister? She must be dithering between gowns, or plucking stray hairs from her brow, or cleaning her fingernails, or polishing her teeth before she bares herself to your glance again.' He shook his head to invite John to share his own humorous tolerance of the fallible sex.

John sat back on his uncomfortable high-backed chair. One of the paintings was new – globular peonies in a *nature morte*. Two paintings – a seascape and church interior, if he remembered – had gone, leaving their faint rectangular ghosts on the wall. The large globe was also missing.

The virginal was open. Two chairs stood askew before it, and a music stand. The two broken strings of the chitarrone had been replaced. The wood and tortoiseshell instrument lay on the virginal's lid as if set down briefly between songs. There were sheets of music both on the virginal and on the music stand by the second chair.

John glanced at Pomona again. Generous to a fault. He already knew that. And he had refused her invitation to stay. He had no right now to go hot with jealousy. He was worse than Harry. He had no right at all! But he could not imagine Marika playing duets with another woman. He saw Coymans watching him and unclenched his fists.

'Why will the business test us?' John asked.

'Those interfering stadholders are determined to legislate against man's capacity to make a fool of himself.' Coymans snorted. 'God failed with the Ten Commandments, but a bunch of Netherlander burghers think they can do better!'

John's attention was now fully caught. 'Can one still deal?'

'"One" can do anything "one" likes,' said Coymans. 'Laws or no laws. "One" just has to find like-minded colleagues.'

'Who are also willing to break the law?'

'. . . the possible law,' Coymans corrected him. 'Anyway, is a law that most men break a valid law or a farce? No, my law-abiding Englishman, that's not the risk . . . And bring my pipes,' Coymans said to the maid who had entered with their beer. At last, he sat. 'You are still resolutely lawful?'

John nodded shortly.

'Rest easy. Most of these would-be laws fade like morning mist. Even the lawmakers aren't sure from day to day what they have actually done. The real risk grows out of their shilly-shallying. The stadholders think they are trying to protect us all from our folly. All they've done instead is introduce uneasiness, and therefore instability, into the market.'

'I'm amazed it has taken so long to grow unstable,' said John.

Coymans waved a dismissive paw. 'That's your own insecurity and inexperience speaking. The trouble is, because the stadholders see fit to interfere in a thing they don't properly understand, more and more investors are growing jumpy and unreliable, like you.' He drained his glass and set it on the floor.

'For example, two days ago, Spiegel – do you remember him? – refused to pay for futures he bought just after you left. Deal made legitimately *in collegio*, date and price agreed, notarized to the hilt. But the price of that particular bulb then fell below the price Spiegel had agreed to pay. He owed more than he could get on resale. So he cited one of those phantom laws, and the dealer is left high and dry . . . The more fool he!'

Real rage suddenly quivered in those four words. Then Coymans recovered his even tone. 'Now the dealer's paying for a lawsuit and the rest of us must pay for his weakness.'

He folded his arms across his chest, rearranged his feet and relodged his smile firmly among his whiskers. 'So, with the law a slippery beast, risk unavoidable, and no guarantee that our enemies will obligingly drop dead at the last moment like old Bols, tell me what miracles you want from me this time.'

Did he always sound so defiant? John asked himself. Did I miss it in my own fear?

Then he heard the brushing of silk skirts on marble and Marika's joyful cry of 'John!'

He attempted a wordless, flustered bow, but Marika flung herself at him, while Erasmus clutched in panic at the back of her waist. Ignoring both brother and pet, she kissed John hard on the mouth. 'I'm so happy you're back! You caught us by surprise!'

Over her shoulder, John met Coymans's eye. Coymans looked away.

'I'm so happy you're back,' she said again.

John wished she had not repeated it. She's making too much noise, he thought. Like her brother.

'Even Erasmus has missed you.' She pulled back the corners of her baby mouth and showed small white pearls. Erasmus dropped to the floor and hid under the virginal, watching John through the bars of an undefined rage.

'Now I won't believe another word you say,' said John. She was as uncomfortable as he was, after their time apart. Perversely, John began to feel more at ease.

'He's getting to know you, my dear,' said Coymans amiably. 'It's time to find a new lover.'

'I shall have to, if you speak like that in front of him,' Marika replied tartly.

Then her gaze and energy settled. She met John's eyes squarely, held both his hands in hers and smiled across the small distance between them. Her hands were oddly cold, but her waist had felt solid and reassuringly real between John's hands. 'But you must have forgiven both of us for our sins, mustn't you, John? You came back.'

'I had no choice with such sirens calling.' He raised one of her cold hands to his lips and kissed it. The fingers turned in his own to caress his cheek.

'Stay,' she said. Then she lifted her chin and gave a strange small laugh. 'Stay for dinner. Justus, have you insisted yet that John stay for dinner?'

With a tremor of guilt towards Zeal, John let himself fall head-first into the dark waiting waters.

The monkey was a furry whisper against John's bare thigh. John hardly noticed. He purged his weeks of control. His blood buzzed. He was flying, swinging high above sharpened blades of diamond and gold.

'Oh God!' said Marika. 'Oh, yes!'

Their damp skins slid against each other. Her baby's mouth and tall strong body opened to him. Her arms locked hard behind his head.

He swung in great arcs, flying sure, sailing blind.

'Stay!' she whispered.

He held her tight and rolled them both over so that her weight was on him. Erasmus leaped away to cling to the bed curtains and glared down with dark witch eyes.

'Stay in Amsterdam.'

At that moment, he would agree to anything she asked.

Later, he lay awake in the dark. The shadowed weight of Erasmus shifted and vibrated against his foot as the beast scratched and picked for fleas. Then it suddenly grew heavier and vanished as the monkey leaped away onto the bed curtains again, leaving a faint memory of the puppy Cassie dreaming heavily at the end of his bed.

John lay spent. Marika breathed gently beside him. The monkey made the curtains swing as it climbed higher.

I'm back, thought John. To another rapturous welcome.

He turned his head again, then swung his legs across the edge of the bed and sat up with his feet on the cool tiled floor. He should feel warmed and sated, but instead he was deeply uneasy.

During the evening, Coymans had not bothered to muffle

the snap of those sharp teeth that John had imagined that he heard on his first visit.

He's more sure of me in some way, thought John. He rubbed his hands along the tops of his bare thighs and wondered what Coymans might think had changed.

'We must change our strategy to match the time,' Coymans had said when he and John had retired after dinner to the little bare parlour on the first floor.

'Change strategy or change principles?' John accepted the white clay pipe which Coymans had lit for him and looked curiously around the room. Neptune still netted his seahorses on the fireplace, but there were fewer canvases stacked around the room than there had been three months before.

'My principles are as constant as the North Star,' said Coymans cheerfully. 'Still those of a realist.'

'How bad is it?' John drew on the thin shank of his pipe and hoped that the inhaled smoke was as powerful against colds and agues as he had been told. He found blessed little pleasure in it otherwise. 'Is it still possible to deal in the normal way – buy, pray and sell?'

'The market is still full of *liefhebbers*, more sure that they will continue to be able to sell at a profit than they are of entering Paradise. Anything is still possible.'

'But . . . ? I hear a reservation in your voice.'

Idly, Coymans straightened a stack of paintings with the toe of his shoe. 'I have risen and stayed aloft because of my keen sense of smell. I'm a rich man because I can see trouble coming before most other men, and change my actions accordingly. I am constant in my inconstancy.'

John watched while Coymans drew lustily on his pipe, exhaled a cloud worthy to transport Jove, opened a wooden shutter and closed it again.

Something serious has happened since I was last here, thought John. The idea had been growing during the evening.

Coymans has had some bad luck. Which could explain the strange nervousness I also feel in Marika.

'The truth is,' said Coymans, as if answering John's thoughts, 'that I want to avoid risk myself just now. I'm a victim of my passions.' He spread his arms to demonstrate the canvases. 'My corn is scattered wide. It's the danger a patron runs. In short, my capital is tied up and not every dealer will accept paintings as payment in kind.'

'So what is your sense of smell telling you?'

'To sell the bear's skin before I have caught the bear.'

John stiffened. 'Isn't that what we did before? Selling what we didn't have? I won't do that again.'

'Nor will I,' agreed Coymans equably, 'not as we did before. Because, while it is quite legal, it doesn't do to be seen executing that process more than once. Investors are suspicious, nervous creatures, quicker to distrust than ferrets. I absolutely agree with you. This time, we must have a real bearskin to wave under their noses.'

'And where do we get this bearskin, if we haven't risked our capital to buy it?'

'We borrow it!' said Coymans triumphantly.

John lay back on the bed with a sigh. He had no more reason than before to distrust either Coymans or Marika. On the contrary, he owed both of them more than he could ever repay. Though Coymans was a villain, he made no secret of it, seemed not even to understand the need.

And that perverse honesty is my protection, thought John. I am always warned. I can always choose to take a different road. As I did this evening.

But when John refused the borrowed bearskin strategy, Coymans had chewed his upper lip briefly, considered the Englishman and said, 'Think it over.' Then he had slapped John on the arm. 'Come on. Enough business for now. Your mind is clearly on other things tonight. We'll talk again tomorrow.'

377

Sitting naked in the dark, John realized that he was cold. He lay down again and pulled the coverlet to his chin.

In the morning I'll visit Gomez and see what I can learn about Coymans's affairs in the last few weeks. And ask about other dealers.

The decision eased him. He listened again to the gentle sound of Marika's breathing and Erasmus scratching at something down on the floor. He thought about the King's soldiers who needed to be paid. He repeated silently the word 'pardon'.

Pardon. Freedom. He could not yet imagine the full import. His mind flashed quickly to the small boy being carried like Apollo through a high bright heaven on the back of a mammoth horse. The horse carried him out through the gate into the park.

Pardon. Edward Malise's face contorted with held-in frustration and rage after Lord Mallender's casually given order. Malise's face turned against the firelight in the East Java Company offices. Flames washed over the face. And here, John closed his mind.

He eased closer to Marika and listened intently to her breathing as if it were a difficult piece of music he was trying to learn. The gentle rhythm crowded his mind. His thoughts slowly dimmed. Finally he slid into sleep, warmed by the long soft continent of her left hip and thigh.

'My cousin's an idiot,' said Gomez, hefting the muslin-wrapped wheel of cheese. 'To make you carry this all the way here to the land of cheeses! And I know him – he hasn't even the humour to see how funny it is!' He waved John farther into his treasure cave over the baker's shop. 'Sit! Sit! Tell me how he looked. He's thirteen years younger than me, you know.'

John suppressed a grin, shifted a gilt clock, and sat on a stool. 'He seemed in health, in his prime, and not a day younger than you, sir.'

'Ahhh,' said Gomez in mock ecstasy and deprecation. He put the cheese down on a pile of silk shawls on top of a stack of books to rummage out of John's sight behind a tower of three sandalwood chests secured with heavy iron locks. At this time of the morning he was still wearing his brocade robe, but his little black moustaches were stiffly waxed to attention. 'Were your clients satisfied with Cousin Jacov?' asked his muffled voice.

'Mightily relieved, if you want to know the truth,' said John.

Gomez resurfaced with a bottle of ale and one Venetian goblet of green and red spun-sugar glass. 'And so were you.' His sharp dark eyes precluded polite denial.

John nodded. 'I'll admit, the metamorphosis did seem like magic, and I don't take easily to magic. It's too easily misused.'

'That's true of any power. Ale?' Gomez poured without waiting for John's answer. 'As you came to see me again without soldiers or your sword drawn, I assumed that you were content.' He handed John the brimming glass. 'Have you come back to Amsterdam just to bring me Cousin Jacov's cheese? Or have you been bitten by the market lust?'

'By lust, not entirely mine. Or rather, by need.'

While Gomez dug for bread and cheese to go with John's ale and his own curded milk, John explained in general terms what was at stake.

'The official money slid my way without firm identification of its source.' He was unsure how much to say. He still had no idea of Gomez's political sympathies.

Gomez nodded. 'Don't tie yourself into knots of discretion. Jacov has written me how desperate the state of the Treasury has grown. The war with Spain cost England too much and the peace is paying nothing back. You're an important man, my friend, if you're trusted with Treasury money.'

'Then your cousin is important, too,' said John. 'My

employers trusted him with a large share of it.' He showed five bonds that Jacov had written to five different names. 'Most, in fact.'

Gomez read them. 'Good. Good. Perez is a sound man. And the others. No problems there.' He refolded Jacov's bonds and handed them back.

'If the money's secure, I'd like to leave it with those men as long as possible,' said John. 'Even more, I'd love to transform the clanking tonnage I have stowed under guard again in the top room of the Widow Padtbrugge's house.'

Gomez suddenly grinned. John noticed for the first time that the old man was missing several of his back teeth. 'I absolutely refuse to risk my precious books again.'

John grinned back. 'Priced above rubies? If any were damaged, I must pay for them.'

'One or two were mauled in disappointment. Not valuable ones. What are you transforming this time? Plate? Candlesticks? Engraved suits of armour?'

'Cash. Fifteen thousand pounds which could not be translated in time into those flimsy shreds of paper.'

'Then it must be the Bank of Amsterdam. Their vaults are stronger than the widow's stairs. You put it in. Only you can take it out. Unless you transfer it to another depositor there.'

'Will the Bank of Amsterdam welcome English money meant to grow to pay for soldiers and guns?'

'No, but they'll ask no questions of an honest Marrano merchant who has helped swell Dutch trade for the last fifteen years. They already hold money for me.'

'The money will be in your name?' Suspicion nudged at John again.

Gomez spread his thin brocade-clad arms. Trust me or not. Your choice.

John took a deep breath and nodded. 'Agreed.' To atone for his suspicion, he added firmly, 'At a small commission.'

Gomez waggled his silver head. 'As you like. Who can

afford to refuse a commission? Not me, not you.' He cut another slice of bread, then carved translucent slivers of cheese which he arranged on the bread like the petals of a flower. He handed the bread to John. 'Are you investing anything for yourself this time?'

John sat relaxed on his stool as if he had set down a great burden. He accepted the slice of bread and heard himself voice a plan which had been uncurling in his brain since the morning he had left Hawkridge House.

'I want to invest my commission from the last time for my cousin's wife, to help replace her own personal portion, which my cousin has borrowed and invested. While he controls all her money, including that private share of hers, she has no defence . . .' He stopped suddenly.

Gomez raised his arched black brows. 'So what will there be for you if you plan to give your money away?'

Applause, thought John wryly. 'The glory.'

Gomez snorted politely.

John watched him saw at the cheese. 'The chance to reclaim a past life.'

Gomez put down the knife, arranged his own flower and looked at John across the bread as he bit down cautiously with his remaining teeth. 'You're a lucky man to want a past life back. Most men live in hope of a better one in the future. Me, for example, I'm still hoping.'

'I'd settle for any future life at all,' said John.

'Ahh,' said Gomez again, this time without mockery. He eyed John and brushed a crumb from his right moustache with the back of his hand. The gesture made John think of a squirrel. 'Am I giving breakfast to a desperate man?'

'None more so.' John tried once more to keep his tone light, but Gomez did not smile.

'*Nil desperandum*. Despair doesn't suit you, son of fortune. You have a face to cause despair, not to feel it.'

'"Fortune favours fools".'

'Try this one,' retorted Gomez. '"Fortune makes a fool of him whom she favours too much".'

John heard a shift. 'Do you mean me, or Justus Coymans?'

'Have you seen him yet?'

John nodded. 'Is he in trouble?'

'A little less bouncing than a month ago, eh?' Gomez barely concealed his satisfaction. 'He's been cursed with a bad debt he can't recover. His latest big buyer won't pay up.' Gomez refilled John's glass. 'And, alas, it's a very large number of bulbs. He got a ridiculously high price on paper for the bulbs he hadn't yet bought, then signed to buy himself five days later, all nicely notarized, before his buyer, Spiegel, informed him that he didn't want so many bulbs at such a ludicrously high price after all.'

John spilled his ale. He set his glass carefully down on the floor. 'Spiegel?'

Gomez cocked his head. 'Do you know the man? An enthusiast with more appetite for novelty than good sense. Until now.' He smoothed his silver hair with one thin hand. Clearly he knew perfectly well that John had sold Spiegel *The King of Kandy*.

'Spiegel is refusing to pay Justus Coymans?' John asked in disbelief. 'Coymans told me . . . Is it Coymans himself entering the lawsuit then?'

Gomez shrugged. 'What else should he do? He still has to pay for all those bulbs even though Spiegel doesn't want them. He's a dealer with a reputation to keep. Spiegel ferries Baltic coal. Couldn't care less. In some circles, he'll have improved his reputation for being hardheaded and tough.'

'I'm sorry to hear it.' The new solidity of this alien land slid and wavered under John's feet again.

'I'm not sorry,' said Gomez. 'It gives me faith in divine retribution. Comforting so long as my own conscience is clear.'

'No,' said John. 'I'm sorry because it means that Coymans lied to me.'

Gomez stared as if he thought the Englishman had gone mad. 'Lied to you?' Then he chortled. The chortle gathered force and became a laugh. Gomez panted and gasped for breath and wiped his eyes with a handkerchief which he pursued among his pockets with a ferocity born of hysteria. 'Coymans lied to you!' He panted, gasped and wheezed in an enormous breath, which he then wheezed out again. 'Li-i-ied! Oh, me . . . Oh . . . Oh . . . Oh . . . !'

'Senhor!' John was half-alarmed, half-angry.

'How dread . . . dread . . . ful that Coy . . . Coymans told a lie!' Gomez wiped his eyes again. 'Mr Nightingale, you have confused me now. I have misjudged your powers of perception.'

'You misunderstand me. I meant that I had trusted his villainy to be consistent,' said John with a noticeable chill on his voice. His black brows met ominously.

Gomez sobered instantly. 'I'm sorry. I'm not laughing at you. It's just too early in the morning to be given the news that Justus Coymans has told a l . . . lie!' He gasped one last time like a child calming down from a tantrum. 'You must see how funny it is!'

'Perhaps I lack your full perspective.'

Gomez nodded. 'I apologize again. You're right. And it's probably better that you be allowed to keep your narrower view. As long as you're on your guard, which I, in spite of my childish display just now, see that you clearly are.' He put away his handkerchief.

'How much should I fear him?'

Gomez thought carefully before he answered. 'I suspect much, but I don't know. It would give me great satisfaction to tell the worst, but in truth, I know only gossip and rumour. And Justus himself shapes both of those so often for his own purposes that I don't know what darkness he might like men to believe when the truth is really much less dramatic. I don't know! I want to be fair.'

John hesitated. Then he asked, 'What about his sister?'

Gomez busied himself with a small inlaid box filled with mother-of-pearl gaming counters. He cleared a space and began to sort the counters into piles of fish, stars and moons. 'Fairly?'

'I think so. I think I already know.'

'A lovely harlot, then. Apart from that, she has charm and intelligence. I've never seen viciousness in her. Who knows what she might have been with parents who lived and a different brother?'

The word 'harlot' lodged like a splinter in John's heart. He had known, but he had not wanted to hear the truth confirmed so matter-of-factly.

Gomez silently counted seven mother-of-pearl fish. 'Anyway,' he said, with a question in his voice. 'As for Coymans, better the devil you know than the one you don't?'

'If the handle of my spoon is long enough for safe dining.'

'Spoons, I have!' said Gomez. He wrote down the number of fish and began to count the stars. 'Handles all lengths. Short as toothpicks, long as cannons, and the devils to go with them.'

'It was those other devils I came to see you about,' said John. 'As well as Cousin Jacov's cheese.'

Gomez sighed as if expectation had finally been answered. 'You don't like your familiar devil any more?'

'He makes me uneasy.'

'What's new?' Gomez swept a constellation back into the inlaid box and wrote down another number. 'But has your need diminished? Aren't you still performing miracles of multiplication?'

'Is Coymans the only dealer?'

Gomez kept his eyes on the little nacreous moons, like a giant's nail parings. 'Justus is perhaps the most determined.

Besides, he wouldn't like to find you in competition when he believes you to be enrolled among his own personal troops.'

'Are you saying that I have no choice?'

'It depends entirely on how much you need to win. Coymans knows how to come out on top. That's why I took you to him in the first place.'

Thoughtfully, John lowered himself behind Gomez down through the hollow tree-trunk staircase and out through the baker's shop. Gomez would bring an escort and cart to the widow's house at noon to deal with the clanking hoard. They parted and John set out, with directions from the old man, in search of one of Coymans's most interesting enrollees. Gomez had been enlightening. There was much at stake. John needed to find more men who might tell him the truth.

He emerged from an alley that led from the Warmoesstraat and crossed the wide water of the Damrak. The arched bridge carried him at rigging level past a jostling of moored ships, packed so tightly on the water that there barely seemed room for the dinghies and barges that eased among them carrying the cargoes to the gaping warehouse doors of the big canalside houses. As he entered the dark hole of another alley, John reflected that the Hollanders left more room for boats than for men.

He crossed two more large canals, turned left just before the city wall and found a maidservant sweeping the *stoep* of the tall, thin brick house with sage-green shutters, three away from the corner of the canal, as Gomez had said. Here John hesitated. He did not know Saski's last name.

'Saski?' John mimed the act of drawing.

The maid welcomed John into the house with the polite alacrity of a servant of a master who lived on commissions. Then she trotted down the twisting wooden staircase to find Saski.

The hall was much more modest than Coymans's, with a tiled floor, not marble, and plain plastered walls instead of wooden panelling. But Saski's walls were even more crusted with paintings in carved and gilded frames.

John could not tell how many of these paintings were by Saski. He had seen only one other painting and those fast, fairground tricks of instant drawing. These pictures were more solid than the sketches, though not as solidly respectable as Coymans *père*. Portraits of soldiers, market women holding fish, a dwarf. A few more conventional classical pieces. John leaned close to the goddess Flora, asleep half-naked in an Italianate meadow while shepherds and children plucked the flowers that grew around her. It could have been a companion piece for Marika's Pomona; the tawny background of ghostly columns and non-Dutch hills was similar. But both face and body of the sleeping goddess were unfamiliar, and her hair was red.

He moved on to what he first thought was a version of the Last Supper. Looking more closely, he saw that it was an allegorical genre piece illustrating the sins of excess.

The central figure was pouring wine into his neighbour's overflowing glass while turned away in careless laughter to the man on his other side. Jugs and glasses had toppled and spilled. White clay pipes lay smoking dangerously on the Moorish carpet that covered the table. The thirteen diners sprawled on their bench or had fallen forward into drunken sleep. A dwarf mounted on a mastiff poured wine from a jug onto the floor. Excess and waste. In the shadows, bony Retribution lurked with his scythe.

John looked again. The man with the overflowing wine glass looked very like Justus Coymans. Next to him, Edward Malise leaned back, his head turned and chin lifted toward the serving maid behind him.

John's heart leapt and began to gallop. He leaned closer, then straightened, berating himself. Like a witch-seeking judge, he saw the devil everywhere.

But there was no mistaking Coymans – the wild hair, arch-

ing moustaches, white, white smile and chilly eyes. In case
any doubt remained, a bulging purse on the table in front of
him spat two golden coins from its mouth. The man held a
pair of dice on his open palm, and his wrist lay across the
stem of a wilting red and yellow tulip.

'Francis and I were both in Amsterdam . . .' Malise had
told the room full of considerable men while John sat on a
stool and stared at the body of the man he had just killed.

John heard the maid's apologetic voice, from below him
on the lower landing of the stairs. She shook her head, which
was all he could see of her.

'I'm sorry. I don't understand,' said John firmly but
untruthfully. He flung himself down the stairs.

'*Nee*! *Nee*!' The maid tried to block his way. '*U mag niet
naar binnen*!'

As John pushed past her into the studio, Saski turned
angrily away from the canvas beside the big canalside warehouse door. 'I'm working,' he said in English. 'Come back
later.'

Fourteen

July 17, 1636. To avoid conception, juniper berries eaten whole (Dioscorides).

Day Boke of Zeal Beester.

Zeal crawled on her hands and knees in the orchard grass. She circled the bee skep twice, searching carefully. She peered through the busy entrance arch. Through wet, puffy eyes, she could see only a furry, buzzing heaving just inside the hive. No dead bees.

Please! she begged silently. Let me find just one! She wasn't sure whether she was addressing the Lord or asking the hive to offer up one of its noble, busy little souls in an act of self-sacrifice.

If it were autumn, she thought, I would have better luck. She sat back on her heels in despair. Please! Make it easy. I can't do anything just now that asks too much of me.

Panic filled her, as when Mrs Hazelton had shut her into a chest to break her insolence. Locked alive into her coffin, she had nearly gone mad, helpless to change what had been unbearable. Now, though she knew that she could do something, the same sense of helplessness was locking up her will. Three days after John left, Zeal had suddenly thought that Harry might have made her pregnant.

She must not conceive! She might come to it, as Harry had said. Woman was born to travail. Zeal did not think that she would escape. But not yet. She was not ready to put her life at risk. Like her older sister.

Without knowing, she had bundled all her fears into one single blinding terror.

Why had she believed Harry? She had known since infancy that promises were made to be broken. When had she ever been able to depend on anyone but herself?

Sitting in the long damp grass, she gave an open-mouthed, full-throated child's wail of grief.

How dare John desert her?

She cleared her eyes with both hands like a swimmer, then began to sob. If he were still here, he would know where to find a dead bee. He had deserted her when she most needed him. One more traitor.

In an off-centre fury, she climbed to her feet and stumbled through the apple trees to the next bee skep. She must find a bee.

She had searched through all *materia medica* in her library and in John's, inside the privacy of her drawn bed-curtains. She had found recipes for avoiding conception, but they either needed impossible ingredients like mule's kidneys or else suggested such commonly eaten vegetables as carrots and radishes that Zeal wondered how any children were ever born at all. Then she found the instruction to eat a dead bee. It was within her power. The idea seemed repulsive enough to suit her terror. Its very awfulness convinced.

She searched the next skep. And the next.

And there on the stone fair-standing of the withy skep lay her self-sacrificing little beast. With a prayer of thanks, she carefully brushed it onto her palm. She watched it and listened for a long while.

It seemed quite dead, slightly curled, with its legs drawn up like a sleeping child. Round and compact in all its parts. Tail striped black and a soft, russety red. Like her, it had once had all those gifts of nature, smelling, hearing, sight, brain and science.

She raised her hand to her mouth.

The chiefest among all insects, created for the sake of man. With government, manners and a sense of the common good. Magicians who collected honey out of the air, from the perspiration of the sky. Builders of combs and wax that gave man light, among the least of its thousand purposes. Such a creature would surely be unselfishly happy to serve her in this hour of desperate need.

She imagined putting the bee into her mouth. Chewing the striped furry tail, snapping the clear scales of its wings between her teeth.

She retched violently. Then she began to sob again, holding the bee tenderly in her lightly closed hand.

Pliny recorded that dead bees might be revived by being laid in the spring sun, by being kept warm by the ashes of fig trees, or perhaps by being placed in the belly of a slaughtered cow. Zeal had no fig trees or dead cows, and it was no longer spring. But she clambered to her feet fierce with redirected purpose, to find a warm place to breed her bee back to life.

By bedtime that night, the bee had still not revived, but she finally found, in Mr Hill's *Labyrinth,* a recipe for an abortifying decoction of *salvia*.

'I thought you must speak English, from your evident understanding at Coymans's table,' said John.

'I speak a little.' Saski shrugged in deprecation. 'Badly. Not a skill to boast. I am working now. Why have you come?'

'To bring you a pencil of English black lead in exchange

for your drawings,' said John. 'Borrowdale's best, and a wooden case to hold it in.'

Saski stood a moment longer as if he hoped John might change his mind and go away. Then he put down his brush with resignation. He called an instruction to a boy bent over a mortar into which he was dripping liquid from a small stoneware jar.

'You are kind,' he said to John. 'But there was no need. What can I give you now? To eat? To drink?'

'Please come with me,' said John. He turned and climbed the stairs again.

Saski raised his eyebrows but followed.

'Who painted that?' asked John, pointing at the burlesque of the Last Supper.

Saski raised his right hand.

'And who is that man?'

Saski peered at the profile that looked like Malise. He shrugged. 'I draw too many men.'

'Have you drawn him before?'

'I must have done,' said Saski, explaining to an idiot. 'I make studies before I paint.'

'May I see the studies?'

The two men assessed each other. Of much the same age and height. John was the broader through the shoulders, browner, darker and rougher, in spite of his fine city clothes, a woodland creature come to town. Saski, though dressed in rust-coloured wool and leather smeared with paint, had milky skin, fine long bones and hair the translucent, pale yellow of an autumn leaf. An angel in mortal disguise.

A fallen angel, John amended, with those sharp, distant eyes and that quivering energy.

Saski saw much the same eyes and energy in the curly-haired Englishman. 'You can see them if you can find them,' he said. He led John back down the stairs to his studio.

The casual speed with which Saski sketched and dismissed

the constantly shifting pattern of life around him had misled. The truth about his work was far more substantial than John had expected. The studio reminded him of Gomez's lair. Saski too, hid his riches from the public eye.

Canvases leaned against every upright surface, stacked twelve deep. They were slotted into open wooden racks along one side of the studio and hung frame-to-frame on the walls. The room was densely scaled like a fish, its flesh and bones hidden under gleaming scales of varnished canvases.

Stacks of drawings, loose papers and portfolios lay on every flat surface. Tabletops, stools and floor disappeared under piles of charcoal line sketches, grisaille drawings, and bald, stark, gesso panels. Here and there space had been cleared for stoneware jars that bristled with brushes, stirring sticks, straight edges, compasses. For bowls of iridescent charcoal chunks, boxes of slim, precisely cylindrical oil sticks, jars of dry, powdered pigments, a dish of eggshells. For pencils, knives, etching needles, jugs of turpentine, glue, paint rags, rabbits' feet, squirrels' tails, feathers and all the other magician's tools that turned a bright white barren surface into a frozen scrap of time and the life that had filled it.

The painted scraps, however, had a weight and density lacking in the sketches. The truths which inhabited the empty spaces of the drawings, only half-snared by the quick, moving lines, were netted and tied down in Saski's paintings by a skin of oil, turpentine and pigments that spelled out every detail of every square inch. In the paintings in the studio, John now recognized the hand which had painted most of those in the hall above.

'Go ahead,' said Saski. He waved an arm at the middens of paper and canvas. 'You may look, but I think you will not find.'

'I need more help than that.'

Saski glanced longingly at his abandoned canvas. 'Boboli,' he said. He threaded his way among tables of bristling paintbrushes and ricks of leaning canvases to the racks along the wall. 'Perhaps . . . Boboli . . . He's dead now. Not a single symmetry in him.' He pulled a large portfolio from the rack and opened it on a table after clearing a stack of canvases on to the floor. 'He was an interesting problem. Like a plant. I could make no easy assumptions about that body. He challenged the truthfulness of my eye.'

John looked past Saski's shoulder at a sketch of the dwarf who rode the mastiff in the painting in the hall. Saski sifted through a series of studies: Boboli absorbed in juggling apples, Boboli dancing on the table, with a false smile and sharp assessing eye turned on his audience. John studied the faces of the men who watched the dance.

'Perhaps not that night,' said Saski. 'Here, you look.' He shoved the portfolio a few inches toward John, and pulled another from the rack as well. 'I am working. Bread and cheese work. Excuse me, please.'

He returned to the large canvas by the warehouse door.

John turned over more drawings. Boboli again. The maid who served at Coymans's table. His heart kicked and beat a little faster.

Anonymous men. Faces he remembered from his first visit. Several sketches of a familiar-looking youth. No one who looked like Malise.

John was almost distracted by a series of flower drawings where Saski had contrived to suggest the ghosts of human faces lurking in the crumpled abundance of roses and the streaks and flames of tulips. Then he realized that he had seen these ghosts rendered substantial in a new still life in a gilded frame on the music room wall in Coymans's house. These were studies for that painting.

Under the last of these, lay a single sheet which bore three charcoal studies of the naked Marika. Three times, she stood squarely on two bare feet with her hands resting as lightly and fleetingly as birds at her throat, her waist, her shoulder, her glorious hip. On the next sheet, the goddess leaned forward to offer a single apple in one hand, again to hold out a basket with two hands, and, finally, in her pose of the finished painting, to pour the cascade of fruit into the grateful farmer's arms.

Lust and rage attacked with equal force. John glared from Marika to Saski's working, oblivious back. John swallowed. Of course, Saski was likely to have painted Pomona. As well as Flora. And how could he have painted the picture if he had not done studies first?

But why hadn't he painted her face on a model's body? This was no model. John knew the intimate geography of that sketched flesh. Even in a country as foreign as this, decent women did not take off their clothes and stand naked before the eyes of any man who chose to gaze. If John were tempted to fool himself, he only had to imagine asking the Widow Padtbrugge to oblige.

John knew that Marika had the heart of a harlot, however she dressed it up, and he had not minded in the least while he was in bed with her. But when Marika had exposed herself to Saski's truth-seeking eye, the artist had possessed her with an intimacy which now seemed to John to be far greater than his own merely carnal exchange.

He turned over the sheet of paper to erase Marika's image. Under her lay another study of Boboli, this time with the mastiff.

John forgot his spasm of jealousy. He was closing in on his quarry. If quarry it were. The next sheet was a study of two men's heads, then came a study of three. The sheet after that showed a triangle of faces. Two men, hungry as wolves, leaned in from either side towards Marika, barely pubescent, no more than twelve or thirteen, but already self-aware and amused. Drawn at least six years ago. The man on her left had the same falcon profile that was turned to the serving maid in the painting in the hall.

John riffled quickly down the pile of drawings but found no more of the man who looked like Malise. He crossed to Saski with the drawing. 'Have you drawn this man any other times?'

'I don't know. Too many to say.' Then he looked more closely at John's intent face. 'My eye tells the truth better than my tongue. Look more if you like. But be careful with the drawings.'

John returned to the hunt. Within a quarter of an hour he had found what he was looking for and wished he had not.

What am I to do with this knowledge now?

He stared at Edward Malise playing cards with Marika as she looked now, Edward Malise in full and three-quarter profile studies and Edward Malise leaning forward to accept a light for his pipe from Justus Coymans. There was no doubt about who it was; Saski had caught his hunger and air of suppressed rage. With both a young Marika and the present Marika. Malise and Coymans had known each other for at least six or seven years, perhaps more.

For a few seconds John tried to persuade himself that nothing was proved. Coymans made a point of knowing everyone. John already knew that Justus would drink with the Devil himself to settle a deal. And Marika didn't necessarily bed every man who ate at her brother's table.

But clear sight had returned.

I should never have lost it. Blinded by lust and greed. At the very best, such generous impartiality in both sister and brother does not argue well for them as trustworthy friends. I can debate with myself as long as I like, but it will only delay the arrival of what I already know is the truth.

'May I buy this?' He showed Saski the drawing of Malise and Coymans smoking together, watching each other from under lowered lids. Proof, John thought. Though I don't know yet of what. But I do know that the friendship of these two men is dangerous.

Saski glanced over his shoulder. 'Take it for nothing. Bring me some more English pencils when you can. Take as many drawings as you like. In five years, I will have no room left for what is happening then.'

John looked around at the stacked canvases and over-flowing portfolios, piled-up fragments of time, Saski's life accumulating relentlessly, snatched at by that always-moving hand. John himself was snared somewhere in those slanting, crinkle-edge heaps, just as Malise had been snared.

John now saw what Saski was painting. 'A fair likeness,' he said, to put off the question he knew he must ask.

A full-size portrait of Justus Coymans was taking shape on the canvas. Startling patches of life-like fur, silk, grey pearls outlining the jacket edge jumped out of a tentative wilderness of charcoal lines. The connoisseur, patron, scatterer of corn. Around him, Saski had sketched the rectangles of empty frames to be filled with paintings Coymans had bought. A ghostly Turkish tulip pot held the skeletons of flowers still to arrive. Saski had nearly finished the face. The white teeth, the pouches below the eyes, the humorous crinkles at the corners which contradicted the coldness of the eyes themselves.

'You don't flatter him,' said John.

'He says he is happy enough with the truth.' Saski became busy with a jug of turpentine and a rag.

'Shouldn't artists show us a better world than our own?'

Saski concentrated on rubbing out a minute patch of paint with his turpentine-soaked rag. 'I can't lie. And therefore I am not rich like others I could name. Anyway, I show Coymans as the world should see him.'

John thought of the painting of Marika as Pomona. The greedy face of the peasant, the goddess gauging her effect. Undiscriminating generosity twisted into its own allegory for harlotry.

He studied Saski's Coymans for what the world should see.

If Coymans wanted a truckling memorial to his success and virtues to set beside that of his father in his hall, he had commissioned the wrong painter.

'What tulips will you paint for him?' John asked finally.

'*The King of Kandy*, of course. His greatest triumph. Would you like to commission a portrait with the *King* as well?' Saski repainted the smooth peninsula of Coymans's right earlobe in the frothy sea of his tawny hair. 'Or do you have greater riches in England already memorialized?'

John thought of the off-set being nursed by Zeal at Hawk-ridge House. 'I have memorial enough, though I thank you for the offer.'

'It is nothing.'

John weighed the coldness in the painter's manner that lay deeper than irritation at being interrupted at work. He wondered if Marika had done more than pose for Saski.

'I shall leave you now,' he said. 'Thank you for this . . .' He held up the drawing of Malise and Coymans. 'And for your time.' He asked the hideous question that he could no longer avoid. 'When did you last draw this man?'

Saski cursed under his breath. He laid down his fine-pointed brush with exaggerated care and turned to John. 'Does it matter?'

'It matters.'

'I suppose it would,' said Saski. The pale skin around his eyes crinkled in a spasm of sharp-edged humour which John did not understand. 'Five days ago. At Coymans's house.'

John suddenly saw the two chairs pushed back from the virginal, the two sets of music and the chitarrone aslant on the virginal's lid as if laid down briefly between songs. And before he could ask himself why, he saw the challenging con-firmation of his suspicions in Saski's light-blue eyes.

'It is more tolerable to be refused than deceived.'

John could hear the questioning voice of Dr Bowler suggest that his pupils might care to debate this maxim of Publius

Syrus. Harry, himself, Cousin James (still alive then), all three distracted by their dogs which had been drawn to the outdoor schoolroom under an oak. John had argued for the proposition, as he recalled. He had known no better then.

Coymans wore a mask of open truth. John had mistaken the disguise for nakedness.

I can't dine with Coymans and Marika tonight!

He knew himself. He would try to hold his tongue, then suddenly blurt out a challenge to them both to tell the truth. Respect the thorn, he told himself. Your hand grabs for the rose. Respect the thorn, or pull back your hand.

If you pull back your hand, you lose the chance of pardon.

Escape from the prison of secrecy in which he had hidden for the last eleven years had not freed him, after all, into the luxury of constant truth.

He set off through the streets with Arthur loping anxiously in his wake. They skirted the semicircular walls of Amsterdam. John hardly noticed the fortified towers and windmills that rose at intervals in its circumference. He stared out through gates, across bridges, without seeing the neat wet fields beyond that blended into the grey, mist-furred horizon.

He would have to face the Coymanses sooner or later.

In the meanwhile, they must go back to the widow's house to meet Gomez and his cart. And his notary.

The accounting was done. The English treasury money rolled away into a warm, foggy Dutch afternoon, Arthur and Sir George's man riding on top.

John stared after them. Still the serpent of doubt bit at the edges of his stomach. If he were Gomez, might he not have pretended to help when the stakes were relatively low – as they must have seemed to a man who lived in a treasure cave? Might he not have won trust and waited cunningly? An expert fisherman spurns the sardine in hope of a whale. What greater whale swims the financial seas than the English Treasury?

He had to get out of this house and breathe fresh air, even damp air. On the way down the spiral stairs, he was intercepted by the widow on the second floor.

To John's amazement, she beckoned him into her parlour and thrust a heavy purse at him. He stood holding it while she gave him firm but unintelligible instructions. She spread her hands farther and farther apart.

'Forgive me,' John said. 'I don't understand.'

The widow repeated both her gesture and her torrent of words.

'*Tulipa*,' she said. Again, she set her hands a palm span apart, jerked them to the width of a cubit, then spread her arms wide. She sighed with frustration, and then smiled to cancel the sigh.

John suddenly understood. 'You want me to invest for you, in tulips?'

'*Ja, ja!*' she cried with relief. She touched the bag and mimed one final growth. '*Tulipa*.'

'It's not the best time . . .' John began.

'*Ja*,' begged the widow. Now she pointed to John, bent to place her palm near the floor and rose onto her toes to show the size of his fortune made in this way.

'I can't,' he tried to say. 'The risk is too great!'

'*Nee?*' she asked in disbelief.

'I'm sorry. I don't think it's wise. Invest in the Bourse. Better to be satisfied with a sure and steady two or three per cent than to lose it all.'

She pointed at him fiercely. *He* was investing, was he not?

John struggled to think how to explain an urgency which overrules good sense.

Now the widow grew angry. Her smooth white brow wrinkled like water before a wind. John could hear in her voice that he was a terrible man who refused to help women in distress.

She clapped both hands so hard against her full, black-encased bosom that she crumpled the fine white linen veiling. Clearly, John selfishly clutched success and fortune to his own bosom.

Her hands fell open. She was disappointed in him. He had seemed such a nice man, such a gentleman.

But then, he was only English, after all!

John caught her drift very clearly there. Then a reference to *kinder*, her children. Her greatest treasures. He could only assume that his stubbornly selfish refusal to share his good fortune was an affront to the children as well. Possibly (he wasn't clear here) he was destroying their future.

She began to cry. Not for effect, he was sure. She turned aside angrily, as if ashamed of her female weakness but with resignation. The movement reminded John of Zeal under the willows among the geese. Tenderness betrayed him into folly.

'Please stop. All right. I'll see what I can do.'

He would set her money safely aside. If he succeeded, he would add a little and return it to her. If not, there would be no harm done.

The widow clearly did not agree with the maxim that it was more tolerable to be refused than deceived. She wiped her eyes, smiled and took the bag from his hand again, quickly as if she feared he might change his mind. John watched, amused but impressed, while she carefully counted it out in front of him, noted the amount on two pieces of paper, signed one for him to keep and gestured for him to sign the other for her.

He escaped at last. He walked even when rain began to fall gently, insinuatingly, as if the clouds had thickened like curds in muslin bags and begun to drip. His hat grew limp and heavy, and his toes numb. It was not in his nature to delay the unpleasant or difficult. He paced the cobbles. Leaned briefly on bridges. He argued with himself. He swore to leave Amsterdam secretly that night. Then he vowed to shake Coymans until he spilled out exactly what Edward

Malise had been doing in that house. Then, just after a darkening of the moist grey sky had indicated sundown, he presented himself at Coymans's house determined to practise restraint and cunning.

Discipline cost him his appetite. Smiling hurt his cheeks. The corners of his jaw creaked when he attempted light remarks. He reminded himself again and again to unclench his fists, which lurked like knotted wood amidst the froth of his lace cuffs. Perversely, both Coymans and Marika were more at ease than they had been the night before, on his first night back, and both therefore were more beguiling. Marika sat back in her chair, laughing while Erasmus leaped and hummocked under her skirts like a bag of drowning kittens. John watched the line of her throat vibrate with her pleasure and the way the candlelight ran brightly along the golden wires of her hair. He imagined Malise's beak feeding on her pink curving mouth.

The image was unbearable, so unthinkable that John lost his grip on his conviction that Malise had really been in Amsterdam, occupying the same spaces that John now occupied. John needed to go back to the widow's house and brand Saski's drawing on his heart.

With ironic detachment, he observed himself begin to devise a bearable argument.

I have constructed a nightmare from a chance resemblance, an old man's dislike of a professional rival, and what I imagined I saw in a stranger's eyes. Trifles light as air.

He leaned back, gazed again at Marika and tested the feel of this argument. It was now less painful to study the lines of her face and arms. Justus Coymans was a smiling villain, but his sister should not be condemned for the accident of her birth. He had always respected her thorns. He watched her laugh again, then he gazed once more around the table.

The party was small, just John, Saski, a ship's captain of the Dutch East Indies Company whom he had met once before, a poet, and a man named Dirck who was playing chess with Justus in the rubble of dinner.

'Who would like to sing?' asked Marika. She raised her eyebrows invitingly at John and slapped lightly at the shifting silken peak of her lap.

She would be presented as a witch in parts of England, thought John, with that monkey always hanging like a changeling in her arms. But he smiled back helplessly at her invitation, unable to condemn her for trifles light as air.

'Tomorrow!' called Coymans from his chess game. 'Tomorrow, Nightingale. You come hunting with me.'

John sang Marika English songs, and applauded her playing on the virginal. The poet attempted the chitarrone without distinction. After the late ale had been served, John excused himself and went to sleep at his lodgings. Marika said goodnight brightly as if she had never expected him to do anything else. Perversely, lust punished John as fiercely that night as it ever had at Hawkridge House.

He met Coymans early, by the Weigh House near the Bourse. Coymans eyed John curiously.

'You came,' he said. 'You behaved so oddly last night, I half feared that you had decided to deal elsewhere.'

John considered carefully before he answered. 'A pupil can begin to think he's been taught enough, and hanker to try his new skills alone.'

Coymans's shoulders eased slightly under his jacket. 'Natural enough! But you're still humble enough to show up today.' He grinned. 'Unless it's to show off the flapping of your little fledgling wings.'

'I'm not arrogant enough yet to spurn my first and greatest teacher, *magister*.'

It was, without doubt, Edward Malise in Saski's drawing. One look when he got back to his lodgings had restored John's conviction.

'How much am I dealing with this time?'

'Twenty thousand pounds.' At the last moment, John's tongue halved the total sum.

Nevertheless, Coymans whistled and twitched one eyebrow. 'And you don't want to cling suspiciously to my coat tails?'

'Experience has taught me to trust you.'

'Do you still refuse to borrow a bearskin?'

John nodded. 'Spot dealing only. Unless you tell me you won't carry on, because I've spoiled your fun.' He breathed in the gust of cinnamon that welled up from the ship anchored below them. 'I also want to play on the regular Bourse . . . that doesn't interest you?'

'Not in the least,' said Coymans. 'Would I deal in two or three per cent, when Flora fetches fifty or a hundred? You disappoint me.'

'I have a Manichaean hunger to widen my understanding,' said John. 'How can I appreciate spice when I haven't struggled to swallow stale bread?'

Coymans bared his teeth cheerfully. 'Amsterdam is as safe a place for a heretic as anywhere.' He slapped John on the arm. 'If anywhere is safe. I assume that you really have that twenty thousand? And how soon should I agree to exchange?'

'Five days, in the normal way,' said John. 'As you taught me.'

Coymans slapped him again, just hard enough to make John suspect buried malice. 'Off you go then, my fledgling heretic. Leave your future fortune to me. I hope I can trust *you*!'

He stood watching John's broad shoulders and long-legged swinging stride until the Englishman's curly russet head vanished among the vegetable baskets and porters' hats of the huge market place.

That night Coymans told John that he had invested

£10,000 in florins in futures for three different bulbs, all rarities selling at so-many florins per ace.

'And I invested myself, as well. You brought me luck last time. I'm counting on you again!'

'How long before we can sell?' asked John. He did not like being implicated, however subtly, in Coymans's own success or failure.

'A week for *Lilith*, a week, more or less, for *The Shepherd of Texel*, and at least two weeks for *Prunelle*.'

'*Prunelle*?'

Coymans laughed. 'You were right to shun her last time – she wasn't moving fast enough. But after you left she gained favour and is still rising. That similar colour break which you threatened me with hasn't come forth yet to challenge her . . . More ale?' He leaned back and snapped his fingers for the serving maid.

John slept with Marika again that night. It was a coldly sexual exchange. She was bright and ingenious. John felt brutal and clumsy, and angry at feeling that way. To atone, he scratched Erasmus's neck the next morning and was particularly nice to Marika over their shared bread and cheese. He must not, would not let himself punish her, without fair trial, for the veil-like ghost of Edward Malise that trembled above her bed.

The next morning, John revisited Gomez.

'I'd like to meet one of your other devils after all.'

Gomez looked alarmed. 'Does Coymans know?'

'No. I'm trading through him like last time. But I have more to invest than he knows.'

'Be careful.'

'I will. But I'm in a fever to test a little of what I've learned.' John's hair radiated from his head as if it had been rubbed with a piece of silk. His brown fingers drummed. His boots danced on the floor.

'I'm glad at least that you decided to spread your risk.' Gomez did not look reassured.

Restlessly, John set off along a narrow twisting defile between stacked carpets and a wall of fragrant barrels. 'Would you help me spread it even further? Deal for me on the Bourse? With my commission money from the last trip.'

Gomez's lined, lean old face took on an expression of guilty pleasure. 'The money meant for your cousin's wife? You haven't already invested it in tulips?'

'I don't know why, but I haven't.'

'Perhaps a pardon and future life are enough to stake on one commodity.'

'Will you do it?' John leaned out of the open double doors to look at the green water far below.

'Of course, if you like. Of course, this is only for your cousin's wife.' Gomez dangled, but John refused to take the bait. 'Just don't expect miracles of Coymans's kind.'

'"Moderation is the silken string running through the pearl chain of all virtues." I can be moderate in my desires.'

'I hope so.'

John spun on one foot to look the old man in the eye. 'Trust me.'

Gomez laughed in rueful acknowledgement. 'Then on your behalf, or rather that of your cousin's wife, I think I shall turn my faculties to such questions as dried Danish cod.' He sipped his bowl of milk. 'Do you still want to meet my devil?'

John nodded.

'You'd best come to supper,' said Gomez. 'Coymans's eyes and ears don't penetrate that door.'

Harry calculated, accurately, that the best way to punish his wife was to carry her back to London. It was still summer and no one of consequence would be there. They were all on their country estates. But Harry thought he would go mad if he listened to one more conversation about how badly the land needed rain and how many years it had been since anyone had seen it so dry and whether the Shir would run dry before harvest time. Revenge and desperation played equal parts in his announcement after supper in mid-July that they would anticipate the autumn season by a month or so.

How dare the little chit look so miserable? he thought with fury. As if it were a penance to appear for the autumn and winter season in London at the side of a handsome husband whose chiefest thought would be to find the best entertainments and most amusing company!

'There's too much to do on the estate at this time of year!' protested Zeal. 'All the crops are just reaching their peak, and with the weather so dry . . .' She saw Harry's lip curl and veered onto a different tack. 'With John gone, you need someone here to look after your interests.'

Two hot patches flared on Harry's cheekbones at the mention of John's name. 'How dare you pretend to care for my interests?' he bellowed. 'How dare you think that you're even able to "look after" them? Apart from your money, you are useless!'

'Oh my,' whispered Mistress Margaret to her half-embroidered stool-cover.

A hit! thought Harry with triumph as Zeal's face quivered and steadied again. If she wanted to make him feel like a villain, he'd give her real cause.

'You're coming to London whether you like it or not. And you'll set about improving your behaviour right now. Tell your woman to pack to leave the day after tomorrow.'

'That's far too soon . . . !'

'I'm sure my aunt will be only too pleased to help. Everyone on the estate will be relieved to be rid of your meddling!'

Mistress Margaret looked at him, astonished and perturbed.

It's not fair, thought Harry, that Zeal should make me feel so evil for doing what I must!

'And you needn't worry,' he added, 'that I'll lay a finger on you again. You can wait for me and weep for shame, madam, for a long, long time!' His exit from the parlour was magnificence itself.

Mistress Margaret stabbed at her stool-cover. She swallowed audibly and glanced at Zeal. Silence pressed heavily down on the mild early evening air.

Zeal sat staring thoughtfully after her husband. She was herself again. Although the bee never revived, her monthly flow had come. Rachel had confirmed the facts for her. She had eluded the planting of a demon. No human child could have been conceived by such a mating of wrath and revulsion.

I suppose that wifely duty doesn't count as such if it's pleasant. Duty makes palatable something we would otherwise prefer to avoid.

She sighed.

Like going back to London. On the other hand, Harry's final threat lifted a cold weight which had lain heavily on her days and nights as she waited for him to repeat his husbandly demand.

Zeal stitched at a stool-cover that matched Mistress Margaret's and considered strategy.

'Thank goodness you're here to see to things,' she said at last to Mistress Margaret.

'Oh my,' said Mistress Margaret thickly. 'Oh my! Yes, well, I shall do my best. But what an inconvenient time he picked to spirit you away, if I dare say it. We're short-handed enough! I don't know how Sir Harry can ask it of us.'

On her way to her chamber to bed, Zeal gently slapped the nearest wall hanging to check for dust. A smoky cloud flew out around her fingers. Her dust. Hers by marriage to Harry, entrusted to her to remedy by John.

I'll be back for you, she told the dusty hanging. Don't think you're getting off.

She would go to London meekly. Pretend obedience. Startle Harry with her efforts to fit in. Drive him to exasperated tedium with her shortcomings so that he would soon come to welcome the idea of sending her back to Hawkridge House. With luck she might be back before harvest, in time to stack the apples in barrels of sand, to boil the fat from the autumn butchering down for soap, and to take part with her own hands in all the other domestic delights which were so far only words in books.

In any case, she had promised John to love Hawkridge House. He hadn't meant her to do it from a London town-house full of bought cheese and market stall pies.

> Dear Cousin John [she wrote by candlelight, inside her bed that night]
> Harry wants to go to London early and so I am forced to abandon Hawkridge House. Please forgive me. I shall leave things in the best order I can but fear for the gardens unless we have rain very soon. Tuddenham bought a most lovely milch cow at Basingstoke to replace poor Iphigenia . . .

She lost herself in a list of fascinating details he would want to know. The fledgling doves, the first honey, the Billiborues in the orchard which were now the size of her fist. At the last, she added, 'I am no doubt being indiscreet but wish you would nevertheless tell Arthur that Rachel misses him madly and pines for his return . . .'

She thought for a very long time, then signed herself 'Your most loving cousin, Zeal Beester.'

She would send the letter from London.

She blew out the candle and resolutely sought sleep. Their kiss kept her restlessly adrift every night in the blurred land between sleep and waking.

To distract herself, she imagined the journey her letter would make, from her hand to John's hand in Amsterdam.

I don't know why they make such a fuss about the Devil finding work for idle hands, she thought. They should worry about idle minds!

⚜

Four days later Coymans sold the *Lilith* options for 200 per cent gain. John settled in five days for cash. The clanking hoard had begun to accumulate again.

For the first time, John let himself imagine moving around England as a free man. He could visit Hawkridge House again, openly. Deliver Zeal's recaptured fortune in person. Watch understanding light up her blue eyes. Hear her gratitude. Take her warm little hand in a cousinly way.

'*Prunelle* is still rising,' said Coymans on the afternoon that they settled. 'Use your profits to buy more of her!'

'But the stadholders?'

'Quiet. Debating their past failures in tones of hushed astonishment.'

'I'll decide by the opening of dealing tomorrow.'

John went straight to Gomez. He intercepted the old man in Warmoesstraat outside the baker's shop.

'No new legislation is expected for the next ten days,' said Gomez. 'Or so my brother-in-law tells me.'

'Go ahead,' John told Coymans the next day at the Petticoat. The same day, he also told Gomez's devil, one Maurits Kramer, to buy *Prunelle* immediately, before news of Coymans's purchase pushed the price up.

By the end of dealing that day, the double purchase by two mysterious buyers had raised the price of *Prunelle* by another 75 per cent.

'Who else is buying?' exulted Coymans. 'I must get to him. He may be fool enough to try to buy a corner. I need to see how much greed there is in his eyes. Let me find that son of a whore! I'll screw him higher and higher!'

Widow Padtbrugge questioned him eagerly each night. She had special delicacies laid on his plate. His tankard was refilled before he swallowed twice. John began to like her less.

On Coymans's advice, John also bought more *Shepherd of Texel*, a modest performer but not spectacular. Two days later, John sold *The Shepherd of Texel* to a syndicate of craftsmen for settlement the following day. In kind.

'I need cash,' said John.

'Take it,' Coymans said.

John stared in dismay at the jumble that the craftsmen had unloaded from the carts into the street outside the widow's house. Carpenters' tools, a saddle, three hogsheads of wine, four barrels of eight-florin beer, one thousand pounds of cheese and a bed with hangings. Eight pigs, trussed head to tail in wooden corsets and still stacked on a cart, shrieked and squealed like unoiled gates.

'What do I want with all those?' At Hawkridge, he would have been delighted, but the widow would not welcome pigs into her neat back courtyard. And while Mallender might accept the beer, wine and cheese to appease the northern troops, he wouldn't find much use for a tester bed with hangings.

A small crowd gathered.

'Don't they have the money?' he asked Coymans.

'Would they be selling their beds and their tools if they did?'

'Let them off. Cancel our deal. I can't take away a man's means of living.'

The pigs were tiring. Their din grew sporadic.

Coymans was shocked. 'They don't want to cancel. They *want* the bulbs!'

But he passed on John's words. The men argued. Coymans argued back.

John shook his head unhappily. These mad men were desperate to make him accept their last assets in the world. They waved papers and stabbed their fingers at his signature.

The widow came out of her door and wanted to know what all those things were doing in front of her house.

'Wait,' John begged her. 'Justus, ask her please just to wait.'

Coymans threw his hands theatrically into the air. 'Take the pigs or take the syndicate to court. They say they're offering fair value in exchange. Take what you can get. You're doing better than some sellers. At least you've been paid. You can resell the goods.'

'Ask them if they will agree to cancel,' said John again.

Reluctantly, Coymans turned back to the men. Suddenly, John was the enemy. There were hostile glares and muttered asides.

'They will bring a lawsuit against you if you try to back out.'

Resigned but still unhappy, John signed the papers which acknowledged his receipt of saddle, cheese, bed, beer, pigs and carpenters' tools.

'You must move those things,' said the widow's neighbour from her own *stoep*. 'You can't leave those things in front of my house.'

The widow entered into an icy exchange between the two *stoeps*.

'Well, my friend,' said Coymans, with visible relish. 'What will you do now?'

'You tell me! You advised me to accept it all.' John kicked a barrel. One of the pigs farted loudly.

The skirmish between neighbours ceased. John sensed the possible birth of a new and hostile alliance.

'Mevrouw,' he called up to the widow. 'Would you do me the honour of accepting one of these cheeses?' He gestured at the mountain range of orange-gold discs, each one larger than Justus Coymans's hat. 'You might as well give one to every house in the street,' he added under his breath.

'I'll sell it all for you, if you wish,' said Coymans, serious and helpful again now that he had had his fun.

'No damned silk purses either!' said John.

'Sow's ears are too small a challenge. Let me see what I can make of the whole sow!'

'Do what you can with the misbegotten beasts!'

Coymans began to explain to the widow that all would be gone by the end of the day.

In the following two days, Gomez changed the cash Coymans realized from the sale of bed, pigs, and the rest into more bonds, which John hid with the others in his mattress at the top of the widow's house. And Kramer told him that the price of *The Shepherd of Texel* had begun to fall as soon as John had sold his bulbs.

His commission was invested in futures on the Bourse. A VOC ship was expected back shortly. John owned £1,000 worth of shares in its cargo of indigo and saltpetre. One quarter of the value of Hawkridge estate.

Coymans danced through the first days of August as nervously as a cat through a puddle. *Prunelle* kept rising. Then she wobbled, without visible cause.

'Hang on,' said Coymans. 'Don't panic. I believe this will pass. And I'm still sniffing around for that other big buyer of *Prunelle*. Why hasn't he approached me yet? But he will! I know these animals. He's waiting for the price to stabilize again. Then we'll see his little snout poking out of the bushes.'

John visited Maurits Kramer at his house on the New Side, near the fish market.

'A rumour of new stock caused the *Prunelle* wobble,' said Kramer, who had lived in London for two years as a boy. 'Do you want to sell?'

'Whose new stock?'

'Not one of the old established florists. A man married to the daughter of a breeder named Bols, who died in June. This son-in-law took over Bols's nursery. He doesn't know tulips, but he is sharp enough to make the most of the existing stock while it lasts.'

John felt his level of alertness change, as it did when he suddenly realized that there was someone near him in the dark. A chilly current trickled through his chest and down into his legs. It's just the association with Bols, he told himself. There's no reason.

But reason could not stop the chilly slithering in his chest.

🌷

LONDON, AUGUST 10, 1636

Zeal thought of herself as a prisoner of war. The image gave her a sense of dignity which was otherwise lacking.

Not Harry's prisoner, just a prisoner here in London. In a prison of eyes and tongues. Walled in by the good examples she should be aping. Sodden with a prisoner's ennui.

She paced out the length of their first-floor parlour, avoiding the cracks. It was too dark to read or embroider, even with candles. The house had no useful garden to speak of, just a lot of hedges, terracing and Harry's stupid fountain that had broken while being unloaded from the ship from Italy.

Harry had gone out again without her, though he forbade her to go out without him unless it was shopping in a convoy of maids. She didn't want to go wherever he might have gone. Dinner that afternoon at Edward Malise's house had been bad enough.

She turned at the end of the room and started back, this time avoiding knots as well as cracks. Dinner ... yes, well ... Rage and embarrassment twisted uneasily together in her stomach. She couldn't remember now what she had said, but Malise had exchanged sympathetic glances with Harry. And Harry connived by looking back. She should have felt triumph but had been humiliated. Her strategy of deliberate failure was more painful to carry out than she had imagined. Her will was weaker than she had hoped.

If she had been older or more experienced, she might have seen that Harry needed to punish her for reminding him every day, merely by being there, that he was a worse man than he liked to think. The fact that she would rather have been elsewhere made Harry even angrier. Zeal did feel that in some way Harry was being unfair, even though she meant him to send her back to the country. Without being able to explain to herself why, she felt indignant.

When Harry broke his promise to her, he shook the unquestioned absoluteness of Zeal's own promises made to him. She had, she frequently reminded herself, sworn in church before God, while he had merely given his word.

She had lain awake at night here in London and before, in her big bed in Hawkridge House, seeking philosophical clarity on the subject of her marriage. In the rawest hours, when night hit the bottom and began to rise again toward light, she even felt angry.

By day she saw that her duty to Harry was still clear and unchanged. Two years ago, even six months ago, she would diligently have observed Lady So-and-So and Mistress Such-and-Such as he had instructed her, and suffered over her own lacks. She would have felt ugly, tongue-tied, awkward, frumpy, dull, and all the other things she read so clearly in Harry's eyes. She still even thought that she *should* be feeling those things. Her duty was to try to put them right, to please Harry, but she couldn't scrape up the will, nor the least shadow of guilt at her failure from the murky bottom of her soul.

Furthermore, her duty to Harry now included the running of Hawkridge House. It had recently begun to seem to her that 'duty' could include knowing better than her husband how to protect his interests. It seemed possible that she must defy him for his own sake. She would have felt that way, she was sure, even if John had not entrusted the estate to her care.

She paused in her pacing and wondered if there were anything she could call for now, any small action to bring alive this shadowed, smoke-filled evening room. She crossed to a window and leaned her forehead against a ridge of the diamond-shaped leading. A horseman wavered past outside the bubbled glass. A lantern shivered and refracted, going the other way. She imagined grabbing her cloak, going out alone to explore the streets. Then she blew her cheeks out and sighed.

What would Harry say to *that*?

In London, with only the tiny garden and small staff, and the practice of buying most food already prepared, she lacked all those fascinating chores which had filled her time at Hawkridge. An idle brain is the Devil's workshop. Everything would be right again as soon as she could escape back to Hawkridge House.

She called for her cloak. She would go down into the little garden at the back of the house, poor thing that it was. It was enclosed by the outbuildings. It lacked the view of the Thames which Harry pined for. It served no useful purpose that Zeal could see, except pure ornament. But it was somewhere else than this room.

'Shall I come with you, madam?' Rachel asked.

Zeal looked at her maid, of whom she had become very fond. She now filled empty afternoons teaching Rachel to read. But Rachel was a Londoner and indecently thrilled to be back where she knew the terrain. She was distracted by kitchen visits and overflowed with gossip about old friends and family who were strangers to Zeal. Apart from Rachel's endless desire to speculate about what Arthur (and therefore John) might be doing among the Dutch herring-eaters, she rubbed Zeal across her present grain.

'No thank you,' said Zeal. She would hide for a little while where no one would watch to see what clumsiness she might commit next. No one would exchange looks with another someone and raise his eyebrows. Not that Rachel did, but the maid was too happy to be apt company.

Zeal ran down the stairs in her haste to escape.

The night smelled of damp coal smoke. The sky was thickly curded with cloud. Zeal leaned on her hands on the stone bench in the niche in the hedge. She counted twelve different dogs barking. Wooden wheels rattled outside the nearest wall. Male voices shouted distantly. In the centre of the garden, the dolphin whose tail had broken on the sea voyage spat a wiry arc of water into Harry's new pool. Zeal listened to its irritating splat. She missed the sheep.

Why didn't John answer her letter? He must surely have had it by now. In her mind she once more traced the letter's progress. From her hand to Rachel's, from Rachel's to a man-servant who took it to the docks where he found a ship's captain bound for Amsterdam who was willing to carry letters and packages. He would haggle over the price, the letter would join one or two others in the captain's cabin or the wheelhouse.

The boat pulled away from the dock onto the grey water she had glimpsed at the end of narrow streets. Drops of sea spray blurred John's name a little but not so much that it could not be read. The boat crossed a sea embroidered with breaking waves and the arcs of leaping dolphins. On the other side, a Dutch urchin would eagerly accept a silver coin to deliver the letter to the house of Justus Coymans, Breestraat, Old Side, Amsterdam. John would open the letter and hear her voice speak.

Male voices rumbled inside Harry's house. Zeal watched a light move across the upper windows. To her horror, the light came down the stairs toward the garden door. The door groaned.

'That's all, thank you,' said Harry's voice loudly.

She listened to a flurry of sound at the far end of the garden.

She pulled both cloak and dignity around her and stood up. She took a step toward the house and stiffened herself for the meeting.

Another man's voice said something too low for her to hear.

'Oh, she'll be tucked up in bed with her dolly,' replied Harry.

Zeal stepped back through a gap in the yew hedge, into a small side *allée* along which she could escape to the house unseen. She knew she did not want to hear anything more they might say.

The men's footsteps moved toward her end of the garden. If theirs were so plain, hers would be too. She was trapped, one way or the other, must stay put. She braced herself for more humiliation.

'. . . endless gyrating tedium.' The second man was Edward Malise. But he was no longer discussing her. 'I have never thought that driving around in circles in a carriage was worthy to be called entertainment.'

Harry sighed his agreement. 'But it must be done, eh?'

Zeal heard the scratch of wool against silk and stone. Someone had sat on the bench.

'Like this duty of mine with which I need your help,' said Malise. 'Can I count on you?'

Harry didn't reply.

'I only want the case to be heard,' said Malise. 'I want nothing more sinister than justice.'

Is this what men talk about then, when they are alone? wondered Zeal. Duty, justice and tedium? Very, very slowly, she inched one foot across the brick path toward the house.

Harry laughed uneasily. 'You're a tenacious enemy.'

'Not an enemy! Must I be his enemy to think that a man should be brought to trial for a crime witnessed by more than twenty enfranchised Englishmen? No, Harry, I've purged hatred from my soul. Don't insult me with an accusation of spite.'

Zeal shifted her weight delicately onto her forward foot.

'No, no,' said Harry. 'I don't!'

There was a pause.

'He tried to kill me too, you know,' said Harry. 'Two days after Sir George's party.'

'That's beyond belief.' Zeal heard a heavy breath in and out and a suppressed delight in Malise's voice. 'I confess, you shock me! In spite of what I already know of him. Ungrateful . . . ! And you let him get away, as he had already escaped me?'

'I, ah, drove him from the estate.'

'To freedom in Amsterdam.'

Zeal's attention jolted from her escape back to their talk. The path crunched under her feet. She froze and held her breath, terrified that the men had heard.

'You're more forgiving than I could have been,' continued Malise. 'Even for family.'

Cassie, or a cow, stepped hard on Zeal's breastbone.

'Would you be willing to swear before a court what you just told me?'

There was a long silence.

'You mustn't ask me to be disloyal to my own family,' said Harry finally.

'Disloyal?' Malise sounded amazed. 'After what he has done, and may yet do if not stopped? Is it disloyal to tend to your cousin's soul?'

'How so . . . ?'

Harry has other cousins, Zeal told herself.

But not in Amsterdam.

'He will one day die with an unexamined crime weighing his soul down to Hell. I would encourage him to subject himself, of his own free will, to the judgement of his peers. I would urge him to take the chance to examine himself and repent.'

Zeal leaned close to the stubbly, aromatic wall between her and the two men.

'I would question my own reasons for shielding a criminal when I knew his full guilt,' said Malise. 'However helpful he might be to me, I would try not to value the personal and particular above principle and the greater good. Unlike Tupper, who knows the truth but has money in this venture and is tight as a clam to protect it.'

'Don't misjudge me,' said Harry. 'I wouldn't want you to think . . . I haven't invested either. But I do owe John . . . we all owe him . . .'

'All the more reason to see him make peace with himself and his fellow man. Believe me when I say that I have put my grudges aside.'

Only someone as hungry to hear ill of John as Harry was would have missed the ringing oversincerity in Malise's voice, or the hint of a threat. Zeal heard both clearly.

'Oh, I know that, Edward,' said Harry eagerly. 'Now that you and I have become friends. I would understand even if you said you hadn't entirely forgiven him.'

But even Malise held back at that point. 'I'll be honest, Sir Harry. I won't pretend that I have entirely forgiven . . . my family suffered at the hands of the Nightingales, after all – my grandfather, my parents, my brother . . . Without being a saint . . .' He gave a tiny cough of a laugh. 'And I've never claimed that.'

'You're honest,' said Harry warmly. 'There are several things I'll never forgive him either, but I still try to behave as I should.'

'Then we are agreed,' said Malise. 'It is important to my peace of mind that you should help me with an easy heart. I won't wound our friendship.'

'You swear you don't mean to hurt him?'

Zeal heard a sudden wobble of uncertainty in her husband's voice.

'I swear. I shall merely have him arrested and brought back to England. Even though I suspect he has been currying favour in high places, I choose to trust the Star Chamber. Hang, pardon or acquit, I will accept the judgement with good grace.'

Hang? thought Zeal in terror. They're both mad. Hang John? She thought she would be sick. But she forced herself to concentrate on what Malise was now saying.

'. . . may be pardoned. Neither you nor I are men to enjoy the sight of a known murderer being fêted and adored through all Whitehall. Therefore he must not return with the profits of his speculations. That's all the harm I intend. To keep him from buying his way free of justice. An old and trusted friend of mine in Amsterdam will see that he leaves the money behind, where it belongs. Your cousin has already tried to suck my friend into his own manipulations. I believe that Justus will be happy to have a chance to live up to his name. I will then bring your cousin safely home for judgement.'

'And what exactly must I do?'

Zeal could hardly hear her husband's words.

'It's not what you must do, but what you must not do. I ask you only not to lie in court if asked whether he tried to kill you. Not to paint your cousin better than he is. Just assure me that you will not feel obliged from a sense of family duty or in mistaken defence of family honour to carry on your late uncle's subversion of justice. Assure me that we are on the same side.'

'I am honoured to serve on your side, Edward.'

'And I to have you.'

Zeal heard a rustle of fabric and imagined their hands being clasped.

'In truth, Sir Harry, the greatest service you can do me is to drop the odd word here and there . . . the man's own family wanting to see justice done . . . Your influence is growing, Sir Harry. I still fight prejudice, particularly among your cousin's cronies in the South Java Company.'

'What I can. What I can. When will you go back to Amsterdam?'

'The day after tomorrow if I can find a constable and some men-at-arms to come with me.' The pleasure in Malise's voice grated like a knife-blade along Zeal's bones. 'Thank you, Sir Harry.'

He wants John to hang! thought Zeal. I can hear how much he wants it. John is in terrible danger.

Then she suddenly wondered, what can he possibly have done?

Fortunately for her, Malise was now impatient to leave. The two men went back into the house, leaving Zeal rooted in the *allée* like one of the yews.

Fear crowded her out of her own body. The real Zeal hovered somewhere else, because being there in that body was too terrible. She remembered the feeling from years and years ago, but not the reason for it. She didn't want to feel that way, ever again. She would die.

Then she jolted herself back to the present moment. Quickly, while Harry was seeing Malise away. She raced along the *allée* and into the house. Up the stairs. Listened on the landing to the men's voices still at the street door. Into her own room and bolt the door. Safe for the moment, to think.

Edward Malise hates John. No question. And Harry's on his side.

Zeal hadn't seen Harry's reasons to punish herself. But she was no fool; she saw very clearly some, if not all, of her husband's reasons to dislike his Cousin John. Like Mistress Margaret's first hatred of Zeal herself, only the other way around. And with more reason, even. Zeal, the unwitting threatener, had been afraid of Margaret Beester and felt humbled by the older woman's superior knowledge, while John had nothing at all to learn from Harry.

While Rachel helped her undress for bed, Zeal thought about Harry's treachery.

He must at least believe he has reason. He must believe that John has done something terrible.

'Rachel?'

'My lady?'

Zeal hesitated, but dire need excused. 'Has Arthur ever said anything about John ... Mr Graffham? I mean, about his past ... something he did?'

'Arthur, gossip?' Blandly, Rachel began to pull the pins from Zeal's coiled hair.

'Oh, stop that!' said Zeal, suddenly beside herself. 'I've seen you kissing him! Don't you ever talk as well? I *need* to know the answer to my question! Please answer me at once!'

'My lady.' Rachel rolled her eyes, which were her most attractive feature, but obliged. 'He never told me what. But he did say that whoever Mr Graffham did it to deserved to have it done to him.'

Zeal pulled away from her maid's hands and turned to face her. 'Rachel, did Arthur ever say that John might hang?'

'Hang?' repeated Rachel, horrified. 'Oh, no. Never that!'

The two young women stared at each other.

'He never said that,' said Rachel. Now she looked as unhappy as Zeal. 'Just that he'd follow him to the end of the earth – and that it might come to that.'

'All right,' whispered Zeal.

'What, my lady?'

Zeal shook her half-released mane of crinkled red-gold wires. The rest of her hair fell. Rachel stretched her hand from habit to catch the pins.

'It can't be that bad then,' said Zeal.

'What can't?'

'What he did. Or Arthur wouldn't have said that, about following. Thank you, Rachel. Please go away now. I need to think.'

'My lady . . .'

'Please go.'

'I don't want him to go to the end of the earth.'

'I know,' said Zeal. 'That's what I have to think about.'

Her pillows were enemies, her coverlets snares. The hangings suffocated her.

I can't ask Harry what John did, she thought. He would guess that I overheard.

She turned, then turned again on the ridges in her mattress. Sat up. Lay down again.

What shall I do?

She would send a warning message to John!

With whom?

Which of Harry's men could she trust? And how could she pay them?

She half-dozed, then woke to wide-eyed, heart-thumping awareness in the dark. Malise did not need to go to Amsterdam if he wished only to arrest John. He could just wait until John returned. Whatever John was doing with money wouldn't change a court verdict if his crime had been so vicious. Malise meant to harm John. She had to send warning.

The diamond panes of the window seemed lighter.

She climbed down from the bed, smaller than her galleon at Hawkridge House but still roomy enough for four. Early autumn had chilled the damp air. She would send a second letter. But a letter would take too long. A cold breeze blew across the floor over her bare feet. She was too cold to think.

Back in bed she found, however, that the cold draught seemed to have cleared her brain. The risk was too great that Malise would reach John before her letter did. The paralysing fog had lifted, giving a clear view of what she must do.

She must get a warning to John. She knew where to find him. She knew when Malise was leaving for Amsterdam. She would send a messenger. She was half-way to solving the matter.

She raised herself suddenly onto her elbows again. Malise's good friend who would take away John's money was named Justus. She had sent her letter to John at the house of Justus Coymans.

Is it a common name there, like John or James? she wondered. Or might her messenger deliver her message into the very lion's den?

She lay a little longer, coverlet up to her ears. Then she sat up. She climbed from the bed again and crossed to her door.

'Rachel,' she whispered into the darkness of the anteroom. 'Rachel, wake up! Come into my bed, quickly. I want to talk with you!'

♧

Prunelle steadied as Coymans had predicted, and then rose again.

Coymans became his old self, noisy, cocksure, and firm as steel under the swirl and racket. However, the uneasiness that had descended on John on his return to Amsterdam would not lift. He sensed unexplained triumph in Coymans's manner, and imagined slyness where before he had seen only open knavery.

'Go play, young man! You're too young to be wasted by care. Let me worry and my sister entertain you.'

Then Coymans found a buyer for *Prunelle*, in a private deal.

'Double again!' he cried. 'Double again! And so easily. I still never found out who that other investor was. I didn't even need to screw his greed to the ground to double our money. We must never part, my dearest Englishman. You are my Midas finger, my golden goose.'

John signed his name in a state of dazed disbelief. His imagination threw itself again and again at the word 'pardon' but could not get a grip. Another self watched coldly from outside, knew that something dreadful would come of this moment and wondered how unthinkingly or otherwise he had been called a goose.

In this double mind, John accepted a celebratory tankard and claps on back. He paid for beer all around. Coymans, in loudest roaring form, embraced John fervently. John tried to hide his recoil.

'What next?' asked Coymans.

'Let a man draw breath, Justus! I'm giddy with a surfeit of gold!'

The King's money had more than doubled. The Company money likewise. The fat packet of bonds worth £70,000 was already buried deep in his mattress at the top of the widow's house. Gomez held another £20,000 for him in the bank of Amsterdam. A small chest held the distilled essence of gold plate, candlesticks and coins. When he had settled all deals, John would have £250,000. Only his own investment in the East Indies ship was still at risk.

The streets were dark and empty that evening when he knocked on Maurits Kramer's door. He smelled blood and

fish. Kramer was eating soup with his wife. A jug of marguer-
ites bloomed on their rug-covered table. Mevrouw Kramer
insisted, through her husband, that John sit and accept a bowl
of pea soup with ham. Then she excused herself.

'Sell *Prunelle*,' John told Kramer. 'As soon as trading opens
tomorrow morning. With a discount for immediate
settlement.'

'But the price is still rising, Mynheer Nightingale. Rumour
of that other new stock has gone quiet.'

'Sell!' John did not like the echoes of Bols's case. And he
had to prove that he could cry 'Enough!'

'All right, all right! You'll still do well enough out of it!'

He may have signalled secretly. Mevrouw Kramer returned
at that instant with a jug of wine and a maid bearing a plate
of fruit.

'Did you hear,' asked Kramer, 'how bad luck is hitting the
tulip trade? Another death, two days ago. An enthusiast
named Spiegel. A loss to us all, a man so eager to possess.'

A cold current trickled through John's arms and thighs.

In his crow's-nest bed, listening to the snores of Arthur and
Sir George's man, John could not sleep.

'Well enough' Kramer had said. Well enough for a pardon.
He could go back to England with honour. It was beyond
belief that he had succeeded a second time. He suddenly
wanted to get out of Amsterdam, back to England. He wanted
to be done with a world where he was told that a tulip was
not a flower but a dried cod or cord of Baltic pine. He wanted
to get away from men who gave their craftsman's tools for
something they didn't understand in the hope of growing
richer than they had ever known. He had to get away from
Spiegel's death and what it might mean.

He would ask Gomez at once to sell his personal shares in
the indigo and saltpetre carried by the VOC ship. Then he
would go home, claim the pardon and reclaim his life. He

would stay away from Zeal. Give up his childish dream of sweeping in to Hawkridge House and pouring gold coins into her lap like Zeus. He would sign on for a voyage with the younger Tradescant to the Caribbean or the Americas. He would discover new plants, mine silver. If he couldn't afford an estate in England, he would carve one out of the new found lands. John Nightingale would be reborn from the Graffham worm. He could not yet imagine all the glowing colours of the scales on his still damp and crumpled wings.

'Ah,' said Gomez. His dark sharp eyes evaded John's.

'What's wrong?'

'I usually say that,' said Gomez. '"What's wrong?"' One finely-cured hand slipped up to cover his mouth.

'What don't you want to tell me?' demanded John.

'Some ale?' Gomez bent out of sight behind the pile of carpets near the spinet.

'No breakfast. Just the truth.'

'There is a rumour,' said Gomez. He popped back up into sight with a goblet and jug. He poured as if he had not heard John's refusal. 'The VOC ship hasn't yet reached the Canaries. She was expected into port there last week. It's early to mourn. Winds can die for days.'

John accepted the offered goblet.

'But there are rumours that she has been sunk. By the English.' Gomez rummaged for his milk bowl. 'I don't know whether or not you find that amusing.'

'Painfully so.'

Gomez nodded in sympathy. 'The shares for the voyage are now worth nearly nothing. They will be worth nothing until the ship is sighted again.'

One thousand pounds as good as lost. As well as the profit they might have made invested elsewhere. This is my reason for dread, thought John. It was nothing to do with Coymans or *Prunelle* after all.

427

'I'm sorry,' said Gomez. 'But these are the risks one takes. Still, I'm truly sorry, if only for your cousin's wife.'

'Can I retrieve anything at all if I sell now?'

'One hundred pounds,' said Gomez with surprising good spirits. 'Still one-tenth of their original price. They're not valueless yet.'

'Then, for God's sake, sell them before they are.'

'I would hang on,' said Gomez. 'The sinking is only a rumour, after all. I've seen this before.' He tapped one well-shaped yellowed fingernail against his front teeth, then twisted the tip of one moustache with a flourish of decision. 'I think, in your place, I might even risk a little more.'

John's commercial ear had sharpened since the early spring in Hampshire. He waited in silent attention for Gomez to explain.

'As the shares now cost so little, you would not lose much more if the rumour proves true. And if it's false . . . !'

'And how do you judge a rumour?'

'After knowing Coymans, you ask me that?'

'I don't *know* Coymans, any more than I know you,' said John with some irritation. Events were slippery in his hands again. It infuriated him.

'Will you buy more shares in the voyage?' asked Gomez neutrally.

It meant staying longer in Amsterdam. But it could also mean recovering the money for Zeal after all. And even some for himself.

'What are experts for if not to advise? Buy the things if you think it's right!' John leaned on the window glass and glared down into the water of the Damrak far below. 'Throw my last five hundred pounds after the rest. I'll borrow my passage home.'

That night Marika began to teach John to speak Dutch. He was a half-hearted student.

Two days later, John took receipt of the profit from

Kramer's sale of *Prunelle*. He felt no exultation this time, just a dark weight of foreboding.

He returned the widow's money plus thirty per cent interest from his own profits on *Prunelle*.

'*Dank*,' she said with glum politeness, clearly disappointed that it wasn't more. She did not ask him to invest any further money for her.

Gomez bought more shares in the VOC voyage. John now owned the equivalent of £6,000-worth of the original shares, as Gomez had bought the new shares at one-tenth of John's original purchase price.

'Others have bought, too,' said Gomez. 'Don't say a word, but the price has risen a little again.'

'Should I sell?' asked John.

'I don't think so. I have also invested in early warning if the rumour is confirmed. There's nothing yet.'

'Be merciful,' begged John. 'My desires may be moderate, but my terror isn't.'

'The longer without confirmation, the better,' said Gomez. But he looked anxious.

The Treasury money doubled, the South Java Company's nearly so. John could go back to England with honour, with only his own loss to regret, and that was nothing beside the chance of a pardon.

He ached to leave Amsterdam. He had done enough. Fortune grated in his ear like the two ends of a broken bone.

I will go back, he decided, ship or no ship.

He asked Gomez to withdraw the money from the Bank of Amsterdam and metamorphose it into bonds for transport back to England.

He was being followed again. He heard someone behind him as soon as he left the baker's shop. He stepped without warning into an alley and waited. No one came after him. Back out in the clear light that reflected off the canal water, he examined the faces around him, each apparently busy with its own private concerns. No sign of his old friends Forehead and the Egg Seller.

Tomorrow he would have Arthur trail him at a distance.

In spite of Marika, how he wanted to go home!

🌷

Zeal and Rachel between them solved the question of finding money to send warning to John.

'For a new gown,' said Zeal sweetly. She could not look Harry in the face. He would see her contempt, born in a yew hedge the previous night. 'And of course, one for Rachel.'

Harry was correctly suspicious. He searched his wife's modestly downcast face.

'And a fur muff for the autumn.' Zeal held out her hands. 'They'll go red in the cold.'

'You order them on account. I'll pay it later.'

'Oh, please, Harry!' Zeal risked a quick flash of her eyes. 'I must practise handling money. Let me try.'

'I can't afford much. Shall I come with you?'

'Let me test what you have taught me.'

I'll have her followed, thought Harry.

'Twenty-seven pounds from Sir Harry,' said Zeal triumphantly. 'And four pounds I've not yet spent on house-keeping.'

'Plus my wages,' said Rachel. 'I'll play the coachman at angel-beast tonight. He always loses to me ... fat good it will do him!'

'More than thirty pounds. How much do you think whoever it is will need for lodgings?'

Rachel shook her head. 'It's only for a night or two.'

'I wish Arthur were here to send,' said Zeal. 'I wouldn't fear sending him abroad with all this money. And I trust him to get the warning to John.'

Her message would never reach John in time. Malise would arrive with his men-at-arms . . .

'I hope Arthur's bravery doesn't go to his head, like last time,' said Rachel. 'Almost getting himself killed fighting for Master John. How many men did Mr Malise say he would take?'

Zeal dared not trust any of Harry's grooms to be her messenger. Much as they seemed to like her, they wouldn't dare accept a mission abroad that must be kept secret from their master. Zeal considered lying, but that would be unfair. Harry would kick the groom in question into the street, and there was not much employment to be had in overpopulated London.

Rachel had suggested one or two old acquaintances, but Zeal could not imagine handing over to a stranger either so much money or the responsibility for John's life. Nor could she ask a stranger to judge whether or not Justus Coymans could be trusted.

She might have sent any one of several men from the estate, but had no time to send for them. Malise would leave for Amsterdam the next day.

While Rachel scorched Zeal's collars and cuffs in the laundry, Zeal tried to embroider. She tried to read, but her books held no prescriptions for such cases. She let herself be driven up and down Fleet Street for an hour in Harry's carriage without seeing a thing. Unwittingly, she offended several of Harry's friends.

Whom could she send?

The groom who trailed her for Harry reported a tedious day.

Zeal went to bed in despair and lay awake most of the night, with Rachel equally restless at her side.

'Let Colin go, madam!' Rachel whispered. 'I'm sure he can be trusted.'

'Perhaps it's the only way.'

At sunrise, Zeal shoved Rachel hard in the ribs. 'Malise has sailed,' she said. 'What shall I do?'

She slid out of bed. She had to do something, even if she didn't know what it was!

Her hair had suddenly prickled on her arms.

Don't be stupid, she told herself. In her sudden panic of revelation, she tripped over a stool and fell.

'Are you all right, madam?' Rachel bent in concern.

'Could Colin arrange us passage?'

'Us?'

'You and me.' If her letter could make the journey, so could she.

By dinner time Rachel brought word that the matter was in hand. At sundown Colin arrived at the stable door asking to see his second cousin Rachel to give her some radishes from a fictitious aunt and the information that if they wanted to leave that night, they must go to the Customs steps before the tide turned just after midnight and look for the sailing barge *Persephone*.

Zeal and Rachel stared at each other. They let out shaky sighs in unison, then laughed nervously.

'Are we really doing this, madam?' asked Rachel.

'It would seem so.'

'I can't seem to breathe right.'

'Nor me,' said Zeal.

Fate was on their side. Harry was supping out.

Just after supper, before the food had been locked away for the night, Rachel was caught in the buttery by Mrs Pollen, the wife of Harry's London steward who ran the house while her husband kept the stables in order.

'Thieving, madam,' Mrs Pollen said indignantly to Zeal.

'I'm sorry to bring bad news about your own serving woman.'

Rachel widened desperate eyes at Zeal.

Mrs Pollen's comfortably upholstered face was flushed with excitement but Zeal saw no malice or glee.

'Mrs Pollen,' said Zeal. 'I must ask you to forgive ill deeds done in a fair cause. I want to draw you into a Christian plot to save a good man's life.'

Within the hour, Mrs Pollen, both shocked and thrilled, had prepared a bag of cold meats, pies, ale and fruit. She also donated nine more pounds to the rescue mission. When Zeal swore to protect the anonymity of all accomplices, Mrs Pollen agreed to delay as long as possible Sir Harry's discovery of his wife's flight. Mrs Pollen did not approve of Harry and hoped young Lady Beester never learned the half of it.

'This way,' whispered Rachel. 'I know the way to Customs steps.'

The housekeeper turned the key behind them. Colin waited in the street to carry their single chest. Zeal and Rachel carried a bundle each.

'Mind the ditch,' said Rachel.

Another voyage, thought Zeal. No more impossible than all the rest. The street looked different to her tonight. The dark lantern-lit tunnel stretched all the way to Amsterdam.

If she had not been so terrified for John, she would have recognized her rising joy. She thanked the Lord that she had asked John where to find him, even if it were in the lion's den.

Fifteen

The widow came scrambling down the spiral stairs as John entered her house. She was clearly angry. She pointed upstairs and shook her head.

John understood the word 'man'.

The widow wagged a reproving finger. Several men. Not allowed.

The world lurched a few degrees towards disaster.

The widow led John up the stairs, still protesting.

'I wasn't here last night,' said John in the imitation of a reasonable voice. He wanted to shove the woman aside and leap up the stairs.

The door to his room was still barred from the inside. The widow faltered in her accusations. John was clearly now outside the door. Who then had barred it?

She called down the stairs. A manservant climbed up. He went back down. He reappeared with carpenter's tools and removed the hinges of the door.

The widow held out her hand for each nail and admonished him to be careful of the wood. The door fell inward with a breathy crash.

There was a moment of stunned silence. Then the widow shrieked. She turned on John. She held him responsible. She screamed in white-faced fury. A dead man lay bleeding all over one of her wooden floors and white feather pillows.

Sir George's man had had his throat cut.

She seized John's arm, intent on flinging him down the stairs. He stood braced against her, hardly noticing her rage. Thank the Lord it's not Arthur! Arthur had been with him. Now stood alive and gasping behind John.

Then John saw that the double shutters of the window onto the street had been split and hung ajar. The rope dangled loose from its pulley, trailing into the street. The money chest had gone. He looked around the little room again. It must be there somewhere. He looked again. It wasn't. But his mattress had moved.

John pulled his arm from the widow's grasp, knelt and ran his hand along the floor beneath his mattress. Nothing. He heaved the mattress up and searched the floor wildly. The pouch of bonds had also gone.

Arthur flung aside his own bedding and clothes, looking under and among them. The two men repeated all their actions, not believing the truth. Then they stood up and looked at each other bleakly. John's legs felt oddly unreliable. His heart thundered. His chest had set like iron against his breath. This was the sensation of death.

All the money was gone. Specie and bonds alike. And all that Gomez had brought from the bank when John decided to leave Amsterdam. Not just the profits but the original stake as well. The company's money, and the King's, enough to muster an army or buy twenty estates.

The fall was too far and too fast. John felt numbed. He saw Arthur waiting numbly for him to give an order that would begin to put things right, but he could not think what to say, nor even move his mouth.

He tried to think what might have happened. Who had it been? The master of the men who had followed him in the street. Any one of the dozens who had followed his dealing and knew how much he must have. Coymans.

The widow took the dead man by the legs and began to haul him toward the door.

'Leave him!' said John.

She shouted back, shook her head and heaved again.

'LEAVE HIM!' bellowed John.

The widow began to beg. Tears ran thickly down her cheeks.

'Wait!' John pleaded. 'Just wait, while I try to think.' He held up both hands, palm out. 'Please wait.'

He turned to Arthur. 'Go fetch Coymans. Tell him I urgently need a translator.'

Arthur raised and dropped one shoulder unhappily. 'Are you sure . . . ?'

'I know, man!' said John. 'I suspect him too. Get him here and we'll both watch every twitch he makes. I must decide about him or I'll go mad. Go!'

He turned to the widow. 'Wait.' He mimed speaking with his right hand. 'I've sent for someone. Just wait.'

The widow cried quietly while they waited. When John was sure she wouldn't bolt, he searched again. He turned out every cuff and pocket and shook each handkerchief and empty boot. He avoided the broad sticky dark-brown puddle around the dead man's head, but lifted even the pillow on which the head half-lay, to feel beneath.

He tried to let the unthinkable into his mind. This was ruin, total, irredeemable, fatal. The scale of the loss was as hard to grasp as the profits had been.

After a millennium, John heard footsteps on the stairs.

Coymans drew a loud sharp breath. 'Is anything missing?' John nodded curtly. To his shocked ear, Coymans's tone was blamelessly exact in its balance of curiosity and dismay. John was almost disappointed not to be more sure of the man's guilt.

Coymans said something to the widow which made her turn on him. Horror and rage seemed equally mixed in her torrent of abuse. Then, still talking, she began to weep again.

'We must call one of the sheriff's constables,' John said.

But he had little hope that anything would be recovered.

'They must have come over the roofs,' said Coymans. 'And one was agile enough to get onto the rope.' He leaned out of the window. 'Not a trick I would care to try.'

A flawless performance or innocence incarnate.

Now the widow and Coymans entered into a lower-keyed but fast and intense discussion. The widow disappeared. She came back with a thick coverlet and some rags which she and Coymans began to wrap around the dead man.

'We must call one of the sheriff's constables,' said John again.

'*Baljuwen*,' Coymans translated. 'It's bailiffs over here.' He and the widow exchanged looks.

'You can say what you like once you get him into the street and away from her house,' he said. 'But she doesn't want it known that she had a murder here. It's not that kind of house.'

'If robbery and murder have been done here, that *is* the kind of house she has.' John stepped in front of the door to the stairs. His legs felt a little steadier but his thoughts were just as confused. 'Leave him there.'

'*Baljuwen* . . . !' The widow was weeping again.

'The bailiffs will fine her,' said Coymans. 'She will be suspected of keeping ruffians in her house. She'll be ruined.'

'Please send for a bailiff.'

Coymans stood up from beside the body. 'Listen to me, Nightingale. You are a foreigner. You don't understand how things work here in my country. You think you will do the right thing, but you will just end up making pain and disaster for innocent people. Let me deal with this mess! I won't cover up anything that matters. I will report the murder of an English serving man. You employed him – you'll have to explain exactly who he was and what he was doing here.' This last sounded like a threat.

'I intend to,' said John. But he was shaken by Coymans's

accusation that he might harm the widow further than a murder in her house had already done. She was right, of course. If he hadn't been staying there it would not have happened, at least not to her.

The widow watched him with wet, angry eyes.

'Tell them what you like, when the time comes,' said Coymans. He spoke briefly to the widow. 'Even tell them where it happened. Be as honest as you like. She just doesn't want the shame of having him found here, and the bailiffs tramping all over her house and frightening her children. Let me deal with the matter now.' Coymans shook his head in warning. 'You must let me, in any case, unless you can suddenly speak my language.'

John looked at the half-bundled corpse on the floor. What Coymans said was reasonable, but he didn't like it.

'I'll set the law in motion.' Coymans put his hands on John's shoulders. 'She'll calm down if you go. Go to my house now. Tell Marika what has happened and that you need somewhere to sleep for a few nights.'

John tried to protest, but Coymans cut him off. 'You don't have many choices, my friend. Clear off now and argue later. I will join you in an hour or two. We'll decide then what to do next.' He clapped John on both shoulders with sudden compassion. 'You've had a shock. Go to my house for some brandy and to draw a breath. Use my man to help carry your things. Go!'

Arthur's gaze said that he had heard nothing more than John in Coymans's voice and manner.

Either he's truly helping me or he plans to cut my throat, thought John. And the petty roguery of Coymans's manipulations of the murder's aftermath made it hard to see him in the more extreme role of murderer. Numbly, John helped Arthur gather up the few clothes and personal articles left in the room.

My best embroidered gloves have been taken! he noted.

Then he saw the irony of worrying about a pair of kidskin gloves. If Coymans did cut his throat, he'd almost welcome it.

When they left, the widow was crouched on her haunches in a billow of black skirts, her arms around her head, rocking on her heels and moaning in despair.

Marika was magnificent. She showed appropriate but not excessive horror. After a few quick questions, she ordered a room to be readied for John, found a bed for Arthur with her servants, suggested a private supper away from the evening's guests, and then left John alone. She offered no consoling caresses.

After Arthur had been led away to the kitchen, John sat on a chest and stared at the green and white tiled floor.

No pardon for you, my boy. Summary execution instead.

He pulled himself away from even this ironic slide toward self-pity. He knew that he most feared the humiliation of failure, of reporting the loss to Sir George and to Lord Mallender. Execution would seem a relief.

He dropped his head into his hands. His fingers dug and twisted through the acorn-coloured hair.

I should have stuck to running an estate.

Well, you didn't. And you have failed.

So do something now to put things right!

He was a prisoner of his own language. If he were not a foreigner, he would never have agreed to allow Coymans to deal with the bailiffs.

He stood up decisively. Foreigner or not, he could not leave this to Coymans. He would go back to the widow's house to regain his grip on the affair, whether Coymans liked it or not.

Before he crossed the first bridge, he knew that someone was following him again. Unreasoning rage lit up the mists in his brain. He had had enough!

For a few yards he toyed with his follower, stopped to buy an apple, to pull up his boot. A large, low hat and a cloak. Too short for Forehead. Could be the Eggseller.

Without warning, John spun round. The man froze in alarm, turned and fled into the sliver of an alley. With his blood thudding in his head and swelling his eyeballs, John chased after. He would kill that fleeing shadow with his bare hands. He pounded out of the alley into a market and stood panting and glaring at three hundred identical hats. Half the men he saw wore similar cloaks.

Two women with baskets looked at him oddly. He had growled aloud in frustration. He had had enough of feeling helpless. When his breathing had slowed a little, he changed direction yet again.

The maid stood squarely in his way, a broom in one hand, more as a weapon, if necessary, than a symbol of industry.

'I must see your master,' said John.

She shook her head and sketched a flourish in the air. He was working.

'SASKI!' bellowed John over her shoulder.

The maid clucked and flapped a hand at him. 'Shhh!'

Two old women stopped in the street and stared up with disapproval. The maid began to shut the door. John shoved his knee against it.

'SASKI!'

The old women sniffed and exclaimed to each other in voices meant to be overheard by the rowdy up there on the *stoep*.

Saski came up the stairs from his studio. When he saw John, he swore in Dutch. Then in English he asked, 'What do you want this time?' His face was pale and angry.

'I must talk with you.'

'I'm too busy.'

'When will you have time?'

440

The light-blue eyes swept John from hat to boot. The painter picked up one corner of his apron and seemed to unscrew his thumb with it. He examined the crimson stain that still remained after wiping. 'Next week. Maybe two weeks. I don't know.'

'I can't wait a week, or maybe two weeks.'

'I don't like you,' said Saski succinctly. 'Please go away.' He stepped back.

With triumph in her eye, his maid slammed the door shut in John's face.

John met Coymans on the bridge by the widow's house.

'It's done,' said Coymans. 'To suit even your refined conscience. The lovely widow is now resigned to the price of keeping her good reputation. Her neighbours will never know as long as the servants don't talk. Tomorrow the bailiff's man will want your evidence.'

'Thank you,' said John. He fell into step with Coymans. It had rained again. The cracks between the cobblestones were still black and wet. The canals glinted like pewter under the dripping trees.

'If I were you,' said Coymans, 'I would thank the Lord that you and I were together in a large company both last night and today. Otherwise I think they'd have one of us for the killer, to save the effort of looking further.'

He looked wearier than John had ever seen him.

Coymans saw John's assessing gaze. 'We're sick as a pair of rain-soaked cats. No question about it, Mistress Fortune is crueller than any woman I've ever known, and that's saying something!'

A rain-soaked cat fitted a part of John's feelings rather well. Another part of him still wanted to catch up with the man who had followed him and knock his head against the cobblestones. He glanced over his shoulder, but his luck was out – there was no one trailing them that he could see.

'Is there any chance of catching the villains?' John asked.

'If I'm honest, not much.'

They walked on in a grim and thoughtful silence to Coymans's house. Just outside, Coymans paused in the street. 'How bad is your loss?' he asked again.

'Everything.'

'La,' said Coymans reflectively. He see-sawed his moustaches for a while, then cocked his head towards the music-room window from which came loud laughter. 'I don't know about you,' he said, 'but I can't face all those chickens in there. Come upstairs with me to hide? Marika will cope.'

Not behaviour John expected from a guilty man. I believe Coymans is having a hard time too, he thought. He may really be trying to do what he thinks is best for everyone.

As he climbed the stairs behind the dealer, John felt a little guilty about his earlier suspicion.

'You don't need to go back to London with your tail between your legs,' said Coymans. He bent forward under Neptune's net to prod the fire.

There were far fewer canvases stacked around the room than when John had last been in the parlour less than a week ago.

'It's not a posture I enjoy.' John paced the panelled room. He quivered with suppressed rage at the man, or men, who had ruined his life, and Zeal's life, and, most terminally, the life of Sir George's man. The earlier paralysis had passed now that he felt he need not attack his host.

Coymans watched him. 'There's a remedy you can set in motion tomorrow, if you like.'

'You're wooing so sweetly that I'm sure I won't like it,' said John.

'It's true that you didn't like it last time.'

O clever man, thought John. To make me ask.

Coymans raised his large red hands in disclaimer, anticipat-

442

ing John's disapproval. 'The borrowed bearskin, my friend. You need no money at all to borrow a bearskin.'

When John didn't answer, Coymans went on. 'You might at least recover your original stake.'

'This sounds like a conjuror's trick.'

'Exactly!' said Coymans. He seemed pleased with this idea. 'Exactly like! Miraculous to the uninitiated. Simple once you understand how it's done. And no magic at all, just a few twists to the expected ways of doing things.'

'By bearskin, I presume you mean bulbs?'

'My prize pupil!' cried Coymans in a manful imitation of his usual exuberance.

'My brilliance stops there, *magister*.'

'You know that when dealing in the normal way, you can borrow stock to settle an agreement? You merely pay an interest rate on the bulbs. And when you've had enough, you buy the bulbs at whatever the going rate may then be and return them to the dealer or grower you borrowed them from.'

'In other words,' said John, 'you try to detect a kind whose value will fall, not rise. Or in the end, you will pay more for the bulbs than you will have been able to sell them for.'

Coymans clapped his hands with ironic delight. 'Oh, well done!'

'Like laying money that a certain horse will fall in a race.' John studied Coymans under his lashes. 'Now, I suspect, we come to the first of those little twists to the expected ways of doing things.'

Coymans grinned. 'And the twist is just your style. You borrow, say, one thousand *Hyperion* worth a hundred florins an ace. Then, instead of greed, you practise renunciation – that *is* your style, isn't it? Generously, out of pity for the poor who cannot normally afford such beauty, you offer your bulbs at ninety florins per ace.'

'And sell well, because you're underselling the going price.'

443

Coymans nodded. 'Then, you offer a few more at eighty florins.' He offered John a pipe. When John refused, he took one for himself. 'And then, you offer them again, at seventy. And so on. Your selflessness is quickly rewarded.' Whewp, whewp. He blew through the pipe, then began to pack it with a large red forefinger.

'Rumours of decline spread like flood waters. Greedier men dump their stocks to cut their losses. Even your soft heart could not ask for better – in the end, even the poorest street-sweeper can afford his own *Hyperion*. And you have made it possible. At this point, your act of charity is complete. You buy one thousand bulbs from any one of the sellers desperate to unload, and you return his stock to the dealer you first borrowed from.'

'A stock much reduced in value.'

'Plus interest.' Coymans grinned. With tongs, he delicately held a coal from the fire to the bowl of his clay pipe. 'The greater good often demands individual sacrifice.'

'I don't think so.'

Coymans paused. Then he sucked in, hslup, hslup. 'You don't think what?'

'That I want to borrow a bearskin.'

'But if you go back to say that you lost the Treasury money . . . ?' He held up a hand against John's denial. 'Where else did you get that kind of money to play with? I'm not a fool, Nightingale. It's either Treasury or the British East Indies Company and neither institution is known for its charity.'

'Odds on, I'll hang for a thief,' said John. Perhaps not, not as a thief. But he still wouldn't relish facing Sir George. Harder even than Mallender, who would probably not be surprised.

Coymans shook his head. 'I don't understand. You could recover everything. Where's the rub? Eh? Where's the illegality? What imaginary transgression sticks in your craw worse than going back to your English masters with nothing?'

My partner in all this is what sticks, thought John. Ungrateful, suspicious wretch that I am. Suspicious without any firm reason.

And I am also a little concerned about all those people who might buy at ninety, eighty or seventy florins. Like the Widow Padtbrugge, doubtless placing her money elsewhere. Who don't have you to steer them away from the rocks.

'No,' he repeated mildly. 'I'm sorry. Not this time.'

Coymans raised his arms and let them fall in resignation. 'As you wish. But I must go ahead.' He waved one hand around the emptied room. 'It won't have escaped you that I'm in a little trouble myself. Someone I expected better of has let me down – it's always a risk in business – but I have already begun to put things right.'

'Do you know an Englishman called Edward Malise?' John asked suddenly.

'Yes,' said Coymans at once. He turned his head, comically searching the shadows of the ceiling. 'Where did that question come from in the midst of our talk of mutual ruin? But, yes, I know the man. His family were Catholic refugees in the Low Countries.'

John had expected a denial. Then he wondered if the response had been too quick, insufficiently surprised in spite of the comic performance. 'And Marika?'

Coymans stared. He blinked twice, then he began to laugh. 'Aha! Now I see! Oh, Nightingale, my friend, when I warned you that my sister was no angel, I thought you were listening. Oh, jealousy, cruel as the grave!' His mirth seemed genuine but not ill-meant. 'Marika loves you now. Does it matter whom she might have thought she loved before?'

'Did she love Malise?' John's voice was harsh.

'My sister lives her life "as if it were spoil and plucks the joys that fly".' Coymans shook his head at John in mock reproof. 'I thought she was teaching you the same Roman philosophy.'

'When was Malise last here?'

Coymans frowned and sucked on his whiskers. 'I can't put a fine date on it . . . perhaps two summers ago. One summer ago? The summer, certainly.' His eyes were steady, but not too much so.

John could detect only the effort of remembering and amusement at John's unexpected frailty.

He has lied to me before, John reminded himself. In vain, he tried to remember whether he had felt a similar frisson of discomfort then, when Coymans had told him about Spiegel refusing to pay a dealer.

But in a sense, that had been the truth. Not entire, but not false either.

Saski claimed that Malise had been in Amsterdam this summer. Someone was lying. And Saski's eyes had challenged him to believe.

'Is jealousy why you refuse to join me?'

'No.'

What was his reason for refusing to try one last time to save something from the ruins?

'I don't have a good enough reason,' he said truthfully. 'Except that I can't do it.'

'It's your choice. I won't throw you out of my house just for spurning my advances.'

John suddenly realized that from the moment they had met on the bridge by the widow's house, not one word of their conversation had rung true.

He had to leave this house. He had to talk to Saski. He was appalled to find, as he gazed in a friendly fashion at the flushed, amiable face by the fire, that the hairs on his neck and arms were bristling like Cassie's hackles in full snarl.

I'll leave in the morning. Find lodgings . . .

He did a quick calculation of his reduced wealth. One bond worth £500 rolled into the cuff lining of each boot, to be kept intact – a tiny drop in the chasm of his debt. A purse half-full of florins, lighter by the price of wine money that day in the White Cat. Whatever more Gomez might be able to lend him against the will o' the wisp of the VOC voyage.

I might as well sail back to England while I can still buy our passage, he thought. Get it over with.

Cold dread flooded back.

He replied to some pleasantry of Coymans.

I will face it, he promised himself. But not with this sense of unfinished business. Perhaps Gomez will give me a corner of his floor or a pile of carpets to sleep on for a day or two until I settle one or two points in my mind.

When he finally excused himself and went to his room, Marika was waiting in his bed.

Her instincts sensed the end.

'*Eeen, twee, drie, vier* . . .' She closed her lips around each of his fingers in turn. 'Now you count for me.'

'I must go back to England.'

A single candle burned on a table near the bed.

She licked his thumb before she lifted her eyes. 'And live in discontent.'

'Why do you say that?'

'You would never have left if you had everything you wanted there. Stay here with me, please. I can give you whatever you lacked. You stay here in my land and be my new country where I can find peace. I'll teach you the language. Your tongue is already shaped for it . . . give it to me, here, between my teeth . . .'

He returned her kiss, in spite of himself. Then turned his head away. She pulled back, gave up. They lay with her neck on his arm and stared up into the darkness.

'Do you know an Englishman named Edward Malise?'

Marika went very still. Her neck tightened on his arm. Then her hands moved in the darkness in search of a resting place. Finally she crossed her arms and clasped her own shoulders. 'He's a friend of my brother's,' she said at last. 'At least, I think he's a friend.'

John heard the dryness as she swallowed.

'Is he a musician?'

'*Merde*!' said Marika. 'Is this all really a jealous inquisition?'

'More than jealousy.'

'Is that why you refuse me?' She sat up abruptly.

John stared at the dark cliff-face of her broad shoulders and ribcage. 'No.' He paused. 'Not that alone.'

'You have refused, haven't you?' her voice asked. 'In earnest? Absolutely?'

'Yes.'

She moved in the darkness. A shadow leaped from the end of the bed as Erasmus jumped into her outstretched arms. The mattress shifted as she rocked gently from side to side.

Suddenly she drew a deep breath. Erasmus screamed. Marika threw him violently away and turned like a fury on John. The coverlets swirled with her rage. John heard a scrabbling thump as the monkey landed on the floor.

'Get out!' Marika screamed. 'Get out! Get out! Now! Go!' John caught the shadow of a flailing arm.

'Get out of my bed! I'll kill you! I'll have Justus kill you! Go, go, go, *go*!' She wrenched her arm away and flung herself face down in her pillows, beyond comforting.

John had his breeches on by the time Marika's maid knocked at the door, and his shirt on by the time Coymans arrived.

'What have you done to her?'

John stared at Coymans's drawn sword. His own lay beneath his cloak, on top of a chest on the far side of the bed. 'I swear that my fault was not doing enough!'

'Has he hurt you?' Coymans demanded of his sister.

She sobbed in long grating breaths. 'Make him stay, Justus! What have you said to make him want to go away? What have you done?' She curled away from them. 'Oh, I want to die!'

'Fetch her a sleeping draught!' said Coymans to the maid. 'Run!' As the woman darted away into the dark corridor, Coymans turned on John. 'Ingrate! Traitor! Diddling both my sister and me!'

John took a careful step back in the direction of his cloak and sword.

Coymans shouted over his sister's weeping. 'Do you think I didn't know you were betraying me through the offices of that old Jew? I could forgive you for that but not for thinking me stupid enough not to know!'

'And did you think I was stupid enough not to know that I was in partnership with a murderer?'

The shadowy bulk of Coymans stopped dead.

'Where the Devil did you get that idea?'

The silence had been far too long.

Then Coymans asked, 'Who am I supposed to have killed?'

John felt his way around the bed to his cloak and sword. 'Is there a choice?'

'Tell me! Why did you say that?'

'Just for fun,' said John.

There was another silence. Marika moaned softly into her pillow. Erasmus rattled something on the floor under the bed. The maid came back with the sleeping draught for Marika.

'Get out now,' said Coymans in a tight cold voice. 'Take everything. Don't even leave one hair from your beard. I want to clean my house of you and your vile ingratitude.'

'No!' moaned Marika.

'Take her back to her own bed,' Coymans told the maid.

'I hate you!' said Marika. Her voice kept coming back from the hallway, growing fainter and fainter as she went to her own room. 'I hate you. I hate you.'

'I will give you five minutes to wake your man and collect

449

your things,' said Coymans. 'Then if you're still here, I will kill you.'

A little later, John and Arthur stood in the wet dark street among a jumble of belongings. John surveyed the salvage from his wrecked life. Spare boots, a short cloak. His razor, comb, writing box. Two shirts, a silk jacket and sleeves, two pairs of sewn woollen stockings and one of knitted silk. A provisions bag with an empty jug, two wooden trenchers and two spoons, and a horn of salt. No treasure chest, no jingling boxes of coins. No leather pouch cocoons for the meta-morphosing wages of the King's soldiers on the Scottish border.

'Well,' said Arthur. 'No room at the inn.' When John remained silent, Arthur asked, 'Where shall we go, sir?'

John bent and began to load himself. 'Warmoesstraat. Unless I've misjudged Gomez as well.'

He had been right about Coymans. Why hadn't he listened to himself? He couldn't say who the man had killed, but a killer he surely was.

Did I mean Bols when I accused him? I think I did.

'I hope Gomez will forgive us for waking him, but I can't think where else to turn.'

The earlier rain returned as a pre-dawn drizzle. Twice, John stopped to listen.

'What is it, sir?' asked Arthur.

'I'm imagining that someone is following us, even now in the middle of the night.'

The dog warned him. Instead of trotting up to the shadowy tree to sniff or raise its leg, the animal stopped four feet away and considered. John watched the animal as he walked past. Then a strip of the tree trunk flung itself across the cobbles at him.

John felt a tug at his jacket back, then heard the rasp of

torn cloth. Turning, he struggled in the folds of his cloak, which had caught on something. His hat was knocked off. His cloak ripped free of the snag. A knife blade glinted dully against the matching sheen of the dark canal water.

John shouted for Arthur and struck at the attacker's knife arm. The blade flew free and slid noisily across the stones into the canal. They wrestled, hampered by their cloaks, feet slipping on the wet cobbles. Arthur heaved and struggled, but could not pull the man off. Finally, John backed them all against the tree. The man threw his head back into Arthur's face.

Arthur grunted and stepped away, hand to his nose. Though the attacker had now lost his hat, it was too dark under the tree to see his face. John wrestled him back into the open, where the water of the canal reflected a faint light.

The eyes were round with fearful amazement. The mouth was compressed into a white-edged snout of absolute rage.

A young face. Not Forehead or the Egg Seller. But familiar.

The youth butted John hard on the chin with his head, crying out with the pain he caused himself.

John released one arm and hit the young man just below the arched meeting of his ribs. He panted and stared down at the retching youth doubled over on the cobblestones at his feet. The boy made a sound like a dying cow and stumbled to his feet. With a dark stain flooding from his nose over his mouth and chin, Arthur prodded him tentatively with his sword, then sheathed it.

A window opened overhead. A man's voice shouted down.

The boy flung himself at John again, fell against him, clawed and clung in turn, croaking out his rage. John heard Bols's name, Coymans's, and his own.

More windows opened.

The boy's voice grew louder as his breath returned. John heard the name of Bols again.

'We must get him to Gomez.' From what John thought he

was beginning to understand, he needed a friendly interpreter. 'Take my sword. Leave everything else for now. There's nothing of value now anyway.'

He clamped one hand over the boy's mouth and pulled his arm up behind his back. 'March.'

'Gomez!' shouted John. 'Wake up! Gomez!'

Arthur pitched cobbles against the old man's window shutters.

Finally one wing of the shutters swung open. A small head in a white cap peered down into the street.

'Gomez! For the love of God, let us in!' called John.

'Who else is with you?'

'Just my own man and a mad child I need you to examine.'

Gomez didn't reply.

The shutters of the house across the street from the baker's shop swung open. A woman shouted angrily at Gomez, almost face to face across the narrow gap.

'I'm a desperate man, senhor!' called John. 'I shall stand here shouting until you let me in!'

Gomez withdrew his head.

Five other windows and two doors had opened before he unbolted the baker's door. He peered through the narrow gap.

'Do I look like a raiding party?' demanded John.

Gomez stepped aside.

'It's old Bols's assistant!' exclaimed John.

Gomez lit the last candle in a glowing tree of eight and set the candleholder on the spinet. 'Sit him there.'

John shoved the boy down on the bench against one wall, between the spinet and a pile of small, folded rugs. The boy collapsed leglessly and stared around in amazement at the treasure cave.

Arthur washed his bloodied nose and went out again in search of their belongings.

'Why did he try to kill me? Find out, senhor. My mind is in a tangle.' John sat on the folded rugs.

Gomez poured three multi-coloured glasses of *eau de vie*, and gave one to the boy and one to John as if they had all just finished a pleasant evening of cards. He asked the boy a question which sounded as casual as a query about the comfort of his seat.

The boy clutched his glass of *eau de vie* in one dirt-grimed hand and talked with the recklessness of despair. He pointed at John with his glass, spilt it, looked at it in astonishment and gulped what was left.

Gomez listened intently, nodding and making little encouraging chirps and grunts. He did not look at John. Finally the boy had drained himself. Gomez sipped his brandy and wiped his moustaches with the back of his hand, still avoiding John's eyes.

'What did he say?'

Gomez coughed. 'To summarize: you have destroyed everything Bols was working for . . . you and Coymans.'

After a pause, John said, 'That is an extreme way of putting it, though I can perhaps see what the boy might mean.'

Gomez coughed again. 'No, I think he means rather more than that.'

John heard a tremor in his voice. Gomez is afraid, he thought. 'Then I don't see his meaning.'

'He claims that you paid ruffians to visit Bols's nursery . . . He wants to know how a man who pretended to delight in flowers could wipe out the lifetime of a servant of Flora.'

'You're still not being plain with me,' said John. 'How can I answer an accusation I don't yet understand?'

The boy followed the talk from one man to the other, tick, tick, with eager eyes.

'You destroyed all the bulbs,' said Gomez.

For a moment, John stared in horror. 'Bols's bulbs?'

'*Ja!*' cried the boy.

'To raise the price of your own,' said Gomez apologetically. He looked away.

'To do *what*?'

'It has been known,' said Gomez. 'To steal or destroy a rival's stock to put up the value of your own.'

John rose to his full height on a surge of rage. 'Hell's TEETH! And you think *I* did that?'

Gomez didn't flinch. 'You're not a man who likes to lose,' he said gently.

'Nor to win at any price!'

'Not if the prize is only gold . . . I had already decided that about you. But might the ransom for a past life tempt you?'

'Unless you're blind, you must know me better than that by now!'

Gomez finally looked down. He licked his thumb and forefinger and pulled the end of his beard into a point as fine as one of Saski's brushes. 'I haven't yet seen where you draw the line.'

John closed his mouth and pulled his head back into his shoulders. He closed his eyes briefly and opened them again. Then he sat down heavily on the rugs. 'Senhor, forgive me. You raise the question I should have been asking myself.' He stared at blue and white *kraacke-ware* cups stacked on an Italian mosaic table then lifted his head and spoke directly to the boy. 'I did not lie to Bols. I share your former master's love of his children and I have already trusted that infant *King of Kandy* to a conscientious and eager nurse.'

Hein looked away.

'He believes that you love Dame Money more than Flora,' said Gomez.

'Is the choice between Dame Money and the goddess Flora always absolute?' asked John. 'Can't the Dame help a man

454

to enjoy favours from the goddess that a poor man can't afford?'

Gomez shook his head. 'That's a fleeting game, my friend, not a choice. Dame Money has her own absolute logic. If you are true to her, you must forsake all others.'

'Though she may have pulled me a little way from myself, I did not smash the bulbs. I do not think that I could bring myself to it, even to salvage a past life.'

'He says that somebody smashed them all, four days ago. You and Coymans had the best reason. You were trying to sell your own *Prunelle* bulbs.'

John hissed in disbelief.

'You must come see for yourself, if you don't believe him.' Gomez listened to the boy again. 'Or are you too ashamed to see what you have done?' He shrugged. 'I merely translate, Nightingale. Don't imagine that I believe.'

I can imagine anything just now, thought John.

'I would like to see,' he said. 'If the young man will swear not to try to knife me again. And will you come too, senhor? To translate? And perhaps to help me clear some things in my own mind?'

When Gomez hesitated, John added, 'If I'm not ashamed to go, senhor, surely you are not afraid?'

Their feet crunched. The floor of the shed was covered in shreds of brown papery skin, yellowed pulp and pot shards. Crushed baskets held puddles of rotting mush. The benches around the walls were sticky with drying juice. The table whose top had been used as a press lay on its side. Damp rotting fragments still clung to the rough wood. Their feet stirred a dreadful stench of putrefaction. Gomez moved unhappily, with little flicks of his booted feet, like a cat on wet snow.

'So many!' said John aghast. 'I didn't know that Bols had so many *Prunelle*.'

'He didn't,' said Gomez after consulting the boy, Hein. 'Only the four breeder bulbs that you saw. But Bols labelled all his new and rare bulbs in a code. Whoever did it couldn't tell *Prunelle* from the rest, so they smashed them all.'

Hein led them across the barn court. The second shed also stank of the rotting pulp that crusted its floor.

'The other two sheds are the same,' Hein said, through Gomez. 'The commoner sorts had labels that could be clearly read, but they paid no attention. Everything is smashed.'

John swore. 'Is anything left in the fields?'

Gomez enquired.

'A few late Serotinas, he says. And he has a dozen pots of different sorts in his own lodging, under his bed to keep them in the dark.'

Bols's grandchild would never have her field in full blow.

'Even if you are innocent,' said Gomez, 'Hein is still sure that Coymans sent them.'

'Does he have any proof that it was Coymans?'

Hein was watching them both from the shadows in one corner of the shed.

'He says he doesn't need proof ... Eh?' Gomez leaned to listen intently to something Hein said so softly that John barely heard.

'. . . Any more than he needs proof,' said Gomez in a strange voice, 'that Coymans killed Bols.' He met John's eyes with defiant bravado.

John held the old man's challenging eyes. 'Tell Hein that I too think Coymans killed his master.'

Gomez obeyed, without dropping his eyes.

'You too?' asked John.

Gomez nodded.

'And is that what you secretly accuse me of?' asked John. 'Is that why you hesitated to open your door to me last night?'

'It's logical. For the same reason that Hein thought you

456

had smashed the bulbs to destroy *Prunelle. The King of Kandy* rose, did he not, after Bols died?'

'Your logic stinks. Is it logical to accuse me of murder when we're here alone, with only a boy to defend you? I argue that this very accusation, in these circumstances, demonstrates your faith in my innocence.'

'*Concedo*,' said Gomez. 'I'm happy to accept your conclusion. But what you have not yet proved is the soundness of my faith.'

'You're both illogical and brave to the point of foolhardiness,' said John.

Gomez half-smiled. 'Nah. Just too old for fear to master my curiosity. Who needs more weary years of life when he can have knowledge?'

'I did not kill Bols, nor have him killed, nor know that he had been killed. I can't prove it. But I can tell you about my own loss. And rupture with Coymans. The story might or might not reassure you. Tell the boy that he has caught me at the very moment my mind became clear. I felt that Coymans had killed Bols even before I went so far as to suspect him. Now I suspect and want to prove.'

'You think you can find proof?'

'I think I know where to look.'

Gomez told Hein. He brushed one moustache with the back of his hand and looked at the littered floor.

'What else, senhor?' asked John.

'Perhaps while you're looking for that proof about Bols, you might keep one eye open for anything concerning another recent, convenient death. Mynheer Spiegel.'

'Spiegel?' John felt no surprise, just amazement at his own ability to have swallowed the news of Spiegel's death so smoothly when Kramer had told him, without more of a lump sticking in his gorge. 'Did Justus lose his lawsuit, then?'

Gomez nodded. 'On a point raised by a new statute, that set a date after which all transactions were void. Spiegel used

457

the statute to avoid paying Coymans. I do hope that you have not badly offended Justus yourself. It seems a dangerous thing to do.'

John told him briefly of his eviction from Coymans's house.

'And half of Warmoesstraat know you came straight to me,' said Gomez. 'Oh well . . .'

'I'm sorry,' said John, stricken. 'I should have seen the threat to you. I had no one else . . .'

Gomez shook his head politely. 'Nah, nah. Don't concern yourself about that. I merely meant that we should try to find that proof of yours as soon as possible. If Justus thinks your accusation of murder had proof behind it, he won't wait before he acts.'

I'll make that superior little limner talk to me, thought John, if I have to break his door down and hang him from his own easel!

Someone had saved John the trouble. When John arrived at Saski's house, a carpenter and his apprentice were pulling nails from the smashed remains of the heavy sage-green front door.

John ran up the steps to the *stoep*. No one stopped him at the door, or in the hall. The empty door-frame made the house feel nakedly vulnerable. John stopped in mid-stride. The hall had been stripped of pictures. The plaster of the walls was chequered with their pale, ghostly marks. Then John saw the pile of smashed frames on the tiled floor.

'Saski?'

One or two of the smaller portraits survived, but the rest had been sliced, their frames broken.

What did I say last night to Coymans? Could I have done this?

John turned over the wreckage, searching for the burlesque of the Last Supper with Coymans and Malise at the centre of the table.

458

'Did he overlook something and send you back again as his messenger boy?'

John straightened and whirled toward the staircase that led down to the studio. The artist had propped both wrists between banister and newel post to steady the pistol.

'You are lucky my nerves are as steady as they are,' said Saski. 'Amazing, under the circumstances. I might have fired without looking closer. I might even have hit you.'

'Who did you say sent me?'

'Our mutual benefactor . . . your whore's brother.'

'Coymans did not send me,' said John.

Saski gave a hard mock laugh. 'After all the nights that I have studied and drawn the two of you together, please don't pretend with me!'

'After all that observation, you should recognize my true ignorance!"

Saski sighed shakily. He withdrew his wrists from the notch between banister and newel post. The pistol rattled against the wood as he did so. His nerves were not so steady after all. 'Come down,' he said. 'See what he has done.'

The air was thick with acrid smells of rosin, oils, animal glue and smoke. A giant hand had carelessly stirred the canvases, portfolios, paints, brushes, jars, jugs, dishes, pencils, pieces of charcoal and chalks. Drawings were torn, crumpled, splashed with paint. Heads had been torn from bodies, skies rent in two. A small fire had been started and died out in one heap of portfolios. Canvases dangled in fringes from shattered, twisted frames. Brush handles had been snapped, jars of pigments and glue thrown to the floor and smashed. Boots had printed themselves in ochre, *terre verte* and black across drawings of faces. Only the portrait of Coymans survived intact, although it leaned precariously against the wall on the half-fallen easel.

Who'd have thought Justus was so vain?

John leaned down and picked up a severed hand drawn in

silverpoint. The wrist and arm lay half-masked by a thick pool of dried gesso.

'Your playmate is a bully,' said Saski.

'He was your patron.'

Saski gave him a bitter blue-eyed glance. 'What did you say to him?'

'Nothing to bring this about, I swear. Why do you think I caused this?'

'He wanted certain drawings . . . studies. I heard him ask.'

'Where were you?' asked John. 'While your accumulated life was being destroyed?'

Saski shivered. 'Hiding, I assure you. Hiding my hands.' He stared bemused around the wrecked studio. 'This is nothing. It will be cleaned. Frames can be mended. There will be room now for the drawings I am yet to do. I was hiding my hands from him, and my eyes.'

John laid the hand back on the studio floor beside the wrist end that reached out from the gesso pool. 'Which drawings did he want?'

'You tell me!' said the painter. He was shivering minutely like the surface of a pot just about to come to a boil. 'He seems to think you learned dangerous things from my work.' Saski was poised precariously on the edge of control.

'I asked him if he knew the man I found here last time, the Englishman, Malise. Nothing more.'

'You have ruined my life,' said Saski. 'I won't find another patron like him, who has not swallowed the old-fashioned dogma that art must only be for moral and spiritual uplifting of our souls. Who does not demand prettifying and lies for his money but will let me show the truth.'

'Clearly, he could not accept certain truths.'

'He could accept the truths but not what he feared you would do with them. "What did you show the Englishman?" he asked me, that last night you saw me at his house, after you went off to bed Marika.' Saski's voice rose. '"What did you show him?"' He raised one hand in imitation of Coymans's jabbing attack. The hand still held the pistol. "'Saski, you have ruined us all!"'

'Saski,' said John gently. He took the painter by both shoulders and eased him down onto a stool. 'Let me take that.' He lifted the pistol from the man's hand and laid it out of reach on the littered floor. 'Bad conscience is pushing Coymans on. Bad conscience means that he knows that some of the truths you have witnessed are unacceptable. And you know they are unacceptable.'

Saski shuddered. 'It is not for me to make those judgements. I record.' His hand drew scribbles on the air. 'I record. I do not judge.'

'Then why are you afraid?'

Saski stared across the studio at the portrait of Coymans. 'I never thought he would be too vain or too superstitious to destroy his own face,' he said reflectively.

'If you have not judged, why are you so afraid?'

Saski still avoided the question. 'I only want to work.'

'At any price?'

Saski raised light-blue eyes full of despair and rage. 'I only want to be able to paint what I see. The rich merchants and stadholders want painted lies. Testimony to their wealth and power that will live after they have rotted back to mud. Justus was different, he cared only for what he could have now. That freed him to free me. We inhabited the same present moment. But now even Coymans has warned me to blind myself!'

'What must you stop seeing?'

Saski stared down at his hands, flexing the fingers as if playing some complex children's counting game.

'You have judged,' said John. 'But like me, you chose to ignore what you knew, because it suited you.'

Still, Saski stared at his hands.

'Or worse, and again like myself, perhaps you secretly

enjoyed riding on the tail of another man's wickedness. I haven't let myself start to tally up the damage yet, but I know I must, sooner or later. Show me what you must stop seeing!'

Saski laughed. 'Do you think I dare, when merely showing you drawings of some other Englishman brought this about?' He lifted a hand at the chaos.

'Yes.'

Saski looked startled.

'You have always dared. You're not the quiescent observer you pretend to be. Every drawing you have ever done for Coymans was a dare. Now he has dared you to go further.'

'That's an interesting way to look at it,' said Saski.

'And it excites you, your life of secret danger.'

'And now you're daring me to go even further.'

'Yes. To the final duel. Unless these smashed canvases, broken brushes and the wiping out of your past life are as much danger as you can take. If so, Justus has also wiped out the rest of your life. He has finished you in this world. Show me what you must not see and we can finish him.'

Saski bowed his head.

'Think how interesting it will be to draw his trial, and perhaps even his execution.' When Saski still did not reply, John continued, 'I think you lie when you say you don't mind the loss of all your work. You hate him for the greatest injury one man can do another – he has taken away the purpose for which you were born. Destroyed the evidence of your past being and forbidden you to continue to be. Unless you can console yourself with the promise of future Paradise, you hate him!'

Saski looked up at the passion in the Englishman's voice. 'Has he done the same to you, then?'

'He was not the first to do me this injury. But without your help, he will be the first that I will have allowed to do so.'

'He was like an older brother.'

'I think you love the sister and hate the brother.'

Saski stood and led John upstairs into the tiled hall.

The studies were under a loose tile in the floor. Saski handed John the first sketch, drawn in his loose, quick lines, of Coymans and Forehead. Coymans instructing, Forehead agleam with knowing malice. A heavy purse sagged in Coymans's palm. Forehead's hand was suspended in the air, greedy, already shaped for the purse, aching to take on its weight.

'He let you see this?' asked John in disbelief. 'When he told me he was a gambler, I didn't know how far he pushed his idea of "fun".'

The second drawing was more detailed, as if Saski had drawn it in the tranquillity of the studio, a *memento mori* genre piece. An old man, working alone by candlelight, looked up startled at an intruder. His fringe of white hair flared in an aureole of alarm, his eyes and mouth signalled that he recognized Death at his door. Death held out a skeletal hand in a politely enquiring gesture. 'Do I intrude? May I come in?' But his face was still covered with flesh and recognizable as Forehead.

'Bols!' breathed John. 'Do you *know* this? Or is it imagination?'

'I don't render falsehood.' Saski was studying a third drawing. 'I didn't need to hide this one, but it goes with the others.' He handed it to John.

John and Coymans celebrating the sale of *The King of Kandy*. There he was, rejoicing in the profit from an old man's murder, unwitting but tainted all the same. He saw on that face the mark of Cain which he had never felt before.

'This won't keep me from using the other two against Coymans, if that's your meaning,' said John, after a long moment.

'It's your risk, your choice.'

'The drawings alone won't convict Coymans.'

Saski smiled thinly. 'Oh, no! Don't even think of it. You won't make me any further witness than these.'

'You didn't happen to draw the smashing of Bols's bulbs?'

'I would have had to imagine too much.'

'And Spiegel?'

'I'm an artist, not a hero. Please take those and go!'

'The drawings alone aren't enough to convict Coymans,' said Gomez. 'But they will set in motion the arrest of old Oly there. He's loyal to the money, not the man. He'll talk, even if Saski stays closed up like an oyster. The drawings are enough to make Coymans lose his attraction as paymaster.' Gomez held the study of Coymans and Oly at arm's length. 'The risk of doing business with him seems unacceptably high. Even if Coymans escapes the law, he won't keep his reputation. Just as in speculation, rumour is as good as truth.'

'Saski's life hangs on how those drawings are used.'

'And so does yours,' said Gomez. 'And mine. Concealment, I understand. Don't try to teach me, young man.'

But the following afternoon, John and Arthur were set upon in the alley between St Anthony's Gate and the Warmoes-straat. Arthur regained consciousness on the floor of the baker's shop, where someone had pulled him, having recognized the English manservant whose master had recently roused the entire street with his brawling and shouting two hours before dawn.

'Where's your master?' Gomez asked Arthur. 'Where's John?'

Gomez and the baker ran to search the alley again. They banged on doors, and peered into the depths of the canal, without result. John had vanished.

Sixteen

He was sitting in shallow water in near darkness, propped against something hard, wet and cold. He put his hand on the floor to push himself to his feet. Chilly water rose above his wrist. Buttocks and back felt like ice. Damp shirt clung to his back. His hand explored. Knife and sword gone.

Terror cut through the painful fog in his brain. Consciousness swept back. He levered himself to his feet, then had to pause while the fog swirled back. When it cleared slightly, he tried to decide where he was.

In a damp stone cell, three feet wide and four feet long. He had been propped against its back wall. The roof was a handsbreadth higher than his head. An opening seven inches square had been cut into a wooden door three and a half inches thick and set with iron bars thicker than his thumb. The walls were slippery as phlegm, covered in a vegetable growth that oozed water like a saturated sponge. Too dark to see his feet, but he heard them suck and slosh in the water on the slippery floor. He had been stripped of his cloak and doublet.

With his eyes closed, for five seconds John believed that the force of his will would dematerialize the wooden door and cramping stone walls. He opened his eyes, half-expecting space and light. The heavy door still closed him into the stone sarcophagus.

Coymans.

Coymans had moved faster than Gomez. Saski had betrayed him. Marika had demanded that he be punished. Whoever cut the throat of Sir George's man decided to shed me as well.

Why am I still alive? Why didn't they just kill me and dump me in the river?

Then he thought, because I'm hidden here. My body will never bloat and bob up to accuse my murderers.

His hands fumbled along the edge of the damp wood, then searched the centre of the door, also covered in oozing sponge. No handle on the inside. Nor keyhole, nor bar, nor hinge. Nothing but thick, wet, blank wood, sliding under his fingers. The iron bars were set solidly into a frame of iron. And though wet, the wood of the door was not rotten but extremely sound. John shook the bars with all his strength. These teeth were tight in their jawbone.

He braced his back against the rear wall, raised his leg and kicked the door. The pain of the shock ran up through his heel into his knee, but the door did not even creak. Renewed terror accelerated his pulse and breathing. He pressed his face to the bars, projected his body out into the space beyond, his back turned to the blackness.

There's plenty of air. You won't suffocate.

He spoke to himself sternly, from as far away as possible. The other instructing self, safely outside the dark, wet, three foot by four foot stone cell, observed dispassionately. You have plenty of air to breathe. You have more than enough room. You are not in unbearable pain. You have nothing to worry about. Not until Coymans or his ruffians return.

All the same, he sucked air through the bars as if storing up a reserve against need.

The thickness of the door limited his field of vision. Beyond the barred opening, he could see the surface of a stretch of water, a stone sea wall close on the right. Directly below the door, a stone ledge protected by a knee-high wall. Beyond

466

and below that, the water eased slowly toward him, into a backwater at the foot of the stone ledge. To the left of the cell, farther out in the channel, the current suddenly stretched and disappeared downstream in wrinkled rills.

The cell is built out from the sea wall, he thought. Or in the pier of a bridge.

The broken stern of a half-sunk, derelict skiff was lodged in the backwater in the bottom right corner of his square of vision. The feathery dust-mop tops of a distant row of spindly trees rose above the sea wall to his right. Above the other sea wall across the wide metallic channel, he saw a blank grey evening sky, without a tree or a sail of either boat or mill.

The row of trees to his right suggested a road.

He shouted for help.

No one answered.

He shouted again. Then he forced himself to be silent. Shouting could swell into panic, to imagining help on the way, and then to disappointment. Imagination was his enemy now.

You have air, said the dispassionate instructor. What's a little discomfort? A wounded dignity? The impatience of enforced waiting? Where's anything unbearable in all that?

He forced himself to leave the little square of light, striped by the bars. With his hands, he searched the black, slimy walls.

Another opening isn't likely, but be sure.

There was a twist he didn't like in the imagination that had built this cell, but he could not yet see exactly what bothered him most. An evil sense of humour would have a man die of panic with escape a few inches away.

He slid his hands over the wet black surfaces of all four walls but found only solid stone. The single irregularity was a row of small squares pierced into the stone at the bottom of each wall, like tiny drains. He inserted a finger into one but could not feel the back of it.

467

His sleeves as well as the back of his shirt were now sodden and chilled. The four inches of water on the floor had soaked through his boots.

He shouted again for help. He would ration his cries. Considered cries only. At controlled intervals.

Outside, the sky was darkening. The treetops had blurred into rounded shadowy shapes like hens roosting on posts. The water was still coldly bright, reflecting the dying light.

You can survive here until morning, said the dispassionate instructor. Then Gomez will know that something is wrong and will go looking for you. Or a farmer or boatman will happen by. One or the other, with luck, before Coymans returns. If you control imagination, you risk nothing more than an ague.

He heard scraping sounds on the stone above his head.

'Is someone there?' Sudden hope battled with equally sudden terror.

The scraping stopped.

'For the love of God! If you are a human soul, and can understand my drift if not my words, get me out of here!'

There was silence above his head.

'Is someone there?' He swooped down into a profound circle of Hell. It was only an animal. A cow or sheep. Then he realized that if it were an animal, a herdsman or farmer might be nearby.

'Help me!'

He waited for the end of silence.

'Why should I?' asked a familiar English voice. 'I put you there.'

The hair rose on John's neck. I should have killed him in the stable yard.

'It's a pleasure to hear you beg,' said Malise. 'Away from the protection of your master, Sir Harry.'

I'm dead, thought John. It's the end of hope and of disappointment.

'Once again, I'm sorry to say,' said Malise, 'I need something from you.'

'My life must have been yours to take while you were putting me here.'

'That too, in time, as I said. But first I want something much easier for you to give.'

John kept silent.

He heard Malise's feet scrape again, moving away. Then they came closer, along the little ledge outside the cell door.

Malise peered into the cell and clicked his tongue. 'Your cousin wouldn't approve of these lodgings. It's just as well that he'll never see them. Nor anyone who might spread the damaging rumour. He is most unhappy, you know, to be linked to you. I was agreeably surprised how readily he agreed with me that it was past time for you to be brought to justice.'

'You're lying!'

'How do you think I knew where to find you?' Satisfaction oiled Malise's voice.

John clamped his tongue between his teeth, already regretting his loss of control.

'Or again,' said Malise. 'Might it have been the scorned Marika? I'm always at her service, though I'd like to skewer that monkey of hers.'

'Did you lock me in this hole just to bait me? Go away. I want to go to sleep.'

'Still pretending to urgent purpose?' Malise put his face against the little opening in the door. 'I suppose we should go ahead before your hands are too stiff to write.'

He shoved a roll of paper between the bars. 'Be so good as to sign this for me.'

John left the roll where it was. 'It's too dark in here to read. You know better than to ask a man to sign a document he hasn't seen or heard read.'

'It's a confession of murder.'

'You don't need it to prove my guilt. You have all those considerable men as witnesses.'

'Oh, this isn't a confession to the murder of my brother. This document certifies that you killed Bols.'

After a long silence, John said, 'But I didn't kill Bols.' He was now too curious to care about giving Malise the satisfaction of his interest.

'You're a murderer. Does it matter which death they hang you for?'

'You don't see the difference?'

'I can see that from your point of view there might be a difference, but from mine there's none. You escaped paying for a murder you committed. You will hang for one you didn't. It seems rather elegant to me. I have no interest in how it seems to you.' When John said nothing, he added, 'And I might find less need to defend myself against a counter-accusation made by a man who has killed twice.'

'Why do you think I'd sign that and guarantee myself to hang? You're mad.'

'You will see why,' said Malise. 'I'll visit again.'

After the sound of Malise's feet was muffled by the dusk, John leaned against the little opening, heavy with thought.

Not Coymans after all. Or not directly.

He remembered their two faces leaning close in Saski's drawing. A falcon and a Chinese lion dog.

He braced his mind against Malise's jibes about Marika and Harry. He made their very plausibility an argument against: Malise knew which weapons to choose to give the most pain, he wanted to cause pain, therefore, they were weapons only.

It doesn't matter who sent me here. I am probably going to die. It should not matter to me, only to the one with the weight on his or her soul.

The rills of the current on his left gleamed. In the faulty light, they seemed to be flowing the wrong way.

Malise has heard of the application for a pardon, thought John. I won't escape him again.

He looked around the little cell.

Again he looked at the rills of the current on his left. They were flowing the wrong way. Upstream.

Imagination! he warned himself. The current had always flowed that way. He had been too panicked at first to observe well. The serpent rills had always come sliding up around the corner of the left wall of the cell.

The light was going, even from the surface of the water.

You can't see which way it's flowing. Don't fill the holes in your physical senses with miasmas of the brain!

He shifted his weight and felt a new resistance against the ankle of his boot.

The hair lifted on his scalp. The calm instructing voice was sucked into a chaos of panic-stricken clamour.

The water on the floor had risen.

Calm!

John moved both feet, one after the other, from side to side against the push of the water. He lifted his right foot and pushed it down through five yielding inches.

You may have mistaken its depth at the first.

But he knew without further evidence that he was in a channel on the seaward side of the last lock and that the tide was rising. That was what Malise thought would change his mind.

For a moment he couldn't move. Then, with dread, he bent to touch one of the row of square holes in the back wall of the cell. They went right through the stone wall. Water slid out in thick liquid worms, feeding the rising lake on the floor. He looked back out of the little barred window. The surface of the backwater already looked higher. This was the twist. This was the death he had chosen over hanging.

How high was a tide? How long did a tide take to climb to its full height? He cursed his ignorance. The Dutch lived with one eye always on Neptune like courtiers of an unpredictable tyrant. Though he had spent weeks in their land of water, he had never asked about such basic facts.

He pulled back his sleeve, bent and touched the floor. The water now came well past his wrist.

Plug the holes.

Too many. He had only his shirt and breeches. If he stripped naked, he could not fill even half.

He rode his panic now like a treacherous horse, in precarious control. Though he was still in the saddle, any slight alarm would throw him.

Why am I here?

Malise wants me to confess to a murder I did not commit. And what part did Coymans play, if any? Malise did not try to hide his connections.

John bent to touch the floor again. The water had climbed half-way up his forearm.

'HELP ME!' he called through the bars. He tried to clamp his lips closed but a second cry escaped. '*HELP ME!*'

If Coymans learned of my last visit to Saski ... Perhaps Gomez had blundered and betrayed. Perhaps Coymans had handed him over to Malise for fun.

Please God! Please use Your will to turn the tide!

The water continued to rise. The little square drains were now far under the surface but he could feel the water pressing out of them, filling up his cell. The darkly glittering surface of the backwater rose and fell in the dusk, sometimes far, sometimes almost seeming to flood over the wall around the ledge outside the door.

God was not going to help him!

John tried like King Canute to press the water back down into its ocean bed. But it kept rising. It was nearly to his knees. John leaned his forehead against the bars in the door.

I think I may be about to die very soon.

Never imagined it like this. All those rehearsals in my mind but never this.

'How high do you think it will rise?'

His own clamouring thought echoed back from outside, above the cell.

Malise was back. His feet scraped again on the stone above John's head.

'I am told that the height of the water varies from day to day, according to winds and the phase of the moon. Sometimes it rises to the roof, sometimes a little less.'

'I thought you preferred fire,' said John.

'All the elements serve me.'

The scraping came again, faded, then sounded again from the side of the sea wall. Feet grated along the little ledge and a man's shape blacked out the faint square of the barred opening.

'Well?' said Malise conversationally. 'Are your feet as wet as mine?'

Move away from the opening! John willed him. Do anything, but don't block the air! Then he brought himself under control again. But he didn't trust his voice.

'I wanted to talk,' said Malise.

Not here just to fish out the waterlogged corpse then, thought John. He swallowed. 'More taunts or to a purpose?'

'Your choice,' said Malise. 'For the first time. A real choice.'

The water was over John's kneecaps. He had begun to shiver in the evening chill. 'You're persistent,' he said at last. 'I almost admire that.'

'Choose. Will you sign, or stay there and drown by inches? I think I'd rather hang. And there is always a chance of the block and sword.'

'If I sign, what do you offer me in return?' John asked.

'A more civilized death.'

'That's a poor bargain.'

'How about a hunting advantage, with you as the stag? I hold the hounds till you've cleared the first meadow.'

'Why are you doing this?'

'Because I want to see you hang,' said Malise patiently, with the air of having repeated the words many times.

'I meant the "why" behind that one.'

'To help out an old friend, who had begun to find you a nuisance.'

'That sounds closer,' said John. 'But not enough for your hatred before I killed Francis. Why did you kill my parents?'

And if he answers, I will know that I die tonight.

After a long silence, Malise said, 'The water is coming over the top of the wall now and beginning to soak my boots. Make up your mind what you're going to do. I want to get back up on dry land. Will you sign?'

'No,' said John.

'You won't sign?' John heard the faintest quiver of incredulity in Malise's voice.

'No.'

John heard a rustling of fabric and wet sloshing of feet.

After a few seconds, Malise said, 'You have at least another hour before high water. I'll leave you to think about drowning by inches. I'll come back one last time before I return to the city.'

John tried to imagine that hour, with the water climbing to his chest. But it was beyond imagining. Dangerous to imagine.

'Give me the confession,' he said. He heard the other man inhale sharply. Then another rustling.

'Here!' Malise could not control the trembling of his voice. He shoved the paper through the bars. 'I brought an oil stick for you to sign with. I feared that the sea might dilute your ink.'

John snatched at the curl of paper, afraid of losing his resolve. He unrolled it. The pale rectangle rattled in his shaking hands.

'Anywhere near the bottom of the page.' Malise offered the oil stick through the bars.

John tore the paper in half, then tore it again. He had to concentrate to control his shaking muscles, tore the quarters into eighths and then into sixteenths. He shoved a fistful of fragments through the bars and continued to tear ferociously as if he feared the document might magically reconstitute itself.

'That's that, then,' said Malise with despair. He did not leave.

'It is. Please go away now.'

'I'm surprised that Justus wanted you dead,' said Malise. 'I find you so much like him – both of you from families of polite footpads and civilized highwaymen, both happy to thrive on the losses of other men.'

'You confuse me with yourself.'

'Do you imagine me to be a villain?'

'I know it,' cried John through teeth which had begun to clatter with cold.

'Unable to live with injustice. That's my worst crime. Before you die, which you will tonight, I want you to admit your own guilt. Your family ruined mine. Usurped our lands and place. Francis and I took three lives. Your father and grandfather took away the continuing life of the entire Malise family. And the courts backed them. If King Henry had decided to take our lands and give them to a clerk who had bowed and scraped a little deeper than all the others, why then God Himself had ordained that clerk must become a gentleman! While we, who had ruled our estates for two hundred years, became nothing. Without lands, without place, without voice.'

'Without Tarleton Court?' asked John.

'Without Tarleton Court, my father died abroad, among strangers who spoke a tongue he didn't know. He died of wet feet and a broken heart. My mother followed him soon after.' Malise leaned close to the little window again. 'My parents for yours, Nightingale. And neither of us has the lands. On balance, you still owe me.'

John imagined that he could still see the pale scraps of paper floating on the surface of the backwater, which had now drowned the ledge and slapped gently against the outside of the door. He had so nearly signed, just to open this door and step out again into the air, onto dry land.

Malise had been gone a long time. It had been easier while he was still there. John was going to have to do the last part alone.

Each man is alone in his death, he told himself.

But not like this!

Some worse. His parents. Would they have preferred this way to their own? He tried to breathe and felt the weight of water press against his chest. The sea was sitting on his heart.

The cold had become a sharp ache that replaced his bones. He didn't know whether he was still shivering or not.

I'll dive, he thought. When the time comes. And then fill my lungs with one deep breath.

Can I call it a breath, if it's water and not air?

Water burned in the lungs like fire. He knew that from swimming. But the pain would end.

He imagined diving and miraculously swimming out through a hidden portal below the surface, swimming free into open waters and surfacing like a whale with the waves breaking from his head.

The water had reached his collar bone.

He shook his head to knock away a memory of drowned kittens. Crumpled and sticky. Smaller than when they were alive. Shrunk by the removal of some vital substance.

O Domine Jesu Christe, Rex gloriae, libera animas defunctorum de poenis inferni, et de profundo lacu.

Save the souls of the departed from the fathomless waters!

. . . ne cadent in obscurum . . . let them not fall into utter darkness.

He felt nothing. Neither fear nor peace.

Is this the time to dive?

Libera me.

He was standing on his toes, with the water to his chin.

Dive now, he told himself. While you still control the time. Dive into death, don't trickle and whimper. Dive!

Oh Lord, deliver me . . . From the fathomless waters . . . From the lion's mouth . . .

I must dive soon, if I'm going to do it.

He poised. Dive!

Then out of his own mouth, with no more volition than if he had been possessed, exploded a great roar of rage.

NOT YET! IT'S NOT TIME! NOT YET!

The sound of his rage spun like a cyclone around the walls of the cell and careened off the rising surface of the water.

I refuse! Not yet!

What have you done? What have you done? he asked himself in a new despair. Condemned yourself to struggle.

But I won't go!

Libera me!

I won't go!

The water rose slowly towards the top of the barred opening. It reached the top. The supply of air was closed off.

Quiet. Calm. Said the dispassionate instructor.

Where have you come from, again, all of a sudden? asked John.

Quiet. Breathe slowly. Gently. Head back.

The weight began to leave the soles of his boots.

Float upward.

The ache of the cold had gone. His body was numb. He hung in the water, his head tilted back, toes of his boots trailing, just touching the floor.

The roof pressed down towards his face. He couldn't see

it, but he could feel the stone squeezing the air like a weighted cheese. Panic began to quiver through his bones.

Calm. Quiet. You're doing well.

What do you know?

You're doing well.

The roof was so close that it reflected back his own breath.

There's still air all around me. On all sides. Calm.

One leg twitched involuntarily and almost drowned him with panic. Calm. He floated again. Toes bounced against the floor. Nose nearly touched the roof.

The air is growing thick. It will turn to treacle.

Nonsense. There's plenty left.

This is not possible.

But you're doing it. Calm. Quiet.

This. Is. Not. Possible.

This. Is. Not. Possible.

Crocus vernus. Crocus neapolitanus. Pseudonarcissus. Narcissus maximus. Hyacinth of Spain. Tulipa praecox. Tulipa persica . . .

This. Is. Not. Possible.

Libera me, Domine . . .

The Great Female Peony. Dodoens Iris. The Susian Iris. Mountain Moly. Rosa centifolia. Rosa alba . . .

When the earth and heavens shall shake and tremble . . .

Then the stone roof lifted and he flew out into the night sky, circled over the sea and flew to the orchard on Hawk Ridge. The setting fruits gleamed like candles among the grey-barked spurs. Zeal and Aunt Margaret were sitting in the branches of the Lady Tree.

Waiting for me, he thought. But he couldn't make them see him. Even though he made his wings whistle like a swan's.

At least they've made friends, he thought. That's some consolation. Then he folded his wings and dived towards the inconsequential gossipy quacking among the reeds of the middle pond.

His toes touched the bottom. He had settled. He stood on the soles of his feet. He was back in the drowning cell.

Panic punched him under the breastbone. He was still in the darkness. The sea still sat on his chest.

Oh God! I didn't die! I'm still here! I can't bear this any more! I will go mad! He tried to thrash out with his arms but the water held them.

Quiet. Calm.

He felt his heels hard against the stone floor. His eyes opened wide in the darkness. His body twisted in fear. Then his eyes found the rectangle of pale light. Still only a narrow slice. But growing. Slowly, but growing.

He pressed his forehead against the top of the opening and breathed the clean air. He squeezed his eyes tight shut. But he began to cry with relief. The tide had turned. The water was going down.

'Mr Coymans?' Zeal asked directions repeatedly. 'Mr Coymans's house? Breestraat? Old Side?'

'Breestraat? Coymans?' People had pointed her onward.

Their successful crossing had filled her with triumphant strength, which faltered only briefly at the docks. Then she had met two helpful English speakers in the street, and Rachel had managed to find two boys to help carry their belongings.

Zeal stood looking up at the front door of Justus Coymans's house. John was inside that strange house, in this strange country, leading a strange life that she knew as little about as that of a New World savage. She could not believe that she was about to reach into that strangeness to tell him that his life was in danger, and that his host might be one of his enemies. The idea both excited and frightened her. She picked up her skirts and hiked briskly up the stone steps to the door.

'Careful, my lady!' Rachel cried as Zeal slipped on a wet, newly scrubbed stone step.

'Please knock,' said Zeal.

'I've come to see Mr John Nightingale,' she said firmly to the young woman who half-opened the door.

The young woman said something which Zeal couldn't understand. She began to close the door.

'Mr John Nightingale!' repeated Zeal a little more loudly. 'The Englishman. He may call himself Graffham.' She put her hand against the closing door. The young woman's black dress was so fine and she wore such glittering stones in her ears that Zeal couldn't tell whether she was addressing mistress or maid.

'The Englishman, mistress. If you please. He told me that he was staying at the house of Mr Justus Coymans.'

Another woman's voice called from inside the house. The woman at the door replied. Then she stepped back.

A second young woman came out of a door into the black and white tiled hall. This one was the mistress, no mistaking now. She wore a yellow dress and the largest, sheerest lace collar Zeal had ever seen. A collar of pearls around her long white neck. A long chain of them held a heavy gold and seed-pearl locket suspended just below the low neckline of her bodice. Another chain twined around her wrist. More pearls hung in her creamy ears, below escaping tendrils of fine blond hair.

A stupid mistake, said Zeal to herself. She wondered if the maid had noticed her uncertainty. And then she thought that her own hair must look like cheap brass next to that soft shining gold.

'Who wants John?' asked the second young woman in accented English. She seemed to glide across the checkerboard of marble squares, magnificent, golden and serene. A hobgoblin nestled in her arms. 'I'm Justus Coymans's sister. Why are you looking for John, my dear?'

Zeal stared in dismay.

'Please come in, then,' said the young woman pleasantly, but with open curiosity. 'You don't look like a raiding party. Come sit down and draw a breath, if you like, before you tell me what you want.' She spoke again in Dutch to the maid, who led Rachel away toward the back of the house.

'Is he here?' asked Zeal urgently, as the door closed behind her.

She suddenly wondered if she had been exceedingly foolish to come unprotected into this strange house, and to have let Rachel be led away like that.

'No, he's not,' said the young woman, with a sidelong look at Zeal. She led the way into what seemed to be a music room.

'But you know him?'

'Oh, yes.' The young woman smiled gently and stroked the hobgoblin, which Zeal could now see was some kind of monkey. She frowned at the monkey.

It was the 'oh' that Zeal objected to. If she looked at the young woman now, or tried to speak, she knew that she would burst into tears.

'Do you mind telling me who you are?'

Zeal gulped and breathed in. 'His cousin's wife.'

'Ah.' The young woman seemed to settle back a little more easily in her chair.

'Lady Beester,' Zeal added quickly.

'John's cousin Harry?'

Zeal nodded. 'Of Hawkridge estate. In Hampshire. In England.'

She raised her eyes and saw the painting. She stared for a long, horrified moment at the naked luxuriance of Pomona, which mirrored so exactly the magnificence that sat four feet

481

away studying her with an interest which was not entirely benign. Then she did burst into tears.

'I don't know why I'm crying,' she said angrily. She yanked her handkerchief from her sleeve and attacked her eyes. 'I'll stop, I promise. Stop immediately.'

'Would you like some ale?' asked Pomona solicitously. 'What can I send for?'

'I'm all r . . . r . . . right!' cried Zeal. 'It's John who's in danger!' Only then did she see from the puffy pinkness around her eyes that the other young woman had also been crying.

Though John couldn't see the sun, the sky had lightened. Perhaps it grew brighter. He couldn't tell. It was a steely grey that diffused light and made it impossible to see the sun. There was still deep water around his feet but he was too exhausted to measure exactly how much . . . and too cold.

'Help me!' he shouted. The permitted call. His voice disappeared into the soft grey sky as if a feather mattress were pressed against his mouth.

The cold had metamorphosed back into pain. His hands shook so hard that he could not hold onto the bars. His legs would not support him. He sat down and found himself submerged to mid-chest. And he could also no longer see out through that small square of grey light. Unless he was looking out, he did not believe that air could get in. So he hauled himself up to lean against the door, clothes stuck to his body like skin, and tried to set his mind adrift among the rills of the backwater and the feathery tops of the line of trees.

An unfamiliar bird distracted him for a time. It clung with wire-thin claws, upside down, from the gunwale of the half-sunk skiff and picked with great speed at the barnacles and algae that grew on the rotting wooden side. John watched the needle beak dart even faster than Aunt Margaret's embroidering fingers.

'No!' he cried aloud, when something he couldn't see startled it and it flipped away. He was alone again.

The water was still going down, but it would rise again.

In how many hours?

Hours didn't matter. He had no way to measure them. He couldn't see the sun.

I'm not sure what I shall do when the water begins to rise again, he thought. I don't know what is left in me.

The past night had joined his mother's bright dancing shadow among unbearable things.

I can't do it again. Not knowing beforehand what it will be. I *can't*!

But it was not his decision. Malise had decided that he must do it again.

'*I* decide what you do. Not you. You . . . insignificant have-nothing!'

The old rage solaced him for a while. Malise had won after all. I should have killed him with the fork and let his men do their best to kill me. It would have been faster. I would have plunged out of my life on a hot current of rage.

You can still dive, he told himself. But now he knew how hard that would be. He hauled his mind back and shoved it out through the bars.

Malise was using other evils to justify his own.

A wind pushed the water into sliding wrinkles that vanished behind the wall of the ledge. For a long time, John picked one wrinkle, rode it on its swift journey to obliteration, picked another, rode it, picked another.

Thought was the enemy.

Desperate hope breeds faith, he thought with irony. He had begun to talk seriously to God. He apologized for his lack of faith. The Lord had freed him from prison once before. Would He consider doing it again?

He was very thirsty. His bladder had emptied at some point into the outgoing tide.

I need a prayer buried among the roots of the Lady Tree. Let the bird come back.

The floor was nearly dry now. But instead of cheering him, it made his heart as cold as his limbs. The lower the water went, the sooner it would turn and begin to rise again.

I can't do it again!

Lord, he begged. If You won't send me freedom, send me resignation! I know I should not fear. My thoughts know that there is only a brief moment of agony before the eternal peace. Why won't my body accept?

He was getting tired of his body anyway, the way it shook and ached.

Then a new thought came to him. What if it were not his mind that balked at repeating the ordeal of the night before? What if his body refused? What if his legs buckled and let him down into the dark water? His numb hands already refused to hold fast to the bars. Who would be deciding then?

He thought he heard the scraping above his head again, but he refused to call again so soon. Hope had become too terrifying for him to admit even the possibility that someone was there.

He wished the bird would come back to the skiff.

The water worms were crawling in through the little drains again.

I think it will still be light this time, he thought. Even through the water, I should see at least a little light.

He staggered slightly and caught himself. He decided to sit for just a little while, while the water was still low. If he shut his eyes, it didn't matter that he wasn't looking out.

How odd that I haven't felt hungry, he thought. Perhaps my body knows that there is no further need.

He hugged his wavering knees together and dropped his

forehead against them. His forehead knew, but his kneecaps felt nothing.

Honey, he thought. Honey on hot bread. And an apple. An apricot warmed in the sun . . .

He jerked awake. Water washed around his buttocks and lapped at his spine. He jolted to his feet, setting off waves that slapped against the stone walls. Leaned on the door, braced his legs straight so that his muscles need do no work. They couldn't.

He heard scraping again.

He couldn't stop himself. 'Is someone there?'

'Don't worry,' said Malise's voice. 'It's only me. I'll stay with you to the end. You won't be alone.'

Please let me out! screamed the animal in the trap. 'You'll have a long wait,' John managed to say.

'Not as long as all that. The next tide will be higher than the last.'

'Brandy?' asked Malise's voice a little later. 'I imagine it's fairly cold in there. Are you sure you wouldn't like a little brandy? It's only Dutch, I'm afraid.' He seemed to have lost his desire to confide.

The water had reached John's ankles again.

If he never spoke again, Malise would never know when he had finally died. John would cheat him of that moment.

'Help me!' he called. His last permitted cry. The last messenger dove flew out across the flood. Now he would be silent.

John leaned on the door and closed his eyes. It amused him that Malise's presence seemed to make dying easier. It tied all those flapping, terrified pieces of himself back together. He did not think that Malise would enjoy the joke.

Malise wanted pleas and gurgling. Apologies and repentance.

Silence and dignity.

On my own terms.

'Are you sure there's nothing you would like?' asked Malise's voice, now sounding faint and slightly ridiculous.

John closed it out.

Not long until it reaches my knees.

The scraping means nothing any more.

John closed it out, along with the imagined voices. His body had begun to shake in truth. His jaw rattled. His bones crashed against each other. Not long before his mind would no longer hold him up. Soon, he would fall and ease under the surface. Time slid through him like water between banks.

There was a scream from the burning coach.

John opened his eyes. A man somersaulted slowly across the square of grey light. While John's jaw banged twice against his upper teeth, the man bounced on the ledge and crashed onto the stern of the half-sunk skiff. A monkey wearing a red jacket screamed again and vaulted from Malise's shoulders back up onto the ledge.

'Let me! Let me!' A woman's urgent voice.

John watched with puzzled interest from very far away.

There was more scraping above his head and a scrabbling and tumbling of clods from the direction of the sea wall on his right. Someone came out along the ledge.

'Oh God, open!' the voice begged. 'Please *open*!'

Another shape tussled with the first outside the door.

'Stop pushing on the door, sir,' said Arthur. 'We can't move the bar if you're leaning on it!'

John fell back against the rear wall and slid helplessly down it onto his heels. Cold water washed him to his nipples. The voices blurred. He was getting into his bed, smelled the musty leather of the headboard.

My candle blew out by mistake. He shrugged. He did not mind the dark.

'It's the water!' said Arthur's voice. 'The bleeding, cursed water, still pushing on the inside!' He sounded close to tears. 'Come on, come on, come *on*!'

'Like this!' said the woman's voice.

John leaned against the wall, hands clenched against his rattling teeth. 'Thank you, Arthur. That's all for tonight.'

The door opened with the sound of ripping silk. The water inside the cell gushed out onto the ledge. But Zeal flooded into the cell with far greater force.

John laughed. Where's Aunt Margaret? Did you both fly here from the branches of the Lady Tree?

He felt her hands, her arms. He clutched at her. She was warm. I've begun to die, a part of his brain said. I've travelled too far from wherever I was, a few minutes ago.

He was too tired to fight the arms that pulled him away. So many arms. Warm. And faces. It's all right, Arthur . . . Zeal. You can't come. A man dies alone. I can't take you too.

He stumbled through space. Not how I expected it to be. Wish I could tell Dr Bowler how the final darkness . . .

'John! John! Oh, John!' She rocked him to and fro, holding tight as if she could quell his shaking. 'Poor, poor John!' she crooned. 'Come back, please. Come back!'

'He's breathing,' said Arthur.

'He's all right,' said Zeal sharply. 'He's going to be all right!'

John turned his face against her breast. He had been bound. He tried to struggle.

'Steady, sir,' said Arthur. 'We're trying to get you warm again.'

John opened his eyes. Zeal's face hung over his.

He woke again. He was lying on the floor with his head on Zeal's lap. She nursed one of his hands as if it were a kitten. 'He's awake!' she exclaimed.

John looked up into the grey-blue eyes. They looked very far away, yet her waist warmed his cheek.

The floor rocked violently under him. John turned his head and saw Marika balancing, with an oar in her hand as a boatman helped her over the gunwale of the sailing barge.

'How are you, sir?' asked Arthur.

There was another puzzle. Where had his man come from? John closed his eyes again. He had also imagined Zeal and Aunt Margaret sitting in the Lady Tree. His whole body was so numb that he no longer felt the water.

'You're going to be all right,' said Zeal. 'Aren't you, John?'

He felt her hand tighten on his. A piece of lace on her bodice scratched his ear. He was lying down. There was no water. The bindings that tied his legs were a dry cloak.

He jolted back to full waking. Zeal's eyes were still above him. The lace still scratched his ear. Her hands were still warm around his. Strands of red-blond hair were glued to her cheeks with damp, like the fuzz of a newly hatched duckling.

'When you ask like that, I wouldn't dare be anything else,' John said indistinctly.

'He's fine,' said Arthur with relief.

John stared in amazement. He had been stripped and wrapped in dry cloaks, comfortably laid on the bottom of Coymans's little sailing barge. Arthur and Zeal sat beside him. Rachel stared at him from behind them. Marika sat on a bench watching them all with her pensive, what-next stillness. The high banks whirled and steadied on either side.

The barge rocked again as the bargee raised the rusty red sail. It flapped and bellied. The wind was behind, the banks slid by amazingly fast. The bargee whistled between his teeth and looked over all their heads.

John let his head fall back again. He would get it all sorted in his mind in time.

It had not been yet. He had been right not to dive.

He pushed away the memory of how close he had come.

'I think I knew you were coming,' he said to Zeal. 'I must have known.'

'Go to sleep.' She raised his hand to her lips then replaced it like a kitten in her lap.

John heard the new possessive authority in her voice and obeyed.

Seventeen

Coymans's house was an empty shell. Their footsteps bounced crisply off the marble floor of the hall. The walls of the hall were bare of paintings, except for Coymans *père*.

Marika led them into the music room. John, now wearing Arthur's best breeches, stood and stared. The rugs gone from tables. Most of the tables gone. Virginal still there. Chitarrone gone. Disordered music and her chair, only the kernel of Marika's life remained in the emptiness. A single maid seemed to be the only servant left. Erasmus paced along one wall as if counting the baseboard tiles.

'Where is Justus?' asked John. He had to explain their danger to Zeal and leave at once. He looked at Arthur.

'Justus is gone,' said Marika.

'Where?'

'Oh, I wouldn't tell you if I knew.' Marika leaned over the virginal and played a chord. 'How could I?' She played the chord again. 'Your little Marrano friend Gomez brought the bailiffs. They were so cross at missing Justus that they took everything else. I made them leave me this . . . and my bed. I said it was mine, not his.' She played the highest note, thin, watery, almost unheard, a tiny, high, cricket click.

'You mean, Justus won't be back?'

'You've seen to that, haven't you? You and Gomez. Justus said you would ruin him.' John could not tell if she were angry.

'He's fled?'

Marika nodded.

She knows, but how much?

'And in spite of everything, it seems that I owe you my life.'

'Not entirely,' said Marika. 'Your cousin's little wife spurred me on. And she wanted the best fun for herself.'

'But the real thanks is to *her*,' interrupted Zeal. She had decided on the barge to ignore all possibilities about Marika Coymans except what she could see. What she ignored didn't exist. What didn't exist could do no harm. 'She arranged the boat and knew where to find you.'

John shot a look at Marika.

Choose what you want to think, said her eyes. I won't make it easy for you. You decide.

'I don't know what we would have done without her,' said Zeal. She decided that she was now overdoing it and closed her mouth abruptly. Her flush began to rise from her collar toward her ears.

Arthur came to her rescue. 'Master Malise was so surprised to see two gentlewomen sailing toward him with picnic baskets and pets that he never suspected a thing till Lady Beester hit him.'

'Till Lady Beester hit him' . . . John heard and would return to that idea. But now he felt a jolt of alarm. 'Where's Malise now? I forgot about him.' Improbable but true in that wonderful fog of his rescue.

Marika shrugged. 'We left him where he fell, draped over that rotting skiff. His men weren't far off, in his boat. They may have saved him from drowning.'

'You let him *go*?'

'What did you want me to do?' Marika suddenly grew angry. 'With Justus gone? Edward didn't kill you after all. I must save what I can for myself. *Sauve qui peut*. Go back to England and fight your own battles there – don't ask me to do any more than I have already done!'

* * *

Zeal listened to John and Marika and pretended she was not terrified by whatever might happen next. John was alive. She had thought the story would end there. Now she was waiting while it seemed to be starting all over again. She could no longer reach out for him as she had in the boat, while he was half-dead. This man was too much alive again, beginning to take charge, thinking thoughts she could not imagine.

She glanced sideways at the picture of Pomona. Then she saw John look at it too. She walked to the window and pretended to be fascinated by the blur outside. She thought she might scream.

After so many impossibilities not found in any of her books – the voyage from London, finding Marika. Meeting Arthur in the street outside Coymans's house, where he had been keeping watch ever since John had disappeared. Then finding John, hitting Malise with the oar, hauling John out of that wet stone coffin. She had been a giantess, a tree in a storm, the storm itself. Now that she was safely back, and John with her, in a civilized if empty house, not ten minutes from a boat that would take them back to England, she thought that her entire being might fly apart into little pieces. Zeal stared out of the window down into the street. She could not make herself turn round to watch John and that woman.

'How did you know where to find me?'

Marika stared at him defiantly. 'Edward stayed here the night you spent in the *torresluis*. I asked him where he had gone that day – you and I sailed near there once. Justus had told him that you had quarrelled with us, and he was jealous enough to want me to know that he had beaten you. I figured the rest.'

Put together with what you knew from your brother.

Zeal decided that she had better turn round. No point in hiding from what you don't want to know. Get it over with.

Anyway, she could no longer deny the familiarity in their two voices. She turned. John and Marika were standing farther apart than she had expected. Their faces looked tight and desperate and a little reckless, like men's when they are about to fight. Zeal didn't know whether this was good or not.

'When Justus told you that I would ruin him, did he tell you that he had already ruined me?' John held himself still as a hawk on the wind.

Marika watched Erasmus turn tail-up inside the virginal case. She seemed to count the pearls on the ropes around her wrist. Then she turned and left the room without speaking. Erasmus shrieked and scuttled after her.

No one moved or spoke after she left. Arthur watched John look after Marika. Rachel watched both men, but gave her mistress a quick, anxious glance.

Life is about to change yet again, thought Zeal in terror. And I can't make it stop. I thought I had stopped it when I married Harry, and now look where I am!

Marika came back into the music room with a small leather-covered portfolio, which she laid on the bare top of a table not worth the bailiffs' time to shift. She turned over the contents, a few pages at a time. Sepia pen and ink studies of seashells. John recognized two as specimens he had left for Zeal in his cabinet at Hawkridge House. Some densely black engravings. Several letters.

Marika gave him Jacov Fernandez's letters of exchange.

John exclaimed and went white.

'Justus left so suddenly,' Marika said. 'He rather forgot to arrange how I would live when he had gone ... Or didn't get the chance.'

'Marika ...' John began.

'Fortunately, I had thought it best to hide a few things, just in case,' she cut in brightly. 'Before the carrion crows arrived to begin their search. I was able to hide these on my person.

So I kept them as well as the virginal. Justus left so abruptly, when he heard that Gomez was on the way with bailiffs, that he forgot to ask me for these, and one or two other things that are none of your business.'

She gave him the stolen bonds of exchange. All of the King's money. Most of the South Java Company profits. Only the value of the chest contents was missing.

'How did you know your brother had these letters?' John asked hoarsely.

'He told me the night . . .' Marika glanced at Zeal's averted face. 'He told me the night that you and he quarrelled so badly. I think he rather took my loyalty for granted at that point.' She rolled her eyes mockingly. 'He thought it might amuse me to learn what a fool he had made of you. The same mistake Edward made.' She pulled herself back from the first hint of hysteria. 'I had already wondered why Edward suddenly came back again from England when he had so recently left, close on your heels, burning with purpose and swearing me to secrecy. I didn't know anything more . . . what he wanted . . . what the two of them had planned . . . your money for my brother and you for Malise . . . that man dead. I waited . . . Then you disappeared and little Lady Beester arrived.' She begged him to believe her.

John said nothing.

'I did not love Edward Malise.'

To Zeal's horror, John stepped forward, lifted Marika's hand and kissed it. Then he took her face in both hands and kissed her hard on the mouth.

'You *are* an angel!' he said. 'And I'll kill anyone who says otherwise. Please forgive me if I have sounded ungrateful. I'm still not quite myself. You have been braver and more generous than I deserve.'

'You don't deserve either of us,' said Marika, looking at Zeal. She half-turned away from John, holding out her arms. Erasmus flung himself from the top of the virginal and neatly looped his black paws around her neck. His tail lapped around her arm like an Egyptian bracelet.

'I think I shall marry Saski,' said Marika. She bent her head to kiss the monkey's head. 'I shall be his model. Upset my neighbours further with my wickedness. Do something useful. At least he always tells the truth.'

'How is he?' asked John after a pause.

'Also still alive.'

Marika's plan for Saski gave Zeal the courage at last to move forward into the conversation.

'Now that we're not so excited by just having done it, I want to thank you again!'

Marika eyed her, not unkindly. 'And now that we've saved this man Nightingale, what are you going to do with him?'

'Do?' asked Zeal. 'Do?' She stared at Marika in confusion. 'Oh Lord!' she said angrily as the purple flush climbed once more from her lace collar toward her earlobes. 'I don't know!'

At which Marika began to laugh.

On the sailing barge back to England, Zeal decided that if Hell were worse than being alive, she would reconsider her childish defiance of damnation. What had she known then, at thirteen, about anything? This was real damnation, in this world, not the next.

She leaned on the rail and let the wind bring tears into her eyes. She could remember how she had felt, back in Marika's sailing barge, still Boadicea, Hippolyta, a giantess filled with the power of a tidal wave, who had swung the oar against Edward Malise's head. That woman had cradled John's head in her lap and looked ahead along an infinity of canal that carried them like an arrow toward the edge of the world.

This boat carried them back to London and to her husband, Harry. Zeal braced her elbows on the rail and dropped her head into her palms. She watched the water curve away from the side of the boat. She had saved John and lost herself. He had become hers. She would never love anyone but John, in the whole rest of her life. She felt older than Aunt Margaret.

She leaned a little farther, to look straight down at the dark line where the water slipped up from under the boat's weight.

Marika had known what Zeal felt, and had laughed as if at a most amusing joke.

The boat spun frothing crystal lines that opened wider and wider behind the barge until they disappeared. If she leaned a little farther, she could fall and ride one of those lines toward the horizon that the Dutch canal had never reached.

Harry had wanted John to die. He wanted Zeal to die, even if he wouldn't admit to either wish. She leaned a little farther.

Wicked, even to think of falling.

But I'm already past wickedness, loving someone besides Harry. And what's more, I don't care!

I'll never love Harry, no matter how hard I try, duty or not. She dropped her forehead onto the rail and drew a shuddering breath. How many years would she have to endure his prodding between her legs and ramming his slimy tongue into her mouth? How many little Harrys would swell her body as her sister had swollen, then tear it apart?

She raised herself up with purpose and looked at the water.

John had been watching her from the stern. He had avoided her after they embarked, as she had seemed to avoid him. He was still too weary to unravel the complex knots in the bumpy strands of their conversation. His body needed to recover. His feelings were disordered and bruised.

He had gone to the dark boundary, gazed across and, to his surprise, returned. He felt that he should have died. His survival distorted the smooth unrolling of time, as if he were a bulge of undigested frog in the belly of a snake. He felt both raw and precious, an unset gem. A gift to himself. Unbelieving, joyful, but a little puzzled and stilled.

However, above that deep, still level in which he was re-entering his life with a sense of surprise, he was tossed on choppy waves. He had made, lost, and recovered an incomprehensible amount of money. He would almost certainly, therefore, earn the royal pardon on which his future life depended. He should rejoice.

On the other hand, he owed much of his success to an amoral murderer (who also took pride in being a patron of art). Other investors had lost so that John could win. Spiegel was dead. Bols was dead, and his granddaughter's field in full blow had been smashed to a sticky, rotting pulp. Even if John's infant *King of Kandy* one day multiplied to cover a field, he would never again feel the pure elation that he and Bols had shared as the wind shivered the gold dust of petals to the ground and bent the tulips into waves like the sea.

Part of my mind will always count both the value and the cost. That rare part of life not ruled by need is now tainted. Coymans's fun had destroyed pure pointless joy.

On the deck of the London sailing barge, John felt the sense of repentance which had eluded him in prison after killing Francis Malise. Now he wanted deeds undone and knowledge ungained.

He watched Zeal following the boat's wake with her eyes.

He had almost certainly been betrayed by his cousin Harry, whom he had trusted to be no more than a harmless fool. Edward Malise was very likely still alive and God knows where, cheated of his lusts yet again and with Marika as a new grievance. Though his avenging devil had turned into a mere bitter and disappointed man, John felt foreboding. Their tale – his and Malise's – was too ancient and too profound merely to stop in mid-phrase.

Perhaps I was saved in order to play out our story.

John's black brows pulled together as Zeal leaned over the rail and looked down intently as if counting fish.

John had been either saved or betrayed by Marika, or both. He most certainly owed his life to Zeal.

How can I begin to know what I feel?

Amongst all those complexities, he had scanted the joy that he should have felt at Gomez's news that the VOC ship had at last been sighted off Portugal. It mattered little that Gomez would arrange for his cousin in London to pay John the profits on his shares in indigo and saltpetre, ten times more than he had paid. Wealth felt less significant than he had imagined it would. Nevertheless, he would enjoy telling Zeal of her windfall when it finally arrived.

He did know that he felt deep, deep gratitude to that small, tense figure on the forward deck, wrapped in a cloak, daring the wind to drive it below decks, but she also angered him. He was angry that he wanted so badly to be standing beside her with her shoulder warm against his, angry that he must take her back to Harry, angry that she was so clearly miserable and there was nothing he could properly do or say to cheer her.

When she leaned farther over the rail, he moved forward, around the roof of the cargo hold. She might slip. The boat might hit a large wave and tip her over.

He felt angry that it would not be his business to feel responsible for her once they docked in London.

When she dropped her forehead onto the rail in open despair, John was behind her across the narrow width of the boat. He saw the nape of her neck, as fine and fragile as that of a dove, and the fine bumps of her spine. Her knot of red-gold hair had slipped sideways, as usual. Golden wires blew in a corona around her bent head.

What an oddly contradictory little body for such an energetic soul, thought John. In spite of Marika's greater height and breadth of shoulder, he had never questioned the fact that Zeal had swung the oar. It twisted his heart to see her so quelled.

He had guilty memories of the sailing barge, barely half-conscious but awake enough to luxuriate in her care. He had turned his cheek firmly against her breasts, which were softer and fuller than he had realized. With difficulty, he had refrained from nuzzling them. She was no longer the child she had been in the orchard, or even, still, on the steps of the porch that night.

He remembered his tweaking of lust when he had looked up the length of her slim bare thighs high in the apple tree. Already a married woman, even then. Best to stay here, safely across the width of the deck.

When Zeal suddenly straightened with resolve, he was jolted into a run. She twisted in terror as he grabbed her.

'Don't!' he shouted in rage. 'Don't you dare!'

'It's you!' She dived into the cover of his cloak. He refolded it around her. After a moment, her muffled voice asked, 'What did you think I was going to do?'

'Jump.'

She was quiet against his chest. 'Just pretending. I think.'

'Don't ever be so stupid!' He still sounded enraged.

There was another pause. Then, 'If you say so.'

She felt as warm, fragile and tough against him under his cloak as a young hawk. He kept his hands locked on the back of her waist when they ached to creep down to find her young buttocks through her skirts. There were things Marika had taught him . . . He should step back, let her go.

'May I stay in here?' the muffled voice asked. 'For a while?'

'Of course.' He tightened his arms.

After a moment he bent and kissed the top of her hair, which was all he could see.

She had begun to shiver. 'I'm getting sick,' she said. 'Maybe I shall die without trying.'

'I think we should agree not to die, either of us, without the other's permission.'

That brought her up for air, smiling a little. She turned and leaned her back against his chest. Her shivering eased. For a long time they both looked out at the wide, flat, grey water and overcast sky.

'Perhaps there will be rain in England, at last,' said John.

Zeal giggled. 'And perhaps it will be fine in Spain.'

He smiled. He kissed the top of her head again.

She went very still. 'John?'

'Yes?'

'We are in between.'

'What do you mean?'

'In between two real lives. We're not really in anything, or anywhere.'

He was startled that she felt the same side-step in time. 'And so?'

She twisted in his arms, making a great coil of wool and silk. She held up her face.

His thoughts were still trying to arrange themselves into acceptable excuses as he kissed her. She kissed him back with her entire being. She kissed his chin.

'You're scratchy,' she said with delight.

John groaned. His rawness had no protection against her. She put her fingers on his mouth. 'Don't say the right thing. I *know*! I'm just pretending again.' Her fingers slipped between his lips.

He closed his eyes and tasted her fingers. He took them in his mouth.

Zeal whimpered. She was trembling, staring at him wide-eyed.

'That's enough, now,' said John roughly. Or he would take her right here on the deck. 'I'm sorry.' He turned her to face the sea, bent her head forward with one hand and kissed her nape. He sniffed at the scent of her skin and hair. Then again, more loudly, like Cassie, to try to turn it all into a joke. She laughed a little, acknowledging his effort. Then he pulled her back to lean against him again.

I'll suffer for this, he thought. We'll both suffer. But I don't care and I want to think that she decided not to care either. Meanwhile, she was right. His next life could wait to begin at the London docks, in far too short a time.

🙵

Secretly, Harry knew that when he shook hands with Malise he had opened the way to more mischief than either he or Malise was admitting at the time.

A murderer should stand trial, he repeated to himself more than once after Malise had left. Even if he is one's own cousin.

Malise's departure for the Netherlands did not free Harry's mind for other matters. On the contrary, it left him in a state of miserable expectation, besieged, waiting for the outcome of a distant battle.

I would sin in the eyes of God if I protected a man merely because he is my own family.

However, this virtuous thought brought no virtuous glow to his cheeks, nor did it straighten his shoulders with pride in his own worthiness.

John never asked me to help him, he thought unhappily. If only he had sworn me to secrecy, and begged me to help smuggle him abroad. Then I would have refused to forswear myself . . . even at the risk of my own damnation.

Harry imagined magnanimously giving John a heavy purse, a good horse, and a concerned, familial, farewell blessing. John then rode away up the curving drive between the beeches with a bowed head. In Harry's mind, it was raining.

But he's too stiff-necked. Too cocksure. Didn't need my help. Despised my extended hand. (Harry remembered yet again his handsome offer on the day of his first arrival, to let John stay on and run Hawkridge estate. And John's ungrateful, almost lunatic outburst in recompense.)

If only he ... but I should not have allied myself with Malise.

The thought kept returning to Harry at the most inconvenient times. It clove through his other thoughts like an arrow. It even caused him, well before time, to roll off from on top of a London widow who was richer than Zeal had been before Harry spent her money. Two days later, Zeal saved him from seriously beginning to dislike himself, by her escape.

He had come back late that night and did not realize she was gone until the following morning when a housegroom brought him her letter with his morning ale. The letter held nothing more than the bare facts of what she intended. No apologies. No sign that it had crossed her mind that a man might not want his wife to go haring off to foreign countries in search of another man, even his own cousin. Not a whisper that she owed her husband respect, obedience and consultation on all her conduct. No indication that she had even considered that he might not want her back after such a trick. She even had the effrontery to tell him not to be concerned.

Indignation, humiliation, fear and disbelief came to Harry's rescue. His guilty misery was translated into incoherent rage.

What did a little chitty-face like that know about buying passage abroad, and going about in a foreign city? What gave her the arrogance even to think that she could?

And she had gulled him out of the money to do it! Made a fool of him, again!

The shame and horror of it made Harry curl up in bed like an unhappy five-year-old. Only his fierce search for words vile enough to describe her – minx, cockatrice, deceiving cunny, harridan, liar, trollop, trull, cheat, rig, quean, swindler – kept him from arriving at several small, cold truths which would have made him burst into tears.

I'll go after her! he decided. By God, I'll thump some sense into her and then lock her up for the next ten years! If she hadn't drowned or been murdered first.

Instead, he rose and was dressed and pretended to go about his normal daily business. His friends and acquaintances mentioned, *entre eux-mêmes*, that Sir Harry was not himself. As none of them was used to seeing his young wife in society, the servants were whispering long before the masters.

I'll go and warn John myself, thought Harry while applauding the actors in a play whose title he had already forgotten.

I'll go and kill the pair of them. He raised his glass to someone or other in a toast.

I'll . . .

When his wife and cousin walked through the door of his London house, both alive, five days later just as he was rising late, Harry nearly buckled at the knees with relief. Then, quite naturally, he again became incoherent with rage.

'And what explanation can you give me, mistress?'

John was clearly still at large and alive. Harry hadn't done anything wrong after all. He had made himself suffer excruciating guilt and fear for no good reason.

'Get out!' he shouted to Zeal's maid, his cousin's man-servant and other servants who hovered to see the new arrivals for themselves, agog to hear Harry's greetings to his runaway wife.

'Wait, Rachel. Please take my cloak.' Zeal gazed up at him with distant politeness. 'Do I owe you an explanation, Harry?' she asked coolly. Before he could find the aplomb to slap her for this impudence, she continued just as coolly. 'If you must know, I was undoing your wickedness.'

Harry staggered mentally but attempted a recovery. 'You're the wicked one! To go . . .'

'Harry!' Zeal's eyes burned with an urgent warning to shut his mouth.

To his own surprise, Harry did.

'I came here only to see your wife safely back to her house.'

Harry turned, vibrant with a new alarm. John looked past him, over his shoulder.

'Safe!' exclaimed Harry. 'And what part did you play in this, coz?'

'Not a noble one. However, I owe my life to your wife.' John turned away to Zeal. 'I'll go to Sir George's house now. Send if you need me, my lady.'

'Oh no you don't!' said Harry recklessly. 'You stay right here!' He would not be dismissed, for whatever reason. 'I demand that you tell me what the devil happened over there.'

John looked directly at his cousin this time. 'Better than I deserved or you intended.'

Harry tried to stare defiantly back, but he felt the marrow of his bones shrivel under the cold force of those direct grey eyes.

When John had left, Harry gathered himself to attack again. 'You both treated me as if I were party to some outrage,' said Harry. 'I have a right to know what you're blaming me for!'

'You already know.'

Zeal stood, eyes down, hands clenched against the front of her skirts. The familiar posture misled Harry.

'If I do, why am I asking?' His indignation sounded genuine.

She raised her head and told him in detail what Malise had done. 'I haven't betrayed you to John,' she said. 'Nor will I. But I think he already knows. He's no fool.' She gave Harry a look of pure contempt.

Harry collapsed heavily on a window seat. 'You had no right to eavesdrop on Malise and me,' he protested feebly. Among other things, he had noted the proprietary tone with which his wife's voice had caressed his cousin's name.

'I'm going to pack now,' she said. 'To go back to Hawkridge House.'

I should forbid her to leave London without my permission,

thought Harry. 'I'm going out,' he said abruptly. His brain wouldn't take any more buffeting. Things needed to be thought about, but not today. Not tonight. Harry intended to become splendidly drunk.

He came home at four o'clock in the morning, slept until noon and was almost relieved to find that Zeal had already gone by the time he rose for dinner the next day.

The day, if not his mood, then improved with the news of the Company's good fortune at his cousin's hands. And the shame of being related to an outlaw was lifted with the news (from Sir George Tupper) that his cousin would have a Royal pardon in gratitude for something or other he had done. The *Boston Maid* was safely past the Canaries on her way home. Harry would be a rich man yet, said Hazelton. There's hope for us all.

Harry smiled and raised his glass with the other celebrants. Where pleasure should have been tickling his innards, he had a cold, heavy lump.

The next day he woke early and could not get to sleep again. He grunted morosely at the barber who helped him waste the morning and decided he was not in a mood to walk in St James's Park that afternoon. He thought he might go out later to admire the new big houses in Covent Garden, where he might buy a house himself when the cargo of the *Boston Maid* had been sold.

But he could not seem to begin anything. As a result he was still at home after dinner, when a mounted messenger clattered into the street. Harry barely had time to peer in half-hearted interest from the window before he realized that the horse had stopped in front of his house and someone was pounding on his door.

When the man had left and he was alone again, Harry finally put his head into his hands and cried.

John had spotted the messenger outside the Thameside inn where they ate at midday and recognized him as a Hawkridge cowman who often won the horse races on feast days. The man's horse heaved and frothed as if it had just completed a rigorous course.

'Tom!' John called. 'Tom Thresher!'

Thresher stared, then recognized John and kicked his horse toward them.

'Tom, what the devil are you doing so far from home?' John was half-prepared for bad news by the time the man reached them, where they were preparing to mount their horses to continue to Hawkridge House by road.

'Well met, sir!' Thresher cried, brimming with horror and importance. 'I was on my way to London to Sir Harry. Thank the Lord, you're going back! Hawkridge House is burning!'

Zeal gave a small moan. 'Is anyone hurt?' she croaked.

The man shook his head. 'Not so far as I know, but it was a right shambles when I set off. Screaming and shouting and all that smoke . . .'

'When did it start?' asked John.

'This morning, before sunrise sometime.'

'Any sign of how it started?'

'Don't know, sir. Tuddenham sent me straight off. I alerted Sir Richard on my way.' The man shook his head as if only now believing his own tale.

'Lady Beester and I will ride ahead. Arthur, you and Rachel follow on with the cart.' John looked at Arthur's face. 'There'll still be plenty for you to do when you get there, I've no doubt,' he said grimly.

John and Zeal set off at once, followed by a mounted groom leading a pack horse. The spring mud had baked sharp and hard into ridges and ruts. When they couldn't ride on the verges, they had to pick their way or else cripple the horses. Whenever they hit a rare smooth stretch, they cantered.

An autumnal smokiness filled the clearings among the trees, seeped into the green tunnels that arched over the road, and thickened the hazy dusk. A heavy lid of dark cloud pressed down on the smoke.

Zeal sniffed and looked at John with anguish in her eyes.

'We're too far away still,' said John. 'That's burning stubble or charcoal furnaces. Don't imagine the worst. It may be better than we fear. From the look of that sky and the dampness in the air, they may even have had rain at last.'

They rode without stopping for supper. Even so, they arrived after sundown.

They smelled the fire before they saw it, sharper and stronger than burning stubble or charcoal furnaces. John leaned forward in his saddle, squinting into the dusk. They guided their horses even faster along the fossilized wreckage of the spring rains. Then they saw the glow through the trees where no light should be.

John kicked his horse into a groaning canter, Zeal's horse beside him. They careered into the top of the beech avenue and reined in abruptly, frozen with horror and a kind of awe. John's hair stood on end.

The roof of the house had already gone. Red eyes glowed where windows had been. Fiery Medusa snakes twisted and flickered behind the walls. The orange-red furnace of her heart made the air quiver like rippling silk. A ravenous marvel from Hell was gnawing at her.

The chapel still stands, John told himself numbly. Thank God, there's no wind! His heart was trying to beat its way out of his ribs. And the barns are still there.

He could not move.

'No!' screamed Zeal in a rage. She kicked her exhausted horse forward down the avenue.

The fire's first rage of hunger had subsided. It burned steadily. Dark silhouettes crossed and recrossed the hot backlighting of the fire. Beyond the west wing, crumpled balls of sparks lay like fallen fireworks along the *allée*.

The hornbeams, thought John with a fresh wrench of pain.

He was falling, in a halo of flames. He watched a piece of fire detach itself and wheel gracefully through the air like a drunken comet towards the brewhouse roof. He was falling off his horse. He grabbed at the pommel to steady himself.

Zeal's horse scudded along the dirt of the drive.

John saw the firelit shapes of men on the chapel roof. With a dry mouth, the seven-year-old boy watched the fiery angel shadow of his mother dance. He fell through darkness, a claw of flame clamped tightly around his head. He gripped onto the saddle with knees and hands. He could not bear to fall again. There was no act of will, as in the drowning cell. John did not decide, he had no choice. Terrified or not, he could not accept this new monster. He kicked his horse down the drive after Zeal.

Sir Richard Balhatchet was there with his estate workers. Aunt Margaret, in a frenzy of organization. And Tuddenham, exhausted. And the manager and workers from the Winching estate. 'John!' cried Aunt Margaret, suddenly spying him. 'Thank God . . . !' Her relief implied that he could somehow change things.

He embraced her and looked over her shoulder at the darting silhouettes. 'Dr Bowler?'

'Back by the ponds. I told him not to try to heave buckets about at his age, but he paid no attention! And Will Pike's passed out from the smoke.'

'I've got three more lines at the back,' said Tuddenham flatly. 'Using the ponds.' He had gone far beyond the limits of his strength in the last six hours.

The noise was deafening. Under the roar of the fire, an irregular drum beat somewhere deep in its core. Voices shouted urgent directions through the orange-lit darkness. A beam fell with a crash.

Those are shouts, not screams, John told himself.

'I'm sorry, sir,' said Tuddenham at his side. 'I'm so sorry. I thought we might save the house. With so many helping, and water at hand, and the still air all day, and the promise of rain, I really thought we might!' He stared with bleak disbelief into the dying rage of flames. 'But everything's still so dry. You should have seen it at midday! Nobody could get near. I had to order the men back. I had to!'

'Of course,' said John. 'You did right.' Tuddenham, too, expected him to take charge.

A line of weary men and women passed horse-buckets of water from the garden pumps to the corner where the chapel joined the main building. John saw the splashes of water explode and vanish in the heat.

Behind the furor he heard the screams of horses, safe so far in the barns, but terrified by the smell of the fire. Tuddenham had already gone. He grabbed a passing groom by the arm. 'Turn the horses out into the pastures,' he heard himself saying. Then, in sudden horror, 'Where are the dogs from the yard?'

'Up there.'

The children huddled high up near the top of the beech avenue, shepherded by two old women. Some slept, wrapped in robes. The large shape of Cassie sat alert, but quiet, in front of them. Near her a pair of pups rolled downhill locked together in friendly battle.

John stood for a moment, a still point in the frenzy. The house was past saving. The chapel was still in God's hands.

John turned his head like a stag feeling for danger. His face found the breath of wind from the north-west. It was rising, perhaps bringing the rain that had been lying heavily on the air all day. But first it would carry the fire. The beast in the fire seemed to shift and rouse itself a little. The barns were probably distant enough to be safe, unless sparks began to blow. The brewhouse was more at risk, just across the little Knot Garden. At that moment, another comet detached itself and spun gracefully toward the brewhouse and barns.

John ran across the forecourt to the front end of the west wing. The heat was too intense to follow the *allée* through the smouldering hornbeams. He climbed the wall into Roman Field and circled round to the back of the house near the dovecote.

Three chains of men and women passed buckets of water from the ponds to the fire, inadvertently frying the odd fish. They moved slowly from exhaustion, but with a numb stubbornness that denied the futility of their effort, which could only dampen the very edges of the buildings. The savage heat forced the men and women nearest the house to retreat and wet down their smouldering clothes before they pressed forward again.

'Dr Bowler?' called John. He searched the bucket lines, but the parson was not there.

'All of you . . . William, Will, Tom, Peg . . .' John diverted one bucket line. 'Go around and start wetting the barns and the brewhouse! Set ladders and put men on the roofs. Get buckets up to them. The house is gone. We must save the outbuildings!'

Smoke-reddened eyes stared at him. John suddenly smelled toasting cheese.

'Save the brewhouse and barns! The hay and corn stores. Or man and beast will starve this winter. You . . . you . . . you . . . and you. Start wetting down the grain stores. You . . . The rest keep on here. Do what you can to save the laundry and dairy.'

John stared briefly in through the *basse-court* gate. The red eyes glared from the back wall of the house. The dog yard roof, the stillroom, laundry and dairy had not yet caught, thanks to the bucket chains from the ponds. They might survive. The rising wind would push the fire towards the front of the house. A holly tree set in a pot outside the dining chamber suddenly ignited and flared like a torch. The heat made the skin on his face smart and drew it tight across the bones.

He continued on around the house into the gardens through the pond gate. '*Dr Bowler!*'

Bowler was in the Knot Garden under a hail of ash and sparks, passing buckets of water through a smashed window of the chapel. A chain of coughing, gasping men passed buckets up a ladder. The top man emptied the water between a gap in the crenellations.

'Get everyone off that roof!' shouted John. 'And whoever is inside must come out! The wind is rising.'

The parson looked at him with blank recognition, as if John had just returned from a short stroll to catch him in the middle of struggling to compose a sermon. 'We're fine. We're fine here. Everyone's off the roof. Don't worry, John!' His wild eyes and frantic, uninterrupted slinging of the heavy buckets belied his apparent calm.

John was distracted by a shout from the brewhouse. The slight wind was rising a little more. The heart of the fire beat a little more quickly inside the shells of the walls. Sparks and misguided comets had begun to arrive in thick showers on the roof around the belltower.

That's enough, John screamed silently to the devil in the fire. You've already had enough!

He climbed the nearest ladder and joined the men on the roof, beating and stamping, filled with an ecstatic indignation. Though the roof was steeply sloped, he moved with the invincible, unrushed calm of an avenging angel. The sparks from Hell died under his feet, his jacket, his bare hands. He shouted, pointing out the enemy to his fellows.

You won't take this! he yelled to the beast. You won't take the rest!

Even here, across the little Knot Garden, the heat from the main fire was intense.

'Stop!' John slapped out a small fire on the arm of another man's shirt. He sucked painfully at the murky air.

How long will it burn? How long must we keep this up?

The sky was too dark with smoke for him to judge the clouds. Then a gust of wind blew the smoke from the main fire directly toward the brewhouse. John choked and gasped. His eyes streamed. His nose ran. A knife sliced into his lungs.

'Get down!' he called. 'Everyone down!' He stamped on another glowing lump that landed five feet away across the roof. Someone beat at a flaring spark in his hair.

'I ordered everyone down,' said John, and choked again.

'We go down when you do, sir,' said the man, as his face disappeared behind a black veil of smoke. He coughed. 'Here's another bucket, sir.'

John moved in a trance, beside himself with fury and determination, from the brewhouse to the barns, to the grain stores, the cowshed, and back onto the brewhouse roof, tucking himself between the cushions of smoke, hauling buckets, beating, stamping, calling orders. He heard the others around him on the roof, coughing and retching in pursuit of sparks.

The wind continued to rise.

Come on, damn you! John urged the damp, sliding air. Bring us rain as well as fire!

The hot shower on the brewhouse roof grew heavier. The Medusa locks stretched and reached, subsided, then snatched again.

The water level in the ponds had dropped faster than the slow Shir could refill them. The water from the pumps now trickled too slowly to fill the buckets. A thin stream of buckets began to arrive up from the mill-pond, but the distance was long and the chain stretched too thin.

Please rain! John begged the black, smoky sky. Oh dear God! Please send rain!

'John!' Zeal's voice. He had forgotten her in his battle with the beast. He hurtled down the ladder to her.

'Are you hurt?' he asked.

'It's Dr Bowler,' she said. 'You'd better come!'

He followed her at a run, into the Knot Garden through the forecourt gate, but did not find the crumpled black heap he expected.

Bowler was near the top of the ladder up to the chapel roof, climbing with one hand and hauling a bucket up with the other. A group of burned and ragged men stared up at him. Smoke trickled from the smashed chapel window.

'We had to come down,' said Cope in shaky apology. His face was smeared with smoke and the blood that trickled from his bruised nose. 'The fire's blowing off the fore corner but the smoke's too thick up there. Four men knocked out by it already.'

'And inside!' added another. 'I swear, sir, even you . . .'

'But he won't heed!' Cope looked up at Bowler. 'And when I tried to stop him going up again, he kicked me in the face.'

'Give me a bucket of water.' A Winching estate groom put one into his hand. John climbed the ladder.

Bowler had reached the roof and was now emptying his bucket between the crenellations. The water exploded into steam.

'Dr Bowler! It's John. Here's another.' John passed his bucket up, then grabbed onto the ladder as a pillow of smoke rolled over the edge of the roof, thick as soot. He put out a hand for Bowler's empty bucket. 'Let's go down for another.' He waited until he felt the parson start to descend after him.

Bowler stopped on the ladder four feet above the ground. 'Give me another bucket!' he ordered, already shifting his hand up a rung to climb again.

'That was the last,' said John gently.

'Give me a bucket.'

'The chapel is going to go soon. You can't stop it with buckets of water.'

'Give me another bucket,' Bowler ordered Cope.

'Hold the ladder steady,' said John quietly to Cope and the Winching groom. He climbed the ladder to get his face above Bowler's heels. '*Magister*, you must come down now and change your weapons.'

'I need another bucket,' said Bowler. 'The roof is beginning to smoke.'

'Water's no longer enough,' said John. 'We need you to explain in your best church Latin to the Master of us all that we humbly request a miracle.' He wrapped an arm around the old man. Bowler gripped the ladder tightly with both hands.

'Why would He listen to me?'

John gripped, twisted, and carried both of them to the ground. Their fall broken by outstretched hands, they landed in a heap, untangled themselves and scrambled into a sitting position.

'What good is praying now?' cried Bowler. He sat, slack as a doll, eyes fixed on the smoke that coiled from the chapel window.

'We must find out!' John stood and hauled the old man by the armpits onto his feet.

Bowler plunged back toward the ladder.

John caught his arm. 'My dear, dear Doctor, I have not yet had a chance to tell you about a conversation I had with the Lord in the Netherlands. At the time I thought it was for lack of any other company, including my proper self. To my surprise, He paid attention. As you yourself are so fond of asking, how can men ever presume to know what might be on His mind? Perhaps He has a miracle in mind for us.' He pushed Bowler toward the forecourt gate, as gently as he could. 'At least go and reassure the terrified children and old women up there on the hill. They need you! Leave buckets to the plough oxen. Go, to the job that only you can do!' He propelled the parson towards the orange-lit forecourt.

Bowler wavered, half-intent on pushing past John back into the Knot Garden.

'Go!' said John. 'Ask for a miracle. Insist, most reverently, on immediate and immoderate rain.'

John watched Bowler's stooped figure climb wearily up the slope away from the fire towards the cluster of children on the brow below the road. If the wind in his face weren't so damp, John would never have put the old man's faith in both God and himself to such dreadful proof.

'Sir!' Tuddenham stumbled urgently out of the murk.

'Has the chapel finally caught?' asked John with despair.

'No, not that. I forgot. With everything else. We got him!'

'Who?' asked John.

'The bastard who set the fire. I'm sorry. I forgot, with everything else . . .'

'Where is he?'

'Tied up in the carriage house. Spotted by . . .' Tuddenham hesitated. 'Well, one of the men was out very early, while it was still dark, coming back from the dovecote, sir . . . checking that it was locked up safely.'

Before dawn? thought John. 'I don't care if the man had a pigeon in every pocket, if he caught our fire-raiser!' He shouted up to the men on the brewhouse roof and started for the carriage house on the far side of the yard.

'He saw someone by the corner of the west wing.' Tuddenham shot John a sideways glance. 'He thought he'd sneak up and see who else might be up to something. Then he saw that the window of the lower gallery was open, and nobody from the house would bother to go out by a window unless they were up to something wicked.'

John took Tuddenham's elbow and steered him towards the carriage house. It took a tug to set the estate manager moving again, as if his muscles had forgotten how to work.

'Got close enough,' said Tuddenham, 'with the hedges of the bowling lawn and all, to see that he didn't know the set of the man's shoulders. Nobody Sam knew.' Tuddenham stopped abruptly at the slip of the name.

'I'll give Sam nothing but thanks! What happened then?'

'Sam tackled him. The villain broke free and climbed the wall into the sheep pasture, but Sam caught him again. Lost two teeth and near enough an eye and an ear, but he raised a racket and held onto him long enough for some others to reach them.' Tuddenham drew a wheezing breath, and John saw how close he was to collapse.

'I thought it was the Last Trump when they first woke me. Then all of us out there in the meadow, wrestling in the dark and trying to sort out one man from another and hang onto the one we wanted. Got him tied, a stranger, far as we could tell, but you couldn't see your hand far in front of your face, started to march him back to ask a few questions. Then someone noticed the fire in the lower gallery. It bit so fast! It was already too late to get at the fire buckets there in the gallery.'

They arrived at the carriage house.

'Bring him out here where I can see him by the light of his fire,' said John. Murder brewed in his vitals. All the rage and frustration that had kept him upright on the brewhouse roof shot like a lightning bolt at the man who stumbled out of the darkness into the wavering orange light of the stable yard. Slight, tough and unfamiliar to John. He had hoped to recognize a groom or serving man.

'Who paid you?' John demanded.

The pair of eyes flickered and looked away.

'Paid for what?' A London voice.

John's entire weight gathered behind his fist. In the eternity it took the fist to travel its arc, John saw Francis Malise fall.

If I had gone ahead and killed Edward Malise in the stable

yard, I would not have spent that night in the drowning cell.

Francis Malise's head hit the stone floor with the succulent thud of a ripe melon.

With a grunt of effort, John forced his aim from chin to belly.

The man sat down on the cobbles with a wheeze. John stood panting in the small circle of hushed men.

'Who paid you?' demanded John. He leaned forward and jerked the man back onto his feet. But the man's legs wavered. He sat again, clutched his belly and wheezed like the garden pump.

'WHO PAID YOU?' roared John. 'Is he worth dying for?' He drew his dagger. 'Now. I have calmed myself. I won't beat you into a paste after all. Instead, I will count to five. On six, I will cut your throat. Don't waste time protesting innocence. One.'

The man looked away. Air finally reached his lungs with a long drawn-out squeak.

'Two . . .'

'John!' Zeal had followed them into the stable yard. She stopped abruptly when she saw the group outside the carriage house.

Squeak.

'Three!'

'John!' Zeal repeated uncertainly. She moved forward in protest. John put out a hand to stop her but kept his eyes on the seated man.

'Four!'

The man groaned and looked at the ground.

'Five!'

John stepped forward. He grabbed a handful of the man's hair and yanked his head back to expose his throat, so hard that the man's scalp pulled his eyebrows up into false astonishment.

'*John, don't!*' shrieked Zeal.

'And this is six.' John positioned his blade under the man's left ear.

'Mal . . . !' croaked the man.

'Malise?'

The man nodded minutely. He could nod no harder without tearing off his scalp.

'Say it loudly enough for all these men and this gentlewoman to hear,' ordered John.

'Master Edward Malise.' The syllables emerged painfully from the crooked throat. The man drew a death rattle breath.

John dropped the man's head and wiped his palm on his breeches. Malise had survived. The fire was an act of spite, a pointless venting of malice by a defeated man.

It was finished at last. The illusion of a duel to the death reduced to a matter for a court of law. How petty the Devil had proved to be if this were the level of his triumph!

John felt icy fingers on his knife hand.

'Please put that away,' Zeal whispered.

He sheathed it, still staring at Malise's arsonist. Then he looked down into her terrified face. 'Did you think I would really cut his throat?'

She took too long to answer. 'No.'

'Then you're more sure than I was, at first.'

'Well, you didn't, so that's all right!'

She put her other hand on his arm. 'Now lift your face. I have good news.'

John suddenly felt how heavy every bone in his body had become. 'Lift my face?'

'Look up!'

Puzzled, he did so. A cool dampness eased his taut, burning skin. Then he felt the whispering moth-wing taps. He hadn't noticed before.

'It's starting to rain!'

'It won't save the house,' said John.

'No. But it could make all your running around on the outbuilding roofs worth while.'

The men around them in the stable yard spread their palms and lifted their faces to the prickling sky.

Zeal stood with her face turned up, her arms spread wide. 'It's growing stronger! I'm sure it's beginning to come down harder!'

'Where's Dr Bowler?' asked John, as the truth of the rain began to seep into the smoke-filled crevices of his brain. 'Does he know that it's raining?' Drops hit his arms through his shirt now, random but definite. The air between them and the burning house glittered with orange refracting jewels that flashed and vanished.

Zeal spun with her arms out, like a gypsy dancer. 'Come on! Come on! Harder! Harder!' Her voice waxed and waned as she turned. 'Bowler has all the children singing hymns. HARDER!' she shouted up at the sky.

The race between rain and fire was neck and neck at the finish. The early drops vanished into the furnace while the growing wind blew the revived flames in long banners out through the windows of the front, across the corner of the chapel towards the brewhouse and barns.

'HARDER!' Zeal yelled at the sky, now on her knees on the slope of the hill. Above her, the dark shape of Dr Bowler waved his arms. A thin occasional sound of singing fought its way downhill against the wind, above the roar of the fire.

'HARDER! Please, God, harder!' With the chapel roof smoking and John back up on the brewhouse roof in a renewed frenzy of effort, Zeal would have agreed to forty days and forty nights without any argument.

The orange jewels in the air turned to golden streaks against the firelight. The streaks crowded closer and closer together.

Zeal stopped shouting. She sat tight and clenched on the grass, watching the race. Unable to look, she knew second by second exactly where John was on that steep, slippery roof.

In place of the twisting serpents of smoke, a mist now rose from behind the crenellations of the chapel.

Zeal leapt to her feet. 'Yes! Oh yes!'

The smoke on the chapel roof was steam!

Then the rain became bundled rods lying aslant the wind. It beat her hair flat against her head, glued her skirt to her petticoat and drenched her skin with delicious cold. She turned towards the brewhouse, with her eyes tightly shut. She was too frightened to look. They were so nearly safe. Nothing must happen now.

John, come down now! she begged silently. Come down now, my love. It's over. Please come safely down! Please!

She peeked quickly. Saw his elegant shape leaning dangerously out from a chimney stack. Shut her eyes again.

Please!

John woke up to bright daylight coming through the stable doors. He lay against the wall of a stall, on a mattress apparently stolen from a bed. He had been beaten black and blue. Or felt that way. His eyelids grated over his eyeballs and his chest hurt when he breathed in. With effort, he lifted his head a few inches.

Bodies lay strewn like flotsam over the barn floor, on other mattresses and piles of straw. Leather fire buckets tilted on their sides. Chairs, chests, a table, rumpled carpets, plates, and paintings had been stacked in unconsidered heaps against the walls. He saw one of his own collector's cabinets propped on its corner with doors agape and drawers half-closed. A smashed eggshell. And a pile of his books. Snores rattled the air around him. Directly above him, a sparrow sat on a beam, head sideways, looking down no doubt in amazement at this strange substitution of rider for mount. Or perhaps merely annoyed at the lack of a grain bucket. John closed his eyes again.

Lord, it felt good to lie still.

The others, including Sir Richard's men, were safely bedded down in the carriage house, in the shelter of the cowsheds or in estate cottages. Even with the rain, he had not risked using the brewhouse last night.

'John,' whispered Aunt Margaret. 'I have some poultice for your burns.' She stooped in a rustling of skirts and peered anxiously into his face.

He protested that he had not been burned. Then the pain of raising himself on his hands made him look at his palms.

'Sir Richard's sending food and drink,' whispered Aunt Margaret, taking one of his hands. 'You've cooked this one properly . . . Though I think most of us will sleep most of the day. And Master Winching will ride over later to see what else we need. And look at your poor frizzled hair!'

'Was anyone badly hurt last night?' asked John. 'How's Sam Beale?' Hero and pigeon poacher.

'Will Pike may cough for a bit. Sam's left eye is swollen shut – I don't know if he'll keep the sight in it. And his ear's bigger than his hand. Young Cope broke his nose but swears he doesn't remember how. Otherwise, some burns and tears, but nothing mortal. But, oh, all those lovely old things! Everything in the west wing gone. We managed to save the dining table and four of the stools. And some of the beds . . . you can see how many there are in here. In the carriage house, let me try to think . . . But someone saved your cabinets.'

John lay back and let his aunt anoint and bandage his hands. Grateful as he was, he wished it were Zeal crouched beside him with his wrist tucked between her knees.

He wanted her lying beside him. He felt her slight weight lift in his arms, warm against him during the one embrace they allowed themselves when the fire had finally died to a hissing bed of coals. He could smell the fragrance of her neck where he had buried his face. He glared up at the sparrow to distract himself and bent one knee up to distract his aunt.

Harry should be arriving today, he reminded himself. To take up the reins, however singed.

Strangely, he felt more grief about Harry than rage against Malise. Malise had always been clear in both feelings and intent. Harry had kissed and betrayed. Worse, Harry had convinced John that he was not a traitor, merely a fool.

Thereby making me a fool as well as nearly killing me, thought John. Being gulled should have stirred up anger of the bitterest, most unforgiving kind. Instead he felt sorrow and, deeper than that, an odd, voluptuous lack of concern.

'Thank you,' he said to his aunt, a little more abruptly than he meant. 'I'll be fine.' However, he wished for the help of a block and tackle by the time he had levered himself up onto his knees. 'I must get up and take stock of our losses by cold daylight. Did we manage to salvage a feather bed for Sir Harry?'

John spent the day overseeing the first clearing of the ruins. In spite of the rain, pockets of hot coals still burned under the ashes. John wanted no more injuries and directed anyone who made it back onto his feet that day to sorting what had been saved from the house. The arsonist had been put into Sir Richard's hands for interrogation and the preparation of a case to bring against Malise.

Normal estate business also still made its demands. When he finally rose, for example, he had been mortified to hear the pained lowing of the cows, still unmilked and swollen, clustered at the meadow gate and crying for relief. Vegetables trampled during the night's rush to and from the pumps needed harvesting or resettling more firmly in the earth. There was honey to salvage from the smoked-out bee skeps in the garden and the bee-boles in the forecourt walls.

Zeal and Mistress Margaret, with their helpers, prodded

the edges of the kitchen wreckage and pulled out iron pots, spits, trivets and knives without their handles. John and Zeal began lists of what they would need to replace. John set carpenters and the cooper to work at once making knife handles, churns, wooden tubs. Aunt Margaret set the older children to stripping rushes for rushlights and candle wicks, and some of the women to sewing mattress cases from a most amazing range of salvaged materials.

'So long as we can eat and sleep, we'll manage the rest,' said Zeal cheerfully to John, as she backed past him lugging one end of a rolled carpet.

Sometime in the mid-afternoon, as he stood in the horse stable beside his salvaged books, gingerly turning over in his bandaged hands the inflated puffer fish which someone had unaccountably saved in preference to his papers, John realized that he was happy. It was a cautious, blinkered joy that admitted no more than the moment, but he felt calm, assured, purposeful and content. He stood quite still. The feeling was absurd, if not criminal, in the circumstances. It would pass. But he would not let it escape without savouring it to the full. He pressed his fingertips very gently against the points of the fish's skin and gazed up at a row of four suspicious sparrows on a beam.

Harry still had not arrived by dusk, nor by the time they all collapsed into sleep again.

The next morning, after his second night in the stable, John's mood swung abruptly to the expected rage. Harry did not arrive but his messenger did, at midday, while John was in the cowshed talking to one of the cowmen, and Zeal hovered, urgent with a question.

John tore open the letter.

Sir Harry regretted that he could not come to Hawkridge. Would John please attend him as soon as possible at his London house?

'Harry be damned!' said John in a fury. 'Doesn't he know

or care what needs doing here?' He crumpled the letter and threw it violently into the nearest byre.

Heartless, self-centred, vicious, insolent pup! Did he think John would dance attendance on a lying, treacherous, pea-witted, puffed-up . . . ?

'They'll feed you something in the brewhouse,' he said curtly to the messenger. 'Then you'll go back to Sir Harry with *my* message.' He stormed out into the stable yard, followed by Zeal.

'Aren't you going?' she asked, masking her delight.

'Why the Devil should I?' For the first time since they had met, John glared at Zeal. The black eyebrows drew together. He bared his teeth as if he wanted to tear out Harry's throat.

Zeal was disconcerted. She stopped uncertainly on the cobbles, blue eyes surprised. 'You're not curious to know what he wants?'

'I know better than he does himself,' said John viciously.

Zeal laughed nervously. John knew about Harry, after all.

'I'm sorry, but you do look funny like that. With your hair all lop-sided from the . . .'

The image of John teetering on the steep brewhouse roof suddenly returned. She drew a sharp breath and shut her mouth. How dare she laugh at him?

She reached out a small conciliating hand. 'Oh, John, I'm so sorry. I didn't mean to mock you. I . . .' At the feel of his arm under her fingers, she suddenly lost her way. It was a beautiful arm. She looked away, flushing, then peeked to see if he was still scowling.

He wasn't. He was looking at her, but Zeal could see him thinking, and not happy thoughts. He was remembering, too. He looked down on her hand, which still lay on his arm. Then he sighed a long, quivering sigh up from his toes. Zeal's hands and feet went cold.

'You will stay here, then?'

Now John looked away. 'You know I can't. Even if I don't jump to obey Harry's summons.'

'Oh,' said Zeal, in a voice so small he barely heard. She took her hand from his arm, tearing her own flesh. 'Well, it's only for a few days, I suppose. We'll do the best we can until you come back.'

When he didn't answer, her heart twisted.

'How long will you be?' she heard herself beg.

'Zeal . . .' he began. 'My lady . . .'

'No!' she shouted. 'Don't you dare!'

'Zeal . . .' said John placatingly. Heads turned toward them from the pump, the carriage house, the horse-and-hay barn.

'Don't you dare,' she repeated more quietly. 'You stupid, stupid man! I'll never forgive you if you decide to be noble and do something blind and honourable like deserting me just now when I need help more than I ever have before!'

Her voice rose again. She glared at him, breathing like a bellows, teeth clenched, eyes on fire. She stretched her face up as close to his as she could reach and said in a firm low voice, 'I know what you're thinking, John. Don't you dare *insult* me like that!'

She kept her eyes fixed on his startled face and clamped her jaw tight.

Boadicea, the giantess, the storm-tossed tree reinhabit me! Don't let me cry! Or wobble!

To her amazement, John began to laugh. He looked away, rubbed his forehead with his long brown fingers and laughed a little more.

Zeal sank back onto her heels and waited.

'Oh, Lord,' he said. 'Oh, Lord!' Then he scooped up her hand and kissed it gently. 'Your most humble and obedient servant would never dare insult you, madam.' He replaced her hand firmly against her filthy skirts. 'But you and I both know that what we wish is impossible. I'll go see what your husband wants with me. I swear that if I can, I will come back to help with this shambles. You know I can't say more.'

That night, Zeal asked Rachel to ask Arthur to steal one of John's gloves. When he and Arthur had left the next afternoon, Zeal climbed the beech hanger to the Lady Tree. With guilty stealth, she buried the glove between the roots of the tree.

'Let your fellow come back to find you,' she told the glove. Then she climbed the tree and sat in its branches, looking down on the lady and out across Hawkridge valley towards the London road, until she heard Rachel calling for her in the orchard a little before sundown.

'I only came,' said John, 'because I was curious to see what other evils could still be lying in wait for me.'

The fair skin around Harry's blue eyes was reddened and puffy. The blond hair had not been combed.

'How bad is it?' he demanded.

'You should have come to see for yourself.' The voluptuous unconcern had gone. He was in a savage mood with Harry now, puffy eyes or not. Savage and unspeakably weary.

Harry looked away. 'I'm no good at dealing with that kind of thing. Anyway, I was too busy here. It was best for you to do it. Is there anything left of the place? What about the furniture and plate?'

'Shouldn't you have asked if anyone was killed? Or how your wife is, or your aunt?' John glanced down at his own red, stiffened hands. Holding the reins on the journey here had been painful.

Harry blinked at the rebuke. 'Was anyone hurt?'

'A few injuries. None dead.'

'Thank the Lord. But what about the house?'

'The walls stand, and the chapel is intact.' John stared into the memory of the red eyes and fiery hair. 'The fire started at the gallery end. Brewhouse, barns, stables never caught.'

'What about everything inside the house: the new feather beds and hangings . . . ?'

'Mostly in ashes. Zeal and Aunt Margaret have started sifting. Some of the chests may have protected their contents. You'll have a list in time.'

'Most of it was old, in any case.'

John looked at his cousin bleakly. 'The hornbeam *allée* is gone. Two stumps remain. And the Knot Garden was trampled by men fighting the fire with water from the garden pumps.' He grinned with sudden wolfish pleasure. 'However, I'm delighted to say that the *basse-court* buildings still stand, even though Lady Beester's cheeses unfortunately melted.'

Harry sighed. 'I'm sorry about your garden, but no one plants knots any longer, not in London.' He looked more distracted but less distraught than John had expected, as if some other matter were weighing more heavily on his mind than the burning of his country house.

'It was almost certainly your friend Malise.'

'Malise? Why on earth?' Harry asked the question with dutiful amazement, but he shook his head woefully as if nothing would ever surprise him again. 'Are you sure?'

'One of the fire-raisers was caught.'

'Malise,' said Harry glumly. 'Well, you can ruin him at last. He won't dare return to Court. Or even England, I suppose.' He raised eyes filled with naked appeal.

He does not deserve my sympathy, thought John. Poor Harry. Then the worms of water began to crawl into the stone cell again. John closed his fists and looked through the window at a solidly present English house front across the street.

Calm. Calm.

And there it was again, that blissful slackening.

It's all a gift, from now on, thought John. Whatever

happens, good or bad, is more than I thought I would have. And whatever it is must not be wasted.

'Cousin . . .' Harry waited with desperate eyes for John to oil the conversational slide. 'I'm sorry . . . if there's anything I need to be sorry for.'

John closed his eyes and waited until the renewed touch of certain death stopped brushing his skin with cold. When he opened his eyes, Harry looked oddly reduced, coloured with falsely assumed significance, like an actor in a play.

'Truly,' said Harry. 'I never meant real harm.'

John sighed. He raised both hands in a gesture of defeat. 'And now you want me to forgive you and forget that you nearly helped to kill me. You're asking too much. I'll probably forgive, in time. Forgetting isn't an act of will.' He picked up his hat. 'And now that I've told you the news you wanted to hear and heard the apology you felt you should make to ease your mind, I shall take my leave. I need to sleep for a fortnight.'

'But that's not why I called you back to London,' said Harry.

'There's more?'

'For the Lord's sake, sit down!' said Harry. 'Please.'

John didn't move.

'Very well. Make it hard for me.' Harry sat down defiantly in his chair-of-grace and crossed his legs. 'As you wish.' He recrossed his legs, folded his arms across his chest, drew a breath, looked out of the window, exhaled and closed his mouth again.

'That night,' he said abruptly. His face grew bright red. His intended words were clearly more painful even than apology. 'That night,' began Harry again. 'When.' He licked his pink lips. 'When . . . we had our falling out the next day.'

John raised coolly interrogative eyebrows.

'Nothing happened!' Harry leaned back in relief at having got it out.

John stared back, refusing to help. He wasn't sure that he had heard right in any case.

Harry was now as purple as Zeal's ears had been when she arrived at Hawkridge House. 'Nothing happened,' he repeated. 'I mean, with my wife.'

John was shocked into speech at last. 'I don't understand.'

'I didn't touch her.'

'She didn't scream for the joy of it.'

'You never know with her,' Harry muttered.

'I do know her,' said John. 'And I know you. You try to wriggle out of every nasty piece of behaviour you can.'

Shaky but resolute, Harry said, 'John, I didn't touch her!'

John was stunned into silence by the baldness of the lie.

'I didn't, and I'm prepared to swear to it, in the Star Chamber if necessary.'

'Is this a new city trick of yours, to lie on oath?'

'I dare say that Zeal would confirm it . . . Do stop refusing to understand me, John! I'm trying to say that I'm thinking of applying for an annulment of my marriage.'

'Ah! You've found a richer woman!'

'No!' cried Harry indignantly. 'That is . . .' Pride asserted itself in spite of his good intentions. 'There are plenty to know now that I'm among 'em.' He threw his arms wide and grasped the carved wooden arms of his chair. 'Oh, Lord, coz. Don't be so fat-witted!'

'From you, coz, that's rich!'

Harry glared, then recovered.

He's surprisingly determined to keep his temper, thought John.

Harry steadied his halo. 'You keep refusing to understand.' A faint shimmering of nobility passed across his face. 'I don't want to imprison her in a life she hates. I would rather give her her freedom again.'

'Now that you've had the use of her money to make some of your own.' John sat slowly on the nearest stool. His heart began to thud gracelessly against his ribs, though he showed his cousin a still sceptical face.

As if on a counter-balance, Harry stood up. He walked to the window that gave onto the street, then he turned to his cousin in naked appeal. 'Coz, could you live with a woman who despises you?' He recovered enough to add, 'Not openly, of course. Not despises, more like disregards.'

John was too distracted by his own thoughts to notice this fine distinction. He closed his hands tightly between his knees. A pardon. Hawkridge burnt. Malise in flight. Zeal unencumbered. Too much light, too much dark. At the same time. He couldn't put it all together into a single reality.

'She pauses in whatever she's doing and waits for me to leave the room,' continued Harry. 'As an adult does with an interrupting child.' Harry leaned forward. 'John?'

John refocused.

'I'm actually rather good at being visible, John.' It seemed important to Harry that John understood what he was trying to say. 'I think I have a knack for it. And for getting others to look after the money side of things for me. I was a little surprised to learn how good I am, in fact.

'But she doesn't see it. She doesn't even understand why I bother. There *are* women, just as rich, who value a man who can make them laugh, buy wine, give a good dinner and knows how to tickle them in every way.'

'There's shame for her if you throw her off.'

Harry finally rolled his eyes to the ceiling and let his halo slip where it would. 'You are an ass! As bad as she is. I swear before God Almighty that you're perfect for each other! I'll visit with pleasure, but I'll be damned if I can live with either of you! If Zeal doesn't oppose me – and I don't expect that she will – I mean to seek an annulment,' said Harry. 'Then you can sort yourselves out!'

Harry had the upper hand in this conversation at last. He stood with his hands clasped behind his back, warm with a number of different satisfactions, magnanimity and self-interest exactly congruent. And his cousin gaping like a landed fish. Harry asked nothing more of the moment.

'What will Hazelton think if you reject his niece?' asked John at last. 'Having invested her portion in the meantime?'

Harry suppressed a grin of delight. 'He's happy enough. I've told him already. Our commercial relationship will continue as before, through the Company . . . The *Boston Maid* has been sighted, by the way. She didn't sink!' Briefly, Harry rejoiced, then he said, 'Anyway, I had meant to make good my debt to her . . . my wife that is . . . by giving her the estate. Of course, it's not worth now what it was when I made the decision. Although then it was worth more than I owe her. Now you say that the barns and stock are safe. Only the wretched house is damaged, and any sensible man would have wanted to knock it down and begin again anyway. So.'

He bent slightly forward, looking for his reward of John's approval.

Harry, the half-aware traitor. Harry, the generous. Harry, standing there wagging his tail, waiting for a pat on the head and words of praise for his generous self-interest.

'She'll need your help,' said Harry, as if to a very slow child. Like Dr Bowler to his own infant self, in fact.

And then John finally realized the full extent of Harry's offered gift.

'What were you planning to do with yourself now that you've become a gentleman again? Will you buy yourself an estate?' Harry was now enjoying himself thoroughly.

'I'm thinking I might enrol for a voyage to Virginia or the Caribbean. In spite of the risk of running into the fugitive Malise out there.'

'I'd be grateful if, first, you could take word of what we've just discussed back to Lady Beester.'

'I could do that.' John stood up, still suspicious. Only my

cousin, he thought, could manage to look both smug and shy at the same time.

The two cousins examined each other, two young men assessing the scars. Harry, blond, tentative and brimming. John, sharp, dark, elegant and still suspicious. He was astonished to feel himself begin to bubble with the reckless, unformed expectation of a child.

'Oh, coz!' said Harry with a theatrical, cyclonic sigh. 'Who'd have thought it would all be so complicated?'

🌷

Dr Bowler stood alone in the carriage drive between the beeches. He had walked up from the forecourt gate. The avenue swept down to the black ruins behind him. Small coloured shapes crawled around and over the ashes of Hawkridge House. The sharp smell of wet ash reached the top of the drive. John felt an unsettled rustling in the atmosphere. A single red-brown leaf twirled and twirled down through the air from the nearest beech, filling John with an unreasonable dread.

Why has the old man come out to meet me alone like that? thought John. His heart and hands chilled. Where are the others? Where's Zeal? Apart from the crawlers on the wreckage, the estate was as still as after the plague.

John had heard the brewhouse bell, faint and urgent, as he and Arthur were passing the entrance to Bedgebury House. Their arrival was expected. He kicked his horse forward sharply, with growing terror.

All the way here, he had dreamed of the seeds of new beginnings. Fields of kings in full blow.

Not a child in sight. Not a cottager. Not his aunt or Lady Beester. Only Dr Bowler waiting alone in his torn black silk coat and breeches, with dirty red ribbons tying his shoes, incongruous among the sheep and drying meadow grass.

Something has happened to Zeal! Or to Aunt Margaret!

'My dear Doctor,' John cried. The exhausted horse caught his urgency and stumbled into a trot. 'What's wrong?'

Dr Bowler raised his arms above his head.

For one second, John thought the old man had lost his balance and was about to topple backward into the grass. John had already begun to fling himself from his horse when the parson brought both his arms down with such a convulsion of energy that he seemed about to launch himself into flight like a large ink-green raven.

'*Deo gratias*!' he sang with open throat and full lungs. Thanks be to God.

The trees of the beech avenue began to sing.

'*Pleni sunt coeli et terra gloria tua*!'

The heavens and earth are filled with Your glory.

From the leaves of the beeches in the avenue fell a shower of notes as clear as falling stars in an August night.

'*Hosanna*!' sang the beeches like a choir of cherubim, from above John's head, on both sides, behind and ahead. He was bewitched into stillness half off his horse.

Dr Bowler turned and waved his arms urgently. A pair of trees farther down the avenue towards the gates chimed in a little late, raggedly but sweetly.

'*Hosanna in excelsis*!'

Time paused. There was nothing in the Universe but that high, clear singing of the trees.

John looked up in wonder. Through the thick swells and swags of the branches, he now saw a child, then another. Then a pair of swinging legs. The truth was every bit as sweet as the magic.

'*HOSANNA*!' For that one splendid second, they all chimed together.

Then the voices began to slide apart, the widespread singers unable to hear each other or to see their conductor clearly.

Most were also still breathless from their mad scramble into the trees when the bell had begun to ring.

'Amen!' sang Dr Bowler.

The two late trees sang on alone, high and true, still behind but unaware.

'AMEN!'

The song ended. A sheep bleated.

'There,' said Dr Bowler with deep, deep satisfaction. 'We managed your music at last!'

John slid to the ground and embraced his old tutor, fighting tears. And suddenly, children began to tumble and scramble from the trees. The avenue was crowded with children and dogs. Cope stepped from behind a beech, Tuddenham from behind another. Zeal was running up from the forecourt gate, skirts clumped up in both hands, with Aunt Margaret rolling, swaying, and out of breath behind her.

'Where the bee . . . !' shouted Dr Bowler urgently into the growing mêlée. 'Where the bee . . . ! And . . . !'

He collected up a few voices, including the maid Rachel and Sam the pigeon-snatcher, who was very loud and terribly off-key. '. . . in a cowslip's bell . . .'

'John!' cried Zeal.

He caught her up and swung her round. Then, in front of everyone, he kissed her hard on the mouth.

Zeal pulled back. Her face was white.

'It's all right!' John shouted to the faces around them. 'I have the right!' He kissed her again.

'You killed Harry?' whispered Zeal in horror.

'On the contrary, I almost like him again.' Then he put one arm around her and the other around his aunt.

'Lady Beester and I have the house family all boarded out now among the cottagers,' said his aunt.

'Merrily, merrily, shall we live now,' Dr Bowler sang.

'And we have made a perfect cooking fire in the brewhouse. And Sir Richard sent twelve huge cheeses . . .'

Zeal walked at John's side, staring up, trying to read his face, feeling his mood but not yet understanding it.

'And we cleared the chapel . . .' chirped Mistress Margaret.

Still staring at John, Zeal finally managed to say, 'And Sir Richard also promised us eight oak beams . . .'

'And that's not the best of it,' said John. 'If I can get a word in edgewise.'

'. . . Under the blossom that hangs from the bough.' By the time the procession reached the gate, only Dr Bowler was still singing, happily, to himself.

Quicksilver

Christie Dickason

The dazzling second book in the Lady Tree trilogy –
available in hardback from HarperCollins

Quicksilver is part romance, part psychological thriller. Richly
evocative and subtly erotic, it gives a fascinating insight into the
myth of the werewolf.

Raised in exile as an English gentleman trying to forget a tragic
past, Ned Malise wanted only to be left alone with his music, his
rich daydreams and his love for Marika. But at the age of thirty-
three, he suddenly began to turn into a wolf. Or so it seemed in
1638, when werewolves were still tried and hanged like witches.

On the run from hunters with dogs, Ned takes refuge with the
woman he has loved from a distance all his life, who must
herself in turn make a terrifying decision. Then Ned finds that
rescue can be even more horrifying than execution.

Set in England and Holland, in a world where medieval super-
stition still warred with the emerging experimental sciences of
the Age of Reason, *Quicksilver* moves from court intrigue to
back-street quacks, from the healing power of music to the
deadly hunger of intellectual ambition. From the horror of
Ned's first unravelling by his Wolf, by way of one of the
strangest yet most satisfying love stories seen outside myth, it
propels the reader to an astonishing but exhilarating end.
Quicksilver resonates with parallels for the modern day and
stretches our understanding of the beast that lurks in man.

ISBN 0 00 224355 5

Earthly Joys

Philippa Gregory

'A hugely readable and unexpectedly moving book'

Daily Telegraph

He is a traveller in a time of discovery, and the greatest gardening pioneer of his day. Yet John Tradescant is a man of humble birth, trusted by the kingdom's greatest leaders: politicians, aristocrats, even royalty. Surrounded by luxury and intrigue, Tradescant gives all his attention to his magnificent gardens, in the midst of a society on the brink of upheaval.

Uniquely skilled at collecting, raising, and nurturing plants, his practical good sense makes him an invaluable servant, as he scours the known world for new and beautiful species, and penetrates the most secret activities at court. Here both King Charles I and Tradescant are in thrall to the irresistible Duke of Buckingham, the most powerful man in England.

Tradescant has always been faithful to his masters, but Buckingham is unlike any he's ever known: flamboyant, outrageously charming, utterly reckless. The court may love him but the people hate him. Every certainty upon which Tradescant has based his life is challenged as his personal world is turned upside down while all around him the country slides towards civil war.

'Vivid and enthralling'

Sunday Times

'Brilliantly true to the period . . . I was entranced'   *The Times*

ISBN 0 00 649644 X

Child of the Phoenix

Barbara Erskine

An epic novel by the bestselling author of *Lady of Hay* and *Midnight is a Lonely Place*.

Born in the flames of a burning castle in 1218, Princess Eleyne is brought up by her fiercely Welsh nurse to support the Celtic cause against the English aggressor. She is taught to worship the old gods and to look into the future and sometimes the past. But her second sight is marred by her inability to identify time and place in her visions so she is powerless to avert forthcoming tragedy.

Extraordinary events will follow Eleyne all her days as, despite passionate resistance, her life is shaped by the powerful men in her world. Time and again, like the phoenix that is her symbol, she must rise from the ashes of her past life to begin anew. But her mystical gifts, her clear intelligence and unquenchable spirit will involve her in the destinies of England, Scotland and Wales.

0 00 647264 8

fireandwater
The book lover's website

www.fireandwater.com

The latest news from the book world

Interviews with leading authors

Win great prizes every week

Join in lively discussions

Read exclusive sample chapters

Catalogue & ordering service

www.fireandwater.com
Brought to you by HarperCollins*Publishers*